THE
OCEAN'S
SHADOW

THE OCEAN'S SHADOW SERIES BOOK ONE

About The Book

This swashbuckling dark adult fantasy is a fractured kaleidoscope of reimagined tales and mythologies set in its own unique, compelling world. With pirates, gods, mythical creatures, and witches, readers will sail into a realm where magic meets madness.

Please Note: This series contains explicit content and dark elements that may be triggering to some. Reader discretion is advised. Within this story you will find explicit romance, mature language, violence, and reference to childhood trauma. This book is not intended for anyone under 18 years of age.

This is Book One in an unfolding series.

To the ones who've guided me along the way,
the ones still here
and the ones now gone.

Chapter 1

Vessa

The briny water fills my lungs as I sink deeper beneath the waves. The liquid salt that should sting and burn me from within barely registers as an itch. Not in comparison to the rage that fills me far deeper than the ocean floor – that I am now approaching at an alarming rate.

The rope bites into my bound wrists and ankles, but I don't care. I don't care that the anchor pulling me down has rubbed my skin raw and that blood now mixes and diffuses in the rush of bubbles that draws the only line between me and the surface. No. All this I could excuse. If the only affront issued against me was to my physical self, I could forgive such a primitive assault. After all, who am I to condemn the same violence I bestow upon my own enemies?

This? This is a matter of authority. Of power. This is personal.

Being the captain of a ship is a challenge in its own right. Being one of the only women to hold such a title... well, let's just say there is a reason I took to the path uncharted. The rules of the world have never interested me. Every social practice, every power dynamic had always been stacked against me - against the women around me. For as long as I could remember, the men in my life had held me firmly in *my place*, as they so eloquently phrased it.

I was to be kind - but passive. I was to be accommodating - but quiet. I was to never strive for more than that which the men around me had already achieved. There was no room for a woman in the adventures the world had to offer. They told me that beauty was all that mattered for a woman and praised me for exceeding expectation in this capacity. For the longest while, I fought with my words, fought against the restrictions placed upon me, both figurative and literal. One of my first memories is staring into a mirror at the face with the black eye, forgetting that it was mine entirely as I pushed the memory of my punishment from my mind. My punishment for daring to say I would be more than what I was told I could become. It kills me that those thoughts even registered with me at such a young age.

When I was deemed old enough to marry, my father sold me off to an affluent man who lived in our humble town. The bride-price he offered alone would have been enough to advance my family to an entirely new social status had I not stolen it from my father's safe the night before the wedding, never looking back as I ran as fast as my legs could carry me to the harbor and sought refuge in a docked ship.

How differently my life might have turned out had I chosen a different path - a different place to hide. How strange a series of events that I found *that* ship docked in *that* harbor on *that* night. Some may hear my tale and think this the most sinister of outcomes for a poor young woman, as I was when he found me. But I see it as the first time mercy had ever been shown to me and the first taste of good fortune that would stoke an addictive need for *more* that could never quite be satisfied.

Captain Vayne found me tucked behind a stack of barrels below the deck of his ship. His grimy face and tattered beard held no horror for me as I stared back at him with all the defiance of a 15-year-old child who refused to be broken into manageable pieces. He was never one to share his words so callously and could never be accused of being an empathetic man, but he once told me - half in the bag from one too many fingers of rum - that when he first found me, all he could see was a lost child, trapped in a conventional life, just burning to be set free. He was the first person to ever see me as something more than a pretty face - to see me as equal to any of the men on his crew. In his own way, he truly saw me as a son, of sorts. Though he recognized the feminine exterior and drilled the fear of the sea gods into his men should any of them lay a finger on me. And they never did. And *he* never did.

I worked my way up the rungs of his crew, never shying away from the more remedial work and never being given special dispensation for what I lacked in brawn and strength compared to my fellow crewmembers. Over time, I became as capable as any man aboard the *Ocean's Shadow.* I went from Vayne being my protector to being the thing that others needed protection from should anyone cross me and my quest to rise the ranks.

I succeeded in this, becoming Vayne's second in command by the time I was twenty-one. For two years, I served at his side until that otherworldly storm came and pulled Vayne and seven other crewmen out to sea, never to be seen again. For days, we searched, refusing to believe his death had come so swiftly and without the dignity of falling in battle. But on the fourth day, I awoke with a newfound darkness in my soul. I dressed in my usual clothes but with one of Vayne's ornate feathered hats and his sword slung at my side. I trudged out of my chambers and up to the deck, only stopping once I stood before the helm.

Vayne is lost to us, but the Ocean's Shadow *will carry his legacy. I stand before you as your captain, unless one of you dares to challenge the authority appointed to me by my predecessor.*

I unsheathed the sword that had become mine and brandished it in a flourishing sweep, addressing the entirety of the crew. Nary a whispered breath escaped their lips as they watched me in silent submission.

Onward, men. I, Captain Duvessa, have plans for this vessel. And we all shall play a part in making that wish a reality.

That is how the *Ocean's Shadow* came to be mine. It has been three years since I became captain. Three years of adventures beyond what even Vayne himself could have dreamed possible.

The anchor hits the ocean floor with a thud, sending sediment flying around me in a clouded fog. I feel the inside of my skull pop from the pressure, but I smile sadistically at the pain, wondering if that is all the ocean has to try and subdue me. I would take this pressure one thousand times over that which I endured as a child.

The anchor now positioned on solid ground, I use its weight to pull myself down until I'm crouched at its side, slicing the rope against its sharp edge until my wrists are free. I make short work of undoing the knots around my ankles. Scaffold knots - *child's play.*

Liberated from all bindings, I quickly pull at the collar of my leather jacket, exposing my neck to the cold water. They had bound and thrown me overboard, still wearing my jacket, presumably so its weight would further prevent me from escaping certain death. Little did they know that simple choice kept them from seeing the very thing that will be their undoing.

The jacket is now off of my body, and it is sinking to the ocean floor. My boots quickly follow. I don't mind leaving them behind. I have others just like them aboard my ship, and even if I didn't, piracy pays handsomely - I can afford a thousand more if I wanted.

I crack my neck before I begin my ascent. My toes stretch wide, revealing the accordion webbing between them as they fan out into powerful fins on either foot. I take a gratuitous breath in through the gills that wrap in spirals along the sides of my neck, now unobscured and freely capable of inhaling with ease.

Pure hatred burns within me, spilling out through my eyes. A smile pulls at the corners of my mouth as I swim toward the surface, where hell awaits those who have wronged me.

Chapter 2

Vessa

Their bodies lay at my feet. *How unfortunate for me.* By the time I reached the surface, their blood was already staining the deck, my crew having slaughtered them of their own accord without so much as leaving one for me. *Thoughtless.*

This blunder is of my own doing. Perhaps I should focus on that rather than fixating on the lack of maiming I get to indulge in for the time being. I am fighting the urge to take out my frustration on a random crewmember as a way to save face. I am a lot of things, but I am a fair captain. One to be feared if anyone steps out of line, but not one to unjustly punish others for my own shortcomings.

It was a miscalculation on my part, choosing to bring the two men we found marooned on the small, uncharted island. Their ship had crashed against the rocks that partially circled the sandy expanse. They managed to swim to safety and had constructed a makeshift shelter out of driftwood from similar wreckages that had washed up on shore. We had easily avoided the otherwise perilous rocks, having had prior knowledge of their location. Skeleton Island is a regular stop for the *Ocean's Shadow*, after all. The island is small, not just in diameter but in height, with no notable mountains or particularly high hills, keeping it unbeknownst to those passing through the region. Those who stumble upon it rarely live to step foot on its shores. Those that *do* rarely live long enough to step foot back off. Except the few instances when numbers are thin and I find myself in need of additional hands.

There are pirates, and then there was Vayne. Vayne was the most notorious pirate in all the realms. Some say he had more wealth than the richest of kings and queens that ever existed, though I think these rumors are ones Vayne started about himself at the various bars and taverns he frequented while docked at port towns. He always did enjoy hearing other people tell tales about his grand adventures, not knowing that the legend himself was the stranger listening in on how the details twisted and turned through word of mouth. *He sounds like a regular god of the sea*, he would often say in response, raising a glass and shooting me a quick wink.

It was always odd being at port towns with Vayne. Our dynamic had never seemed at odds with expectation to me, until I started to hear the whispers of certain towns folk of ports we would frequent more regularly. Some people were content to mind their own business. Others took issue with the young woman living aboard a ship with dozens of men and who was the constant companion of the much older captain himself. Their small minds could only conceptualize me as a sexual being, diminishing their impression of who I was or what I could become before they even learned my name. In my mind the term *whore* became synonymous with *deviant,* and *that* I could work with as an identifier.

As much as Vayne loved hearing stories of himself, I hated hearing the rumored tales in which I was a character. Over time, they became almost comical to me with just how far they were from reflective of my reality. This restructuring of my own perception kept me from murdering every person who spoke my name in these such tales. I did still, however, continue to fantasize about the various creative ways in which I would disfigure them for propelling such atrocious lies. *Whatever subdues the mind, I suppose.*

We pirates are creatures of habit. Order and regularity are a safety net to us. Routine can keep us from losing our sanity altogether during long stretches out at sea. That never bothered me so much, since the ocean was the place that saved me by swallowing me whole, demons and all. But the need for structure was engrained in me by repetition and habit from the moment I stepped foot on the *Ocean's Shadow.* Skeleton Island was the place where Captain Vayne kept his treasures and, therefore, where much of my treasure resides. Of course, some remains on the ship itself, but his legacy and his wealth far exceed the capacity of one singular vessel. And he never wanted to expand, like so many others desire. He never wanted a fleet, only one individual ship that was entirely his to control. He was a paradox that way. Always wanted more treasure, more esteem, more adventure, but never wanted more than the wood beneath his feet and the ocean in the horizon. At times, I wonder if he even wanted the treasure at all or if all of his conquests were just to keep from being held prisoner to convention. Maybe that likeness was what he saw in me all those years ago.

There is always someone on Skeleton Island. We would never leave our life's work so carelessly unattended. I rotate crewmembers to monitor the island each time we stop to unload and regroup on the only piece of land that any of us consider to be a stationary home. Some of them dread their island shifts. Others kiss the sandy beaches in gratitude for the reprieve. I never felt too strongly about it either way, but have yet to feel any sense of nostalgia for the place now that my station as captain prevents me from undertaking any lengthy land-dwelling obligations.

Skeleton Island can be called nothing else. If not for the ominous rocks surrounding her like the ribcage of a giant protruding from the water's surface, she is named for the piles of skulls and bones that litter the beaches. Courtesy of decades of protecting what is rightfully Vayne's. Rightfully, now, *mine.*

The piles of useless flesh now littering my deck were taken captive by my men when they were found huddled in their primitive shelter their first night on Skeleton Island. The interlopers should have been killed upon my order once I arrived back at the island. My men are under order to keep all captives alive until I return, however long that may take. There are, of course, extenuating circumstances where this rule may be broken. But such executions are not indulged in lightly, lest they risk invoking my wrath.

More often than not, my order to kill comes moments after I lay eyes on the captives of Skeleton Island. It takes but a moment's glance to recognize that a person is not who I am looking for. The order to kill these men should have come. The words had almost slipped past my lips when I froze dead in my tracks as I heard their begging prayers to her.

Delesseria.

Their prayers, of course, fell on deaf ears. Delesseria was never one to return the affection of her disciples, few as they are in modern times. They give. She takes. Whether they know it or not. Whether they consent or whether it's forced upon them.

But *I* heard them. *I* answered their prayers with my own brand of mercy. I *spared* their lives with the understanding that they would divulge to me everything they knew about the sea witch, Delesseria. I *spared* their lives with the understanding that joining my crew was the only way they would live to see another day.

After days of abusing my hospitality, after guards were dropped and trust began to take root, they decided that death was their preferred option.

They made their move in the dead of night. My head had barely hit my pillow, still fully dressed from the previous day. I'd been working at my desk, charting new courses for upcoming expeditions. I had planned to close my eyes for an hour at most before I would resume my work, but the weight of my eyelids pulled me quickly into much deeper sleep than I intended. I did not hear them when they entered, gagging my mouth as they pulled me from my bed and onto the rug in my captain's chambers.

They spewed their profanities – the typical conglomeration of words that small men tend to direct at a woman of power in their feeble attempt to break her down under the weight of their insecurities. If my mouth hadn't been stuffed with a filthy rag, I might have laughed at the predictability of their words. If they wanted to verbally grate me, they'd have to try a lot harder than that. At the core of their assertions was the fact that they would not yield to the orders of a *worthless whore*, no matter how tightly I had my *sniveling men* wrapped around my finger. The unfortunate cretins thought they could simply step into my shoes and take my place as co-captains once they got me out of the picture. They underestimated just *how* tightly I hold the reins of my crew.

Secondary to their justification was the fact that they would not allow any harm to befall their beloved Delesseria. The devout acolytes mistook *my* charity for *her* divine intervention. A mistake my crew prevented me from correcting myself. Death at the hands of other men was too good for these wretched scum. I'd have relished the feel of my blade disemboweling them, belly to sternum, watching the light fade from their eyes as they realized I would be the last thing they would ever see.

Bygones.

They bound my arms and legs, tied me to an anchor, and tossed me overboard. Not before removing my gag to allow me the civility of final words. I used the opportunity to spit in the closest man's face and scream for my crew before they hurled me over the edge of the ship. It was by sheer luck that the anchor did not hit me on the way down.

They hadn't known about my abilities. How could they? The only ones who know are the members of the crew who have been around since it happened. They don't know all the details of how it came to be, but they know what I have become. And I have heard whispers amongst the crew of variations of the actual tale. I have to admit, some of them are pretty close to the reality. Others are as far-fetched as some of the stories Vayne used to fabricate about his own escapades.

It all happened six months ago...

There is a chill in the air, despite it being the midst of summer. We pulled into Puerto Destino not three hours prior. Already, most of the crew are littering the various pubs and brothels the small seaside village has to offer. They'd become restless and needed a night on the town to blow off some steam. I can't blame them. They are like children that way. I learned their tells long ago. They are easier to manage if I give them a little leeway to tend to their more basal needs from time to time. And I find that, on occasion, I enjoy a good reprieve from the stench of rank men. A win for all parties.

I hook the heels of my boots into the rung of the wooden stool I sit on at the bar. Barra de Placer is quiet tonight. It has been quiet every night I've ever been here. That is what I like most about it. Plenty of rum and plenty of solitude. Most of the crew tend to favor the more... full-service establishments in town. I used to accompany Vayne to such places on occasion. He liked to keep a close eye on his men, to remind them that even on dry land he was always watching. Nobody bothered me when Vayne was around. Eventually, I would retire to the ship and Vayne would saunter off to some rented room with whatever harlot won his attention that night.

After Vayne was lost at sea, I stopped going along with the crew. One too many instances of patrons thinking I worked for such debaucherous establishments. After a while, I got tired of threatening to maim people when I was supposed to be unwinding. So, instead, I would find the dives. The quiet places most people walked right past on their way to the excitement of a roaring nightlife. The types of men that frequented those bustling places weren't what I was seeking anyhow. I far preferred the quiet nobodies who would accompany me back to my ship for a whirlwind night and fuck off before the sun finished rising. More often than not, my one-night stands would flee the ship in an anxious whirl as, one by one, my burly crew returned to the Ocean's Shadow in varying states of disarray from a night of wild, bawdy devilry.

I polish off the remainder of the rum in my glass, placing it on the bar top with more force than I intended, drawing the attention of the bar wench whose back was turned to me.

"Another, when you have a moment," I requested.

I have a soft place in my heart for working women. I doubt that working in a dank tavern is the fulfillment of her deepest wishes. But I respect the hell out of her for doing something more with her life than wedding and bedding. The last thing she needs is some rude patron demanding more of her time than it takes to pour a glass of rum. Patrons should leave her the fuck alone to do her work without needing to perform false joy in the interaction. I'm grateful for the service. And I'd be grateful for a chat, if she felt so inclined. But she does not owe me social interaction. She owes nobody anything. I hope she knows this.

It is rare that I meet an unencumbered woman in my line of work. At least not one who isn't trying to sell something. So, when I do, like this stoic barkeep at Barra de Placer, I notice. And the part of me that remembers what it was like to be restrained smiles just a bit as I silently acknowledge the likeness in our mutual fight.

I sense a presence behind me, but I do not turn to face it. I let it move around me to lean into the bar at my side. A pair of elegantly weathered hands fold together as they press into the surface of the bar.

"One for me as well, dear," a distinctly feminine voice chimes.

I steal a glance at the woman beside me. She is older than me, late thirties or early forties. She is quite striking. Long, fire-red hair that accentuates the amber in her eyes. Rounded, apple cheeks with the dimples of a more youthful person. In fact, looking at her more closely, I would almost say she is younger than I initially thought, but something about her eyes... they feel older than life itself.

We exchange polite smiles and sit in silence while the barkeep returns with a clean glass, refilling mine before setting it down and filling it as well.

"Anything else?" she asks us both.

"I am quite alright, thank you," I reply with a nod and a fleeting smile.

14

The other woman says nothing as she continues to stare at me from my side. After a moment of hesitation, waiting for any semblance of a reply from my new companion, the barkeep says, "Well, let me know if you need anything else." She walks clear across the room and busies herself cleaning a table that I have it on good authority was already clean. The redheaded woman slides herself onto the stool beside me, now turning her attention to her glass of rum.

"I always did have a fondness for the stuff," she says, lifting the glass and taking a conservative sip.

"Hmmm," I grunt in agreement, hoping she will take the hint that I am in no mood for idle prattle.

"Maybe too much of a fondness," she sets her glass down and returns her scrutinous gaze to my face. "They say too much of a good thing will kill you. I'm not so sure I buy that."

"Yeah?" I say, more dismissing than engaging. I take a gratuitous gulp.

"I have lived a life of, let's say, restriction." She settles into her seat, picking up her glass and swirling its contents as she speaks. I watch the amber liquid whirlpool between her fingertips. "For the longest time, I listened. I obeyed. Moderation. Propriety. Father knows best." She shakes her head, taking a heartier sip from her glass. I startle slightly, being suddenly pulled away from the hypnotism of the rum dancing in her glass.

"I know a little about that myself," I confess. I don't know why.

"I can tell that about you." She smiles, eyes fixated on her glass.

"Can you?"

"Yes," she looks up at me briefly from the sides of her eyes. *"Like recognizes like."*

I don't know why, but my heart speeds slightly.

"The ship that came to port today, that's yours?" Her question lands as more of a statement. *"The one that flies under black sails."*

"What makes you say that?" Few people know or recognize me as captain, fewer still outside of nautical circles. Most assume Gareth is captain of the Ocean's Shadow. Gareth is my appointed first mate, and the closest thing to a friend I have.

"I know power when I see it."

I take a hard look at the woman and wonder who she is. *"Like recognizes like?"* I ask.

She chuckles softly. *"Indeed."*

"Yes, that is my ship," I again confess without fully understanding why.

"The Ocean's Shadow," her name sounds like music on her tongue. *"I have to confess, it's nice to see her manned by, well... someone other than Vayne."*

"You know him?" I still struggle to use the past tense with regard to my former captain.

"Knew. It seems. You are her captain after all, right Duvessa?"

"I seem to be at a bit of a disadvantage. You know who I am, but I haven't the slightest notion who..."

"I am a fellow traveler," she cuts me off. Anger riles beneath my skin at the disrespect, but I remain quiet. *"I am no captain, but I have seen you around from time to time."*

"*I don't recall you,*" *I shake my head as I look her up and down. With a quick jerk I polish off the last of my rum. "And I am always privy to what's happening around me.*"

"*You wouldn't know me,*" *she smiles coyly. Her demeanor shifts and she seems smaller. "Just a fly on the wall, taking in the world as it passes by.*"

The barkeep materializes in front of us, and we order another round. I don't recall how many I've had at this point. We continue to drink, and a few more people enter the tavern. Our conversation turns casual - friendly. We are joined by a group of men who take a liking to the redheaded beauty who keeps handing me taller and taller glasses of rum. I feel looser than I have since I took on the responsibility of being captain.

"*Let's play a game!*" *The redheaded woman raises her glass. We are all standing around a tall, circular table. Two of the men only remain standing because of the support from the table beneath their forearms. I am dizzy but not so gone that I cannot walk in a reasonably straight line, though I feel my control slipping further from my grasp.*

"*Aye, lass,*" *one of the more vertically apt men smiles wryly as he clinks his glass against hers. "I have one particular game in mind that I'd like to play with you.*" *He steps close to her, melding into her as he begins to kiss her neck. His face is engulfed in the flames of her hair, and she laughs at the intensity of his approach.*

"*All in good time, my dear,*" *she brushes him aside with complete authority. I think I have grown to like* her. "The game I have in mind is far more... group oriented."

The same man turns his gaze on me and licks his bottom lip. I want to cut the skin from his face. "I wouldn't object to that," he eyes me head to toe.

She reaches up and grabs his jaw with her entire hand. Though dainty in form, her fingers squeeze with an intensity demanding all of his attention. "I don't share, darling." Her tone is void of all the lightness that proceeded. As if switching back to another personality entirely, she releases him, smiling again to the group, "Let's play the wishing game."

The wishes each man confesses are as predictable as they are lighthearted. I spit a mouthful of rum on one man's face as I laugh at his very specific wish for bodily harm to befall his abhorred boss. Another one wishes for something I am almost certain he can pay for at any number of brothels in this town alone.

I am having, dare I say, fun. First time in a long while. None of the men are overtly flirting with me, and I greatly enjoy the dynamic. It feels similar to the more lighthearted moments with my crew, which are few and far between. Only now, there is no pressing need for me to maintain authority. Just lighthearted banter. It dawns on me that this lack of inhibition is not something I have ever experienced before, even in my drunkest state, and I wonder what is different now. The thought leaves my mind before I am finished considering it.

"And what do you wish for?" The redheaded woman places her hand on my shoulder. I didn't remember that she was there. The sudden recognition of *her proximity makes me feel small, and I can't seem to make myself feel large again.*

"I..." I try to think of words, of wants, but all I can do is feel small. "I don't know."

"Come now, everyone wishes for something at some point." She runs her hand down my arm and hands me another glass of rum. I don't want it, but I take it and simply hold it in my hand.

I haven't felt this small in years. Not since before. I feel a connection to my younger self that I sometimes forget from the pedestal of power I carved into a throne. I am feeling swept up in emotion and I can't seem to push it down.

"What is your wish?" she asks again.

"I..." I falter. I search.

"Come on, girl," the man to my right laughs. "What is it you want more than anything?"

The word girl grates my ears – cuts me like a knife. I am more than all these men combined. Better than them in every conceivable way. Why had I allowed my guard to falter? Why did I let a few simple moments of lightheartedness make me forget how these men see me in comparison to them?

"I want everything that I deserve – everything that I desire." I am speaking only to her. They were never listening anyway. "I want to search the very depths of every ocean in every corner of the world. For as long as I live and breathe. I want every treasure in the world, not for the sake of wealth, but for the pleasure of taking what others say I cannot have."

I feel an odd sense of relief at the admission, having never put the sentiment into words and certainly not aloud. One of the men makes a joke about giving me what I deserve, and I resolve to kill him later.

"Is that your wish?" the redheaded woman's eyes are locked on mine.

"Yeah," I say with earnest, "that would be my wish."

The energy changes. The night feels over, and I have the sudden urge to leave. I swallow the final glass of rum in a single gulp. "There's a reason wishes get lost in the stars," my voice is weighted down by every indignity I have ever endured. "Even they know it's too late for us down here."

I start to leave, turning my attention to the man to my right. I trace my index finger along the collar of his jacket, looping it beneath the fabric above his chest and gently pulling him to follow. He does.

We are at the door, about to step into the chilled night air, when a nagging voice in the back of my mind compels me to turn and say, "I never caught your name."

"Just call me Delesseria," she replies with a smirk.

I laugh, finding her joke amusing. "Sure. And I'm the queen of Martyrra."

But it wasn't a joke. I know that now.

After I'd left Barra de Placer, I took that inconsequential man back to the *Ocean's Shadow*. I spent the night using him for all he was worth, which did not account for all too much, and by the time the sun rose the next morning, he lay deceased – bloodied and battered on the floor of my bedchambers. I hadn't bothered to wipe the man's blood from my face or body as I redressed and made my way to the deck, ordering the first crewmember I saw to clean up the mess in my room. We would dump his body after we set sail and put enough distance between us and Puerto Destino that it wouldn't wash up on shore.

The only tell of what would come to pass was the unbearable itch that festered under my skin like a burn in the midst of healing. In hindsight, I know that it was the change of the very composition of my being. At the time, I disregarded it as a parting gift from my filthy little friend – like a final word that he never got to speak. Nothing a few weeks of tinctures wouldn't clear right up.

Nothing really changed until the night of the first full moon. That first time was sudden. No gradual building of my condition. One moment, I was wholly myself, the human I had always been. But once that moon reached its apex in the sky, I felt the skin flake from my neck into gills. Felt them lift off of my flesh, gasping for something the open air could not provide. I felt the fire burning in my hands and feet, the ripping of skin and sinew as thick and powerful webbing knitted together between my preternaturally dexterous digits. Felt the breaking of my bones as they restructured themselves to accommodate these flaps of skin, flexing wide upon command to create humanoid fins.

It took time to relearn certain basic motor skills. Walking. Writing. Tying ropes into knots. Anything involving precision became foreign and crudely executed. Until one day, it wasn't. Now, I can barely remember what it was like to move through the world with my previous anatomy. The easiest skill to master was learning when to breathe air through my lungs and when to filter breath through my gills. I credit this to the instinct of life. The first skill any living creature masters is the art of breath – how to take what you need without thought and without asking permission.

It is easy enough to conceal my differences from outsiders. The webbing of my feet folds neatly between the bones and is only really noticeable when I flex them into fully erect fins. They are even less noticeable in my hands, only reaching as far as my first knuckle, and can be reasoned away as a mild birth anomaly at a passing glance. When I spread my fingers, the webbed skin thins and elongates, but when I relax, they can sometimes go completely unnoticed. I typically wear leather gloves and boots when in the company of strangers or when I am on land, where I have limited control over my interactions. This is more of a personal preference than an act of self-preservation. I don't like people staring at what makes me different.

My gills are localized, swirling in intricate loops behind my ears, down the sides of my neck, and across the tops of my shoulders. I dress with all the modesty that men's clothing provides, though mine are tailored to my dimensions and fit snugly to my form. My signature leather jackets, which hang loose and long on my relatively short frame, successfully conceal my gills in their entirety. The weight of the fabric also helps to keep them from involuntarily moving, though I have long since mastered the skill of keeping them dormant when they are not in use. In the beginning, they would lift and gasp against my will. I find that regular breathwork keeps the mind clear and my bodily control strong.

I am subtly using my breathwork now to calm myself as I stare down at the bodies by my feet. As I do, I find myself wondering if any of the information they had fed me regarding Delesseria was even truthful or if it would send me off on another wild goose chase. My face heats with rage, and I kick the slack-jawed skull in front of me. It does little to elevate my anger.

"Toss them. Let the sharks finish them off." I bark to no one in particular. All twelve crewmembers on deck move into action, though it really is only a one- or two-person job. I must be doing a poorer job of self-containment than I thought.

Still sopping wet, I make my way to my chambers in unhurried steps. *Rest.* I would dry myself off and rest. Then decide whether to follow the lead or to discredit it.

There was a time when I thought Delesseria had given me a priceless gift. But she has taken more from me as payment than I'd have ever agreed to part with. If all she'd wanted were riches, I'd have happily paid the price. But she stole from me something more precious than any tangible treasure. And for that, I will find her. I will take back what is mine. And I will have my revenge.

Chapter 3

Azure

I hate the feel of those first few steps on dry land after spending weeks at sea. It feels like the earth itself is trying to swipe a rug from beneath me at every stride – like I cannot rely on its support in even the most mundane of circumstances. I shouldn't blame the land when it is, in truth, my own body that rejects its stagnation. When on the water, even at rest, I am moving – doing. On land, it is possible to be in complete stillness, and that is when the thoughts creep up from where I relegated them years ago.

I continue walking – despite how my adjusting legs make my gait appear similar to that of a drunken sailor when, in fact, I haven't had a drop to drink in days. We'd run out of anything that could remotely dull the senses almost a week ago, one of the many reasons I ordered my crew to dock at the closest port. But I leave this task for someone else to complete. I have more important business to attend to.

It is not by mistake that we ended up here. This destination was by design. I scan the length of the main road that stretches along the coastline and cringe at how much it has changed since I was a boy. Escondida looks nothing like it did when it was still my home. What was once a quiet seaside village with vast expanses of untouched land is now paved over with cobblestone streets and rows of buildings - some residential, others business establishments.

Rural Escondida didn't stand a chance after they found her wealth of pixy dust. Tiny gemstones so small they almost look like specks of sand mixed into the rocky shores and mountains - small enough that they might grace the diminutive fingers of the mythical sprites themselves. When they built the first mine, people started to flock, all trying to get a taste of the fortune such opportunity might provide. The people came, more mines were built, and inch by inch, my childhood home disappeared before my eyes. From the rubble of the degraded sections of land, buildings were erected to accommodate the sheer number of people who came to call Escondida their home. Some came and found their fortunes. Others were not so lucky and found themselves unable to afford to leave, having spent what little money they had to come here in the first place. But that did not stop more from coming. Even the slightest sliver of hope that they might find an easy out from their own personal hardships was enough to keep the people flocking.

Pixy dust sparkles with more colors than the human eye can even detect. More precious than diamonds, these gems are coveted by the wealthiest of the wealthy, who brandish them in gaudy jewelry or ornate trinkets. Others go so far as to have them woven into fabrics and commission garish gowns or suits to be tailored just for them. Pixy dust being found in Escondida was something of a marvel since it was thought that all sources had been depleted. The Escondida mines are the last ones in all the realms. Well, they *were*.

The mines are barren now, though there are still those who venture into them, clawing at the crumbling earth with their last shreds of hope. Despite the many buildings in the central village, more people live on the streets than in the buildings themselves. Not that the buildings are vacant – there are just more people than resources now that the wealth has dried up. Few people manage to leave, and Escondida has become something of a graveyard. Bodies line the tunnels of the mines, many of them literally dropping dead trying to find a scrap that they could sell or barter for food or shelter. Others take the route more dignified and throw themselves from the rocky shores into the ravenous waters below. In Escondida, everything was once vibrant. Now, it is various shades of grey, comprised of muck and grime.

My walking has leveled into something more natural in form as I approach the stone building. It stands smaller than some of the others around it, only one story tall compared to the others, which tower at two or three. I am in the heart of Old Escondida, the section that was once the residential village before the mines and the first place to experience development with the initial immigrants. As it stands today, it is an abhorrent mix of old charm and developed uniformity. Those buildings that remain untouched from the old Escondida are the only things I can stomach looking at whenever I am here.

Fortunately, the building I am entering is one such structure and the only one I have any obligation to enter.

Escondida Bond & Trust is the only reputable establishment that still holds my parents' legacy. Everything else that bears their name I've dragged through the mud ten times over in the twenty years since their passing. If I could have, I'd have done the same with this place and never looked back. But legality prevented me from doing so.

"Ah, Azure, my boy," Braun calls from behind the counter. "Is it that time of year already?"

The smile that pulls at the corners of my lips is not entirely forced. The genuine cheer in Braun's voice, paired with the sense of nostalgia that even the scent of this place instills in me, makes my heart feel less heavy. Though, I know it will not last.

Braun is not my blood, yet he is family. He was the one who took me in when news came of my parents' demise, and he became somewhat of a father figure to me. My parents were merchant sailors, very successful in their trade. Braun was a mutual friend of theirs and the person whose business they entrusted to safeguard the entirety of their substantial fortune. Father never left Mother behind. He spent most of his time sailing to various places across the realms, and he once told me that he couldn't leave her behind otherwise he would never see her – and then what was the point of their union? But that never stopped them from leaving me behind.

I was twelve when they passed. Possibly eleven. I do not know for sure. I had celebrated my twelfth birthday with Braun while they were out on business. All I know is they left when I was eleven, I celebrated my twelfth birthday, and within a matter of a week and a half, news came that their ship had been caught in a terrible storm and torn to pieces by the winds and waters. No survivors.

To say that I was devastated might be an over-exaggeration. I was sad, undeniably. But I was far from lost. After all, very little had changed for me in my day-to-day routine. More than anything, I was angry. I was angry at all the time I spent without them when they would leave me behind in Escondida while they would sail off on their grand adventures. I was angry at all the promises they had made to spend more time with me, to take me with them once I was older. All the promises that they had now broken without so much as leaving me a glimmer of hope that this time they might actually follow through. I was angry that they had left me behind one final time.

Braun mourned them. Probably more than I did. If anything, I mourned the idea of them. At least before their absence was filled by the knowledge that they were out there in the world. Now, they cease to exist entirely, and I can feel that absence like a sustained breath.

I moved in with Braun shortly after we held their funerals. The ceremony felt empty considering there were no bodies to burry. I never believed in the benevolence of the gods, and therefore, I did not put much stock in the prospect of existence beyond death. But I went along with the dog and pony show for Braun's sake. He seemed to heal more quickly after that. I moved my belongings from my parents' house into the room in Braun's home that I used whenever they'd been away. I did not mind when he sold my childhood home to developers to help offset the cost of supporting me in my adolescence. I'd spent more time at Braun's place anyhow. I found that I barely missed the old place. Except for the way it smelled.

Braun let me work in the bank when I turned thirteen. Perhaps this is where I first fostered my interest in wealth. Before handling the bits of gold and coin that patrons would hand me to lock away in the back vaults, I never gave wealth much of a thought. After all, my parents had been wealthy beyond measure, so it never dawned on me that there was a flipside to existence opposing comfort and security. When I learned about economic disparity, I became transfixed with the notion of gain - the joy of taking something simply because you can and keeping it all for yourself. Over time, I found I reveled in the feeling of other people handing me the profits of their life's work and found it increasingly challenging to release my hold on their emblems of wealth as I placed them safely in Braun's vaults.

When I was good and addicted, I learned that my parents had indeed left me the entirety of their wealth. It was all mine to do with as I pleased. With one caveat - the funds were to be released to me in yearly allowances at a fixed rate until the money ran out. I was sixteen when the first installment was paid to me. I was sixteen and one month old when I sailed away on the one remaining ship from my parents' merchant fleet, with the ambition of doubling, tripling my newfound wealth by whatever means possible.

That first year, I failed miserably. I lost every penny I had been given for that year within six months. When the money ran out, the sorry excuse for a crew that

I had acquired along the way all dispersed, leaving me to man the ship alone on my final stretch back to Escondida, where Braun greeted me with open arms and a stern scolding. I returned to working in the bank, but once the next year's payment came on my seventeenth birthday, I was back on my ship and setting out once more on the same vague quest.

It went like that for the next few years until I found my footing and established myself in the field of piracy. Each year, my crew grew with my wealth, and over time, my reputation spread. The boy captain. An entrepreneurial prodigy. No mentor. No assistance. Though some discredited my authenticity because of the financial assistance I received from my inheritance. Part of me wished this bit of information was not common knowledge for this very reason, but in the beginning, my existing wealth was a bit of a selling point for acquiring a crew to man my ship. I try to ignore the snide whispers and focus instead on the legacy I have built for myself. After all, if wealth was my goal, I have more than accomplished it. Who cares what help I have gotten along the way?

"Braun," I grin as I extend my hand across the counter. "Always a pleasure to see you."

"None of those formalities, son," he steps around to the far wall, making his way out to the patron side of the bank. "I swear you act like I didn't help your mother change your diapers when you were a wee babe." He pulls me into a firm embrace, and I try to relax my muscles enough to make the exchange feel genuine on my part. I doubt I succeed. But Braun knows that such physical expressions of sentiment make me uncomfortable. Still, for him, I try.

"Happy birthday," he says, releasing me from his embrace, just enough to place his hand on either of my shoulders and squeeze. "Feels like just yesterday that you first stepped behind that desk and..." he shakes his head. "Anyway. No matter. I guess I know why you are here, lad." He steps back towards the side wall and gestures for me to follow. "Indulge an old man, son. Join me for a whiskey and cigar first. I get you all of once a year – at least let me make the most of what little time I have."

One of my brows lifts playfully, accompanied by a half-smile, "Twist my arm." I follow him into his office.

"This is still your home as far as I'm concerned, so I won't bother telling you to make yourself at home," Braun takes two glasses off a shelf, setting them on his desk. "But please, take a seat. Take a load off." He nods to the leather chair in front of his desk. I slide into the seat, and my muscles melt into the familiarity of its feel. I marvel at how I am the only thing that has really changed in this room for as long as I can remember. Even Braun. If not for the grey hairs and wrinkles circling his eyes, I wouldn't have noticed he has aged.

"It's good to see you, lad," he fills both glasses, sliding one across the desk towards me.

I grab the glass and take a drink. "It's good to see you too, Braun." It isn't a lie. Though I left and never looked back, I am grateful for all Braun has done for me. He is the closest thing to family I have left and even before that was true, he was the person I was always closest to regardless. The whiskey burns beautifully in my throat and I savor these first sips after so much time without. "So, how have you been?"

I see a momentary flash of something in his eyes, but it is gone before it registers. "Oh, you know. Life," he dismisses. He opens a desk drawer and retrieves a cigar humidor, taking two before returning it to its slot in his desk. "And you, boy?"

"Oh. You know. *Life.*" I match him word for word in mocking mimicry. We both know he does not approve of my life choices. Even though he has long since given up trying to lecture me or convince me to do something else with my life, I know that he hates hearing about the details of my escapades. So, I don't tell him much. Stories that find their way back to him by word of mouth he simply reasons away as tall tales or exaggerations.

"You know, your old life is always waiting for you back here." He hands me a cigar.

"Braun," I say in dismissal.

"Azure," he says in disappointment.

That is how we usually leave it. A simple acknowledgement of who the other is. The apathy. The disapproval. The acceptance. Regardless of all the complications, we always get past it. Always making the most of the short exchanges we have each year and pretend like everything is fine.

"I'm selling the business," Braun does not look me in the eye, instead focusing on lighting his cigar.

"Oh?" I prompt. I am trying not to immediately ask what that means for me and my inheritance, instead focusing on what it means for him. "Why is that?"

"It's just time," he says, tossing me his matchbox. I catch it with one hand.

"But this place has been in your family for generations," I note. Lighting my own cigar, I inhale until the tobacco flares to life in the bowl, smoke puffing in my mouth. Leaning forward, I let the dark cloud slip from my lips. "You still have a few good years left in you, old man." My words are said in jest, but the muscles in his face tighten as he continues to stare at his cigar. He takes a long drag.

"Braun?" I push. I cannot conceal the subtle notes of worry in my voice.

"I do, kid. I do." He drinks from his glass. "But I'm afraid a few good years is all I have left."

"What is that supposed to mean?"

"I'm sick, kid." He taps the end of his cigar on the edge of an empty mug, causing ashes to fall like dirty snow.

"What do you..." I start, head shaking.

"I said I'm sick," he cuts me off, sternly. "Doesn't matter what I have. I'm sick is all. Nothing the healers can do about it. I've made peace with it. I suggest you do the same."

"And how do you expect me to do that?" My voice is harsh, grating. I am trying not to be angry with him. For telling me he will be leaving me just like my parents did.

"You left first kid," he snaps. He knows what I am thinking. Knows that I am reeling. Knows just what to say to make it sting more. "I'm just returning the favor."

"Fuck you," I growl.

"No kid, fuck you." Braun slams his glass on the desk. "I did everything for you. Took care of you. Took you in when, quite frankly, I did not have to. I raised you as my own and worked hard to keep this business profitable so that one day you would have something to rely on besides just the money your parents signed over to you with their deaths. And what did you do? You pissed all over it. I'm sorry that what I had to give you wasn't good enough for the likes of your spoiled ass." He downs the last of his whiskey before refilling the glass. "The gods never granted me a family. You were all I got. And I was fine with that. *Am* fine with that." His demeanor softens as the fire in him dies down. "I am fine with that, kid." He takes another, slower drink, trying to drown just how much he means it. "I just. I wish I could pass this place on to you and not have to sell it to some stranger."

My temple pulsates from his affront. I am trying not to react as I would with my crew, remembering that to him I am that small child he knew and loved, not a pirate captain. I can't lash out with him. Another part of me is shocked that Braun spoke to me at all in such a way, since he never raised his voice or lost his temper with me as a child. I calm myself and force my voice to soften.

"You don't have to sell at all, Braun. You said you have years, don't you?"

"That's just an estimation, son. Who really knows with these things." His eyes meet mine and I can feel the apology that he will not be able to verbalize. "Regardless, I won't be spending my final years this way. If I'm going to keel over soon, I want to spend them doing all the things I haven't gotten to until this point."

I can't help but feel guilt for this, as if my presence in his life as his ward had kept him from truly living. Kept him tied down in one place. For the first time, I wonder if maybe he wanted out as well.

"Even if I kept the place for the time being," he continued. "It would only be a matter of time before it got sold off. At least this way I can take the money and live lavishly, for a while."

I finish off my glass and pour another. I don't look up as I ask, "What about my money?" The pause that follows is deafening. I can hear the unvoiced sigh in Braun's silence, the disappointment.

"It always comes down to that, doesn't it, kid?" He leans back in his chair, crossing one foot over the opposite knee. "I thought I'd feel bad telling you this, but honestly, it feels like a weight off my shoulders now." He sips his drink and smiles. "It's gone kid. After today, that's the last of it. You're final installment from your inheritance. Your parents' account's all dried up."

My jaw would have dropped to the floor if I wasn't already clenching my teeth so tightly. My parents' fortune was always an infinite figure in my mind, something I could always fall back on. How could it be gone? Not that I am reliant on it. I have done well for myself in my less than legal enterprises, but the stability of the trust. It was always a safety net. A lifeline.

"It's not about the money," I refute.

"Then why do I only ever see you one day a year? The first day that you are able to cash in on your yearly stipend?" He is laughing now, as if something about the conversation is funny. "Nah, boy, all you care about in this world is good, tangible treasure. I can't fault you now for something I have known all along just because I am on my last legs."

I extinguish my cigar, no longer caring for the distraction. "That's not true and you know it."

"Sure, kid. Sure." He places his cigar between his lips and puffs. "I'll get your coin, kid. I'll close out your account and that will be that. No more obligation. No more reason for you to keep coming back here."

I huff, annoyed at the pity he is basking himself in.

"In a way it's better. I won't feel compelled to stick around. To be here waiting in case you decide to show back up. I can just go peacefully wherever and whenever the hell I want. I can..."

"I could stay," I say. It is my turn to cut him off.

He stares at me for a time.

"What?" his voice wavers.

"I said I could stay," I repeat.

"You wouldn't." He is tentative in his words, almost childlike. I detest how much I relate to the hope clinging unwillingly to his eyes.

"I will," I promise, though it burns in my throat as I do. "I can stay here with you. Or... you come with me." Even as I offer it, I know he will say no. Hope he will say no.

"I couldn't, kid. This sickness makes me queasy enough as it is. I couldn't stand sea sickness on top of that."

He couldn't stand to have to see firsthand what I've become.

"Then I could stay," I affirm. My mind is still screaming at me to shut my mouth. "Make up for lost time."

The way his face glows, even as he tries to hide it, makes me nauseated. More so with myself than anything else. "You don't have to do that, boy."

"It wouldn't be for you," I lie. "I want to, for purely selfish reasons. I assure you." I augment my voice in jest.

He laughs.

"Stay the night, anyhow," he counters. "We'll see how you feel about that declaration in the morning."

We finish off our whiskeys, and together, we head down the street to the pub, the only decent one that still remains. Though it is owned by different people now, it is the same place he used to take me on special occasions when I was young and is the place we have gone to every year on my birthday since I left. We eat a hearty meal and have a few more libations before heading to Braun's cottage on the outskirts of town. Even with all the development, his place is still on the border of emptiness.

I haven't been back here in years. At least ten. I enter and am met with the familiar scent of must and pine.

"Room's all made up for you," Braun gestures in the direction of my old bedroom. He didn't know I would be staying. After all, I never do. I step into my old room, and it is exactly as I had left it. But there is no dust, and the linens are clean. I find myself wondering if he keeps the room tidy all the time or if he cleans it fresh each time I come into town, in the hopes that I stay, even for a short time. My heart pinches at the thought, and shame takes the form of a tear in my eye, but I force it back down. I don't deserve the catharsis of shedding my shame through tears. I deserve to carry it with me always like a brand on my wretched soul.

I sit on the edge of my old bed and I feel too large for it. I feel too large for the room itself, and I find myself feeling anxious and trapped between the four wooden walls and low ceiling. I feel the floor wrapping up my ankles and trying to root me in place. When the tightness around my throat starts to constrict, I step back into the main room. Braun has already retired for the night, so I exit the front door and head back towards the main strip of town. Finding my way to the nearest bar, I order myself yet another drink.

I am joined by a few of my men, who had clearly spent their entire evening getting three sheets to the wind. They are speaking jovially about some misbehavior from earlier in the day, a brawl of some kind, but I am not listening. All I am doing is thinking of Braun and the fact that his time is limited. Thinking about how I made him a promise it just might kill me to keep. I'm not sure if any part of me even meant it when I told him, assured him I would stay.

"Ah, he better pray to Delesseria herself that we don't run into him again while we're at port," one of my men says to another as they finish reveling in the beating they had given a dock worker for some perceived slight.

"What did you say?" I state more than ask.

"Just that not even the gods themselves could help him if we see him again," my crewmember laughs nervously.

"Corkin, you blithering idiot," another jabs him in the side. "The captain doesn't want to hear your peacocking about such trivial matters. What happens at port stays at port. Aye, Captain?"

The men raise their glasses and voices in a toast, but I pay them no mind. My mind is elsewhere.

Delesseria.

"Meet me back on the ship in an hour. Sober yourselves and the rest of the crew. We set sail at dawn," I order. After grumbles of discontent, my crew sets off to collect any other inebriated stragglers.

I return to Braun's cottage and make it a point to enter as soundlessly as I can manage, given my own mild inebriation. I find a scrap piece of paper on the table and write out a quick message.

Be back. Don't sell. I will make this all right again. Going to find a sea witch and see about buying you more time.

I leave the paper on the table, where he will find it in the morning. He will know that I mean to return because the last of my parents' money is still in the vault at Braun's bank. Even if he doesn't trust that my compassion for him will bring me back, he will at least know that I'll come for it. In truth, I would toss the coin to the bottom of the ocean if it meant Braun would get better. In this moment, money means nothing to me. Not when the prospect of losing him is looming over me like a dark shadow. I cannot sit idly by, waiting out the clock of a dying man. Even if that is all he wants from me.

Chapter 4

Vessa

I woke feeling ravenous. Near-death experiences will do that to you.

I have a hearty meal brought to me in my chambers, devouring it while I'm still in my sleeping trousers and tunic. I am pouring over the maps on my desk as I eat. I'd lost more time than I am accustomed to, with the necessity of sleep and the inconvenience of attempted mutiny taking up the bulk of my day. It is now early evening, and I have made my decision.

I will follow the bloody lead.

There is a high probability that the intel those two sniveling weasels fed me is nothing more than prevarication meant to throw me off my mark. To protect *her.*

But I have no other leads.

At the very least, this will propel me forward. Elsewise, I would just be floating aimlessly adrift. No more or less likely to find her by doing that than on a wild goose chase.

Their lead will take me to a place that everyone in the realms knows, though I myself have never been, and where the richest of the rich would never dare set foot, lest their sparkling reputations become tarnished by the squalor that plagues its shores... *Escondida.*

The men had confided to me – when they were still masquerading as willing comrades – they'd heard rumors that Delesseria frequented Escondida, preying on the souls of those too desperate to do anything but sell theirs to her in exchange for an ounce of good fortune, having found none in the now barren mines. They claimed that they'd been heading there when their ship was caught in a storm, and they washed up on the shores of Skeleton Island.

While I retain reservations as to the trustworthiness of their intel, the logic tracks. I should have considered it before, that she might hunt in such places of desolation. That I might use that information to turn the tides and hunt her all the same. All this time I'd been trying to chase her. Lure her to me, to find just the right place to reel her in. But Delesseria is no mere fish to be caught. She is a predator of reason. One that I need to stalk. Hunt. *Kill.*

If my calculations are correct – which they always are – and if the wind remains our ally, it will be nearly a two-week journey to Escondida. That means there is still one more chance for her to make me hers before I reach its shores. I pinch the bridge of my nose between my fingers to alleviate the building ache in my head. With a heavy sigh, I think about the night ahead. How close of a call it was being thrown to the waters last night, in particular. *What if it had been one day later?*

Downing the last dregs of coffee, I use the same dirty mug to pour myself a conservative shot of rum from my desktop decanter. It is ornate crystal, held in place atop the wooden desk by hand-crafted, decorative iron bars that have been drilled into its frame to keep it stationary on even the roughest of seas. This having been Vayne's quarters when he was still alive, he'd had the bars fitted to his desk so he would *never have to compromise on the finer things in life.* A value I inherited from my predecessor.

I down the shot in one gulp and briefly consider pouring another, but I need to remain sharp for the coming night. So, I refrain.

I dress in my usual clothing – dark, fitted pants, a loose-fitting white tunic, leather jacket, and boots. Stepping out the door of my chambers, I slip on my feathered hat – which comes to a single point in the front and two in the back – and make my way up deck. As I walk, I curse myself for letting it get so late in the afternoon on the eve of a full moon.

The only remaining sign of the slaughter from the night before is the outline of their bloodstains on the wood deck. Not that there is any blood remaining. Rather, the crew scoured so vigorously that the marks of their soap and rags have yet to fade. I find Gareth, my first mate, at the helm, staring off into the horizon with a look of calm about him. I approach wordlessly.

"Captain," he says in greeting, without averting his eyes from the ocean ahead.

"Gareth." I come to stand at his side, fixing my gaze forward as well.

We stand in silence for some time. Neither of us has much to say leading up to nights like tonight. The awkwardness of it. How habituated we have each come to it. Rather than find the words to discuss it, we'd rather keep things simple. It's easier that way.

"Tell the crew we will be heading to Escondida," I break the silence.

"Already heading in that direction," he confirms. "But I will let them know it is now the official order."

I nod. "Good."

I am tired. I am certain Gareth knows this, otherwise he'd have stepped aside for me to take the helm. I am certain he knows because he is as aware of what today is as I am, and is the only other person in all the realms who knows my secret and bears the responsibility of keeping me safe.

"It's about that time," I tell him, lowering my voice so that it is almost a whisper, though I know we are too far from any of the crew to risk someone overhearing our conversation. "I'll be needing you soon."

"You tell me when, Captain," he glances at me briefly from the corner of his eye. "I'll have Starkey take over for the evening when you need me."

Gareth was a part of Vayne's crew when I first stepped foot on the *Ocean's Shadow*. Had been for several years before I came into the picture. He is a few years older than I, twenty-nine to my twenty-six. He turned eighteen a week after I joined the crew. Our friendship was not instantaneous but forged over years of solidarity in hard work and proximity. Those first months on board, he avoided me altogether. But in all fairness, most of the men on Vayne's crew avoided me unless orders thrust us in the same vicinity. Once my place amongst the crew became established, and the novelty of a young girl being a part of their numbers became normalized, one by one, the crew started treating me like everyone else. Except Gareth. While Vayne considered me like his child, Gareth treated me like a sibling. Always looking out for me. Standing up for me back when I was too young and weak to hold my own. Always in the shadows if I ever needed him. Over time, he became my best and only friend. The only one I have ever honestly had in my life. The relationship I formed with Gareth is how I always imagined family felt.

That's what makes this whole thing so awkward.

"Meet me in my chambers in an hour," I order, averting my eyes as I make my retreat. I do not wait for his reply. I know he will come. He always does.

I make my way to the galley. Though I just ate, I throw together a plate of food and bring it with me to my chambers. I won't be able to leave again until morning and will not permit anyone to enter until that time. Besides, I find that food can be a good distraction while I wait.

Setting the filled plate on my desk, I risk a second shot of rum for the day. I still have half an hour to work it out of my system. Besides, one shot does little more than steady my nerves with my level of tolerance. I passively go over my maps, clearing the food off the plate at my side as I wait.

There is a knock at the door. A courtesy. He does not need to knock tonight. Tonight, I am not in control.

Gareth enters my chambers, walking a few steps in as he assesses the room. His shoulder-length hair is tied back. Darker brown at the roots, the golden hues that fade into the ends are lost in the small bun that's held tight at the back of his head. The stubble on his face and small circles under his eyes tell me he hasn't taken the time to rest much in the past few days. Unfortunate, since I'd prefer him to be well rested tonight.

"Vess," he nods in greeting. It's never captain when we are alone. He takes off his jacket and tosses it carelessly on the bed before rolling his sleeves up past his elbows, revealing the tanned skin of his forearms.

I cannot help the tight burning in my throat as angry words die unvoiced inside of me. It is not in my disposition to allow indignity to fall on me. Nor is it in my disposition to ask for help from anyone. Only Gareth. But this is unavoidable.

"Sun's pretty much down, Vess," Gareth sits on the edge of my bed, facing me where I remain seated at my desk, though I have turned in my chair to face him. "How are you... feeling?"

Anyone else asking me that question would get a swift punch in the face for how uncomfortable it makes me. The expression on Gareth's face makes it look as though I had. I hate how uncomfortable this makes him, but when we are out at sea for months at a time, I don't have any other options.

"In all honesty, the drive is getting strong," I confess. I cannot lie about this or downplay it. "We need to get started."

I think I hear an irritated sigh escape his lips, but I could be mistaken. After a moment of hesitation, Gareth stands and walks over to the chest at the far wall of my chambers. My chambers are directly below the stern end of the deck, with the mizzenmast running through the center of my room. I rise from my desk, locking the door to keep anyone from entering. I make my way to the mizzenmast, leaning against the wide wooden pillar, pressing my hip into it with folder arms. I hear Gareth close the chest and feel the pounding of his boots as he walks towards the bed, tossing the contents of his arms onto it before turning to face me.

"Don't you want to get a bit more comfortable?" He asks casually, but I can tell he is stalling.

With my own exasperated sigh, I push myself from the mast, taking off my leather jacket before tossing it on the bed. I untuck my flowing white tunic from the high waist of my black trousers, unbuttoning the shirt and tossing it atop the jacket. My thick strapped under top is slightly wetted with sweat from the heat of the day, trapped beneath the dark leather. I press my back into the pole, sliding myself to sit at its base as I start unlacing my boots and tossing those off to the side as well. Flexing the digits of my toes, I opt to keep my stockings on, to conceal that one bit of my abnormality. Not that Gareth would care either way. It is me who doesn't want to look at it now.

"Ready," I tell him.

He nods.

Gareth takes a pair of steel wrist cuffs from the bed, coming to crouch behind me on the other side of the pole. I let him clasp them around my right wrist, looping it around the pole before clasping the other cuff on my left wrist. I test them, pulling hard against the restraint. They hold, cutting into my wrists.

"Too tight?" Gareth asks, with genuine concern.

"They're fine." In truth, they are a little tight, but the slight pain actually helps to distract me, so I do not complain.

Gareth continues, not requiring instruction on what to do next. We have gone through this process enough times now. He ties my torso tightly to the mizzenmast, my spine pressing into the wood with just enough pressure that I cannot move and the rope will not budge. Lastly, he binds my feet together with another rope for good measure.

Gareth sits on the floor in front of me, back pressing into the side of my bed as he lets his head slump back against the mattress, his forearms balancing atop his bent knees. We do not speak for a time. We have tried banter in the past but always run out of words as the nights wear on. After a while, we got used to sitting in the awkwardness of the silence. We speak if there is something to say. But we no longer try to force it. Try to mask the discomfort with idle prattle.

He cannot leave. He has to stay the night. Each night of the full moon, he needs to sit with me like this. Not just to make sure nobody comes in but to make sure I do not break free. The whole reason we do this in the first place.

I'll never forget the first and only time it happened.

It has been two months since I first met that woman. In truth, I had forgotten her entirely until one month ago when I transitioned into this... thing. I have done well thus far in keeping my condition a secret from the crew. Save for Gareth. He is the only one I have confided in thus far. All in all, he is taking it in stride. Maybe it is easier to remain calm when it isn't happening to your own body.

I watch the moon rise, almost feeling its rays on my face like the sun. It feels warm. Inviting. Unlike the open air, which is abrasive to the touch. A few members of the crew remain above deck, but I am alone at the stern, watching the night sky and hearing them sing to me.

No, not the stars? The water. The ocean itself is singing to me. Calling. It pulls me like the tides and all I want is for it to pull me close and wrap itself around me. I want to feel the moonbeams radiating through the waves and washing me clean.

I am on the edge of the ship, bare feet balancing on the thin rail. I don't recall taking off my boots or stockings. I feel a cold breeze and realize my jacket has also been stripped from my body. The wind is cold. Too cold. The moon feels warm. My mind is telling me to jump. That the water is warmed by the moonbeams and that everything will be better if only I...

Splash.

I don't recall making the conscious decision to jump. I don't recall taking that leap or falling to the water's surface. I feel the slap of the water like a sheet of solid ice.

It feels like it breaks every bone in my body. I hear her voice, its siren call, and I internalize the verification that this is the woman from the tavern. Delesseria.

I don't hear words, only sounds that I somehow understand. My body is moving but I am not controlling it. She is pulling me by invisible strings, manipulating my every movement. I don't know where I am going but the warmth and comfort the moon promised is nowhere to be found. I know it is her because I can feel her. Even when her call is silent. I am diving deeper. Deeper. The darkness is permeating. I can no longer see, but my body keeps moving. Down. Down. I am terrified, but my body does not react to it. The terror is entombed inside of the puppet.

"Dear, sweet child," her taunt echoes in my head. "Careful what you wish for around a sea witch."

I try to ask her all the questions reeling in my head. But my body is not mine to control. She must be in here with me because she answers – in my voice...

"I want to search the very depths of every ocean in every corner of the world. For as long as I live and breathe. I want every treasure in the world, not for the sake of wealth, but for the pleasure of taking what others say I cannot have."

Her voice is laughing in my head now. "You've gotten your wish, darling, haven't you? Look at you, one of my precious little creations. No longer bound by human limitations. You can access all those sunken treasures you so desperately want... for as long as you live and breathe." *She punctuates the last two words. "How* fortunate for me that you don't breathe under water. So long as you're beneath the waves, you are mine."

There are bits and pieces I see. Flashes that register like distant memories or nightmares as they happen in real time. Though the details come in fragments, I feel every second of my enslavement. I scream and I fight from within my body but nobody hears me and the panic consumes me.

Weeks. Two weeks have passed and I have been awake for all of it.

I see light above and I swim towards it. First, it is my body moving without my consent. Then it is me, in complete control, desperately flailing to reach the surface. The further I go the foggier my memory becomes, details unraveling into nothingness with every stroke. I cry when the air fills my lungs and the tears mix with the saltwater. Weeks of terror, anxiety, and rage release at once and I scream into the air. Over and over again. I scream so much, I lose my voice, my vocal cords rubbing raw from the abuse.

I don't know how they found me. How Gareth found me. Maybe it was my screams. Maybe it was dumb divine luck. I have no concept of how long I was at the surface before the Ocean's Shadow came upon me.

Gareth threw a rope down for me to climb aboard, but the weeks of constant motion without rest or reprieve left me too feeble to grip the rope, much less hoist myself up the side of the tall ship. Gareth dove into the water, gathering me in his arms as the crew pulled us both to safety.

I black out while we are still suspended in the air, halfway up the side of the ship. I come to when I hit the deck, having been pulled over the rail by two of my men. Gareth scrambles over to me, shaking me and asking if I am ok. I try to speak but my voice is gone. He picks me up from the floor and hugs me tightly. I black out again as he carries me to my chambers.

We would tell the crew several days later about my condition. About Delesseria. They had seen my anatomical augmentations – my fins and gills. I could no longer keep it from them. What I would continue to keep a secret was that pull from the ocean on the full moon. How Delesseria could control me if I was in the water on a full moon, and could continue to control me as long as she wanted. She had made that clear through her taunts as she forced my body to bend to her whims. She made sure that I knew I am hers to control.

What she did not tell me was that she could only take hold of me during the full moon, when her powers were strongest. Being a water goddess, turned sea witch, legends say she draws her powers from the lunar cycle. While she could only take hold of me during a full moon, she can keep that hold so long as the moon is visible. All this we surmised through folk tales of Delesseria and through assumption based on my own experience. The day I was released from her control was the day of the new moon. I haven't been back in the water on a full moon ever since and she has never been able to ensnare me again.

That is why I have Gareth tie me up each full moon. The call is too strong for me to fight. I will never again let myself be lost to the will of another. To Delesseria. If my theories regarding the new moon are incorrect, I have no idea how I broke free, if she released me or why. If I did break free of her control, it was by absolute luck. I doubt that I'll be so lucky a second time. If she released me, then who knows if or when she would do so again should she sink her talons back into me. If ever I find myself in the water again on a full moon, she will own me, and there is nothing I will be able to do but bow to her will and be the good little pawn that she can manipulate and sacrifice as she sees fit. That is why I have to find her. Why I have to kill her.

Until then, Gareth and I will pass each full moon like this.

I feel bad for Gareth. I do. After the first few months of this, people started to notice. Then came the rumors. I wanted to come to his defense, but he stopped me. And he was right. Dignifying it would only make it worse. Whispers and jeers that Gareth was *the captain's plaything* stoked like fire over these months that I've been... whatever it is that sea witch turned me into. The interpretation of our friendship became recontextualized by the rumors as did Gareth's position as first mate. Though I ceased intervening when I heard passive jeers at Gareth's expense, per his request, I did put my foot down regarding respecting their first mate. Anyone that had a problem with the hierarchy of authority, and who hadn't learned their lesson after a few good lashings, could walk the plank. I should, in theory, be more emotive over the fact that I inevitably sent more than one person off the plank for that very reason... but I feel nothing over those losses. I'd kill them each again in a heartbeat for Gareth.

I feel the call of the water vibrating in my head. My knees bend and straighten, and my hips try to push up, putting pressure on my hands. My body is fighting against the restraints. The need to get free and jump into the ocean is getting stronger as the moon continues to rise.

"What can I do?" Gareth asks. He always asks.

"I can fight it a little longer. I just..." my legs kick powerfully out, my feet slamming harshly into the floor, pain zinging through my heels. "Get me a shot of rum."

"You always say that makes it worse," he isn't condescending but reminding me in earnest.

"Just do it," I press. "Just one. To take the edge off."

He goes over to my desk and fills a glass. Kneeling by my side, he lifts the cup to my lips, gently tipping it back so I can sip the liquid at my leisure. It burns my tongue, and the distraction is welcome but fleeting.

My shoulders writhe against their binding ropes. My arms are pulling against the cuffs, and I can feel the cutting of the metal into the skin of my wrists. She is pulling me hard tonight.

"Shit." I hear Gareth before I register the sensation of blood dripping down my hand. "Vess..."

"I'm fine," I soothe. "Just a little blood." I hiss as my arms pull even harder against the cuffs. "Damn fucking hell, the pull is really strong tonight."

"She's going to make you cut off your hand, Vess," Gareth has repositioned himself to kneel behind me, concern dripping from his voice. He is grasping my forearms, just above the wrists, fighting against them to prevent further damage. The added restraint builds the tension in my body, and it fights to seek a new outlet.

"Gare," my head starts rocking back and forth as I fight the urge to slam it into the pole. "I need you to..."

"There has to be a better way than this, Vess. Look at you," he scolds. "I hate this. Hate doing this to you. Hate seeing what you do to yourself."

"Gareth, grow a pair and get over it," I spit at him. I wouldn't otherwise speak to him so crudely, but the pain and pressure inhabiting my body has shortened my already bantam fuse. "Just tie my goddamned head down," I order.

I can feel his apprehension, but he obeys. He takes the strip of cloth we use for this singular purpose. It is softer than the ropes but strong enough to hold. I bite it between my teeth as he wraps its length around the pole and secures my skull in place. We've tried various other iterations to keep my head from banging against the mast, but this is the only version my involuntary flailing hasn't been able to slip free of. After the first time, Gareth had suggested that securing me to the bed might prove more comfortable. But my reaction was less than receptive, and he hasn't dared to criticize my methods since. While I'm certain he has a point, and I know he meant nothing by it, the mere thought of being trapped in such a vulnerable position turns my vision a blinding red.

"Was that so hard," I bite my words through the thin fabric.

Gareth walks to the desk, mumbling incoherently as he shakes his head, and pours himself a hefty glass of rum. He downs it, then pours himself a second. Sitting beside me, he sips the second libation slowly.

"This is mental. You know that, right?" He takes another sip, then mutters under his breath, "The things I do for you..."

"Yes, Gareth. Thank you so much," I jape, words slightly stifled by the cloth. "This really makes my whole month."

He snorts, but his face is bereft of all humor.

"I won't stop until we find her, you know," Gareth says after a moment of silence. "I won't let this be how you live out the rest of your life." His brown eyes glow with sincerity, and I know to my very core that he genuinely means what he is saying.

"Neither will I."

Gareth sits with me the rest of the night, periodically cleaning the wounds around my wrists and holding my arms at bay during fitful bouts to minimize further damage. Other times he talks about old memories, stories from our youth, trying to distract me from the long hours ahead.

I know that morning has broken when the last whispers of the pull go dormant in my mind. My body is once again my own and I am safe.

Gareth releases me from my binds and helps me to stand. I walk around the room, prompting the blood to return to my legs, stretching my arms overhead as I do. Examining my wrists, I see why Gareth had been so concerned about them. In addition to the cuts, which had stopped bleeding some time ago, dark bruises circle my wrists in thick bands. They look worse than they feel.

Which is saying something, since they hurt like hell. Making my way to my desk, I pour a brimming glass of rum. I drink it part way down before pouring the remainder of the decanter, topping off the glass. *That should help the sting.*

"Vessa?" I turn to face Gareth, who is now sitting on the edge of my bed.

"What?" I inquire.

"I really think you should consider what we were discussing last month. What I keep trying to discuss with you."

"For the last time, Gare," I am too tired to have this discussion with him again. "I will not just..."

"If you take a furlough, go off on land for a bit, far away from the water," he is speaking with an intentional evenness, trying to sound reasonable. Trying to *handle* me. I find it infuriating. "She can't get you if you are too far from the ocean to be drawn to it in one night."

"*Gareth,*" I mimic his feigned, level tone. "This is *my* ship. And I will not be bullied out of living my life because some cursed *sea witch* is threatening me."

"It would only be temporary," he pleads. "Let me take the ship. I can find her for you. I can kill her. End this. She has no claim on my soul. Me... the crew... we can operate outside of her radar. How do you know that she doesn't know exactly where you are at all times because of that absurd pull she has on you?"

"Gareth, she's an ocean goddess," I laugh, taking a sip of rum as I step in his direction. "I think it's safe to assume she knows where everyone is at any time on the open water."

"But if you let me..." he starts.

"Gare, if I didn't know any better, I'd say mutiny is afoot with how you keep asking for me to give you my ship."

"Oh, *ha-ha*," he orates his laugh in jest. "Just because you are the captain now doesn't mean you can just throw mutiny in my face to change the subject and ignore what I'm saying," he hooks his fingers under my belt, pulling me a step closer to where he sits on the edge of the bed. "That tactic may work on the rest of the crew, but you and I both know damned well you love me too much to do anything about it, even if I *were* vying for the *Ocean's Shadow*."

"You seriously overestimate your worth to me, Gareth," I smile. He laughs as well, taking the glass from my hand and downing a gulp.

"Hmmm," he croons. "You're hoarding all the good stuff in here, Vess." He takes another sip before handing the glass back to me. "Careful, or you'll become one of those cliché lush captains who can't find true north, much less their way to any viable treasure."

"Careful, Gare," I gulp down the remainder of the glass to prove a point, the moral of which I am not entirely certain. "Or you'll find yourself taking a long walk off a short plank."

"Ah," he chortles. "Joke's on you. I actually fancy long walks. And even longer swims."

Our fleeting merriment is cut short by a series of gunshots sounding above deck. A single shot rings from just outside of my chambers and the lock is shot from the door. Out of instinct, Gareth grabs me by the arms, pulling me closer as he rolls us off of the bed, positioning himself to lay on top of me on the floor. Protecting me from any stray bullets.

We hear a bang as the door is kicked open, and several pairs of feet stomp into the room.

I cannot see from beneath Gareth as one of the men steps closer. A gruff voice smirks, "Well, what do we have here?"

Chapter 5

We left Escondida as I ordered. For two days we sailed in the vague direction of *away* before I finally admitted to myself that I had no specific plan for how to find Delesseria. But I was moving, and that kept me from feeling completely helpless.

Prior to learning of Braun's impending mortality, my plan had been to cash in on my yearly stipend and set off to acquire additional ships to add to my humble fleet. I have three to my name as it stands, having sold some and lost others to the seas. The *Queen Marie* looks different under black sails. The last of my parent's remaining vessels, and named for my mother, I feel a particular nostalgia for it and use it as my primary ship. Rarely do I venture off on another and leave it in the care of my crew – though I know they would protect her with their lives.

After seeking counsel with my three first mates – one for each of my ships – half a dozen of my homing hawks were released with missives inquiring as to the whereabouts of Delesseria. Each would follow their usual routes, locating specific ships and land sites alike – allies I have bought throughout the years. Upon receiving the note, some will likely laugh off the inquiry as a fool's hope for something that doesn't exist. Others will know her to be as real as any land dweller. It is upon these few believers that my hope relies.

As I await the return of my hawks and their accompanying responses, I have opted to continue the ambition of acquiring new vessels. I have designated this a necessary task, more so now that I plan to search for Delesseria. More ships mean more sea can be covered in this endeavor. This is what brought me in the direction of *Puerto Destino*, traveling parallel along a moderately trafficked shipping passage.

With two ships on one side of the arbitrary line and one on the other, any passing vessels would be fully surrounded and boarded before they might ever flee their pursuers. Positioning them far enough away, and with the keen eyes of my crew, the *Queen Marie*, the *Cannon's Wrath*, and the *Victor's Trove* are rarely spotted by oncoming ships. And if ever they are, each is faster than the gods and can easily overcome any feeble attempts at escape. All vessels pale in comparison to the speed of my triplets.

All except one.

That is why I rub my eyes as I see her like a mirage in the distance.

Can it be?

My nemesis' ship sails off in the distance, so far she is but a speck. Corkin had spotted her mere moments prior from the crow's nest. After calling down to me, and my climbing the lengthy rope ladder to its peak, my heart nearly stopped as I pressed the telescope to my dominant eye. That they had not spotted us is nothing short of a miracle, if I believed in any such benevolent divinity.

The *Ocean's Shadow*. The most prized vessel in all the realms. The property of my nemesis... *former* nemesis.

News came of his passing years ago and while the thought of appropriating his ship had crossed my mind, I've never quite been able to find her. I'd heard his replacement is a young man who had been in Vayne's charge since he was but a small boy. Gareth is his name. Little is known about this new captain of the *Ocean's Shadow*, other than that his men are kept on a tight leash and even when they come to port, he remains onboard his ship – not even venturing out to the bars and brothels in any of the villages. Vayne having never been one to boast on the achievements of anyone but himself, I assume that much of Gareth's claim to the role of captain happened behind closed doors, so to speak, and remains unknown to those beyond the confines of the ship.

We packed as many men and weapons as we could fit inside our dinghies. From the low vantage point of these oar-propelled boats, and aided by the blinding light of the rising sun reflecting off the water's surface, we were able to easily approach the behemoth of a ship without being spotted by their lookouts. Once we reached its wooden sides, one by one, we climbed aboard using overhanging ropes to hoist ourselves upward. Swiftly and silently, we made our way across the ship, killing anyone who crossed our path before they could sound the alarm. Accompanied by two of my men, I made my way below deck to where I knew the captain's quarters to be – having been aboard this very ship once before in a meeting of truce between myself and Vayne. That meeting had resulted in our temporary treaty of peace, which remained intact until the day I learned of his passing.

Standing outside of the door, I cannot prevent the malicious smile that possesses my face.

Mine. It will all be mine.

Bang!

Gunshots boom from above and I know we no longer have the advantage of stealth. I have seconds before the man inside this room comes bolting out with weapons of his own, ready to fight for his possessions. A fight he will indeed fail.

Bang! I blast a bullet through the lock of the door, effectively destroying it. The door is still intact, so I kick it open with more force than necessary, getting lost in the dramatics of the moment.

I step inside, followed by each of my men. We are joined by two more who came to our aid when the first of the gunshots rang out, ready to support their captain.

Sidestepping the bed, I see the figure lying on the floor. I lower my gun, knowing all too well that four other weapons are aimed at the target of my attention. Captain Gareth.

It takes a moment to interpret the tangle of limbs and hair. Laying supine on the floor beside the bed is a woman, partially unclothed, in pants and a thin undergarment for a shirt. Her long, dark brown hair is strewn across her neck in wild tangles, partially covering the milky white of her face as well. Hovering above her on hands and knees is who I can only assume to be Gareth.

"Well, what do we have here?" I snicker at the scene before me. "Sorry to interrupt. Captain Gareth, I presume?"

The man hesitates for a moment as he lingers above the woman. Still positioned above her, obscuring my full view, he reaches with one hand onto the bed and pulls down a white tunic. He drapes it over the woman before pushing himself to kneel, though he still has one knee on either side of her hips.

I hear four clicks behind me, and I know my men have cocked their guns. "I wouldn't move so brazenly if I were you, captain. My men are eager to protect their own and will not hesitate to put you down."

Neither the man nor woman move from where they are, both recognizing that they are effectively being held at gunpoint, though the man is breathing quite heavily as anger boils inside of him. Stepping past them, I make my way to the other side of the room, circling around the pillar that stands near center in the open space. I kick my boot on a pile of rope and chains strewn beside it before turning to face Gareth, who is now tracking my movements.

"Pity to have broken up such," I pause to accentuate the feigned drama of my words. "*Romantic escapades.*"

While my back was turned, the woman had slipped on the tunic and is now kneeling in front of the captain. Neither has so much as spoken as of yet. I continue to pace the room, looking for any weapons that might be within reach of the two captives. When the girl starts to reach beneath the bed, I hear her before I see it.

I turn to face the girl, now clutching a small dagger as she lunges towards me. I raise a hand to my men in silent order not to fire. Instead, I grab the girl by the wrist, twisting until she is forced to turn around or have her arm snapped in two, wrapping my arm around her waist as I pull her close.

"I wouldn't do that if I were you, love," I croon in her ear. "Now be a good girl and drop that knife."

I squeeze harder on her wrist and she hisses at the pain. Metal clangs on the floor as the knife falls from her grasp. "That's it, darling." I loosen my grasp on her wrist, though I continue to hold her flush against my chest. Feeling a slight slickness beneath my fingers, I lift her hand and examine her wrist. It is marked with cuts and bruises, droplets of blood collecting along shallow abrasions that cuff both wrists. Indignation flares as I piece together her wounds with the pile of rope and chain on the floor.

The sick bastard. Then again, maybe she is a willing participant in his less than savory proclivities. After all, she just attempted to attack an unknown stranger to defend him. It would be uncharacteristic of an abused captive to fight off her own would-be savior.

"Hmmm," I whisper in her ear. "Maybe you aren't such a good girl after all." I don't fully understand what compels me, but some primal urge drives me to bring her hand toward my face. Gently brushing my lips along the tender flesh of her wrist, I press a kiss to her racing pulse.

She moves too quickly. I squeeze her wrist, but not before she clenches her fist in my hair, pulling my head sharply to the side. The suddenness of her actions startles me, causing me to lose my grip on her waist ever so slightly, but she takes advantage of the brief misstep, shifting to the side as she swings her elbow sharply into my solar plexus. The wind is knocked out of me, forcing me to relinquish my hold on her. She pivots quickly to face me, landing a solid left hook across my jaw before the gun goes off.

A warning shot by one of my men.

Upon hearing the shot, she lifts her hands in defeat, though a look of sheer vengeance still shoots from her eyes like daggers. She spits on my boots and says, "You have no idea."

I rub my jaw, spitting a mouthful of blood on the floor beside me. I examine her where she stands, taking my time to really see her for the first time. A wicked grin possesses me – my interest in this woman officially peaked.

"I intend to," I smirk.

"Vessa," Gareth speaks for the first time. "*Behave.*"

The woman standing in front of me goes rigid as a statue. The fire of rage in her eyes turns to something much darker. Colder. The anger is still there, but it is accompanied by something much more potent... *hopelessness.* I feel a shiver in its absence, my instincts pushing me to bait her, if for no other reason than to bring that fire back to life.

"Yes, Captain." Her voice is a husk.

"Respect," I deride. "I like that."

"I wasn't talking to you," she snarls through gritted teeth. Her eyes flare once again with that fire I am finding I enjoy stoking far too much. "You are no captain to me."

"A minor inconvenience, I assure you." I nod at my men and two of them approach Gareth, who is still kneeling beside the bed. "One that is easily rectified."

With a nod, the remaining two men approach the woman, seizing her while Gareth is being dragged from the room and up the steps to the deck. A slur of profanities shoot from both hostages as they kick and flail against restraining hands. But it is no use.

The crew members of the *Ocean's Shadow* are being held at the points of guns and by the edges of blades. Many more have been rendered corpses and are sinking to the ocean floor. They are now outnumbered three to one with no real possibility of their overthrowing us now. Those still alive are being offered a choice.

Join my fleet or die.

"Captain!"

"Captain!"

The cries from the crew of the *Ocean's Shadow* for their captain disgust me in all of their loyalty. Why would they remain loyal to this unworthy scum when they could join an absolute empire such as my own? No matter. They can die for their stupidity. They are replaceable. Crew members are easy to acquire so long as poverty thrives. And by today's standards, they are ripe for the picking.

"Silence," I bellow across the ship and I slowly step towards the helm. I revel in how quickly everything falls quiet in response to my command. I imagine they have witnessed enough slit throats this morning for them to understand that I mean business.

"I, Captain Azure, have commandeered the *Ocean's Shadow*. I have taken her captain hostage," I gesture to where Gareth and the woman are being held just off to my side. "And now I mean to take her crew," I pause. "Lest each of you face a watery grave."

"Fuck you, you sniveling..." A knife slices through the random crewmember's neck before he can finish hurling his insult. His body is tossed over the side of the ship without so much as my lifting a finger. My crew is well trained, unlike the loose-lipped hands of the *Ocean's Shadow*.

"Anyone else?" I ask a silent ship. The waves splash against the sides of the ship. "Excellent."

"Now," I continue, "as I was saying. Who among you will submit to my authority? Who will forsake your... *captain*," I spit the title like a bitter taste. "And sail under my order?"

Silence.

"Very well," I sigh dramatically. "The ship is all I really need."

I am about to give the order to slaughter them all when I am cut off.

"Wait!" Gareth steps forward as best as he can while still being restrained by my men. The woman looks out at the crew, eyes darting between them. Captain Gareth continues speaking.

"Men. As your captain, I have led you through many battles, many journeys over the years. Some of you have known me near my whole life. You know me to be an honorable man, in all the ways that count. You know that this ship, this crew are all the good I've known in this world and the only thing I would ever die for. So, hear me when I tell you, this battle is over. This journey has ended. Live to fight another day. Let your captain live on in your future actions. Fight another day. For those of you that don't, I'll see you in your nightmares. For those of you that do, I'll see you wherever filthy swashbucklers like us go in the afterlife. The captain is the heart of the ship. Keep this ship alive. Keep her alive."

There is a silence that fills the air after he stops speaking. A silence that is too deafening to process.

"How sentimental," I jeer. Members of my crew snicker to themselves as well. "Unfortunately for you, mate, it will be rather difficult to accomplish that task when you are in the bellies of the sharks below."

As if on cue, my men start to drag the dejected captain towards the plank.

"No!" The woman, Vessa, starts to flail against the restraining hands holding her beside me. She is fighting, pulling against them, trying to reach Gareth. Guttural shrieks cut from her throat like razors. "No!"

"Keep her alive!" Gareth yells the command to the crew that was once his, who now stand idly by, eyes downcast as ropes bind his hands behind his back. A long rope is knotted around one of his ankles, an anchor tied to the other end. One of my men slides the anchor to the very edge of the plank. Every bump of a wave threatens to send it careening off, pulling Gareth unwillingly over the edge.

"Gareth!" Vessa wails, tears streaming down her face. He meets her eyes and a single tear slips down his face. His jaw tightens as he tries to remain composed. There appears to be genuine emotion in his eyes. Not fear for his impending doom, but sadness for the pain this woman is experiencing. Perhaps pain for his own loss of her in death. All I know is, for some unknown reason, I want to make him hurt all the more for it.

I grab Vessa by the arm and pull her away from the men restraining her. I pin her to me as I had before, her facing away at the doomed man now being lifted onto the plank.

"Gareth!" she cries again.

"Dropped the *Captain* already?" I sneer.

"Please, let him live!" she is begging now. Only to me.

"Darling girl, you can't barter for something if you have nothing to give in return." I bury my face in her hair, inhaling her scent before bringing my lips to her ear and whispering, "And as I've demonstrated, I am more than capable of simply taking what I want."

I feel her muscles go rigid beneath my hands and I want to spin her around so I can see the anger burning in her eyes. But I also want her to see her captain make his venture into the abyss. Want the agony on her face to be the last thing he sees.

"I take your silence to be a verbal contract," I orate to my newly acquired crew. "The *Ocean's Shadow* and all her assets are now mine. *You* are all mine," I bark. "On with it," I order.

The blood from the bodies tossed overboard has lured several great white sharks to the ship. They circle below as Gareth takes his first tentative steps. There is something thrilling about making someone take their own life, watching them take the very literal steps that lead them to certain death. There is a power there that I cannot help but relish, even if I know it damns my soul for all eternity.

"Better hope the whites have had their fill by the time you hit the water," one of my men taunts.

"Wonder if it's worse to drown or worse to be torn to shreds while you're still alive," another scoffs.

"How's about you switch places with me, and you can find out for yourself," Gareth growls.

"Eh." The man spits on Gareth. "Move it along, before your banter bores me to death."

The jeers continue as Gareth makes his way to the edge of the plank. It seems to take longer than it should, every step an apprehension. When he reaches the end, he turns toward me. A look of pure villainy on his face.

"Please," Vessa begs. She continues to beg, going still in my arms, having abandoned her attempts to break free of me, trying instead to convince me to spare him in exchange for her submission. "Please. No. Please... Please."

"Shhhhhh," I whisper in her ear, in a mock soothing tone. I stroke her hair and as I do, Gareth looks like he wants to walk right back over to me and pry her from my hands. But he can't. And he knows it. All he can do is reconcile the urge.

His eyes drop to meet hers and I am enraged that he gets this final moment. *I want to tarnish it.* Cupping her jaw, I pull her closer, crudely kissing the side of her face. But she does not react to me. And his eyes never leave hers.

His gaze softens as he nods to her, still holding her stare. Not once does he lose his composure. Not once does he let himself embody defeat. He only smiles at her softly, then takes one final backward step off the edge of the plank, disappearing as he falls.

She screams.

Seconds pass before the rope goes taught and the anchor is pulled down as well.

When I release her, she is at the edge of the ship in a flash.

"Keep her from doing anything reckless, like jumping in after him," I order.

I have never before witnessed keening, but that is the only way to describe the sounds and contortions I observe as this woman deconstructs before my very eyes.

She doesn't see him again. The body never resurfaces, the anchor dragging it to the ocean's depths. An hour passes and the men disperse as the new order is being set forth by my men to their new crewmembers. The bustle behind me dies out as I sit, fixated on the woman. Keeping an eye on her to ensure she does not jump in after her fallen captain like a lunatic. But she does not try. Her wails die down to whimpers, and she stays like this for some time, leaning over the rail of the ship, peering down at the water below.

I rise from the barrel I've been sitting atop and come to stand beside her. "Aye, you must have really grown to love your captor," my taunting words hold less cynicism than before, though they are far from kind. "I hear that happens to lasses like you."

She does not respond.

I examine the emptiness in her face as she stares out across the ocean. I brush my fingers against her hair, yearning to see the reanimation of her flame. Craving it like an addiction. "Let's see how long it takes you to forget about your captain entirely and think only of me."

Her face grows hard, silent tears betraying her attempts to bury her emotions.

"So many tears." I trace the back of my index finger along her bruised and bloodied wrist. "All for a man who did *this* to you... interesting."

She cries a little bit harder.

"Ah," I tsk. "You'll be better off with me, love. I know how to treat a woman."

Chapter 6

Vessa

I never knew I had a soul until part of it was ripped away. Until it sank to the bottom of the ocean and all that was left was its absence in the vacant wound of my chest.

Vessa, behave.

Not an order, but a question.

A code.

I knew what he was saying. Knew how the series of events was bound to play out thereafter. Knew it was going to happen.

We were children then. At least I was. Struggling to find a way to force myself to abide by the regulations set forth by Vayne now that I too was a member of his crew. I found it all too familiar, all too challenging to abide by a set of rules imposed on me by yet another man, having undergone such restriction by my father prior.

"This is different," Gareth assures.

"How do you figure?" I toss a small pebble into the bay from where I sit upon the dock of some port. I am not yet acquainted with its name. We have stopped for a short time to replenish supplies. Gareth has been tasked

to keep an eye on me by Vayne, though neither brought the order to my attention. Even if the order hadn't been given, Gareth has taken it upon himself to remain close by whenever Vayne is not around.

"For one, it was your choice to be here. Your choice to stay." He follows suit and tosses his own pebble casually into the water.

"So?" I argue, with childlike petulance.

"So, it is completely your choice if you want to follow these rules. If you don't like it, just walk off into that town and don't look back," he points vaguely behind us to the rows of buildings and fish stands.

"Gross," I roll my eyes. "Not much of a choice. The rank stench of a fishing port or the rank stench of a bunch of sweaty men... I'd much prefer a swift death, thank you very much."

"Well, the sea is right there if you want to hurl yourself into it, princess," Gareth smirks. "You've got a lot of fire, kid. It'd be a shame to lose you to Davy Jones so soon. And truly embarrassing for you to have it happen in such shallow water." He nudges me playfully in the arm, causing me to laugh, despite my bitter mood.

"How do you stand it?" I ask in earnest. "How do you stand being told what to do every moment of the day?"

He sits for a time. "It's never bothered me much." He scooches slightly away from me as he reaches for another rogue pebble on the dock. "Before, before Vayne and all this, I never had anyone who cared enough about me to teach me how to be in the world. To care enough to give me rules or restrictions. All I had were the streets and myself, and that's a lonely way of living. I guess when Vayne found me, when he gave me a roof over my head and a floor beneath my feet, I found it a small price to pay to be given chores and tasks - rules and restrictions. I guess I was grateful to have been given a purpose beyond struggling just to keep on living. I didn't mind working hard for the man who cared enough about me to take me in."

"Didn't mind?" I inquire as to the tense.

"Don't. Don't mind," he corrected. "Me," he continued, tossing the pebble off into the distance. "I am content just as I am. Unlike some of the others, I have no ambition for more than working on the Ocean's Shadow. I like the work and loathe the thought of having more responsibility than I already have. This..." he lifts his arms to gesture to our ship, which is docked just off to our left. "This is enough for me. This is all I ever wanted."

"What if I want more?" My eyes focus on my hands. I don't know why, but I still struggle to speak of my ambitions aloud, for fear that they will be dismissed. Destroyed.

"Well, all the more reason to play the game," Gareth nods his head slowly as he smiles. "Behave."

I groan in disgust at the word.

"No really... think of it as playing make-believe," he smiles.

"I'm not a child, Gareth," I protest. "Don't patronize me."

"Fine. A long con if that is more to your fancy. A set of rules that you abide by for the time being, until the *game changes." He turns to face me. "Until you change the game and you make the rules."*

"Sure," I dismiss what I perceive to be his placation.

"I'm telling you. Fake it. Behave until the time comes that other people have to abide by your restrictions."

He was the first to believe I could rise through the ranks if I wanted. Over the years, it became a running joke of sorts between us. *Behave.* Whenever either of us had a hard day, we'd say *behave.* A subtle reminder that whatever hardship was ailing us in that moment, it was temporary. All we had to do was behave until we got the chance to change the game. Until we got what we wanted.

And that day came when I took the mantle of Captain and I named Gareth my first mate. That was when *behave* became less of a promise for the future and more of a failsafe – a code, should anyone attempt to take what was ours.

Vessa. Behave.

Two such simple of words.

Vessa. Behave.

In those two words, he conveyed what we both understood to be the right course of action. Let them believe Gareth to be the captain of the *Ocean's Shadow.* Let the chips fall where they may and let all those remaining pick up the pieces once the waves settle and we can regain the upper hand. For him, for me, for all the crew, this ship is our very soul. It was our salvation from the cruel confines of a traditional life that did nothing more than keep us trapped beneath the thumbs of society.

We were not wanted there and we could not survive under those conditions. So, we made our own fate. We took to the waters, giving ourselves and our allegiances to the sea itself. There is no alternative for us, no going back. Going back, losing our freedom... that would be worse than a mortal death.

Our ship is our home. Our very soul. An emblem of the freedom we took against the will of the empires that tried to control us. It is the whole we will protect at all costs. Even if that cost is paid in the blood, flesh, or lives of our own.

The moment I saw how few remained of my crew, I knew we had no options. I knew they would kill the captain. Gareth knew it too. Until his final breath, Gareth refused to fully relinquish his desire to protect me. He'd often profess that he would die for me, for his captain, if ever the need came for such a dire outcome. It wasn't until I watched him walk towards the watery grave that should have been mine that I actually believed him.

I stare off the edge of the ship into the now calm waters below.

How could I have let this happen? Why did I not confess my true position? Perhaps they might have spared him. Or else, they might have found it all the more ammunition to kill him. Kill the man found in such odd of circumstances with me in my chambers. Would they have even believed my claims?

No. They would have killed him. His death must have been inevitable for me to stand by and swallow my truth. They would have killed him and tossed me over as well for good measure. But could I not have saved him?

Could I not have cut my bindings just as I have done before and saved him?

No... No... It is the morning after the full moon. Delesseria still holds power over the waters. I decided... *we* decided that it was too risky to venture into the water so quickly after the full moon for fear that she still might be able to ensnare me as she had before.

They hadn't so much as drawn blood. No mortal wounds were inflicted upon him. His death, which should have been my own, was inflicted by the singular means that bears no threat to me.

I would have lived.

But how could we have known? How could *I* have known that the means of execution would involve neither bullet nor blade? Too much risk... there was too much risk.

Gareth was willing to die for me. *Did* die for me. Died to protect me as any member of my crew has sworn to protect me as their leader. Would they have let me die to save him, or would they have played into our ruse in order to protect me? To force me to live to fight another day?

This outcome was inevitable.

There was nothing I could do.

... there was nothing I could do...

The demon who had stood beside me, taunting the loss of my friend, had left me alone after his final words. Though, I still felt the burning glare of eyes on me. I have no idea how long I have been standing here now. I could stand here the rest of my life and still be unable to tear myself away from this moment. An unknown man steps to my side and places his grimy hands on my upper arm, pulling me to the side.

"Enough o' that," he snarls in an abrasive tenor. "Cap'ain said to give ya as much time as ya need, but I'm starvin' 'ere. Ya done wasted enough time starin' at nothin.' Nothin' lef' to see and nothin' lef' to mourn."

He is pulling me deeper onto the ship, but my eyes remain fixed on the water. It isn't until I am being led back down the steps that my attention returns to the present. The man whose iron grip is relentlessly dragging me forward is one I have never seen before. One of *his.* He leads me below deck and down the narrow hall towards my chambers. He roughly shoves me through the door. The violence of the action causes me to lose my footing and stumble onto the floor.

"Don' bother lookin' for any o' the weapons yer cap'ain left stashed in 'ere. We done searched the entire cabin and found 'em all," he gloats.

My mind considers the false board beneath my bed where I keep a flintlock pistol on hand. I make it a point not to look in its direction.

"Aye, even the one beneath the floorboard, lass."

I keep my face neutral, struggling to hide my disappointment.

I glare at the man in the doorframe. I do not speak. Do not ask any questions. Will not give him the satisfaction of denying me information upon request. I will piece together the context of my circumstances as the situation progresses. I doubt very much that there will be more to it than that which even the dullest of imaginations could conjure. I will simply bide my time and wait for the moment to strike. Wait until my remaining men have engrained themselves into the foundation of *his* crew. Wait for them to find the weaknesses. To report back and together we retake my ship.

The door closes and the lock is turned, both having been repaired since the earlier brawl. I am left in silence as the walls close in around me and the ambient silence rings in my ears.

For now, I sit.

For now, I wait.

For now, I will replay the events of the day on a loop in my mind and try to convince myself that this... was unavoidable.

Chapter 7

Vessa

I sit unmoving for quite some time. My limbs are stiff from remaining still for so long. My entire body is buzzing with fatigue from its inability to relax the tensed muscles that have barely released since Gareth stepped onto the plank.

Eventually, I rouse myself enough to search the entirety of my cabin. As the man had said, they'd found all of my hidden weaponry. Even the mundane items that might, if wielded by a more creative sort, be used to inflict some element of harm.

They had been thorough.

I inevitably relent to the notion that there is no single item remaining that could be used in either defense or offense, so I sit atop the trunk by the wall and stare out the circular window. The water level is much closer from this vantage. I wonder if, had I been down here when it happened, I would have been able to witness Gareth take his very last breath. Or maybe he had been screaming when he slipped past the surface. I hadn't been able to hear over my own wailing. The fact that I don't know is an itch beneath my skin that no amount of scratching could subdue.

If I wasn't so numb at present, I might be inclined to feel embarrassed at the severity of my reaction, involuntary as it was. At the way I begged some man to spare the life of another. My cheeks flush red as I decide instead to cling to rage as my anchor to reality. Rage at what was done to Gareth. Rage at the power that was taken away from me when I needed it most.

Rage at *him*.

Like a demon conjured from hell, there is a clanging of metal as a key fumbles into the lock. The knob turns and the door swings open at a casual pace. He saunters into the room as if it has always been his, eyes fixed on his hand as he slips the key into his jacket pocket and pulls the door closed behind him.

For a creed that spends their lives under the sun's heat on the high seas, we pirates certainly brandish a great deal of black and leather. This man takes it to another level altogether.

The tops of his black boots are nearly indistinguishable from the leather fabric of his pants, which leave little to the imagination regarding the musculature of his stature, yet are not so tightly fitted as to hinder functionality. A black linen shirt, the top third of which is lazily unbuttoned to reveal a carpet of pitch-black chest hair, goes nearly unnoticed beneath a blood-red snakeskin vest. Two rows of shining brass buttons line the front of the vest, which match the rows of identical buttons that run the length of his black leather trench that falls to his knees. The thick collar of the coat is popped, framing

82

the intricate design etched into the leather that runs across the tops of the shoulders and branches down the length of each sleeve.

He steps leisurely toward my desk without so much as acknowledging my presence. Slipping off his hefty jacket, he drapes it across the back of the desk chair before slowly rolling the sleeves of his black shirt to just below his elbows, framing the chorded muscles of his forearms. His back is to me as he faces the desk. Running his fingers through his raven hair, brushing it from his face with his rugged hands, he sits in the chair and starts to rifle through my maps and papers.

Instinctively, my spine straightens as he shuffles the articles around my desk, observing weeks' worth of my work. Courses charted. Plans made. I wait for him to say something, anything, about the information he is gleaning.

He says nothing.

The bastard is not even dignifying my presence.

Without averting his eyes from the sprawled papers, he reaches behind him, retrieving a metal flask from the pocket of his jacket. Unscrewing the lid, he takes a pull before placing it on the desk. I continue to observe him from my station on the trunk.

After some time, he collects the various papers into a pile, rolling the map and binding them together with a brown leather string.

"Corkin!" he calls. I jump at the juxtaposition of the bellow from the silence that proceeded. An average man of medium height enters the room.

"Yes, Captain?" Corkin asks from the door.

"Take these back to the *Queen Marie*," the captain extends the pile of papers in Corkin's direction. Corkin takes them in his hands as the captain transfers the stacked rolls of maps into his arms as well. "Lock them in my quarters. It seems we may have a newfound destination."

"Aye, captain." Corkin shuffles out of the room, awkwardly maneuvering the already cracked door further open with his elbow. Another man, presumably one left to stand guard outside of this room, reaches in and closes the door, leaving me alone with the captain once again.

The *Queen Marie...* I've heard that name before. Vayne's primary competition. The spoiled rotten aristocrat turned pirate out of sheer boredom. *The thorn in my arse*, as Vayne endearingly referred to him. I'd never seen the man, the rival of my predecessor. Not close enough to retain any information as to his features. And when their truce kept the *Queen Marie* and the *Ocean's Shadow* an ocean apart, their rivalry was pushed to the back of my mind entirely. It hadn't occurred to me that news of Vayne's passing might negate the terms of that truce. After all, Vayne had kept the details of the ceasefire to himself. He merely told me, *it is done*.

"*Queen Marie?*" I break the silence of the room. "That must make you Captain Calder."

"Aye. Though I thought I'd made that clear upon our initial meeting. Must not have heard me over all your wailing," he turns on his heels to face me, leaning into the edge of my desk. His flask is once again in hand.

"Captain Azure Calder, at your service." He mockingly bows in my direction before sipping briskly from his flask. "And you are... *Vessa?* If I heard your *dearly departed* correctly?" He overly accentuates the alliteration. "I've heard of you... *Duvessa.*" He lifts his flask-bearing hand to point in my direction, head tilting as he glowers at me. My breath catches as I wonder if he truly knows who I am in relation to my ship.

"Have you?" I force neutrality in my tone.

"Vayne's girl," he nods. "Before he met a similar fate to your Captain Gareth." He tilts his head as his gaze rakes over me. "It seems you are quite the inheritable commodity of this ship," he grins.

Ahh. So, he doesn't know who I am. Only heard the false whispers of *the captain's whore.* Good. I can work with that. Yet, it is taking everything in me to feign unimportance. To *behave.*

"You know nothing," I state dryly.

"I know enough." Calder leans further into the desk.

I huff in response.

Calder pushes himself from the desk, slowly stepping in my direction as he speaks. "I am, however, more interested in what *you* know." He ceases walking and leans against the mizzenmast, several feet in front of me. It takes an intentional effort not to shift away in response to his proximity. I do not want to give him the satisfaction of my discomfort.

"Who says I know anything?" I again fight to keep my voice neutral, though a sappy sweetness can't help but saturate the clearly false words.

"I'm no fool, Duvessa," his voice darkens. "Rumor has it you've been aboard this vessel for quite some time. Been through at least two regimes. Regardless of the form your confinement has taken, whether your shackles have been literal or figurative, you do not strike me as dim." He drinks again. "I do not for an instant believe you have spent nigh on a decade aboard this ship and know nothing of its secrets."

"I don't know what you expect me to tell you."

He steps closer and I cannot help my automatic response to shift backward, pressing further into the wall. I curse myself internally for the reaction.

"I guess I will have to find the right questions for you then," he presses one hand against the wall beside my face. My jaw tightens as I swallow my rage that he dares to approach me. He leans closer and whispers in my ear, "What fun we will have as I pick through that pretty little mind of yours."

My fists clench as he presses a kiss against my forehead.

Behave.

Chapter 8

I felt the blood boil beneath her skin. Felt the mixing of anger and anguish that threatened to burst with even the slightest additional provocation. My kiss transformed into a smile as I pushed myself away, making for the door. Passing the desk, I grabbed my jacket, slinging it over my shoulder.

I said nothing as I exited the room, locking the door behind me. I could have told her that I was leaving for the evening, to spend the night aboard the *Queen Marie* in the comfort of my own quarters. Could have told her that I alone held the key to the room that will serve as her prison and that there was no risk of harm befalling her this evening.

But where is the fun in that?

I left her to her own devices and at the mercy of her own mind as I returned to my original ship. One of, now, four in my fleet.

I sit at my own desk, continuing to review the notes and maps of Captain Gareth. How fortuitous that his own obsession just so happened to be the very sea witch I myself am pursuing. Delesseria is scribbled madly across the various parchments in detailed notations. His reasoning for this obsession is of little interest to me, though I may try my hand at gleaning this information from my new fixation when I see her next. Who knows, this information may prove useful to me in some unforeseen capacity.

I find my mind wandering at the thought of her. Wondering as to the strength of her reaction to Gareth's demise. Wondering if she'd have felt so strongly if it had been Vayne she watched fall to his grave. *Had she cared for Vayne as she did Gareth?*

Perhaps she had cared solely for Gareth all along. Perhaps they had connived and conspired in killing their captain, and that was how Gareth came into possession of the *Ocean's Shadow*. Or perhaps she just knows how to play the game to her advantage.

I pinch my brow between my thumb and forefinger. My eyes ache as they struggle to keep reading the fine print in the light of my oil lamp. The dark of night calls to me, my mind unable to consider sleep just yet. I take my pipe and tobacco from my desk drawer and make my way onto the deck.

The night is peaceful, yet I feel confined. The open air is not enough, so I climb the rope to the crow's nest and command the lookout to leave me in peace until I say otherwise. I sit alone, high above the deck below, higher still from the ocean itself, and light my pipe. Deeply, I puff the embers to life and lean back as I gaze up at the night sky. I feel a weight lessening in my chest.

THE OCEAN'S SHADOW

A star shoots across the night sky, disappearing into the blackness beyond. I find myself remembering when Braun would take me over to the cliffs at night when I was still a boy. We would sit at the edge, staring off across the sea. He would tell me that if I wished upon a shooting star, the wish would come true. There was a time when I believed this with all of my heart. After that, there was a time when my belief slipped and I told myself the only reason my wishes were not coming true was that I was failing in my belief – that if I could just wish it even harder, believe in it even more, then my wish would be granted. I clung to that desire to believe, unable to let such childish notions go entirely. Until one day, I just stopped believing.

No wishes. No magic. No happily ever after. A boy can only experience so much disappointment and loss before he stops opening himself up to the pain. Now I take control of my desires. Rather than wish and hope and pray that they'll be granted, I simply take them. Action is the only form of magic that one can truly rely on.

Just because there is magic in the world doesn't mean everything will be alright. There is still cruelty and selfishness, all the darknesses of mankind that control and gatekeep it. Any measurable goodness can only reach so far. But darkness? That exists in infinite abundance.

I fix my eyes on the *Ocean's Shadow*. She is nearly imperceptible in the darkness of the night, though the stars shine brightly tonight. She looks every bit a shadow, with her dark brown frame and black sails.

Mine. She is mine.

How contradictory it seems that I will use her and her resources to track down magic itself. To track Delesseria, the sea witch, and force her to use her magic to save Braun. I take a puff from my pipe and burn away the incongruity rather than contemplate it.

I feel a sense of joy, pride at having finally taken Vayne's ship – the jewel of the ocean that is now entirely mine to possess. I let myself revel in this feeling before it fades, as such pleasures always do. I have refilled my pipe and burned through its contents before I make my descent from the crow's nest. I order the lookout to return to his post before making my way to my quarters.

Despite the excitement and success of the day, I feel empty. Tired. I kick off my boots and lay at the edge of my bed, legs hanging over the side. I stare up at the ceiling and sigh. The room is loud with silence. I try to focus on the crashing of waves, but the ocean is too calm to provide me the respite of ambient noise.

I haven't been able to sleep since I left *Escondida*. I keep playing the scene in my head. How I expect it would have played out.

Braun wakes up. He remembers I agreed to stay. He smiles as he dresses for the day, eventually making his way to the kitchen. He lights his stove and boils the water as he brews a stiff pot of coffee for us to share. He sits in his chair as he watches the sunrise out the front window of his cottage. I always did sleep late when I was a lad. His smile grows as he contemplates how the simple things like this remind him how peaceful our life once was together. He pours himself a second mug of the strong brew. Then a third. The coffee goes cold and he contemplates putting on a second pot, fresh and ready for when I stumble out of my room. He thinks that maybe I ended up sneaking back off to the pub after he fell asleep the night prior. Again, he finds joy in the possibility, again comparing it to a habit of my later years when in his charge, when drink and women started to capture my fancy. His scoldings then held no more weight than they would now if he expressed his displeasure. Again, he smiles, thinking how the exchanges of the past hold the warmth of nostalgia now that time has passed. He waits... and he waits. Until eventually he goes to knock at my door. He waits some more until finally, he reaches for the handle, slowly pushing the door open, peaking in to catch even the slightest glimpse of my presence. When he finds the bed still made, the joy whooshes out of him as he realizes that I had not stayed. He returns to the main room and only now sees the piece of paper lying on the table. He reads it, then crumples it into a ball and tosses it into the refuse basket, reaching for something stronger than coffee.

Or maybe he awoke with a sense of knowing. Perhaps he knew as he settled his head upon his bed that night that he would wake to a lonely cottage, as he has every day for years. He coughs as he rises from bed, head spinning from the whiskey he drank the night prior. He does not regret the hangover. In fact, he is thankful for the painful distraction from the betrayal he feels from his abandonment. He does not bother dressing before he ventures into the cold empty kitchen. He starts the coffee. Pouring himself some hair-of-the-dog, he sips and stares at the flame of the stove. He does not bother looking in the spare room, he knows he is alone. The kettle is whistling. He is unsure of how long he has been standing there. He removes the kettle from the flame and as he pours the steaming water into the pot, he spots a piece of paper on the table. He recognizes the ornate calligraphy. He would recognize it anywhere. But he is too exhausted to read it. Can't bring himself to care. He is already disappointed and already knows what the paper will tell him. He is alone. He takes the paper, draws it near the stove, and watches it go up in flames between his fingertips. Before the flames reach his skin, he tosses the last sliver of paper onto the floor and stomps it out before the fire has a chance to spread. He sets the pot of coffee and a mug by his chair, bringing the bottle of whiskey as well. He polishes both off and falls back asleep before the sun fully rises.

Or maybe he let the flames light the cottage. Maybe he let them spread, same as the loneliness, devouring him entirely.

I rise from my restlessness and go to the trunk at the foot end of my bed. I open it and retrieve a bottle of whiskey. I do not bother with a glass as I take a pull of the brown elixir. I drink until my head buzzes.

Loneliness is the saddest of all afflictions. I do not wish it upon even the worst of my enemies. When I wished upon those pitiless stars in my youth, I wished for there to be no more loneliness in the world. For everyone to have someone or something that made them feel seen and wanted. Fulfilled. Like they held some worth in the world. More than whatever illness threatens Braun's life, I wish I could cure the loneliness I know he has felt for years.

THE OCEAN'S SHADOW

I return the bottle to the chest before climbing back into bed. I close my eyes and replay the possible scenes in my head as sleep continues to elude me.

Chapter 9

Three days pass in near-constant solitude. Twice each day someone enters the room, leaving food and water on the desk. I am grateful for the attached latrine for my private quarters, though the chamber pot has not been tended to since my ship was commandeered.

Not a single bottle of alcohol was left after the search of my room for weapons. Presumably to keep me from using the glass as a shiv against them. Granted, I would have refrained from doing such a thing since I am not one to act callously without a grander plan. No point slicing my way out of this room if I am just to be locked back inside because we are in the middle of the ocean with nowhere to go. Besides, if I did strike now, I would lose my cover. If they know what I am capable of, my windows of opportunity will become far fewer. Better they not see me as a threat for the time being.

I have spent these days in contemplation. Considering the possible outcomes and paths forward. I have tried listening to words spoken outside of the door, but nothing useful has been uttered. I can hear the pounding of feet above as two crews work together in one cause, though my men are but biding their time in false submission until they see a window of opportunity for us to regain control. It crosses my mind that all it would take is one betrayal for Calder to learn of my position. I do not allow myself to linger on this possibility. If I lose trust in my crew then I will be well and truly alone.

No. They will come through for me, just as they always have.

I try not to think of Gareth, though I fail in this endeavor. Each time I close my eyes I see his face as he stood atop the plank just before he stepped off the edge. I did not sleep that first night. And what little rest I've had in the days since has been plagued by nightmares that replay his death over and over again with added gory details. The tears have stopped though, in my wakeful state. But the pain has not subsided.

I ate only small amounts of the food the first day. In part because my appetite had been diminished by grief, but also to test that there was no poison added to the mix. When my body felt no adverse reactions, I ate the meals in full the next day. It would make little sense in any event that they would poison me. If death was wished upon me, a dagger to the throat would be just as effective and a great deal simpler. Regardless, taking that precaution gave me something to do that first day of my confinement.

It is the afternoon of the fourth day. I finished my morning meal over an hour ago. After having completed a series of exercises to both keep myself sane and keep my strength at its peak, I start pacing the length of the room. Each hour that I have been forced to remain in confinement has made the walls pull closer and closer together, and sitting still does nothing but hasten the process. I am so much on the brink of insanity from the mundanity and lack of fresh air that I am almost grateful when I hear the key turn in the lock and Calder enters.

"Anxiously awaiting my return, I see," he taunts. Already his smugness annoys me, but this is the first human interaction I have had in days. "I must have made quite the impression on you."

"If the impression is that you're a narcissistic bilge rat, then yes," I sneer. "Quite the impression indeed."

He chortles at the insult. Seems to absorb it as fuel. "My crew wants for few luxuries, though I've heard rumored words of lesser men from poorer ships turning to a grimy bilge rat or two to fill their impoverished stomachs." He steps further into the room. "I'm sure my newly acquired crewmates will be thrilled to learn they'll no longer need to consider such plebian acts of desperation."

I huff in response. *The bastard is trying to get a rise out of me.* I bite my tongue.

"Or if that's your way of saying you want to devour me, all you have to do is ask, love." He raises a brow, grinning playfully as he stares at me through his dark lashes.

I want to set him on fire.

His accent is posh. A denotation of his aristocratic upbringing, but with the slightest twinge of a seafaring dialect that he must have acquired over the years. He relishes in the sound of his own voice, made evident by his proclivity for multisyllabic words. He thinks too highly of himself. A condition likely exacerbated by the low bar set by the ill-educated seamen he is surrounded with by virtue of his chosen trade.

"How underwhelming an offer," I bite, failing to keep my temper in check.

His eyes darken. "You should be so lucky. After all, I've seen the company that's kept you all these years."

"Luck has held no bearing in the outcome of my life," I speak without consideration for the implications of my words. Fortunately, the ambiguity of the sentiment leaves him to misinterpret my intention.

"Lady luck was in your favor when she sent me to your aid." He looks like he genuinely believes this. Like he sees himself as the hero to Gareth's villainy. The savior of the feeble damsel.

I try to embody the interpretation of me he has chosen to see, burying my every instinct to skin him alive where he stands. Unable to subdue my authentic self entirely, I find an enigmatic compromise. "The transfer from one master to another is hardly an advancement in fortune," I snarl.

"But with a considerable upgrade in view," he gestures to his entire body in a sweeping motion. "Some might argue it a significant improvement indeed."

"I prefer a view with considerably more personal liberties, thank you very much," I snark.

"You're quite welcome, lass." He is sitting on the edge of the bed now. I stand across the room, having countered his progression into the space with my own retreat.

"You're quite abrasive for a harlot." His gaze hardens as he observes me. "It's evident that this Gareth was more to you than a mere captor. Tell me -" he sits forward, resting his chin on his folded hands as his elbows press into his knees. "What exactly was the nature of your relationship with the former captains of this ship?"

I keep my face stoic and my explanation vague. "I think that is quite obvious."

"Indeed, love." He lounges back onto his elbows, making himself comfortable and all too casual, like he has never once questioned his right to do exactly as he pleases. "Yet it is evident by your mutual displays of affection that the former captain held you in higher regard than any pirate I have ever seen for their..." he considers his words. "Someone of your station."

I stare blankly.

"Tell me," he continues. "What do you know of your former captain's interests in Delesseria?"

Fuck. I had hoped he would have seen my notes and disregarded them as a fool's quest. Unknowing as I am to his personal interests in Delesseria, I keep my answer misleading.

"The sea witch?" I laugh, hopefully not too inauthentically. "The fool got it in his head that he could wish himself an entire fleet to maximize his profits... Don't tell me you believe in such childish fairytales as well." I use my apathy in hopes of prompting a telling reply.

"Never said I did, love." His charisma falters momentarily, and I note how quickly he changes the subject. "You call your former master a fool," he notes. "While I'm entranced to hear such wavering veneration for the brute, have no disillusions that such disrespect will be tolerated where I am concerned."

A river of insults flow through my mind. They build behind the dam of my tongue, struggling not to burst with the urge to let them spill freely.

"Answer me one thing," I demand, though he hears it as a request.

"Perhaps. Depending on the inquiry."

"What is your plan for the *Ocean's Shadow*?"

"Why should such complexities concern you?" His eyes narrow. "Your individual death is not in my personal interest. Does that information not suffice in easing your worries?"

"To the contrary," I lie. "It only makes them grow."

"Ironically, an affliction from which I too suffer when it comes to thoughts of you," he smiles, wryly biting his lower lip.

I consider what it would be like to bite that lip clean off of his face.

It has been quite some time since anyone has spoken to me in as crass a manner as Calder. The vast majority of the people I see consist of my crew. None of which would dare attempt such flirtatious, albeit demeaning verbiage unless they secretly harbored a genuine death wish. Calder is trying my last shred of patience.

Yet... beneath the anger. Beneath the sadness and the apathy and the slew of negative emotions, there is... something worse. Something that burns like acid in my core. Like a phantom wave felt on dry land after months at sea. I can't quite name the sensation, nor can I see it, nor express it without sounding foolish or mad. But it is there. And it washes over me briefly before it recedes, leaving me cold and empty. I felt it earlier in this exchange and I have felt it now again as he commandeers the conversation towards promiscuity.

It fades and I reply, "I hope it's terminal."

"It kills me, yes," he answers too quickly.

It kills *me* that he is quick witted. It's harder to despise the enemy when they possess even a modicum of intelligence. Far easier to abhor the inane. But he alone is responsible for Gareth's death, and in that, I feel no apprehension in hating him.

"Divine," I say, and I wish I hadn't. It feels like I am trying and failing to have the last word, like a petulant child. He chuckles and I fear he has the same impression.

"Divine," he repeats, with less levity than my own performance.

He pulls a flask from his jacket pocket and unscrews the lid. Tilting his head back, he takes a hearty gulp. My mouth waters as it contemplates whatever libation tempts so near to me after days of forced abstinence. It is not a conscious decision as I lick my lips.

"Good god, woman," he snickers, wiping a drip of liquid from his lips as he laughs. I don't know why I hate being verbally branded by the term *woman*. After all, I am one. Never claimed to be anything less. Something about the way it is so often used against me, it lands like an accusation of sorts. "You look practically ravenous. Come," he pats his hand on the bed beside him, extending the flask toward me. "Better not to drink alone anyhow."

My desire for the drink wins out and I tentatively approach where he sits on the bed. I take the flask from him but do not remain in close proximity, choosing instead to continue walking across the room. Sitting atop the trunk beside the wall, I take a long drink.

Whiskey.

It burns delightfully down my throat. I take a second gulp. And a third.

"Easy, lass." The flask is pulled from my grasp. I did not hear him approach. Or follow? He is standing in front of me now as he peers down at me from his towering height. "Nobody likes a lush." He leans back on his heels, some unknown expression twitching at his lips. "Very unbecoming of a lady."

I try to grab it back out of spite, but he tightens his hold on the metal container and tsks. "Such poor manners, darling." He takes a gulp without breaking eye contact. "Lucky for you I'm an excellent teacher."

Everything about this man is grating. I try and fail to keep from reacting to his ever-baiting conversation. "You really are quite cocky," I narrow my gaze. "And don't go for the obvious quip. If you truly are as clever as you seem to think, you really should take more pride in your banter."

His smile is annoyingly sincere. "I take pride in all of my endeavors, love." He takes a step back and leans against the pillar behind him. "But I'm glad to hear that you're so invested in my betterment as a man. If you're interested, I can think of more than a few ways in which you can help me to further grow in such a manner." His lips narrow as his eyes rove across my body.

This man is infuriating. I strangle the words I want to say to him, knowing all too well his kind. No matter what I say, no matter what point is made or how eloquently it is spoken, it won't make a difference. At best, I will receive a juvenile quip. At worst, he will act on one of his previously implied threats.

I have no plans in the immediate other than to simply bide my time and make it through the unfortunate situation I am in. Once my circumstances change, when there is footing to be found, then I can make my move to regain control of my ship - and take his as well for compensation. What happens between now and then... well, the chips may fall at the gods' will. I will work with whatever path presents itself and will take the fewest steps possible back to my position of power. Whatever it takes. There is nothing so precious to me that I would not sacrifice it willingly to get back my ship and destroy this man in the process.

I pull my knees up into my chest, retreating further into the wall. Being reactive has proven ineffective, so I try a new approach. He already made the assumption that I was Vayne's and Gareth's whore - willingly or by duress - so I will play the role he has already assigned to me. I decide to try my hand as the unwilling victim. I am under no disillusion that this will dissuade him from forcing himself on *the poor captive of the Ocean's Shadow*, if that's what he decides to do, but if he tries, it will make it all the sweeter when I ultimately kill him.

I muster the meekest voice that I can emulate, and I hope it doesn't sound as fake as it feels. "Please, don't hurt me," I all but whimper.

I hate how my words and voice remind me of...

No. I am not that person anymore. I have no affiliation with her. Not the life she lived nor the people who held authority over her like reins on a wild stallion, broken of its will. The depths of my wandering mind must have breathed life into my feigned persona because Calder's face softens as he examines me. I try to suppress the misplaced gratitude I seem to feel in this moment for my past traumas.

"Wouldn't dream of it, love." For a moment he looks uncomfortable, thrown off his axis. Then he smiles, though the playful energy from earlier no longer reaches his eyes, giving him an eerie mystique. "Unless of course, you begged for it."

I think my reaction is genuine when my muscles tense throughout my body.

"Tell me." He breaks eye contact, stepping away until he leans, half sitting on my desk. "What do you know about the trajectory of this ship? Do you know where your captain was headed or remember anything about where he has gone on recent conquests?"

I am quick to reply so it does not appear that I am calculating my answer. "I know that we are in a *ship*, in the *ocean*, somewhere in the realm of *Martyrra*. Beyond that, I am not entirely sure." I play the ignorant fool. "The captain was not exactly forthcoming with such details. Why don't you ask the crew? I'm sure they would be far better help than me."

"Oh, I have," he nods. "Just hoping to corroborate a few details."

Shit. What did they say? My crew understands the sensitive nature of my quest to find Delesseria. They know not to divulge any semblance of information about my condition nor give anyone the slightest inkling of where she may be. Too many people might be compelled to pursue her and try to force her to grant them a wish. If someone else gets to her before me, I fear she may disappear before I get my hands on her. Then I'll find myself back at square one. I venture a guess that they'll have flipped the narrative. Told Calder that all the places we have already ruled out are actually the places we are headed next, sending him sailing back to everywhere we know definitively she is not.

I take the chance.

"The best I can do is tell you we came from the west and are headed somewhere vaguely east, based on the rising and setting of the sun." Even if this does not corroborate what was said by the crew, this bastard will likely reason away any inconsistency as my being *confused* or *ignorant.*

He looks at me, unblinking, for a moment. "Hmm," he nods his head slowly, eyes still locked on me. "And where was the last port you docked?"

"I have no idea. Most ports look the same to me from miles offshore. And by the time the ship docks I am locked away inside the ship until we depart. I haven't stepped foot on dry land in months."

The last part was a partial truth. Besides Skeleton Island I really have not left my ship in quite some time. I have been sending Gareth in my stead whenever we stop at port villages. In part, to throw off Delesseria if word gets out that someone is looking for her. She will be expecting me if she learns that a woman fitting my demeanor is inquiring as to her whereabouts. She has never met Gareth, and one more man added to the mix of sailors already looking to strike a bargain with her would likely not raise suspicion.

The more paranoia-driven reason why I prefer not to leave my ship is the fear that she can somehow sense my ship wherever it goes and that if I leave it unattended for even a moment, she would command the ocean tides to carry it off to her. Then she would have leverage over me. Would be able to force my hand by making me come to her to reclaim what is mine, leaving me to barter and bend to whatever conditions she demands for the return of my ship – that large piece of my soul that I simply cannot live without.

"You haven't left this ship in months?" If I didn't know any better, I would say that pity fills his eyes. *I want to slap it off his face.*

"That's correct."

"And when you are near civilization, you are locked down here?" He gestures to the room.

"I don't know what you want me to say."

"Why?" He asks in genuine earnest.

"Why what?"

"Why bother locking you up?"

"I guess he didn't want anyone to see me. Or didn't want to risk my running away. Both, maybe?" I shrug my shoulders as I flounder. I don't understand why he is asking these things. And if I don't know why, I don't know how to answer.

"You'd have tried to run? If you had the chance?" his head tilts.

"I... don't know." I am at a continued loss for what to say. "Maybe."

On the one hand, this scenario is entirely made up. There are no correct answers to this line of questioning. But on the other hand, if I paint Calder a picture that misaligns my allegiance with Gareth, maybe I can convince him to trust me. To give the window of opportunity I need to strike. I run with that notion.

"Things weren't always good with the captain. It was worse with Vayne. So, when Gareth took up the mantle of captain, I was... grateful, I guess. Grateful that it was a little better." I pause for dramatics. "He loved me, in his own way. Gareth." A twinge of emotion hits me at the truth behind that final sentiment.

Despite the intentionally dark implications of my words, there is great truth behind them as well. Life was far from perfect when Vayne was still around. He was a savior of sorts for me, a father figure who gave me an escape from my previous life. For that, I am eternally grateful. But he was far from an idyllic leader. He had a temper and a penchant for violence. Both of which were exacerbated when he drank, which he did too often and to excess – a meaningful criticism coming from me, since I myself drink habitually. Toward the final years of Vayne's life, he became something of a tyrant, turning his violence on the crew at the slightest provocation. Even I had been on the receiving end of his wrath on countless occasions. Only once did such interaction result in my sustaining debilitating wounds that bled and bruised for weeks after. Nothing that hadn't happened to every member of the crew before, but it was the first and only time Vayne truly harmed me more than I could so easily compartmentalize. Gareth ministered to my needs while I convalesced, bedridden for two days after. Vayne steered clear of me until I was no longer exhibiting visible signs of the altercation. I think he regretted it and did not want to see the result firsthand. He never apologized, and we never spoke of it again.

Vayne loved me too. In his own way. As I did him. And I needed him. So much so that I convinced myself the entire skirmish had been my own fault. That I deserved to be hurt as punishment for stepping out of line. I swallowed my words of anger and told myself to behave. Not just in our secret way but to well and truly behave for the man who saved me. To snuff out the nagging thought that I deserved better than the abuse I had endured because I knew damn well what it was like to have it worse. Gareth never made me feel like withdrawing and burying myself alive from within. I can't say the same for Vayne. For that, I loved Gareth all the more.

I realize that it has been silent for a time. I have been staring at my hands while I fell deeper into thought. I lift my eyes to where Calder is still sitting atop my desk. His eyes are fixed on me, yet miles away. Dark. His jaw is tense as he grips his flask with white knuckles. His jaw twitches sharply as he averts his gaze, bringing the flask to his lips. As he drinks, his chin juts out, accentuating the sharpness of his long jawline. I watch the muscles of his neck tense as he swallows. The action bleeds indignation.

"Well," he stands suddenly from the desk and strides toward the door. "If you haven't left this ship in months, it is high time we remedy the issue."

My heart skips a beat as he opens the door. I do not want to be left alone in this accursed room again, and my body seems to panic at the prospect of continued solitude.

"What do you mean?" I ask, trying to prolong the social interaction.

"Tonight, you will dine with me aboard my ship."

Chapter 10

Azure

She is silent as she glares at me from across the table. Bringing her here may have been a mistake. If the many glancing faces from outside of the window panes are any indication, I would venture a guess that a great deal of ogling occurred on her trip between the captain's quarters of the *Ocean's Shadow* and mine on the *Queen Marie*. Those of my crew who had boarded the *Ocean's Shadow* when we took the ship had seen her then. Those who remained on the *Queen Marie* had not. Even now as we sit before an ornately set table, several members of the crew pass by the open windows in frequent rotations, trying to steal a glance at the beautiful woman in my company. They are trying to be subtle about their obtrusiveness, but the frequency and volume of each interloper make it difficult to ignore.

I cannot blame them. She is spellbinding. And not just by comparison to the courtesans of the port towns we frequent. She is more than beautiful, she is... *galvanic.*

She is wearing the cream white dress that I'd had brought to her. After rummaging through the entirety of the *Ocean's Shadow* those first days of ownership, I came to realize that there were no women's clothing aboard the vessel. Besides a few toiletries in the captain's chambers, where I presume she resided based on the utter lack of feminine touches elsewhere in the ship, there was no indication that a woman had spent years of her life aboard the vessel. The dress she wears now is one I pulled from my mother's old trunk. Call me sentimental, but I hadn't the heart to remove it from the ship that was her namesake.

The dress fits her well, albeit rather snugly against her waist and breasts, accentuating the slenderness of the former and the fullness of the latter. *Far be it for me to complain.* Elegant lace creeps up her long neck in a modest collar, spreading downward into sleeves of matching fabric that sweep over her shoulders, closing with pearl buttons at her wrists. The flowing length of the skirt drapes down to the floor, disappearing beneath the table. Her swarthy brown locks hang loosely in messy waves that fall over her shoulders down to her waist, effectively shrouding the aforementioned tautness of her form. Her pale complexion is a near match for the dress itself, though the light radiating from the moonlit sky reflects off of her skin in a way that makes her look like the true source of its luminousness.

Her mossy green eyes continue to glower at me. I can't help but revel in the scorch of their fire.

"You haven't touched a bite, love." I nod at the bounty of food overflowing across the table. I refill my glass of wine and top off hers as well, though she hasn't touched the goblet.

"I guess I have performance anxiety," she says dryly. Her eyes flicker to one of the windows before fixing back on me.

My cabin is above deck at the stern end of the ship. A crescent of windows at the back of the room looks out onto the horizon behind, while a row of windows at the front face out to the deck, where her spectators congregate. The remaining two walls are simple wood that extend into the sides of the ship.

With an abrasive air, I stand, sauntering over to the deck side windows. The men scurry off, busying themselves with whatever task they'd been pretending to do to mask their gaping intentions. One by one I pull the curtains shut.

"There," I return to sit across from her at the table. "Now we have all the privacy in the world. Is that more to your satisfaction?"

She does not answer, but her eyes drift to a dish filled with roasted poultry and root vegetables. Unconsciously, she licks her lips as she fixates on the food.

"Dig in, darling. No point in denying yourself the luxuries at your disposal."

"I doubt you know anything about denying yourself," she jabs, as she plucks a cooked parsnip and sets it on the plate in front of her. I take her affrontive conversation as an attempted diversion from the fact that by taking this food she is relinquishing a bit of her control. She continues to fill her plate with food from the various platters on the table. As she takes her first bites, I smile, feeling as though I have won an unspoken power dynamic.

"Why would anyone want to intentionally deprive themselves?" I refill my own plate.

She thinks for a time.

"Power," she offers.

"How do you figure?" I raise a brow.

She sips tentatively from her goblet. Her expression changes into one of elation when she finds the wine to be of her liking, and she drinks more fervently. I can't help the twinge of pleasure this gives me.

"If you don't allow yourself luxuries, you don't grow to need them. If you don't need them, they hold no power over you." She reaches for the bottle of wine.

I tear the bottle away before she has a hold on it. "Careful, love," I tsk, "or I might start to think certain libations hold power over you." I smirk as I pour her another glass.

Her jaw clenches. "We all pick our poisons. Desire is different from necessity."

"Desire can be a necessity," I counter, refilling my goblet as well.

"Agree to disagree." She drinks, then nods towards her glass. "Have anything stronger?"

"You really can hold your liquor, love," I note. An observation, not an admiration. I stand and make my way towards my desk. Opening the drawer, I retrieve a bottle of whiskey.

"Courtesy of my life at sea," she picks more meat from the platter of poultry. "Had my first drink pretty much the moment I stepped foot on the *Ocean's Shadow* at fifteen. Haven't looked back since." She chews on a strip of meat. "Over a decade of drinking, I'd hope my tolerance is evolved."

Fifteen?

She was *fifteen* when she was taken by Vayne? How mortifyingly young. Practically a child. I feel my temper rising at the thought of one so young being subjected to such a fate. I feel... *sympathy* for her. *Unusual.*

"That's... young," I grimace, stepping back toward the table.

"Not everyone shares that perception," she says, still chewing. "Some girls are already married off at that age."

I come to stand beside her, pouring the whiskey into a clean glass. "A primitive practice," I state plainly.

"And forcing yourself on a woman of any age isn't?" she accosts.

"Who said anything about forcing myself on anyone?" I peer down at her, face contorting in repulsion.

"Your lewd comments. Targeted implications. It takes no herculean effort to piece together your intent." She sips her whiskey, apparently unphased by the situation as she perceives it.

"*Lewd comments?*" I mimic, returning to my seat. "I'd hardly call light flirtations lewd."

"If you see that as light flirtations, I'd hate to see what you consider to be blunt."

"Nothing wrong with being salacious, love." I smile, drinking whiskey directly from the bottle. "In any event," I lean back into my chair, "violation isn't really my thing."

She looks somewhat startled as she swallows. "Then what is *your thing*?"

"Look at you, trying to get to know me," I smirk.

"Trying to learn more about my enemy?" She glares. "Yes."

"Come now," I chime. "Why do you have to see me as your enemy?"

"Let me think," she snorts. "Maybe because you killed my friend and stole his ship?" She presses her forefinger against her lips, feigning earnest contemplation. "Or maybe because you locked me up for days, dressed me up like a doll, and paraded me in front of your crew like some novelty?" Her eyes pierce me. "If your intentions truly are as *noble* as you claim them to be, explain to me what exactly it is you want from me."

"I wouldn't dream of branding my intentions as noble," I reply curtly.

She huffs.

What do *I want from her?* Indeed, I kept her alive because she is of no use to me dead. She may know more information than she has let on thus far. Further, I am not in the habit of harming innocent people. Gareth had to die. Not only because I needed him gone in order to take his ship, but also... because of what he did to her. I can't explain the rage that washed over me when I saw the blood and bruises wrapped around her wrists. Such a visceral reaction has never consumed me so entirely, never commandeered my rational mind and driven me to crave retribution for something done to another. Of

114

course, I am the master of my own reactions and downplayed any overt displays of my displeasure in the moment as I embodied the role of enigmatic captain, but that only made the internalized fury burn molten inside me.

What I want from this woman is something I have never before known, and I have no words to describe the sensation in full. I want more than the obvious, what any man wants from a resplendent woman. I want *more* than anything that could be taken from her. I want to possess her, body and soul. I want her to be mine, of her own volition.

I have never wanted a living being this way before. I want her with the same fervor that I yearn for treasure. For property.

These feelings are foreign to me. And I've had no models from which I could begin to emulate what to do with them. My parents were not around enough for me to derive any patterns of behavior between them. Nor did Braun keep female company, at least not to my knowledge. All I have is my own basal instincts and desires, that I have never been very good at keeping in check.

"Why am I here, Calder?" She pushes.

"*Captain*," I correct, with a flash of irritation. "Though you may call me Azure if you please when it is just the two of us."

Her jaw tics. "Why am I here."

I bring the bottle of whiskey back to my lips and drink. "You said you haven't stepped foot off that ship in months. While I can't do anything about getting you to dry land at present, I thought a change of scenery for the evening might provide you some reprieve from the mundanity of repetition."

Her spine straightens as her eyes quickly dart out the window. When they settle on the *Ocean's Shadow*, she seems to relax from her momentary panic. I raise my brow inquisitively, but it goes unnoticed as she sips from her glass, her mind appearing to wander.

"Though perhaps you prefer the crudeness of your unrefined prison?" I sit forward, her eyes meeting mine at the movement. "What do you think of my ship?"

"It's garish," she replies too quickly.

I laugh. "I think you mean refined."

"No. I mean garish." She picks up a corner of the cloth covering the table. "I mean, honestly. You're a pirate, not a socialite." She drops the corner in disgust like she is flicking away an insect. "What is this... lace?"

I smile at her utter lack of appreciation for elegance, so contradictory to her innately elegant features and movement.

"Came with the ship," I simper.

"Did the ship come with a stove, because you could stand to burn a few things." She examines a matching cloth napkin, looking utterly repulsed. "I have to say, these do little for your image as a ruthless pirate."

Did I see a smile ghost across her face? I can't tell if I am more transfixed with her playfulness or her rage.

"Can I help it that I appreciate the finer things in life?" My eyes darken as my smile grows.

"I think you should try," she mocks.

"There you go caring about my betterment again," I taunt. "Better be careful, love, or I'll start to think you care about me."

"Careful, *love*," she mimics my accent on the endearment. "You're starting to sound delusional."

I chortle and take another drink. I offer her the bottle but she declines.

"We're moving," she says.

"Pardon?"

"The ship. *Both* ships. We're moving," she clarifies. "East, from what I can tell."

"Aye," I confirm. "What of it, lass?"

"May I ask where we are headed?" Her voice gets softer.

"*East*," I offer. While I enjoy her company, and though I feel... *something* for this woman, I am not in the habit of divulging information of any kind to those with no need to possess it.

"I take it you are also obsessed with the sea witch?" Her voice remains soft, tentative. "You pirates and your puerile wishes."

"Not all wishes are puerile," I scold.

A tide of sadness ebbs and recedes as I briefly think of Braun. When I look up from the table, my eyes meet hers where they are narrowed onto me.

"Even if you managed to find her, do you really believe that she would be bothered to grant you a wish?" she asks with sincerity.

"I wouldn't go so far as to say I believe," I avert my eyes to the bottle that I am swirling in my hands. "More that I hope very, very much."

117

"Why?" She presses but without the truculence from before.

"That," I stand and begin to step toward the door. "Is not your concern."

I toss the now empty bottle of whiskey into the bin beside the bookshelf. Twisting the handle, I pull the door inward. As it swings open the hinges creak.

"Where are you going?" She stands up as she asks.

"Where are *we* going," I correct. "How about a tour of the *Queen Marie*?"

Chapter 11

The ship was... ornate. Nothing like my humble home. While the size between the two was comparable, the sheer amount of refinery and detail that went into crafting the *Queen Marie* was nothing short of mesmerizing.

Calder led me out the door of his cabin onto the deck. Immediately, we were met by spectators that probably hadn't seen a woman they hadn't paid to keep their company in... well, the gods don't even want to know how long. Not that my current predicament is anything shy of coerced. Though they openly gawked at me as I walked about the ship, Calder's presence kept them from spewing the same jeers they had when I was first brought aboard this ship.

In addition to all the refinery of the *Queen Marie*, a notable difference between my ship and his is that the wood is meticulously polished. Unlike the *Ocean's Shadow* whose worn and weathered structure denotes her years of rigorous service on the high seas, the *Queen*

Marie looks as pristine as if she were on her maiden voyage.

"I've never seen a pirate's ship so... *polished*," I say, descending the steps that lead below deck. As I speak, I run one finger across the shine of the woodgrain.

"Like I told you before, I take pride in all of my endeavors. That extends to the various things that belong to me." He extends his hand in offer to assist my dismount of the final steps. Intentionally ignoring the gesture, I sidestep him when I reach the bottom. "It helps that she was kept in perfect condition until she came into my charge and was made to go on account. Before then, she was but a merchant vessel. The crown jewel of my father's fleet."

I huff. "So, it is true then. You are just a bored man from an affluent lineage, turned buccaneer for, what... sport?"

"My health actually," he sardonically sneers, wincing his face in irritation. "I don't see why you are so judgmental about it. After all, didn't your beloved Gareth inherit all his spoils and properties from the former Captain Vayne? I don't quite see the difference between the two positions."

"Everything he had, he worked damn hard to achieve," I bark. "Nothing was just handed to him." *Nothing was just handed to* me.

"I beg to differ," he continues, his tone turning sing-song. "I received a handsome sum of coin from my, as you said, *affluent line.* Did not Gareth inherit a sizeable fortune upon his predecessor's demise as well? The crew. Were those men not already in place for him? And let's not forget the *Ocean's Shadow* herself. Was acquiring a ship not yet another obstacle your dear Gareth did not have to tackle? He never did quite acquire any additional vessels either, did he?" He shrugs dramatically. "Given that I acquired the entirety of my crew all by my lonesome *and* I have since acquired multiple additional ships in my fleet, I would argue that I am actually a far more accomplished captain than your dearly departed."

My face reddens in response to the accusations being unknowingly lashed upon me. *I* earned every ounce of power and prestige. Against all odds, *I* took rank above all other men in our crew. The mere comparison of my achievements with this... simulation of a man, makes my blood boil.

"And how many ships have you now lost to the ocean's depths?" I spit.

"Mere pawns, all of them," he dismisses. "Some losses are to be expected. So long as the gains outweigh them, I'm happy to lose a bit in the name of collateral damage."

"And here I thought you took pride in all of your endeavors," I mock. "Where is the pride in defeat."

"I wouldn't call loss defeat," his voice reaches a neutral timbre, making it appear to ring with a degree more sincerity than his previously playful tone. "Loss is an inevitability. There is pride to be had in things we lose, just as much as those we still possess."

He continues walking down the hallway. He tells me what each room is, stopping to allow me to enter and observe some, while completely surpassing others. Some of the rooms are less gaudy, more akin to expectation of a pirate vessel. Especially the crew's quarters. Those are quite apparently inhabited by the sea scum that man this aquatic palace.

"Your parents must have been very successful merchants," I note. "This place *is* impressive." We descend to another level of the ship. "It's odd. Your crew looks like any other Jack Tar. They look so... out of place in this setting."

"Do I not look *out of place?*" He asks, opening another door to show me a room full of barrels.

To the contrary. This man looks right at home. Though his appearance has been roughened by his years at sea, there is still an element of refinement about him. Perhaps it is the lingering elegance from his upbringing. Or maybe it is the charismatic arrogance that seems to animate him.

"I just mean, this ship feels too elegant for the life of a pirate," I deflect.

"What is the point of piracy if not to possess the finer things in life?" He closes the door and heads back down the hall from whence we came. "Besides. The crew cleans up quite nicely when the occasion calls for it."

"And what such occasion calls for a well-groomed crew?" I ask.

He smirks. "Wouldn't you like to know."

We ascend the steps. "The lower levels are mostly storage. And the brig, I guess, but that's just housing whiskey barrels at present. Not much interesting to see down there." When we reach the top deck, he starts to lead me back towards the cabin.

"Wait!" I stall partway to the door when I see where we are heading. "Can I... stay out here for a while? It's just. I haven't gotten to breathe much fresh air. I just need to be outside for a while."

He nods and motions back toward the deck in a grand bowing gesture. I instinctively smile and I hate myself for feeling grateful for the permission. I bite my tongue and walk toward the side of the ship. Leaning my forearms against the rail, I gaze out at my ship, which sails parallel to this one off in the distance. I wonder how my crew is doing. Wonder how close they are to instigating a coup to reclaim my ship.

My eyes lift toward the sky. It has been less than a week since the full moon. Yet, already I am concerned for the next. Without Gareth, I am unsure how I will get through it. Unless I get free from the captivity of Calder before the next full moon, there is little chance for me. Unless, of course, he keeps me locked completely away, fortified from the night sky and unable to force my way to the call of the sea. Perhaps then I can evade Delesseria's control for another month. Give my crew more time.

In this moment, I wish that I had confided my full condition to at least one other person besides Gareth. Now my crew is unaware of the time restraint I have for them to free me. Even if they do manage to retrieve me before the next moon, who *could* I entrust to assist me through the night? Or, what if they try to liberate me from Calder's capture on the night of the next full moon, unknowingly opening one cage just to have me leashed by Delesseria?

As I feel the invisible walls closing in around me, I push these thoughts from my mind. I breathe in the night air and try to allow myself this fleeting moment of forced peace while it lasts. It is short-lived as I feel him take position beside me, also staring out across the water.

"It's peaceful, isn't it," he says.

"It was." I continue to stare out at my ship.

"Aye," he chortles. "It's hard to find a moment alone when confined to a ship."

"Harder still with you around."

He snorts. "If you don't like the company, all you have to do is say so, love."

"I don't like the company," I reply dryly.

He lifts his hands in mock defeat, smirking as he backs away. I feel my muscles release their tension with each passing breath.

I continue to gaze across the dark horizon for some time, unmoving in my position. Eventually, I turn around and scan my surroundings. The deck is mostly vacant, save for a hand or two busied with some remedial tasks. Calder is nowhere to be seen.

For a beat, I consider taking this moment to run but quickly diminish the instinct. There is nowhere to run at present that isn't plagued with Calder's picaroons. And though I could easily swim away as far or fast as I want, I will not leave my ship. Better to bide my time in the immediate. Build his trust. Wait for my moment to strike. Calder having taken me throughout his ship, I already accomplished the first task I deemed pertinent in preparing for my escape. Familiarizing myself with the space. Now all I can do is work on building trust and lowering Calder's guard.

With this in mind, I walk toward the center of the ship and hoist myself atop a barrel, pulling my legs to cross beneath me. The fabric of the dress bunches around my ankles, but it keeps me warm as I sit back and gaze up at the stars. The night is annoyingly peaceful in contradiction to the chaos of my current situation. But the powers of the night act to soothe me of my worries and I find myself sighing as I unwind with the sound of each crashing wave.

Hours pass and I remain alone, undisturbed atop my wooden barrel. My mind wanders and empties until I am sitting meditatively without thought or care. Just lulled into a false sense of tranquility. At some point, my eyes begin to flutter, growing heavier with each unconscious yawn. From my peripheral, I see a figure climbing down from the crow's nest. When it reaches the deck, it approaches, but I am too tired to care.

"Vessa," he croons, placing a hand on my shoulder. I turn to face Calder who stares me dead in my heavy eyes. "That's what I thought. On then, lass." He pulls me into his arms and starts to carry me, tucked against his chest.

I am too tired to protest. My days of unrest have taken more of a toll on me than I had initially thought. And the sounds of the ocean and cool night air did nothing but further submerge me in the tides of slumber.

When we reach the cabin door, he repositions me to balance in one of his arms while he uses the other to push the door open. He carries me past the threshold, strides across the room, and places me gently on top of the bed, taking care to position a feathery pillow beneath my head. I must be less in control of myself than I think because I nestle my cheek against the plush surface, curling onto my side without so much as opening my eyes.

"There you go, love," he says as he drapes a blanket over me.

Instinctively, I pull the top of the blanket up and over my shoulder, nuzzling my chin to lock it against my neck. I sigh as I breathe in the refreshingly pleasant scent of the fabric. My eyes are shut, and the cushioning of the warm bed pulls me the rest of the way into sleep.

I feel a hand brush against the side of my face, and I don't know if I am dreaming as I lean into its warmth.

"Pleasant dreams, love."

Chapter 12

Azure

There was something enticing about having her walk the corridors of my ship. I haven't had a woman aboard the *Queen Marie* in... well, ever. This ship is the last remaining connection to my parents, a place that was so intimately theirs that the thought of keeping female company where the ghosts of their memory still lingered felt wrong to me. I am not entirely sure why I broke this rule for her now.

When we returned topside after the tour, I had every intention of locking her back inside my cabin and leaving her be for the night. Sleep has been evading me still and I figured I would take watch to help pass the long hours 'til sunrise. But she had asked so... *simply.* None of the disdain that previously saturated her obstinate tone. Like a siren call, I felt compelled to oblige.

She stood so peacefully, watching the waves, that I found myself entranced by her stillness. Though I found my ascent to the crow's nest after some time, my gaze kept falling down to her like a victim to her hypnotic pull. When I felt the promise of the sunrise lingering in the darkness, I noticed her energy start to drift from where she sat, balanced on a wooden barrel. When she started to sway against the lulling rocks of the ship, sleep threatening to send her falling to the hard floor, I clambered down to the deck and carried her off to the comfort of my bed. She barely roused in my arms, where she felt so small, almost deflated from her wakeful state.

The bulky tulle of her dress encompassed her as I lay her down upon the mattress. Yet, the exposed skin of her cheeks pebbled with goosebumps against the chill of the night air. Not wanting to stir her more than I already had, and not wanting to risk her waking and losing this captivatingly delicate version of her just yet, I procured a folded blanket and draped it over her. She cocooned herself in its warmth and drifted further into slumber.

I sat across the room in my leather chair, where I like to sit reading on the rare occasions I find myself with time to kill. I filled my pipe with tobacco and let the action of smoking occupy my hands as I watched her chest rise and fall as she slept. I only realized I had started to doze off when I was startled awake by her stirring.

A quiet moan, stifled by sleep, escaped her lips as she tossed against the blanket. Her brow furrowed in displeasure as she protested against something conjured by her own subconscious. The nightmare faded, her face soothed, and she returned to her restful state of neutrality.

I sat for some time wondering what demons plagued her when her conscious mind was unable to keep her safe.

The serenity of her repose proved too powerful to refuse, and I too found myself sleeping more soundly than

I have in months. I am not sure what woke me, but when my eyes flutter open, they fall upon her mossy green stare across the room.

She is sitting upright in the center of my bed, the blanket draped across her lap. Her hands are wrapped in the fabric, trifling with the edges of the cloth. Leaning back in my chair, I stretch my arms, feeling the delectable cracking of my spine as each vertebra pops into alignment. I curl my fingers behind one of the window curtains and peek outside to see the sun well risen in the sky.

"Morning, love," I say as I rise from my chair. I run my fingers through my hair, brushing the ebony strands out of my face. "I trust your slumber was restful?"

"It was," she replies.

I feel her eyes tracking me as I walk across the room and pour myself a glass of water from the decanter on my bedside table. She shifts away from me as I approach, and I pretend not to notice the subtle action. I down the water before refilling it and handing her the glass. She stares at it for a moment with an empty gaze before taking it in her hand.

"I'm surprised to see you drinking something that isn't inebriating," she scowls before taking a sip.

"Every vice needs its balance," I sit at the edge of the bed. "Besides, it's you who seems to have the problem."

She scoffs, then swigs the rest of the water. I extend my hand and she sets the glass in my palm. I refill it and take a sip before handing it back to her.

There is a knock at the door. "Captain?"

"Enter," I call over my shoulder.

The doorknob rattles for a moment before twisting, and the door swings open. In walks Fritz, the ship's cook, balancing a tray. When he steps into the room, his eyes are fixed on the floor.

"Breakfast for you, Captain," he says as he goes to set the tray down on the table where I usually dine.

"Bring it here, Fritz," I order, patting the empty space on the bed in front of me. When I do, Fritz looks up to register my command. When his eyes track Vessa, I grab the glass from her hand and take a drink.

"Apologies, Captain," he nods his head in respect. "I didn't realize you would still be having company this morning. If I'd have known, I'd have brought out a second place setting."

"No matter, Fritz," I smirk. "The lady and I can make do with sharing. We've already shared so much as it is." I place my hand on her knee as Fritz sets the tray in front of us. Vessa slaps my hand away, shifting further back as I chortle. "Don't be shy now, love, just because we have company."

She looks at me with utter irritation but says nothing.

"That will be all, Fritz." I wave a dismissing hand in his direction as I stare at Vessa. "Shut the door on your way out. And tell the rest of the crew I don't want to be disturbed."

"Aye, Captain," he confirms before exiting the room.

"I don't understand you," Vessa states, issuing me an inquisitive glare.

"What's not to understand, love?" I reach for the singular mug and fill it with hot tea.

"You talk like that. So shamelessly suggestive, crude even. One innuendo after another. And yet..." her eyes float towards the chair before narrowing back onto me. "Last night you had every opportunity to..." her words trail off, but her meaning is clear. "Yet you didn't." She pauses, expecting a reply, but I do not speak. "Why?"

"Why didn't I crawl into this bed and have my way with you?" I state bluntly, blowing against the steam radiating from my mug. I take a shallow sip before continuing to speak. "As I told you before, not my way, love."

"Why the back and forth? One minute you're nothing short of derogatory, the next you're almost... *pleasant.*" She looks bewildered, which makes me titter.

"Careful, lass. Or I'll start to think you're developing a fondness for me." I pluck a grape from the tray and toss it into my mouth.

"Stop telling me to be careful. And stop calling me love," she exasperates. "What is your game, Calder?" she takes the mug from my hand and downs a swill.

I smile.

"No game. Strictly business." I skewer a piece of sausage with the fork and bite into the savory morsel. "As you have already noted, I have a certain fondness for refinement. I guess no matter how many years I spend at sea, I can't quite shake the gentility of my upbringing entirely." I plop the rest of the sausage in my mouth and take my mug back from Vessa's entitled grasp. Seeing that she had drained it of its contents, I refill it from the pot.

"When I first set my sights on this life, when I was still building my empire, it was... *challenging* for one of my social standing to be taken seriously among the scalawags of this *less than ethical* vocation. In order to overcome the stereotypes of weakness that clung to me from my aristocratic past, I cultivated a *persona* of sorts. Someone rougher. More ruthless. Someone to be feared. Some elements remain subterfuge to this day, while others... well, let's just say I am no longer the boy I once was. The line between the pirate I created and the pirate I am is ragged at best. Besides," I grin. "It can be rousing to create a little chaos. Helps pass the time anyhow."

"So, assault is where you draw the line, but when it comes to murder, your conscience is clear?" she scoffs. "Intriguing sense of morality."

"Again, business. Death is an unfortunate risk we all take when we sign on for this life." I set down the fork, extending the handle in her direction. She pushes it aside and reaches for a piece of sausage with her fingers. I track the ill manners as she proceeds to consume various food items using her hands.

"And this has worked for you? Pretending to be a noxious prig?"

I smirk. "Evidently, yes."

She tosses a fig in her mouth, chewing as she speaks. "I feel compelled again to ask. Why am I here? If death is such a simple command for you to issue, why not kill me like you did Gareth?"

"I have no reason to wish you dead, Duvessa." I stand and walk towards my desk. "You are not to be punished for a life you didn't ask for. I will grant you your freedom when I can release you to the safety of civilization. In the meantime, so long as we are at sea, trapped on a ship with no one but objectively filthy pirates for company, I will keep an eye on you. Under lock and key when the situation calls for my immediate absence."

"How fucking noble of you," she jeers.

I tsk at the rudeness. "Besides, I am growing quite fond of your company. Such refreshing hostility."

"And when do you anticipate we will arrive at *civilization?*" she inquires. "Just how long should I expect to have to endure your company?"

"Ouch," I jokingly clutch my heart. "You wound me." She rolls her eyes. "I'd settle in love. We have weeks ahead of us on our journey."

"And where, pray tell, exactly will we be docking?" she presses.

"In due time," is the only answer I offer.

"And what of the meantime?" she continues her line of questioning. "What exactly am I supposed to do until we arrive?"

"Like I said, make yourself comfortable." I gesture to the room. "Consider this your space. You will stay here until we arrive at port, where you may leave this ship and never return if that's what you want to do. Pass the time however you wish. You may leave the cabin only if I am present – otherwise, you will remain locked in here, where only I have access."

She nods her head slowly, processing my words. "My clothes," she picks at the sleeve of her dress. "You can't expect me to wear this. It's... *uncomfortable* and *impractical.*"

"I'll have some of your things brought over for you from the *Ocean's Shadow*."

"Why not let me return instead?"

"Why do you want to return to a ship where you were kept prisoner for so many years?"

She is silent for a beat before she replies. "Trust the monster you know." She shakes her head and her energy changes. "Besides, being here, it's just moving from one prison to another."

"But with a considerable upgrade, remember," I smirk. "But no. I want to keep you close. I am still unfamiliar with my newly acquired crew from that vessel, and I do not trust them to follow orders."

"And you trust your own men?" she presses.

"I trust no one entirely," I admit. "But it is decided. You'll stay here where I can keep you close."

I am too enraptured to let you go.

"And if I don't want to?"

"Consider it a prison if you must. You might not like my methods, but I am doing this for your own good." I go to exit the room, having spent too much time avoiding my duties already this morning. "So long as you are in my charge, no further harm will come to you."

I step outside and lock the door behind me.

Chapter 13

Vessa

Almost three weeks have passed since my first night aboard the *Queen Marie*. To my utter disgust, I find that Calder has not earned but stolen my trust with each passing day. Like a weathered rock, my coarse edges have been smoothed by the repetitive waves of care and courtesy thrust upon me. It has gotten to the point where his presence no longer sets me on edge. I almost feel, dare I say, comfortable here. I remind myself that this comfort is merely the result of habituation to my circumstances, though this does nothing to remind my body that it needs to be on guard and ready to move at a moment's notice.

A trunk of my clothing was brought to me the same day I requested it. I have been donning my usual ensemble ever since, with the exception of my hat, jacket, and weaponry. This small bit of normalcy has provided me a modicum of comfort in my confinement. Calder has taken to dining with me each morning and evening. Most nights I am alone in the cabin. While I tend to keep the blinds shut during the evenings to maintain privacy, the few times I have peeked out at night I've caught glimpses of him either standing near the helm or climbing up into the crow's nest. Always near. On a few occasions, I have awoken in the mornings to find him sleeping in his chair across the room or have heard him tiptoe inside when he thought I was still sleeping only to sit at his desk and work by candlelight.

My days are spent mostly reading. I find that Calder has a fairly impressive collection of books. I am surprised by his proclivity for literature and the vast array of genres he has acquired. I am less surprised by the anthologies of nautical lore, many of which reference Delesseria. My knowledge of her has always been through word of mouth – initially, by the stories my father told to keep me afraid of going near the ocean, which inevitably kept me trapped in my hometown. While that fear proved effective for some time, when I reached the point where I favored the possibility of death over continuing my life as it was, I quickly learned that these tales were largely false. I gave her little thought after that, not caring to know if her existence was that of reality or fiction. That was until our paths crossed. As I read through the various accounts of Delesseria in Calder's books, many of which were written by esteemed scholars, I found a few overarching trends in her story. Much of the information affirmed and clarified theories and assumptions I've cobbled together. Most notably, these accounts taught me of her true origins.

Delesseria was once a goddess. Her father, Triton, was the king of all the seas in all the mortal realms. A god himself, he fathered many progenies, few of whom lived to adulthood, him having destroyed them for fear that they would grow too powerful and attempt to overthrow him. But Triton had a soft place in his heart for his first-born daughter, Delesseria - named for the red algae bloom where she was conceived and for the corresponding redness of her fiery hair. Her mother having been a siren, Del - as Triton endearingly referred to his child - sang a song that enraptured her father the moment she was born. Though her powers grew, Triton turned a blind eye to the strength she possessed and the risk she posed to his crown.

Had her hunger for more not fed her obsession with acquiring infinite power, she may have lived a pleasant life at her father's side. But when Delesseria sacrificed her own mother in a ritual meant to magnify her magical abilities, Triton could ignore the threat of his daughter no longer. He stripped her of her title, though he could do little to restrain her abilities. While he could not diminish them or rid her of their existence entirely, the best he could do was constrain them by tying them to the cycle of the moon. She could still engage in some of her more simplistic tricks at any time, but for magic that harnessed greater power, for *that,* she had to wait until the moon was full.

When she fell from Triton's graces, he deemed her a sea witch - an enemy of the crown. While he did not have it in his heart to slay the only person he ever truly loved, he made a proclamation that any sympathizers to her plight would be deemed guilty of treason, punishable by execution. An order for her own death was issued as well, though some claim Triton never intended for this to come to pass since he never offered a bounty for her head. Due to the lack of monetary incentive and the likely terminal risk of going up against the most powerful being that ever graced the oceans, few have attempted to slay the witch. Those who tried have been lost to history.

Book after book, I devour Calder's wealth of resources regarding Delesseria, feeding my fixation.

When I am not reading, I use the large space to exercise as much as I can, to keep myself prepared for the moment my crew comes to my aid. I have yet to hear word from a single one of them. I tell myself this is because there is no way for them to reach me on the *Queen Marie*. How could they, when Calder continues to keep my crew sequestered to the *Ocean's Shadow?* Once they fully gain his trust, once they are granted more leeway, they will come. I tell myself *they will come.*

Each night, after Calder and I finish eating whatever meal Fritz delivers to the cabin, Calder allows me to roam the deck. Often, he keeps his distance, either clambering up to the crow's nest or keeping busy with some odd tasks. Other times, if dining together provoked some type of conversation, most frequently in the form of an argument, he will remain in my company until we have exhausted all words and silence falls upon us. Only then does he leave me to my peace. Never has he ordered me to retire to the cabin. Rather, I remain under the stars until I either tire or bore and return of my own volition. Always locking the door behind me. I have not let myself get so tired again that Calder has had the excuse to carry me off to bed like a child. It unsettles me that in my half-asleep state, I had been comfortable enough to let him do this in the first place. I am *always* on guard, and the fact that this occurred unnerves me to no end.

I can always tell that Calder has checked the locks of the door when I retire for the evening. Often, I am still awake when I hear him twist the handle, checking to see if the interior lock has been engaged, then hear the shifting of the keys from the outside as he locks the exterior ones as well. Other times, I wake to an empty room and check for myself the status of the door locks. The interior locks give me nothing but the illusion of safety and control. Calder holds the keys to each lock. He can enter or lock me inside at any time.

I have kept track of our course over the past few weeks. The large windows of the captain's cabin and the stars of the evening sky have proven useful in my piecing together an idea of where Calder is heading. Torrence, if I had to guess. One of the many places we already checked for Delesseria before setting our sights on Escondida. We are now a mere three days from the shores of Torrence. I look forward to the return, and not just because docking should mean I'll encounter my crew and finally get my shot at reclaiming my ship. Provided Calder fulfills his promise and lets me go.

I came to love Torrence during my short stay in the coastal island village. My sights had set on the village, known for its poor living conditions and lack of significance in the economic world, as a possible location to find Delesseria seeking to strike a deal with one of its impoverished citizens.

In all of my travels, all I had ever heard of this land was how downtrodden those were who lived on its shores, and how each and every person lived in squalor, with little more for a home than a shack and none with so much as a single coin to their names. At the time, it seemed like a prime location for Delesseria to strike.

I was shocked when I was greeted by the local peoples of Torrence. The village itself is nestled into the west coast of the island, with quaint hovels woven into the rocky shores. Each home is small, containing only one or two rooms in the entire structure. They are constructed of stacked boulders, cut and weather-worn tree trunks, and roofs made of brambles, leaves, and grasses. Not a single home is sectioned off by any type of fencing to denote distinguishable property. The peoples of Torrence do not believe in such distinction or division of land and resources. Their community thrives on the notion of *what-is-mine-is-yours* and that the lands are everyone's to celebrate. Even the roofs over their heads they are happy to share with any person who is without, and will gladly lend a hand in the construction of another hut in their village for anyone wishing to stay indefinitely. They denounced currency generations prior, and while one may be tempted to label their method of exchange as proximal to a bartering system, such a definition would be incorrect. The people of Torrence give willingly and without the expectation of return, though the gift of returned fortune is something the community takes pride in. They want for nothing because all they could possibly want is within their reach. All that they value they find from within themselves.

Because of their lack of value in the material world, or what those outside of the island's borders consider to be wealth, Torrence is not a frequent stop for ships. Those that do are welcomed by the locals, but any attempts to buy or sell tangible goods prove unfruitful for passing merchants. And there is nothing on the island of interest to sailors of lesser repute. From the economically centered eye, Torrence is a poor village. I have never seen a richer place in all my life.

The pristine coastal village is the only part of the island that has been cleared. The rest of the land is lush, vibrant rainforests filled with every plant or variety of wildlife one could imagine. What the forest provides the people of Torrence, they return tenfold in respect for all that call it home. What they harvest, they sow for future growth. What they hunt, they do in moderation and with great care taken to ensure the longevity of each species. And the roars and rumbles they hear in the dark hours of the night, they do not fear, for they are but the calls of the many denizens of the jungle with which they coexist.

During my last visit to Torrence, I did not technically step foot on its shores. I did, however, have members of one of the well-established families aboard to dine with me and discuss my reasoning for visiting their lands. Though they had not quite understood my desire for material wealth, having placed no value in the momentary workings of the world, they alluded to little judgment of my obvious profession. They had, however, expressed great distress at my stated desire to find Delesseria.

Sea Witch.

Devil.

Evil incarnate.

They warned me that pursuing such a creature would bring nothing but torment to me and anyone who dared to make a deal with such a monster. They warned that nothing I could possibly attain from her could be worth the price she would tack on to the exchange. I feigned to be touched by their warnings and kept the particulars of my situation to myself.

In the three weeks I have been separated from my ship, I have slowly lost my irrational fear that Delesseria will somehow steal her away from me. I have not been there to monitor her every action and still, each day I watch as she sails alongside the *Queen Marie*, so close and yet too far. In this realization, I feel a sense of anticipation at getting to walk along the shores of Torrence and soak in the quiet energy that seems to whirl through the village with the wind.

My only apprehension is that one of the locals with whom I dined will recognize me as the woman they met almost two months ago. Even if they do not see or recognize *me*, they may recognize my *ship*. I hope that their unfamiliarity with such grand ships might blind them to their differentiations. Or perhaps they will be too blinded by the dazzle of Calder's vessel to pay much attention to mine. Then again, they have minimal interest in such *dazzle*, they may well find mine to be of more interest.

No matter. I will mitigate the issues as they arise.

In the meantime, I need to get through the next few days. As I consider everything that comes next, everything I will need to do to reclaim my ship and make an example of Calder, I feel... *conflicted.* On the one hand, he is but another man who has wronged me. Taken my ship while his androcentrism kept him from even realizing that the vessel was mine. He demeaned me. Stole from me. Kept me captive for weeks. Yet, he has been *kind*, in his own arrogant way. He thinks he is keeping me safe, which I don't know if it enrages me that he believes I need his assistance in the matter or, oddly, touched by the effort. He has left me to my own devices to relax in a way that, frankly, I have never had the luxury of doing in my entire life. I feel rested for the first time in years. Relaxed by days passed reading and evenings spent star gazing. My body feels well-nourished from what has truly been the most delicious food I have ever consumed in my life. Sometimes, while we are dining, I contemplate how I will keep Fritz alive after I reclaim my ship, just so I never have to go another day without his culinary skills. All the other luxuries I have been indulged with on this ship I can give up, but I would truly die without Fritz.

I have spent my whole life working. Working for others. Working for myself. But always acting to propel myself forward and accomplish everything I want in life. And that itch will always scratch at my mind. But it had kept me from indulging in the simplest of joys life has to offer. Good food. Quiet nights. Restful moments. I've had a taste of simple joy and, for the first time, I wonder how much of it I have missed out on in my life. And how much of that has been my own fault.

Even his company has been a pleasure. The smell of him still lingering on the sheets even though he has not slept in his own bed since it became mine for the interim. The sound of his breathing as he sleeps across the room on his leather chair.

EHLINGER

Comfort. I think the feeling is comfort. And I am none too familiar with the concept.

I really should be the opposite of comfortable, given every condition of my predicament. Yet, the vein in my forehead, which pulsates at the most aggravating of triggers, and the knots in my shoulders, that bind me to my anxiety and rage, have soothed and subdued to the point that they are nothing more than a haunting threat of what I have to look forward to upon my reinstatement as the captain of the *Ocean's Shadow.*

Chapter 14

We arrive tomorrow. Until now I have kept our destination secret from her. I am not even entirely sure why. It's not like her knowing that information would make any kind of difference in the outcome of my plan.

More than anything, I think I have enjoyed the idle conversation with her over the past several weeks. Whenever anyone talks to me, they are talking to their captain first and foremost. With Vessa, well, she has made it abundantly clear that she does not think of me in such esteemed regards. While that defiance would enrage me with any other subordinate in my charge, with her, I find it enthralling.

She speaks to me and it is nothing short of casual, disrespectful at times. The pure audacity of it entices me more than anything or anyone ever has in my lifetime. I find that no matter how much time I spend with her, how long I watch her from afar while she stares at the night sky, I want more.

Slowly she has, dare I say, warmed to me as well. A less insightful man might not be privy to the signs, but I can tell she is begrudgingly opening up to me. Little things about her posture. Her movement. The way her eyes no longer track me when I walk about the room. She has habituated to my presence and no longer considers me a true threat. Even her speech, I find our topics of conversation now air on the side of lighthearted, at times, though she persists to inquire as to the *Ocean's Shadow* and the specifics of my plans for the vessel. But those moments of lightheartedness? I relish them.

And she no longer pretends to be asleep when I retire to my room for a moment of shuteye. Now she just *is* asleep. Like her body began to trust me before her mind has been able to relinquished that control. It makes me smile when I hear her muffled snores beneath the sheets.

She hasn't drunk as much in the subsequent weeks since her arrival aboard the *Queen Marie*. I wonder if her habitual drinking has been a conduit for coping with whatever hardships befell her during her years on the *Ocean's Shadow*. I get a misplaced sense of pride when I consider that her time with me has negated her need for such a crutch. Misplaced in that, all of this... this time spent together, these quiet moments I have come to cherish, they are all coerced. None possible if I were not holding her captive. No matter how harmless the intentions.

I have never claimed to be a good man in any sense of the word. I am that which I am, and I have no desire to be anything conceivably better than the man I've been at my worst. In fact, there are times I wish I were worse. Like when I feel regret or shame for leaving Braun. I wish I were the type of man who felt no remorse for such things. After all, I feel limited remorse for those I kill. At least those people aren't left to suffer. They are given as dignified a death as any man of the sea can hope for. Swift. Final. No painfully lingering moments to regret and dwell, and feel. Just a moment of numbing fear, then oblivion. *Peace.*

There is no peace for a man with a conscience.

I see no sense in senseless pain. I have no qualms drawing blood if there is a viable reason to do so, but causing pain purely to satisfy a basal need is nothing short of archaic.

I heard that Vayne was cruel. A common trait among leaders in this profession. Perhaps that is why I came to hate him so, not just as a rival in trade but knowing that such scum polluted the waters. I win no awards for mercy, but at the very least, I possess self-control and calculation.

I find myself wondering, far too often than I likely should, just *how* Vayne has hurt Duvessa over the years. Each image my imagination conjures feeds the rage inside of me and makes me wish he had not already been claimed by Davy Jones' locker so that I might have the luxury of inflicting on him the slowest and most painful death that even I could imagine. Some nights I sit awake, watching her gaze out at the star-reflected waters or listening to her oceanic breaths as she sleeps, and I daydream all the ways I could make him suffer for what he's done to her. Even when the brutality of my imagination twists my stomach, and I start to question my own depravity, it never feels like enough to settle the score.

The thought of arriving at Torrence, at having to keep my word and let her go, *bothers* me. I had hoped that this odd fascination I have with her would dwindle over these past few weeks. I thought that continued exposure to her poor manners - her *petulant disrespect* would make me grow irritated with her presence. But my fixation has only gotten stronger. With each passing day, I find myself increasingly aware of her presence. The smell of her in the briny night air. The sight of the moon reflected on her skin. The way she moves with equal parts elegance and arrogance. The absentminded little tells she has on the rare occasions that I do make her uncomfortable. The way she bites her lip when she is thinking or rubs her thumb against the knuckle of her index finger when she is trying to control her anger. How I enjoy toying with her to see the extents of her control over that glorious rage.

I do not wish to tell her that tomorrow is the day she regains her freedom. Do not feel prepared to acknowledge that reality. Yet, she is far more knowledgeable than she lets on. By how she has been acting, watching the navigational tells, I am almost certain she already knows.

She sits at my desk, scribbling something into a notebook when I enter the cabin. I bestowed the small totem to her upon request. Interested as I have been as to the contents of this journal, I have respected its privacy and not so much as stolen a passing glance at its open pages. Though the temptation to do so has been significant.

Fritz has already set an ornate meal on the table. As I slip off my jacket, I sling it over the back of the chair that has become *my side of the table*. I pour myself a goblet of wine and fill a second for her out of habit.

"I'm surprised you haven't started without me," I say, carrying both goblets toward the desk. I set hers down at her side and she quickly uses her hands to shield the drying pages of ink. "I'm not peeking, love. Cross my heart and hope to die." I jokingly sign a cross over my heart and grin as she glares at me. "I swear, love, if looks could kill I would have been a goner quite some time ago." I take a sip of my wine.

She continues to hold my gaze, still shielding her papers from view. I roll my eyes in mock irritation and take my place at the table.

"Your precious pages are safe from my *devilishly handsome* eyes," I fill a bowl with some of the savory, aromatic stew. "Now come, join me before this gets colder than it already is."

She remains seated for a few moments, lifting the pages and blowing gently to dry the ink the rest of the way. When she is content that the risk of smudging has passed, she closes the journal, setting it beneath a stack of other books before sitting across from me at the table.

"What exactly do you work on all day in here anyway?" I inquire while ladling stew into a second bowl and handing it to her.

"Just keeping myself sane," she takes the bowl and sets it in front of her. "Busywork, really."

"Specificity truly is your gift," I note, passing her a basket filled with freshly baked biscuits. I take a bite of the

149

one in my hand and it melts in my mouth in a buttery whirl. Whatever stipend I issue to Fritz, I know it isn't enough to measure the extent of his abilities. Another reason I rarely venture off on any of the other ships of my fleet. *Fritz.* All other cooks pale in comparison. Not even the finest of restaurants offer food quite as delectable as his.

"You're not exactly the king of specificity yourself," she takes a bite from one of the biscuits. Her conversation ceases briefly while her eyes roll to the back of her head from the sheer ecstasy of the experience. Only once she swallows does she continue. "You won't even tell me where we are going."

"Torrence," I offer.

"Torrence?" she slurps a spoonful of stew. "Oh."

"You feign surprise," I state, seeing her indifference to the news for what it is. "Why, when I have no doubts you figured out our destination days, maybe weeks ago?"

"I had my suspicions," she takes another bite of bread and forces herself not to get lost in its decadence once more. "Doesn't really matter to me where we end up."

" *We?*" I taunt.

"*I,*" she clarifies. " *You* will dock your ships and then *I* will take my leave. You do still plan to be a man of your word, yes?"

My eyes narrow. "But of course. Once we arrive tomorrow, you'll be free to do whatever you please."

"Tomorrow?" she seems startled by the news. "That soon?"

"Indeed," I examine her. I think I see a flash of something in her eyes. It seems sad. Regretful. But it is gone before I can name it properly. I take a long drink from my goblet. "I've heard this *Torrence*, is quite the quiet place. Very remote. A land less traveled, one might say."

"Hmm," she nods in agreement as she sips her own wine.

"You've had the pleasure?" I inquire.

"No," she shakes her head, reaching for another roll. "Just heard the same thing. Very small. Not much to it."

"And you would stay there?" I push.

"Why not? It's not like I have many options out here."

"You could always stick around, try for the next port." My offer is sincere but is stated in jest. It almost sounds like a dare.

"I'd rather take my chances jumping ship," she laughs. There is a measurable lightness to her tone. She really has softened to me.

"It is not often ships stop off at Torrence, love. You could be waiting quite some time for rescue." I realize I've made a mistake before she even voices her replying words. She changes the energy of a room without having to say or do a thing.

"Who says I need *saving*?" Her eyes go dead as she stares at me. She gulps the rest of her glass and reaches for the bottle. "And why *not* stay there? It sounds peaceful. Who wouldn't want a little bit of peace in their lives?"

"Sounds far too dull for the likes of me, love," I grab the bottle from her hands and fill her goblet for her. *Chivalry.* "Isn't a life at sea far more interesting? Adventurous?"

"Far less so when you're locked away in a room all day," she snips.

"You've spent a decade at sea," I ignore her attempt to rekindle the same argument about my locking her up each day. I refuse to have it for the millionth time. "What are a few more weeks if it means finding somewhere more suitable to live."

"Anywhere will be suitable for me, provided you aren't there." Her tone is mocking, and I know she only partially means it. But the part of her that *does* hooks beneath my skin.

"Well, then you will be quite happy in Torrence once I leave you there to rot of boredom." I refill my own glass.

"Good."

"*Good.*"

We continue eating in silence. After finishing the stew, we move on to a course of broiled swordfish. Fritz prepared the dish with ample lemons, which we stock in constant supply to keep the crew from developing scurvy. The men, myself included, grow tired of the flavor, so Fritz does what he can to shroud it in other, more palatable tastes. Today, the lemon mixes with potent garlic, which, in combination with some additional spices, has transformed the tangy lemon into a savory complement to the slightly charred swordfish.

"Damn," she groans in ecstasy as she shoves more fish in her mouth. "I will admit, I'll miss *this*." She uses her fork to gesture to the bounty of food decorating the table. "Fritz is a true artist. Where did you find him anyway?"

My jaw clenches as I chew. A twinge of jealousy strikes me like lightning at the thought of her missing Fritz and not me. "That rapscallion? Oh, he's been with me since the beginning." I take a sip of wine to drown my misplaced jealousy. "He was the chef for the *Queen Marie* when she was still my parents' merchant vessel. After they passed, he spent some time traveling the realms. Working his way around, picking up tricks of his trade from all over the world. Eventually, our paths crossed... Oh, *where was it?* One of the islands of the Red Sea? It was pure chance. Anyhow, he joined the crew. Perhaps out of a sense of loyalty to my parents. Perhaps he missed the call of the ocean. He's been with me for six years now."

"How did your parents die?" she asks.

Her tone is gentle. Gentler than I've ever heard her speak. She has never inquired as to my personal life before and the sincerity of it all sets me on edge. *Yet –* my instinct is to confide in her. And I don't stop myself from doing so.

"Shipwreck," I offer, fighting to keep my tone indifferent. "They went off on one of their smaller vessels. Crew of only four men. They never returned. Lost to a storm. Fortunately, good old Fritz wasn't along on their journey, otherwise we would be eating far less desirable fare." I smirk as I shove another morsel of fish into my mouth.

"I'm sorry," she states, holding my eyes. I don't care for the way the eye contact makes me feel dissected – *exposed* – so I avert my gaze to my plate. "How old were you when it happened?"

I take my time to finish chewing. Swallowing, I rinse the taste with wine before I answer. "Eleven or twelve. I was twelve when news reached me, but they departed when I was eleven."

"Oh," she sounds pensive. "So, you celebrated your birthday in their absence only to learn that they had passed?"

"It wasn't the first celebration to be missed," I say, dryly. "But it was certainly the last." I force a fleeting grin across my face, but I can't seem to hold it there.

"I'm sorry," she coos. It sounds oddly soothing. She reaches across the table for the bottle of wine and refills my glass, but not her own.

"I don't need your pity," I say.

"I wasn't offering it to you," her tone hardens a touch, but she smiles. "I've never known my birthday." Her gaze grows distant and she looks almost perplexed. "My family was... *cold.* Controlling. I... I *know* I was born in the spring. I have vague memories of celebrating my birthday when I was very little. Before mother passed. But those fade more and more the older I get. I don't even know if they are real or if I made them up in my mind." She sips from her glass. "Either way, I choose to believe them."

I am looking at her as she speaks. It's her turn to cast her eyes away, fixing them on nothing in particular. *Lost.*

"How did she pass?" I ask.

"I honestly don't know." She hesitates for a moment. "I think my father killed her."

Silently, I choke on my wine, taken aback by the cavalier nature of such a dark admission. Forcing myself to swallow the rejected liquid, it cuts like a razer on its way down. I remain silent as she sits in what appears to be deliberation.

"She was never sick. At least I don't remember her as such. She was always so... strong. Powerful. Comforting. The only times she wasn't was when my father was screaming. She'd tell me to hide and I would. I'd shut my eyes and all there *was* was the screaming and the darkness. Eventually, I would fall asleep wherever I was hidden. And the following day, I would always wake to the sound of my mother's voice calling for me. She would be... *worse for wear*, but she would try to hide it from me."

I take my flask from my pocket and place it on the table in front of her. She does not look up, but she takes the canister. Unscrewing the lid, she takes a slow drink before continuing.

"She was going to leave him. I remember that. I *think* I remember that. Said we were going to run off in the night and never look back." She takes another drink. "Then that night," she swallows some complex emotion. "It happened like any other night. The screaming. The pleading. The hiding." She shakes her head. "Eventually, I fell asleep. Forced myself to sleep because I *knew* that if I could *just fall asleep*... yes, the darkness would take me for a time, but then I would *wake up* and everything would

155

be better. And mother would be there to comfort me, and we would run away, and everything would be ok. But... she wasn't. She was gone. I waited where I was hidden. Waited for hours. But she never came to find me. She wasn't there when my father found me, enraged when I said I was too scared to come out from under the bed. She didn't come when he turned his violence on me and I called out for her over and over again. He told me she would never come back. That she left me. That she cared more about herself than her own family, so she left me there with him. All that was left was the darkness, and I would never wake up to anything different."

Silent tears run down the side of her face. She turns away to shield them from me but doesn't lift a hand to brush them from her face. "So, *yes*. I think he killed her. I refuse to believe that the one person who loved me would have left me in that horrible life."

It is chilling just how stoically she speaks, even as the tears stain her cheeks.

Tears begin to flow more readily down her face, though she refuses to submit to their unyielding authority. Her sobs are silent. Strangled. But they come nonetheless. I don't know what possesses me but I find myself standing beside her. I kneel at her side, wrapping my arms around her in an embrace. At first, her muscles go ridged beneath my touch, but eventually, her body relaxes. She allows her forehead to rest on my chest for a moment and her tears soak the fabric of my shirt. I hold her until she pulls away and repositions herself in her chair.

"I'm sorry," she wipes away the lingering tears from her face. "I don't know why I told you that."

Her face flushes in embarrassment.

I feel a sense of unease myself, not quite knowing what to say. I clear my throat and stand. Brushing the phantom wrinkles from my shirt, I return to my own chair.

I struggle to push down the burgeoning rage that threatens to overcome me.

"What happened to your father?" I prompt.

"Oh, he's still alive and well I imagine," she snickers, taking another pull from my flask. "I ran away when I was fifteen. The night before he tried to marry me off to some older man in our village. Stole the money the bastard gave my father to *buy me* and - well, I never looked back."

"And where does he live?" I clench my fist beneath the table. Her father has just been added to my list of things to take care of in this lifetime.

"Small village called Lythren," she states. "Poor as sin and no place anyone should ever set foot unless they're looking for hell on earth."

She closes the flask, tightening the cap as she extends it toward me. I reach across the table, my hand brushing against hers as it transfers between us. Slipping the flask back into my pocket, we continue to eat in silence.

Tomorrow will be a sad day indeed.

Chapter 15

Vessa

I don't know why I opened up to him last night. Perhaps it was the knowledge that I would be killing him soon and no matter what I confided, it would die with him in due time. That and all this time I have had on my hands the past several weeks has left my mind to wander to places I haven't allowed it to go in years. To feel emotions that I've buried so deeply inside that I am surprised they have not yet suffocated and died, as I long since thought they had.

I had not realized how much Gareth's death had reopened the wound of losing my mother. One moment they were there. The next, gone. Leaving me to suffer the fate of some cruel man. Leaving me to fight alone. To pick up the pieces of their absence and force them into whatever life I can manage to scrape together without them. Both dead because they loved me. Both abandoning me in death.

I am disgusted with myself for confiding the loss of my mother to the very man who killed Gareth. I'm disgusted that it happened. That I felt comfort in him.

Disgusted that I trusted him in that moment. Disgusted that I have come to trust him at all. How could I so easily forgive and forget such trespasses as he has inflicted upon my life? How could I disrespect Gareth's memory in such a way? How is this Calder any better than my father himself?

He has been kind to me. *Is that all it takes?* Am I so pathetically simple that being shown the slightest modicum of compassion or respect subdues me and makes me easily pliable?

Perhaps it is that he has endured a similar loss. Perhaps it is that I have been lonely in my pain. Gareth understood. Gareth had been my companion in grief. Yet... *Calder.* Something felt different. The connection. The knowing.

I hate him. For everything he has done. For making me trust him. For making me feel... *compassionate* towards him.

For making me think twice about whether or not to kill him.

I *need* to kill him. Need to end this. To kill whatever deranged emotion I feel for him brewing inside of me like a poison.

Today, he will die.

I am fully dressed in my usual attire - boots, pants, tunic, and jacket. I will have to acquire a weapon at the first opportunity. Once I do, I can strike - once my men are in view and I know I am backed in my effort. I am pacing the cabin floor, contemplating the various scenarios that might transpire as I slay the beast when he enters.

"Care to join me, love?" Calder asks from the now opened door.

"Land ho!" a voice bellows from across the deck.

"Almost time to part ways," he continues. "Grant me the honor of your company for the terminal part of our voyage?"

I hate that I don't hate him. Hate that my betraying heart is fluttering as he speaks. *It must be the anticipation of my sword gutting him.*

I nod with an unsettlingly genuine smile and follow him out of the room. He gestures for me to follow as he walks across the deck towards the bow of the ship. As I walk, there are far fewer eyes staring at me than the first time I walked this deck. Calder's crew has grown accustomed to my presence. I feel the warmth of the sun on my face and realize this is the first time I have been outside in the height of the afternoon in quite some time. I stop walking for a moment, close my eyes, and breathe in the sun-warmed air.

A strong hand takes hold of mine and gently prompts me forward. Calder leads me the rest of the way until we are standing at the very front of the ship, looking out across the water at the sliver of land in the horizon. Though the crew is busied behind us, we are in relative privacy. I brace my hands on the rail and again close my eyes. Feeling the gentle mist of the ocean against my face, I inhale the briny scent of the sparkling sea. I feel rejuvenated by the energy of the day. I stay like this for some time, allowing myself the simplicity of the moment. The calmness.

"Tranquility is a good look on you." Calder breaks the silence. He is leaning against the rail at my side, watching me. I roll my eyes at him for ruining my fleeting bliss. "As is utter disdain," he smirks.

"How fortunate for you, since you're on the receiving end of the latter emotion quite consistently," I snip with and twinge of sarcasm.

He laughs. "How fortunate indeed."

He procures his flask from the inside pocket of his jacket. He drinks before offering it to me. I take it and do the same, hoping the alcohol will help smother the budding feeling of guilt at the anticipation of killing Calder. *How dare he make me feel guilty after everything he has done?*

I take another swig.

"So," he takes the flask from my hand and drinks before returning it to me. "What will you make of your freedom?" he asks.

Take back my ship.

"I'm not sure," I deflect.

"Come now," he presses in a playful manner. "There has to be something you want out of life. Some harbored dream you've kept all these years."

I find myself genuinely considering the question. "I honestly don't know anymore," I explain.

"Everyone has something," he continues. "What did you want more than anything when you were a child? What did you want to grow up and become?"

"Happy." *I have never said a more honest truth in my entire life.*

"Ambitious," he nods as he looks out across the waves, no mockery in his voice. "I hope you find your happiness, Duvessa. I've never met a more deserving person in all the realms."

We stand together, watching the sliver of land grow progressively larger as we approach until what lays before us, like a glorious oasis, is the lush forests of the island's jungle. We have approached the uninhabited side of the island. The ship's sails are manipulated and we begin to circle the coast. It becomes evident that we have reached their humble port when several smaller vessels and one goliath of a ship come into view. From my last visit, I know that the smaller boats, which are primarily propelled by oars - though a single sail may be attached to each in order to travel greater distances - belong to the local peoples of Torrence. The larger ship, which trumps the size of both the *Queen Marie* and the *Ocean's Shadow,* is one I have not before seen. I figure it must belong to visitors to the Island.

Excellent. More people to help me blend in with the crowd.

The *Queen Marie* stops beside one of the docks and a wooden ramp is lowered from the side of the ship. The *Ocean's Shadow* is close behind and pulls to a second dock across the way.

"Home sweet home," Calder says to me as he steps toward the ramp. "Though it appears luck is in your favor if you indeed wish to leave this place." He nods to the unfamiliar ship. "Coming?" He extends his hand toward me. I do not take it, but I follow as we descend the ramp onto the dock below.

The dock sways with the waves, but the sensation is ripped away from me when I step firmly on dry land. It feels wrong not to have the rhythm of the ocean beneath me. I continue walking, following after Calder, waiting for the stagnant earth to feel normal, even though it never has.

Torrence is a small place. While the entirety of the village can be seen from the docks, the village is situated among the rocks set back from the shoreline by a short distance. Once we are close enough to make out details of the village, the evidence of carnage becomes apparent.

Bodies litter the ground. Bodies dressed in the modest island garb of the local Torrencians.

"Good gods," Calder mutters to himself. He puts his arm up to stop me from stepping on a body that I had not noticed, having been distracted by the piles of others off in the opposite direction. "Careful, love."

He pulls a knife from his boot and hands it to me. "Take this. Whatever happened here, I don't like the idea of you completely unprotected."

I take the knife and clasp it in my hand as I continue to scan the distance.

"What happened here?" I ask of no one but the gods themselves. "These poor people."

Members of Calder's crew have filtered into the village and started to congregate behind us. "Search the village, men," he orders. "See if you can find any survivors. Pair off. These intruders must still be on the island somewhere."

The crew mutter their understanding, but before they can follow the directive, a single man comes into view ahead of us. I hide the dagger behind my back before he notices it.

"Well, hello there," the man calls in a disturbingly friendly tone. His clothing is similar to our own, making him easily distinguishable from the creed of the fallen island folk. I instantly clock him as one of the intruders.

"Pleasantries seem a bit beyond us, given the circumstances," Calder says. His voice is cold, but not combative. He sounds authoritative, staking claim to the upper hand. "You did this?" He nods in the general direction of a pile of bodies.

"Aye," the man nods, not even pretending to be ashamed or attempting to deny the crime. "But there is no need to squabble, lad." The man raises his hands in indication that he means us no harm. "I can tell by your sails that yours is a... *less reputable* enterprise. I can assure you, there is nothing of value to you here. Set sail from here and we can part ways without a drop of bloodshed. Well," he smiles. "Without any *additional* bloodshed."

"What then is your business here?" Calder growls. "If there is nothing of value, why slaughter an entire village?"

"Enterprise, my good sir." The man lifts his hands to gesture to the surrounding jungle. "An entire island of lumber waiting to be stripped and sold. Exotic fauna to skin and sell. Ample land thereafter to auction off to the highest bidder." He looks around at the stone huts that comprise the village. "Once these atrocities are knocked down, this will be a lovely place to develop into... well, that's for the buyers to decide, I guess."

He takes a step toward us, bringing him but a few paces away. Calder's hand flinches over his sword hilt. "All resources for a more merchant-minded entrepreneur. Not so much a pirate." His eyes drop to the sword at Calder's side before taking a mental count of the men standing behind us. "I'm happy to send you on your way with a small token of appreciation for your *discretion*." He smiles, again lifting his hands to indicate his lack of interest in a fight. "Perhaps there is something aboard my ship that would be to your liking?" His eyes lock onto me as he swallows. I tighten my hold on the dagger behind me and scowl.

"Perhaps," Calder replies. He appears to be considering the proposal. For a moment, I think he will take him up on the offer. But then Calder's eyes fall to a small heap, mere feet from the man's boot. The body of a small child. A little girl, still clutching a doll that is now soaked in her own blood. The moment Calder processes the bloody scene of the child's final moments, he unsheathes his sword and lunges toward the man with a guttural cry. Pure rage propels him as he brings his blade down upon the man.

But the bastard has produced his own weaponry and blocks the blow with his own sword. Suddenly, dozens of men start filtering out from the forest edge. Dozens more turn the corners of the streets and start charging us. Our crew begins to parry and riposte against the oncoming attackers.

Sensing a presence behind me, I pivot on my heels, slinging Calder's dagger into the neck of an assailant. I pull the blade from his neck as he falls to his knees. Slipping the dagger into my belt, I take the sword of my fallen victim. I lose no time before jumping in to defend the crew against the oncoming offensive. From the corners of my eyes, I see men running from both the *Queen Marie* and the *Ocean's Shadow* towards the ensuing battle. Soon all hands are engaged in the bloody fight.

My body sings with the opportunity for movement and the exhilaration of the fray. Though it has been weeks since last I held a blade in my hand, my muscles embrace the familiar dance, and soon, the movements are less calculated than instinct-driven. I smile as I mortally slice and stab. I must look mad in my lust for blood.

Calder is moving with all the grace of a stormy sea. The might of his sword clashing against *one... two... three* opponents at a time. Like waves on a restless sea, his sword falls in jagged lines that somehow look graceful. Calculated by a larger design.

I continue fighting with Calder in my periphery. I disarm the man before me, stabbing him through the heart before another approaches and starts to swing. One of Calder's three falls to the ground, dead, as does the man before me. I join in against the remaining duo fighting Calder. Soon, they split so that we are each dueling one-on-one. I watch as Calder falls backward until he is lying on the ground. Having broken his fall with his elbows, his opponent approaches and swings his sword high above, bringing it down swiftly toward Calder's unprotected chest. He lifts his blade just in time to block the attack, but their blades do not separate as they each press unyieldingly against the other.

I continue to fight my own opponent until the moment comes when I see an opportunity to strike a fatal blow. I do not even bother waiting for the body to drop before I am running toward Calder, his opponent still firmly above him. With one swing I slice the man's head clean from his body. Calder rolls away, just before the torso collapses on top of him. But the spewing of the blood has completely covered us both. I look down at him, where he still lies on the blood-coated earth, staring up at me with an unreadable expression. I reach out and offer him my hand.

"You're welcome," I say, helping him to his feet. There is no more time for conversing as several more men come barreling toward us.

We continue with the battle.

I catch glimpses of familiar faces, members of my crew fighting alongside Calder's, working together to slay a common enemy. Seeking vengeance for the fallen innocents of this peaceful village, who never asked for anything yet offered all they had. One by one, the enemy falls until there are none left standing.

I am kneeling in the street, sword still in hand as I catch my breath. Blood covers my hands and face, itching my skin. I stare out across the village at the blood, and rock, and sand. At the bodies and destruction. All around me, the crew is scattered in a similar state as mine. Just taking in the enormity of what lies before us.

I see Calder off to my left, kneeling beside the very same child that sent him over the edge. He too is blood-soaked. His obsidian hair, falling forward into his face, is coated slick with blood, but he doesn't seem to care. He brushes a strand of the girl's hair out of her face as he gazes down at her. Reaching down, gently, he closes her eyes. I feel a sense of gratitude that I did not see the look of fear that must have entombed in her eyes at the moment of her death. Feel gratitude for the girl that Calder took that moment and looked that fear in the face, letting her be seen in her final moment by someone other than the one who cut her down.

With more tenderness than I thought him capable, Calder brushes the back of his fingers against the girl's cheek.

He runs his fingers through his hair, tossing it back and out of his face, revealing the stain of tears that must have fallen for the young girl. He brushes them away like they never existed. Cracking his neck, he turns to look at the rest of the carnage.

"Thank you, my friends," Calder speaks loud enough to address the men who have now crowded closer to their captain. "I'd never dare to call us honorable men by trade. But you all fought honorably for the honor of these fallen comrades." He shakes his head, seeming to swallow any lingering emotion. "How many have we lost?"

"Only three, Captain," someone calls.

"I want names," Calder's voice scratches.

Another person steps out from the crowd.

"Jerico, Martel, and Harting," he answers.

I witness each name hit like a rock, Calder's eyes falling to the ground as his jaw tics. He remains unsettlingly still as he tries to hide the onslaught of emotion, but it only seems to magnify the potency of the moment. It looks like he genuinely feels the loss of each member of his crew.

"We will need to bury them," he says softly. "We have a lot of work ahead of us, men." As if on cue a loud roar sounds off in the distance of the jungle. "And we will have to complete it before night falls. Who knows what stripe of beasts roam these forests at night that might be tempted by the flesh of the departed."

There are mumbles among the crew. Some are in agreement, others in irritation at the order for additional labor.

"Shovels are aboard the ship," Calder orders. "Work in rotations if you must but do not stop until each person is buried."

"Captain," I hear a man speak from somewhere behind me. "It is the custom in Torrence to burn the deceased. Torrencians are very adamant about sending the spirits of their loved ones back to the heavens," the voice chokes out with authority. "Plus, it keeps the carnivora from digging them back up."

I recognize that voice.

"Besides, it'd certainly save us all some time in disposing of *this many* bodies," the voice continues.

"Is that so," Calder turns his attention to the man behind me.

I turn around and see the source of the information. *Harker.* A member of my crew. An older gentleman who was a part of Vayne's crew long before I came into the picture.

"And how is it you are so versed in the customs of Torrence?" Calder asks.

Fuck. Because when we were here last there was a funeral. Harker can't let him know that without confessing we had been here before.

"I was born and raised here as a lad," he states. "Joined Vayne when I was a young man." His eyes briefly meet mine, but are gone before the action can be noticed. "Haven't been back since."

Good man, Harker.

"Hmm," Calder assesses Harker. "Very well, then. Change of plans men. Build three pyres. One for the Torrencians. One for the *bastard scum,*" he kicks the boot of one of the slain foes. "And a small one for our own fallen men. The tides will come to bring their ashes out to sea."

There are nods and mumbles of acknowledgment as the crew breaks apart. Additional orders are being issued down by the hierarchy of Calder's command. Some people head for the tree line to gather wood. Others start to sort through the bodies and carry them down towards the sandy beaches where the pyres will be erected.

Calder approaches Harken and I fear he has seen through the lie. That he has figured out that my crew has been here prior. I grip the handle of the sword in my hand and prepare to strike.

Harker seems on edge as Calder approaches, but he stands his ground. Reaching out a hand, Calder places it on his shoulder.

"I'm sorry for your loss, mate." He squeezes Harker's shoulder, meeting his eyes with a look of sincerity. "This land was once your home and, therefore, these people your kin. What befell them was a tragedy, the likes of which not a single one of them deserved."

I tilt my head as I watch tears swell in Harker's eyes. He is a far better liar than I gave him credit. I wonder how often he has lied to me in so convincing a manner.

"Take the night off, my good man." Calder pats Harker's shoulder, taking out his flask and offering it to him. Harker takes a drink and the tears subside before they get the chance to fall.

"Thank you, Captain," he says handing the flask back to Calder.

"No, thank you for your insight. What is your name?"

"Harker, sir."

"Thank you, Harker. You fought well today. Now take the night and mourn your losses. If anyone gives you grief, tell them to come speak with me."

"Aye, Captain," Harker nods at Calder then starts walking. He nods at me in a cordial fashion as he passes, then heads toward the *Ocean's Shadow.*

"And you," Calder turns his attention to me, where I am still kneeling in the street. "You fought well also, lass. Terribly well." He steps toward me until he is looming above me. "All this time I thought I was keeping you safe from the crew. Perhaps it is their safety from you that should have concerned me." He smiles, extending his hand to me. I take it and he pulls me to my feet, the sword remaining on the ground.

Calder walks away and starts assisting his crew with sorting through the bodies. He starts with the little girl. I watch as he nestles the tiny doll in her arms as he lifts her in his own. She looks so small as he cradles her. In this moment, I hope for a consciousness after death, so this little girl can know the last person to touch her was kind. He disappears off toward the beach. My hand shakes until I clench it at my side. I start helping with carrying wood from the forest.

Hours pass and the pyres are erected. The first one lit was the one constructed with the least amount of care – the one for our vanquished foes. Their bodies had been stacked with little concern for who these people *were,* but rather with contempt for what they had done to the kind people of Torrence. There was no ceremony to the lighting of this pyre. Nor were words spoken beyond Calder's, who said, without the knowledge of anyone listening, *may these flames be the first in your eternal damnation.*

The second was the pyre for the Torrencians. Calder himself sought out Harker and offered him the honor of lighting the pyre. He returned with Calder to do just that, really selling the narrative that these were his people. Harker lit the pyre but made no speeches, so Calder stepped in and spoke on their behalf. Harker watched the flames of the Torrencian pyre for some time before returning to the *Ocean's Shadow* without having spoken a word.

The third and final pyre lit was the small one for our three fallen crewmates. Their bodies were lain out shoulder to shoulder, arms crossed over their chests, and eyes closed, giving them the appearance of a deep sleep. Calder lit the pyre himself and said a few words before offering the crew the opportunity to say a few of their own. People took turns, telling humorous anecdotes about past escapades with the deceased. This went on well into the night, never really stopping as, soon, the spirit of alcohol began to feed the crowd's enthusiasm. I came to realize that all three casualties were from the *Queen Marie*'s crew. None from mine.

The pyres burn bright in the evening sky. I make my way to the shore and use the cool water to clean the blood from my hair and body. The salt stings the wounds I sustained during battle. Just a few superficial cuts to my arms, but the sting of the salt makes them feel deeper and more painful than they really are.

I want to fully submerge myself in the water. To strip naked and allow myself to thoroughly clean the blood from my body. But I am already beginning to feel the call of the ocean. The moon will be in full force tomorrow evening. The excitement of the day almost made me forget that I will need to figure out a way to restrain myself. To keep from plunging into the water, giving Delesseria the opportunity to claim me once again. I am pondering the possibilities when he approaches.

"Only me, love," he says while still a respectable distance away.

I glance at him as he wades into the water beside me. I am bent forward with my hair partially submerged in the sea, working out the last bits of lingering blood.

"You know that would be a lot easier if you just got in the water," he notes.

"I'm fine," I say, dipping my hair a little deeper.

"That you certainly are," he grins, dramatically tilting backward to observe my ass, which is noticeably sticking out as I bend forward.

I stand up, flicking my soaking wet hair over my shoulder, doing nothing to prevent the strands from smacking him in the face.

"You know what I love most about this beach?" I gesture down the shoreline. "The sheer size of it. You could go literally anywhere else on this coast."

"Hmm," he purrs. "Glad to know you're impressed by size." He smiles, too proud of himself.

"Go away, Calder," I roll my eyes.

I roll my sleeves past my elbows, my jacket lying in the sand behind, and begin scrubbing my forearms. Calder takes off his jacket and tosses it back onto the shore by mine. His boots are stood beside mine as well, also on the shore.

"I was surprised by your swordsmanship," he starts to unbutton his shirt, but his tone loses its flirtatious energy. "Where did you learn to fight like that?"

I don't respond to the question, not quite sure if I want to tell him a partial truth or lie entirely. "Does it matter?"

"No," he purses his lips, lightly shaking his head. "I was only curious." He pulls the unbuttoned shirt from his arms, crumples it into a ball, and tosses it to the shore as well.

He reaches forward, cupping water in his hands, and splashes it across his face. In the brief seconds that his eyes are closed, I steal a glance at his bare chest. He has accumulated a few new cuts and bruises from today's battle, which complement the scars of past skirmishes. I must be standing in a sand divot because he looks *insanely* tall beside me. Taller than I have ever before perceived him to be. The scrapes and bruises across his body do little to distract from the taught muscles that cover his exposed form. His strong arms and shoulders are well shaped by years of labor at sea, his calloused hands making it abundantly clear that he partakes in the ship's upkeep. His chest and abdominal muscles are sinfully defined, sharper and harder than anyone I have ever seen, slanting down at the base of his abdomen and disappearing beneath the confines of his pants... *which he is now unbuttoning.*

I immediately avert my gaze and hope that he did not notice my gawking. I assume he has not when he continues.

"You saved my life today."

"That I did," I affirm.

"You didn't have to," he continues. "You could have let me die. After everything I have done, I wouldn't have blamed you."

There is a moment of silence. "Well, I didn't."

"And I thank you for that," he turns his face to look at me. "I am in your debt, Duvessa. You have earned my trust and I fear I am not deserving of yours."

I am facing him now, our eyes having met, and I can't seem to look away. He flashes a sad smile. "I *am* sorry, you know. For everything. For keeping you locked away. For underestimating you. For... *Gareth.*" He half whispers his name like the word was strangled out of him. "I can't take back what I have done but know that I reflect on my actions with regret for how they have affected you. Though, had our tale not played out this way, I might not have gotten to know you. And I feel all the better for having met you. Even if under these... *unique* circumstances."

A flash of Gareth haunts my memory and I can't stand to look at Calder any longer. I break his gaze and splash water on my face, then busy my hand by wringing the water from my hair.

"I believe this goes without saying, but I am abiding by my promise. You are free in every sense of the word. Go wherever you'd like. Do whatever you'd like. Or," he pauses. "Or you could stay. If you'd like."

My hands stall and I decide that my hair is dry enough. My head is spinning. In part from the reek of burning human flesh that now permeates the air. In other part by the queer juxtaposition of expectation and reality. What should be and what is.

He should be dead. I should *not* have saved his life when I could well have left him to die or run my blade through him myself. I *should* have killed him. I should *want* to seek justice for Gareth by killing the man who stole my ship and killed my greatest friend in the world. I should *hate* Calder with every fiber of my being.

I should not so *easily forget* all the ways that he has wronged me. I should not want to *reach out* and *touch* the devastatingly gorgeous man in front of me and *bury* myself in his exorbitant charm and *suffocating* arrogance. I should not fixate on all the little things that make him appear to be a good man when *everything else* proves just how wicked he truly is.

Whatever propelled me to save his life was not of the conscious mind. I feel that subconsciousness clawing its way to the surface now, trying to establish a place in reality. I shake my head and make my way back to the shore, grabbing my boots and jacket.

"I'll be making camp with some of the men along the beach," he calls to me over his shoulder. "Feel free to take refuge in my cabin for the night, if you wish. I will not disturb you."

I see an object hit the sand in my periphery. Calder's pants are now balled up beside the rest of his garments. Without much thought given to the act, I turn to look at him where he stands, wading deeper into the water. The moon gleams against the rippling muscles of his back, and I don't know if it is the call of the ocean or his mesmerizing form that makes me take a step forward. But I stop myself from going any further. Rolling my eyes, I start walking down the beach toward the dock.

"Pleasant dreams, love," he says, before diving beneath the water.

My feet lead me to the dock. I could go to my ship. Spend the night in my own quarters. But for some reason, I find myself walking up the ramp of the *Queen Marie*. I close the door to Calder's cabin behind me, not bothering to lock it. I change into clean clothing, using the water basin and rag to clean any remaining streaks of blood from my skin before I do.

For a brief, gratuitous moment, I look outside the back windows and catch a glimpse of Calder, now on the beach. Redressed and lacing his boots.

I pull back the sheets from the bed, climb inside, and fall asleep surrounded by his scent. And I do, indeed, have pleasant dreams.

Chapter 16

I wake still half in a dream. I try to linger in it as long as possible. It's less lonely there. Less complicated.

When I finally do relent to consciousness, I find myself utterly alone. I make my way onto the deck, my eyes adjusting to the morning sun. Again, not a soul is in view aboard the ship. The makeshift camp along the shore, however, is bustling with men engaging in various tasks to deconstruct the temporary shelters they had erected the night prior. An aromatic scent wafts in my direction as I descend the ramp onto the dock and I follow it across the sand.

A collection of hot embers glow where a fire recently died. A large kettle hangs above it, suspended by three iron stakes and a chain. Directly to its side sits an iron grate lined with coconuts.

"Morning," Fritz almost sings as I approach. "Just in time, the pot's almost empty." He stirs the dregs of the pot with a wooden spoon.

"Smells wonderful." My smile is cut off by the loud growl of my stomach.

With a slight laugh, Fritz produces a machete from seemingly nowhere, swiftly slicing the blade down on one of the coconuts. Picking it up, he pulls the cracked shell further apart, lifting it to his mouth and drinking the clouded liquid that seeps from within. Once the flow subsides to a few labored drops, he slips his fingers between the fissure, pulling until it splits in two. Setting one half aside, he fills the other with the thick, spiced oats from the pot, handing it to me along with a spoon.

"Thank you," I lift the shell slightly, nodding my head in appreciation.

Fritz waves me off with a brief smile.

Our every interaction has been awkward at best. I have rarely seen him beyond his taking trays of food to and from Calder's cabin. And every time he does, he sheepishly averts his eyes. I've tried to strike up conversation with him before, but he has never been receptive to the attempts.

I take the meal and walk off toward the shoreline, where I sit secluded from the rest of the camp. I eat staring out at the waves. I am halfway through the porridge and starting on the meat of the coconut before I am interrupted by a nudge to my shoulder.

Calder is standing beside me, a mug of coffee in hand, which he extends toward me in offering.

"Morning, lass."

A knot forms in the back of my throat as memories from last night's dreams are pulled to the forefront of my mind. I feel a flush wash over me, but I work to keep my expression neutral. I am grateful he cannot read my mind or this would be a far more awkward exchange.

I take the mug, sip, and nestle it into the sand beside me. "Morning."

I am slightly surprised, offended even, when he then walks away, returning to the camp and leaving me once again to my solitude. I expected some kind of irritating banter. Yet, here I am, having not received so much as a smile from the bastard. I huff, noting that I don't need the headache of his presence this morning anyway, and continue eating in peace.

The coffee grows cold long before I swig the final sips, but it is effective in rousing my energy.

Today I will connect with my crew. Today I will decide how to proceed.

I have barely stood, turning toward the village, when I hear a commotion stirring near the forest edge.

Swords are drawn by the crew as two men emerge from the tree line. Seeing the unwelcoming greeting, both men raise their hands above their heads and stop approaching the village. I cannot make out the words being spoken, for there are too many voices speaking at once and I am too far from the heart of the clatter. I reach the spectacle just as Calder starts to speak.

"State your business," he orders the two intruders.

The eyes of both men are filled with fear, darting around to the various swords and weaponry pointed in their direction. Both men appear to be in their forties, though their athletic builds give the impression that each is very apt at running and climbing. Likely far more capable of endurance pursuits than any member of either crew.

"We are," one of the men starts. He takes a moment to clear his throat of the overt tone of fear before continuing. "This is our village. We were attacked by men aboard *that ship*," he points toward the offending vessel. "They slaughtered our people. Some of us were able to flee, but not all unharmed. If you are friends, then please help us. If you are foe, I beg of you, let us return to our people – those of us who remain. We will not disturb you. Take whatever you want. Just leave us in peace."

The second man looks around at the stains of blood on the ground and the absence of bodies. A look of concern floods his face.

"What happened to the bodies?" the second man asks, his expression heating with anger. "What is *your* business here?"

Calder looks over his shoulder at the crew, gesturing for them to lower their weapons. "*We mean you no harm.*" His gaze returns to the two Torrencians. "We came here in the hopes that you would be able to help us. But it seems fate decided to turn that table on end."

Calder takes a single step forward, causing both men to take a corresponding backstep. Raising his hands, Calder mirrors their previous indication for peace. *They do not appear to trust so easily.* Understandable, given the circumstances.

"We arrived on your shores and found the carnage inflicted by your previous visitors. We... *took care of them*, then laid your dead to rest on the shores." He nods his head in the direction of the pyres. Both men track the gesture, their eyes softening when they fall on the remnants of ash blowing in the wind. "We did not know there were survivors, or else we would not have overstepped in such a way." Calder lowers his hands and bows his head in respect. "On behalf of my entire crew, please accept my condolences for your losses."

"How do we know you aren't lying to us? That you aren't working with the others?" The second man glowers.

"There would be nothing to gain from lying to you. Trust me or don't. It matters little to me." Calder's voice hardens. "Ultimately, your lack of trust in us would only harm you further, if you reject our help. Which *you yourselves* have requested."

The first man shoots a glance at the second, whose face fades from angry to merely apprehensive.

"We would be happy to assist you in any way you need, but that choice remains yours to make." Calder takes a step back, upturning his palms as he flashes them a charismatic smile. "So, what will it be, gentlemen?"

The two men exchange glances, sharing unspoken words. Finally, the second man speaks.

"*Fine.*" His eyes latch onto Calder. "Those of us that survived fled to the other side of the island. Some are too injured to make the trek back to our village. Those of us who aren't are too weary to carry everyone back who needs the help. We can live off the land for a time, but we are too exposed to the elements. The injured especially need to be returned to the safety of shelter."

Calder stares at the man with a neutrally pleasant face, nodding his head slowly as if waiting for further instruction. This second man has deeply irritated Calder.

When Calder does not speak, the second man shakes his head in irritation. "So, will you help?"

"Oh," Calder feigns surprise. "I didn't hear a request. Only an outline of your predicament."

"You couldn't figure that out on your own?" the second man spits. Neither he nor Calder break eye contact.

"Please, sir," the first man implores. "Help us retrieve our wounded and return them to our village."

"No," Calder smiles, still psychotically staring at the second man. "I want to hear it from him."

He intends to force him to *ask nicely*. To beg.

The air grows tense as they exchange warring glares in an unspoken battle for power. Calder smiles like a madman, an eerie juxtaposition with the darkness in his eyes. He stands his ground, unmoving, like a snake about to strike. The second man burns with rage, refusing to relent his pride. The first man nudges his friend, muttering something about putting their families first. Eventually, the second man breaks.

"*Please*," he spits the words like poison. "*Help. Us.*"

Calder's smile grows, but his eyes remain cold and distant. His voice is sickly sweet in his reply. "Why of course, lad. We would be happy to come to your aide."

Calder turns, issuing orders to the crew. He instructs twenty men to embark on the journey to retrieve the villagers and the rest to remain and guard the ships. Upon further discussion with the two villagers, it was determined that the retrieval party should be expected to return by early evening. As the selected few begin to gather their weapons and supplies for the trek, Calder walks in the direction of the camp, presumably to do the same.

"You too, love," he says, passing to my side.

"What?"

"I'd like you to accompany us through the jungle. *If you don't mind,*" he smiles. "I know I'd feel far safer having a swordsman like you watching my back." He nods in the direction of the second man, who is now sitting on a rock talking to his friend. "I have a feeling I just made a new enemy today, as it were. So, you just might have your work cut out for you." He pats my back before continuing towards the camp. "Borrow a sword from one of the crew. They are in macabrely ample supply since yesterday."

The man is literally arming the person who has been planning to murder him for weeks.

I too make my way down to the beach. I see a group of men surrounding a pile of swords, where they had been collected and placed after the battle the previous day. Harker and Starkey are the only faces I recognize. The rest are Calder's men. The two from my crew barely glance at me when I join the group. I meet their eyes momentarily and subtly nod.

We cannot speak now. Far too many eyes and ears are on us.

I pick up a sword, walking away as I buckle the scabbard across my waist.

We depart within half an hour, following close behind the two Torrencians who lead us through the dense jungle as assuredly as if one were walking down a cobblestone road. As it happens, not a single member of my crew was selected to join on this quest. I surmise that Calder must not yet trust them in full.

Calder falls in step with me near the back of the party, though we do not speak as we walk. The sounds of the jungle are loud as we tread through the heart of it, and I find myself in a peaceful, meditative state at the ambient sound.

As we walk, I scan the area – looking for any place that might serve as a relatively safe location to bind myself during the full moon tonight. Nothing stands out. I worry that I will have to use the ship and risk being caught. I wish I could use my quarters on the *Ocean's Shadow*, locking myself in, but I am not sure if the room is being used by another since Calder took possession of it. That, and Calder has the keys and can enter the locked room at will. I decide that finding a random place in the jungle, far from the village is the best option for maintaining my secrecy.

I realize quickly that my modest canteen does not nearly hold enough water to keep me comfortable in this humidity. Even Calder has yet to reach for his flask of whiskey, unwilling to risk further dehydration. At the suggestion of our guides, we left our leather jackets at the village, and I am quite glad not to have the added layer slowing me down. Our cotton shirts are clinging to us, having been long since saturated with sweat. I let my hair fall over my shoulders to obscure my gills, just in case the sweat has made the fabric of my shirt transparent. I feel them itching to breathe the moisture clinging to my shirt as my lungs struggle to take deep enough breaths to regulate my body temperature. How the Torrencians can navigate these jungles so seemingly unbothered is a marvel to me. I would do anything to be back in the cool breeze of the seaside.

In spite of the discomfort, the jungle is... *beautiful* doesn't seem like strong enough a word. There is an element of magic about this place that hangs as thick as the mossy epiphytes that surround us. I'd never known there were so many shades of green to behold. Like the blues of the seas, the forest's hues paint pictures of life and death. Of calm and calamity. Of every conceivable emotion known to man and those that only the earth itself can truly understand.

I feel the warring of infinite realities in my desire to remain and my need to return to a place where my breaths are less shallow and the world does not feel like it is buzzing around me. Return to the quiet familiar.

"Here," Calder hands me his canteen. "You look like you are about to pass out."

"I'm fine," I say and even I know that my voice sounds tired.

"Take it," he all but shoves the thing in my hands and forces me to drink. "Good," he grins and I can tell he too is drained. "Finish it."

I try to hand it back, offering him the last remaining sip, but he flashes me a glare that tells me I would need to exert more energy than I can spare in order to convince him to take it. So, I down the last drops and hand the emptied canteen back to him. There were only a few swigs remaining when he gave it to me, but already I feel the water reviving me.

"Thank you," I say through parched lips.

"Any time, love." He doesn't look at me as we continue following our party.

The more docile of our two Torrencian guides falls back, stalling until he is stationed at Calder's side.

"We will be arriving shortly," he offers. "There is a cold spring near where we are camped. We can rest and refill before making the return journey."

"Thank you," Calder musters enough energy that he appears unphased by fatigue as he speaks.

"No. Thank *you*," the man counters. "We are in your debt for what you have done for my people." He glances ahead at his friend, who is now solely leading the group. "And I apologize for Calco. He's had a difficult life. And now, with the losses he suffered yesterday, certain old wounds have been reopened. His grief takes the form of anger."

"I can understand that." Calder glances briefly at the man named Calco, who is walking slightly ahead of everyone else. Alone and silent. Calder meets the eyes of the man beside him. "I didn't catch your name."

"Raigorn," he extends his hand toward Calder, who receives it in a single shake.

"Captain Azure Calder," he drops his hand, then nods toward me. "And this is Duvessa."

"*Mrs. Calder?*" he asks, nodding at me.

"No, no," Calder seems to blush. Or maybe he is more overheated than I thought. "Just a patron of one of my ships."

"Apologies, miss," Raigorn expresses. "*Miss...?*" he prompts.

"No surname," I reply coldly. An impressive feat in this sweltering climate. "Just Duvessa."

I feel Calder's eyes on the side of my face, but I continue looking ahead, ignoring his interest.

"Well, Duvessa, thank you as well for whatever part you played in the events of yesterday and for your assistance here today."

My throat tenses at the expression of gratitude, not quite sure how to respond and uneasy under the attention. Fortunately, Calder steers the conversation away from me once more.

"The raiders," his voice turns somber. "There is nothing stopping more opportunists from trying to take your lands. There are vast enterprises out there that would do anything to take this place for themselves."

"We know that," Raigorn sighs and I wonder how he has the excess of breath to spare. "But there is nothing we can really do to stop them."

"You can prepare yourselves," Calder offers. "Arm your people to defend what's yours."

"The land isn't *ours*," Raigorn counters. "But I understand your meaning." He shakes his head. "All we've ever wanted was peace."

"Well, there is no peace to be had. Only taken," I interject, my words sounding far more bitter than I intended.

"The raiders' ship," Calder continues. "At the very least, it could be a means to deter outsiders. By keeping it displayed in your port, it could give the illusion of a more strong-armed nation. At worst, it could be a way to flee, should you find the need to do so."

"I'm not sure," Raigorn protests warily.

"Their ship is now yours," Calder dismisses, unwavering in his assertion. "Do with it as you see fit. But heed my words, there will be more intruders who mean you harm. Your compassion for others is no longer a virtue when the safety of your people is at risk."

Raigorn bites his lip in anxiety as he measures Calder's words.

"I appreciate your insight. I will not dismiss it so easily." Raigorn nods, then leaves us to return to the front of the group.

I wonder what impact Calder's warning really had on the man. For their sake, I hope they abandon their optimism for something far more practical.

"No surname?" Calder asks once we are again alone, beyond earshot. "What about that family you told me so much about?"

"I never should have told you about that." I shake my head at the memory of how uncharacteristically open I was with Calder about my past. And how his interrogation feels like he is making a joke of my history.

"Surely even such terrible people as they possess a surname," he presses.

"None worth remembering."

"I know for a fact that at least one in their line is not only worth remembering but worth forgetting everything else entirely." His hand brushes against mine before taking it and lifting it to his lips. The act takes me by surprise and I realize we have stopped walking. He is staring up at me through dark eyelashes as he kisses the back of my hand.

"No," is all I say as I rip my hand from his, continuing to walk.

"No what?" he catches up and continues walking at my side.

"No to everything," I shake my head. "No to *them*. No to *you*."

"No to *me*?"

"Yes."

"Well, which is it? Yes, or no?" He smirks and I want to slap him.

"Don't be a child, Calder."

"What have I done, except try to learn more about your origins?" His eyes narrow in enacted bewilderment. "You wound me with your harshness, Duvessa."

"No, I don't," I rebuke. "This," I point my finger back and forth between us. "This is all a game to you. You are bored, so you are trying to get under my skin. Trying to get a rise out of me. I don't want anything to do with it, Calder. I am not one who enjoys games and I am not one who can be so easily manipulated by your false charms. Save it for someone with a little less self-respect than me."

Calder stops walking. In an instant he grabs me by the elbow, pulling me back to face him. I try to yank my arm away, but he pins me by both shoulders, peering down at me.

"Let it be known that *this*," he shakes me slightly to emphasize the word, "is no game to me. If I were bored, it would not be your skin I'd be trying to get under. And there are far more gratifying of ways to get a rise out of you, love."

As if to prove the point, he leans down and presses his lips roughly into mine. I am stunned by the suddenness of the act, but I do not pull away. Nor do I pull away when his hands slip from my shoulders, one wrapping around my waist, pulling me flush with his chest, the other gentling fisting in my hair, tilting my head back as he kisses me harder. Deeper. My palms slide up the length of his arms, taking in every inch of his hard muscles. My hands are lost to the dark strands of his hair as my fingers curl at the nape of his neck.

As suddenly as it started, it stops. He steps away, and I somehow feel cold in his absence, despite the heat of the jungle. His eyes are locked on mine. It feels like he is looking down into my very soul and is disgusted by what he sees.

"Don't play games with me either, Duvessa. I fear neither one of us would survive it."

He steps past me, walking off in the direction of our group. He catches up with them before I collect myself enough to follow after as well. By the time I gain enough ground that I am once again at the back of the party, Calder has made his way to the front and is now conversing with Raigorn.

I try to condemn myself for letting him kiss me. For kissing him back. Maybe it is the heat getting to me, but for some reason, I can't. My heart is fluttering in the aftershock of the collision. His lips pressed against mine. The feel of his arm wrapped around me. Of being pressed against his strong chest. His fingers clenched in my hair. My cheeks heat and I can feel the blood pulsating in my lips as they lust for more of him. *But I cannot seem to hate myself for it.* All I can feel is the wanting of more.

These feelings overtake me for the rest of the journey. We reach the destination and I am shocked by how few Torrencians are here compared to the bodies that littered the streets of their village. People are scattered throughout a clearing, nestled between a circle of trees. The canopy is dense enough to provide limited shelter, though the more able-bodied of the survivors have crafted meager coverings from branches and leaves that are sheltering those who are more gravely injured.

The survivors are in varying states of distress. Some appear to have settled down since they were forced to flee their village. Others are still fraught with the anguish of watching their loved ones getting slaughtered before their eyes. Wounds of varying degrees of severity are cleaned and bandaged to the best of their ability using the fresh water of the stream and some large leaves that have successfully stopped any excessive bleeding. Some of the wounded seem as though they will make full recoveries. Others, I fear, will not make it through the journey back to their village, much less the night.

The villagers have crafted makeshift carrying devices out of vines, twigs, and leaves, allowing one person to lay atop the leafy cot while being lifted and carried by a person at either end. Between the twenty men from Calder's crew and the villagers who are strong enough to help, we have just enough able bodies to carry the injured. The return trip is slower than the way there. Though we had been revived by the clean water of the river, having used it to replenish our canteens and to cool ourselves before departing, we quickly tire with the added weight of so many additional travelers.

One benefit of the slower pace is that I have more time to scan the distance. I am paired with a Torrencian woman. Together, we are carrying a child of roughly ten or eleven. Her son. He is quite small and weighs hardly anything between the two of us. But the added awkwardness of carrying the cot slows our pace so that we are near the back of the group. Due to the high number of people on the return trip, we have broken into two groups, each taking a slightly different path back. Ours is taking a coastal path that adds some distance to our journey but has granted a reprieve from the extreme humidity of the central route. The cool ocean breeze makes the return journey far more bearable. I pass several decent options for where I can retire this evening to wait out the moon. I will retrace the path this evening, bringing the ropes and chains I have already stashed at the forest edge, and see how much distance I can put between myself and the village before the moon rises too far.

The boy we carry is worse off than I originally thought. At one point, he begins to cry and the woman instructs me, with all the authority of a mother, to set the cot down so she can comfort her child. He tells her the pain is too much to bear and that he wants to die. Begs for it. He has a deep laceration to his left leg. It looks more severe than any wound I have ever endured, and it reminds me of many a fatal blow I have seen over the years. I find myself yearning to comfort him, the only way I can. *With a lie.*

I stand at his side as his mother cradles him in her arms, sweat and dried blood caking her face. She tucks his head beneath her chin and rocks him side to side as she too cries at his pain.

"I've seen worse, kid," I tell him, deadpan. "I know it hurts like hell, but that is just a flesh wound. You will be ok. I promise." I am impressed by how honest and unwavering my words sound. I almost feel relief for him.

I can tell the mother knows I am lying. I can tell by the look in her eyes that she knows her son is already dead. I can also tell that her mind cannot bear that knowledge without shattering into a million pieces, so she is allowing herself the sliver of hope that what I am saying is true.

I retrieve my flask from my back pocket and unscrew the lid. I know it will dehydrate me, but my nerves are shot at the sight of the kid. I take a sip before extending it towards the lad.

"You seem a bit young to me, lad, but perhaps your mother will make an exception this one time?" I glance at the mother - who nods - and I hand the flask to the boy. "Go on, lad. Take it. It'll help ease the pain. Besides, I hate to drink alone. You'd be doing me a favor." He takes the nearly full flask and sips. His face scrunches at the astringent taste of the whiskey I'd taken from Calder's stash, but the lad forces himself to swallow it. "Atta boy. Or I should say *man* since you can stomach that stuff."

The boy takes a second sip, tentative at first but then he takes a much larger gulp. He wipes his tears and smiles slightly. He offers the flask to his mother, who declines. He then extends it back to me, but I shake my head.

"You hold onto that. Better your mother and I don't have any, lest we slalom our way off the edge of the cliff." I earn a chuckle from the lad and he screws the cap shut, nestling the flask beneath his arm. "Have as much as you'd like. Plenty more back at the village."

The mother nods at me in thanks, wiping the swirls of literal blood, sweat, and tears from her face, and together we start back off for the village.

By the time we arrive, the sun has started to set. I still have time, but worry I might be detained by Calder or won't have the luxury of excess time to be more covert in my retreat into the forest.

Two of the villagers take the cot from us, ushering the mother to follow as they carry the boy off to one of the hovels. Before they do, the lad takes my hand, stopping me from leaving.

"Thanks, lady," he says handing me my flask. I shake my head, again declining its return.

"Thank me tomorrow, kid," I smile.

As the boy is carried off the mother takes my hand.

"Thank you," she says, squeezing my hand in both of hers. "Please, stay with us this evening. Let us repay you for your help and your kindness."

My body tenses. I've never been accused of being kind. I'm not sure I feel deserving of it or care for the way it makes my stomach slither.

"I can't," I tell her.

"Please," her eyes grow more sincere. "Please, I must repay you. In whatever way I can."

I think for a moment, but time is running out. Looking around, there is no one else in earshot. I make a rash decision and pray to the gods that it is the right one. "If you want to repay me, there is one thing I need."

"Yes," she smiles. "Anything."

"Tomorrow morning, once the sun has risen. Follow the same path we just took with your son. I will need your help."

"What kind of help will you need?" she asks, gently.

"I can't say anything more right now, just," I cup her hands between my own, gazing imploringly into her eyes. "Just please come."

She stares at me for a few moments, but she ultimately nods her head and smiles. "Of course. I will come."

"Thank you," I nod my gratitude and give her hands an encouraging squeeze. "Now, go. Take care of that son of yours."

Once she disappears into her hovel, I make my way to where Fritz is distributing plates of food to the crew. He first fed all the returning Torrencians, who are now congregating around the funeral pyre where their fallen loved ones had been cremated the night before. They sit holding hands in some type of ceremony of grief. Some are singing. Others praying. Some are keening. Others laughing. Whatever form their grief is taking, they are experiencing it together. United in loss. United in the life that remains.

I take a plate from Fritz and sit quietly in the sand off in the distance, making short work of the meal. I turn my back so I am facing away from the villagers. It feels wrong to be so near to them in their hour of grief. At least my averted gaze can give them some semblance of privacy.

Like a dog to a bone, Calder is at my side in a matter of minutes.

"Tired, lass?" He offers me a coconut shell filled with water, which I accept but say nothing. "Come now. Silence is too cruel a punishment for whatever perceived indiscretion you've decided to blame me for."

"You mean for kissing me against my will?" I say dryly.

"You were more than willing, love." His voice is so low he almost growls. He brushes the back of his hand against the side of my arm, but I pull away from his touch.

"There are people mourning the deaths of their families over there and you think it's appropriate to try and seduce me?" I jab.

"I'd say what is inappropriate is to pretend that you are some helpless victim when you are clearly the furthest thing from it." His eyes darken. "If you truly wanted me to stay away from you, I would do just that. But you and I both know..."

"I want you to stay away from me," I cut him off.

Part of me really means it. But the part of me that nags in the back of my chest flares with guilt at the silence that follows.

His jaw tics, his gaze drilling a hole through my skull.

"Your wish is my command, love." He theatrically bows to me, extending his arms wide in mock adoration. "Let me know when you figure out what it is that you truly want."

He stands and starts to walk away.

"I will be staying with one of the local villagers this evening," I tell him before he gets too far. "No need to avoid your cabin tonight."

He stalls for a moment. I think he is going to turn around. To say something. Do something. Come back over and kiss me again. But he continues walking off toward the *Queen Marie.*

Chapter 17

She kissed me back. She wanted me to do it. And still, she played the victim. Pretended I was some deplorable bastard.

As if I would ever need to resort to such imposition.

I don't even know why I kissed her. I wasn't planning to do so. I wanted *her* to come to *me*. For her to have to endure every moment of my presence without so much as a peck on the cheek. For her desire to build and fester until she wanted me so badly that she came to me. Asked me. Begged me.

And I went ahead and ruined it. Like a mere child unable to control himself. She accused me of playing games when it is she who is living in a fantasy – feeding her self-imposed delusion that she does not want me exactly as I want her.

How could I not show her just how much of a liar she truly is? Force her to reconcile that fact with her own physical reactivity.

I spent the rest of the trek avoiding her, choosing to focus on the task at hand rather than fixating on how she tasted. How she melted beneath my touch and wanted me with every fiber of her being. How much I wanted her in that moment.

The stubborn liar.

By the time I made it back to the village, she had not yet returned. I made it a point to be in the section of the return party that took the alternate route from her, trying to put further distance between us for the time being. The man I helped to carry had suffered a gash to his upper leg. Though not a mortal wound, it was enough to prevent him from putting any weight on the leg without brutal pain. Many of the villagers had wounds that left me to ponder how they managed in their initial retreat from the village. I resolved that adrenaline was a powerful tonic for their physical performance. Now that the excitement of fear had worn off, many would have been stranded in the depths of the jungle.

We helped the villagers to their respective homes. I offered the services of Doryn, the healer I employ on a permanent basis for the *Queen Marie.* He is not technically a member of my crew, having made it abundantly clear when he agreed to work for me that he would not take rank amongst common pirates. He did, however, wish to see the world and escape his home village after plague took the lives of his wife and two children. With a broken heart, and no desire to replace the life he'd lost, he decided to move on in the same way I had years ago. By staying in constant motion. Now, his primary residence is one of the private cabins aboard the

Queen Marie, though he travels between the various ships in my fleet from time to time. He has been staying aboard the *Ocean's Shadow* ever since I took possession of her.

Staying in the captain's quarters, Doryn has been slowly rectifying various ailments of Gareth's crew. Now that they are among my ranks, their health is a top priority of mine. The few times I have ventured over to the *Ocean's Shadow* in the past weeks, I have seen the progressively increasing vigor of my new crewmembers as their health has been restored. Along with this, I've noted the progressive increase in their perceived acceptance of me as their new captain. I am, however, not so naïve as to assume they yet feel a sense of loyalty towards me just yet. *That will come with time.*

Initially, the villagers denied the assistance of Doryn. However, when he noted the early signs of gangrene on some of the more serious injuries, one by one, individuals began requesting his treatments. The evening buzzed past as Doryn scurried between patients, ordering members of the crew to constantly retrieve supplies from the ship. I helped as much as I could, but once I started to feel that my presence was becoming more of a hindrance, I retired to my cabin to change out of my soiled linens and busy myself with books and maps.

I must have dozed off because I wake with my face pressed firmly against my desk and a crick in my neck. At some point, Fritz must have entered the room because there is a heaping plate of food set on the table. I curse myself for allowing Fritz to see me napping like a child but immediately devour the meal. Some kind of roasted meat, presumably some animal they hunted on the island, and a tuberous vegetable that tastes like butter and melts on my tongue.

The night is well on its way when I finally emerge from my cabin. I stand on the deck for a time, watching the villagers as they encircle one of the pyres and mourn their losses. My mind wanders to the day of my own parents' funerals. How, like these villagers, I too had no bodies to mourn. Only the ashes of the lives they left behind. I feel a sense of knowing for their particular brand of hardship.

I think about Braun. How he mourned so openly that day. How glad I was that he did. It seemed right – *respectful* that he embodied the very essence of grief and sorrow. How I wished that *I* could have given that final gift to my parents.

But I couldn't.

I find myself wondering if I will be able to do so at Braun's funeral. If I will be able to bring all of that sorrow and grief to the surface or if I will stand over his grave like a cold statue. An unfeeling monument to a life lost.

I push the thought from my mind, not wanting to consider the scenario. It will not come to that. *Not yet. Not if I find her.*

I am walking back to my cabin when I see Vessa sitting in the sand just down the beach. I make my way off the ship, procuring a halved coconut shell filled with water, and approach her. I have no intention other than distraction when I sit beside her. But of course, her ever-testing contentiousness ignites yet another spat between us.

She serves the purpose of distraction, as my mind now fixates on my irritation with her and nothing else. I make my way back to my ship and pace the length of the deck. As the sun dips further into the swallowing horizon, I climb up into the crow's nest and light my pipe. I hope that watching the sun sink beneath the waves and the soothing act of smoking will help purge me of my frustration.

From this high vantage point, I see Vessa walking toward the forest edge. Nobody notices from ground level as she disappears into the jungle. I wait for a time, but she does not return. Finding myself scanning the village, I look to see if she, for some reason, reemerged elsewhere and is already back amongst the safety of civilization.

I do not see her.

An hour passes and the sun is almost fully set. I remind myself that she is a capable woman and not my responsibility to protect. *But I do not recall her having a sword when she ventured off into the jungle.* If she had, surely, I would have noticed.

Another hour passes and night has fallen. The moon shines brightly in the sky and, still, I cannot seem to shake her from my mind. I tell myself not to, that her petulance is not deserving of my compassion, but I find myself climbing down from the crow's nest. I check my cabin, just to be certain, but of course, she is not there. I walk through the encampment, which my crew has reset for the night, having previously deconstructed it thinking we would set sail this afternoon. Having spent the day as we had, another night on land became the plan.

I do not see any sign of her, so I continue on to the village.

I begin knocking on doors. I hate myself for this compulsive need to find her and know that she is safe. Rationally, I wish I could turn around, return to the ship, and forget about her entirely. But my rational mind is not at the helm as I keep moving forward.

The answers are all the same. Nobody has seen her. I hear the growl of some distant animal and my mind races.

Knock.

The door creaks open and a woman peeks through the crack of the door. She glances over her shoulder, raising a finger to her lips to silently shush me before slipping out of the door and closing it behind her.

"Sorry," she half whispers. "My son is finally sleeping. How can I help you?"

"Apologies, ma'am," I match her volume out of respect, but urgency still animates my tone. "I am looking for someone. A woman."

"The woman who helped bring us back from the jungle?" she asks, biting her lip.

"The very one," I affirm. "I saw her go off into the jungle earlier and I have not seen her since. As a ward of my ship, it is my responsibility to ensure she is safe."

The woman's eyes grow distant and she looks to be in contemplation.

"Is she here with you?" I inquire.

"No," she answers and I believe her.

"Do you know where she might be?"

The woman examines me for a moment. "She was kind to my son. Helped me carry him all this way. I do not want to betray her trust."

"Ma'am," I soften my voice, trying to sound as unthreatening as possible. "I assure you I am only trying to help her. She is... *important* to me. If you tell me she is safe, that is all the verification I need."

She narrows her eyes. "I can't say that she is."

"What do you know?" I can't help the slight darkening of my voice. She must register the change because she takes the smallest step backward.

"You are the captain of those ships, aren't you?"

"Indeed," I confirm.

Her eyes shift to search the surrounding area. When she sees that we are alone she continues. "She asked me to come looking for her in the morning. Along the path we took to come here. She said," she lets out a breath. "She said that she would need my help. Now, I don't know what she meant by that, but it sounded urgent. She made me promise that I would only come once the sun has risen. She was very insistent."

"And what path was that?" I push.

"That one right there," she points to a trailhead across the way. "Along the cliff's edge. The trail splits partway down, but if you stay left, it will keep you on the correct course."

"Thank you, ma'am," I say, turning to leave but she grabs my arm before I take more than a step.

"Help her," she says. "For what you've done for us all, I feel that I can trust you."

"I will," I nod at the woman. She releases my arm and I stride for the forest trail.

I don't know how long I walk. The only sounds that mark the time are the thumping of my own heart and the irregular calls of nocturnal jungle creatures. I reach the fork in the trail and keep left, as instructed. My feet want to run, but even with the brightness of the full moon, the forest is so dense that I fear I might surpass her entirely if I am too swift.

It feels like hours pass before my ear discerns a tellingly human sound.

Crying.

I walk in its general direction.

"Vessa?" I call out into the night.

The crying stops at the sound of my voice. Oddly, the absence of the cry makes me hone in on the direction of its origin. Like the light of an extinguished flame that lingers in the darkness, I can still sense it in the void.

"Vessa?" I call again. Still, there is no answering sound.

The edge of the cliff draws nearer as I approach. I see a glint of silver as the moon reflects off of something metallic at the base of a tree. Drawing closer, I note a pair of leather boots set neatly at its side. I realize that the silver glint came from a length of chain that wraps around the trunk, attaching to...

"*Duvessa?*" I sidestep the tree and look down at her where she sits, facing out over the cliff across the water. Vessa is thrashing against ropes and chains that bind her to the tree. The knots are crudely fashioned at her side but are thick enough that they hold her tightly against the trunk. A length of chain is also wrapped thrice around her abdomen, held tightly in place by a padlock. Her outstretched legs are tied from knees to ankles with rope, her wrists bound with chain on top of her lap. Her jacket is balled up and nestled behind her head, which she presses back into the bark.

"Vessa," I say again, kneeling at her side. Instantly, I grab my knife, reaching for a length of rope.

"Don't!" she practically growls.

My eyes narrow, perplexed. "*What?*"

"I said *don't*," she kicks her legs and pulls her wrists against their binding chains. "Leave me, Calder."

"What happened?" I reach once again for the ropes at her ankles.

"Do *not* cut that rope," she orders. Her teeth are practically bared as she squirms in discomfort.

"Who did this to you?" I bark.

"It's a long story. Just…" She hits her head against the trunk of the tree, gritting her teeth as the jacket slips from its blocking position, the base of her skull colliding with the rough bark. "Just leave, Calder."

"Not likely."

"Please," she *begs*, but I am not sure it is to me that she is speaking. "Please," she says again as burning tears well in her eyes. *Tears of rage.*

Her body flails angrily against her bonds, her head crashing back against the tree with more force than before. She releases the deepest, most guttural scream. A manifestation of hell's fury itself.

"Gods, Vessa," I exclaim, using my arm to block the blows of her head. Her skull crushes against my arm with so much force I fear she might crack the bone. "Vessa, *stop.* You're going to harm yourself."

She laughs maniacally. "What a novel fucking idea."

"What in the hell is wrong with you?"

"*Nothing,* just *fuck off,*" she spits.

"Clearly," I cringe as she thrashes her skull against my arm once again. "This is all very normal behavior."

Her response transcends words as she somehow thrashes harder. Blood begins to coat her wrists and I use my free hand to try and prevent her from pulling any more against their chains. She screeches like a banshee, kicking and headbutting me from the side. I stumble back at the force and she hits her head harshly against the tree.

"Fuck this," I mutter, taking my knife once again in hand. She continues to wail as I cut the ropes from her legs and from around her waist.

"Calder, no!" Her voice is manic. Almost panicking as she tries to deter me from setting her free.

But I am not of the mind to be dissuaded.

I lift my dagger, bringing it down with a clang against the chains circling the tree. I repeat this several times, to no avail. Vessa continues to yank and thrust against the chains, berating me as she does. I ignore her pleas and warnings, deeming whatever state she seems to be in as unfit to make decisions as to what is in her best interest. Blow after blow, I bring my dagger down on the metal links, cursing as they refuse to break. I am seriously considering ripping the whole damn tree from its roots when I notice a glint of silver in my periphery.

Could I be so lucky?

I scramble across the grassy earth, grabbing the tiny piece of metal with desperate hands. I lift it into the moonlight and examine it. A small polished key.

I do not take the time to consider how carelessly it had been dropped by Vessa's assailant. Rather, I celebrate the small piece of fortune as I rush back to her side. When her eyes fall on the key, they look different. Suddenly calmer. Hers but... *unsettling*. The moment she sees the key she ceases movement altogether. Her eyes gleam with something unidentifiably foreign to her.

"Yes," a gentle smile unnaturally tugs her face, looking nothing short of misplaced. "Hurry, please."

The voice is hers but the way the words fall from her tongue is not her usual cadence. She sits deadly still, like the calm before a storm. A shiver runs up my spine as I fit the key in the lock.

Click.

The chains fall from her waist and arms and I make quick work of unwrapping them from around her. She remains calmly seated, only moving to lift her wrists to me so that I might liberate those as well. I unbind them and gently pull the metal from where it dug into her bloodied wrists. The moment she is free she abruptly stands and starts running toward the edge of the cliff.

I am stunned into stagnation for only a split second, but it was enough time for her to get a significant advance before I started to make chase.

"Vessa?" I bellowed. A question. A command.

She stops in her tracks, as though she ran headfirst into an invisible wall. Her body seems to convulse as she struggles to take a step backwards. "You will not have me," she screams into the air. She takes another forced step back. And then another. Each one leaden, appearing to take a significant toll on her remaining strength. She roars in protest, seeming to fight an unseen force that pulls her forward with the strength of a hurricane. But she again falls quiet and her steps start leading her towards the edge of the cliff once more.

"No!" I yell. Her brief retreat gave me enough time to catch up. I wrap my arms around her and we both topple to the ground. She pushes to get free of me, but I roll her onto her back as I straddle her from above, holding her in place. She kicks and scratches and claws at me, spitting threats and insults like venom. I clasp her hands by the wrists and pin her arms above her head.

"What is wrong with you?" I beg for clarity. I have no idea how much time has passed since I found her in this state. How long I have been fighting her, my adrenaline on high. I grow warry from the energetic and physical strain and all I want is for it to end.

She shrieks like a banshee, loud and sustained. The wailing pierces my ears and I don't know what to do.

I want her to stop.
I want her to be ok.
I want her to be silent.
I want her to be calm.
I want her...

Abruptly and without thought, I plunge my face to hers, our lips clashing in a primal kiss. Urgent. Demanding.

All her rage from before is channeled into the kiss as she presses her face deeper into mine, biting my lip like she wants to devour me. She tilts her head and her tongue slips between my lips, the familiar taste of her filling my mouth. I groan as I relish the flavor that has consumed my thoughts since this afternoon. Licking the underside of her tongue, she shivers, body arching into mine.

I release my hold on her wrists, lowering myself until I am lying flush against her luscious form. My forearms press into the earth on either side of her face as I continue to pepper her with fervent kisses. Her skull presses into the grass as my tongue explores every inch of her mouth. She links her arms behind my neck, pulling herself closer to me – though there is no proximity to be gained.

My hands fist into her hair, tugging to expose the radiant length of her neck. I lower my lips to her throat, kissing my way down to her clavicle. My lips find a rough patch of skin at the top of her shoulder, but its juxtaposition with the silken softness of the rest of her flesh does not bother me. It is all her.

And all I can do is worship.

Liberating one of my hands from her hair, I pull the collar of her tunic, ripping the top buttons from its neckline. The fabric falls over her shoulder and I pull it further down until both of her breasts are exposed. I kiss my way down her sternum until I am nestled between them. Her hands weave into my hair as I crane my head to the side, circling my tongue around her peeked nipple. Releasing my hold on her hair entirely, I drag my hand down the length of her neck, her chest, until it cups her other breast. I smirk against her skin as she arches into my touch. I squeeze – *harder* – lightly nipping her between my teeth.

She becomes unhinged, hurriedly bunching the fabric of my shirt from behind, dragging it up my back with desperate hands that claw into my skin. I push myself up to kneel above her, pulling my shirt off the rest of the way overhead. When I toss the garment aside, she is sitting up, her legs still trapped beneath me. But she doesn't seem to mind. Her hair hangs long over her shoulders, shrouding her from view. Even still, she is the most agonizingly beautiful thing I have ever seen.

I cup my hand behind the nape of her neck, pressing her beneath my gaze. Her eyes close, a peaceful smile tugging at the corners of her lips. She looks so thoroughly herself, the way she did on nights when she would sit alone, staring off across the water.

I could stare at her *all night.*

With no discernable provocation, her eyes dart open and she stares out at the sea. There is no peace found in her gaze. Her muscles tense and her jaw clenches.

"What is it?" I ask, gently stroking her cheek.

She nuzzles her face into the palm of my hand. Strands of her hair fall away from her shoulder, revealing the flakes of skin my lips had previously discovered. They shimmer like abalone in the light of the moon, wrapping like swirls of seagrass across the tops of her shoulders and along the sides of her neck. They lift and fall as she nervously swallows, and I know that it should disturb me, but for some reason, it does the opposite. I find them hypnotic.

I want to lick them and feel as they writhe beneath my tongue.

"Kiss me," she whispers.

Needing no other provocation, I oblige.

I lose time in her mouth.

Holding her.

Caressing her.

And she matches me, in all our mutual desire.

Our rendezvous does not escalate further than it already has. Not for lack of desire nor her attempts to do just that. I smirk against her lips as her fingers drift to the buttons of my pants. I feel her lips pout when I move her hands away.

While I would love nothing more than to take her here and now, the image of her distant gaze prevents me. I do not know what possessed her so tonight. What caused her to behave so erratically. And while I could not prevent myself from touching her, could not peel myself from her right now even if I wanted to, I retain enough control to save such pleasure for a more assured moment. When I know she is of undeniably sound mind.

Only then will I possess her body in full.

Hours must pass because I watch as the sun rises, with her wrapped in my arms. She fell asleep some time ago, breathing softly as she lay nestled against my chest.

THE OCEAN'S SHADOW

I use my thumb to gently stroke the scaley flecks of skin along her neck, watching as they react to me. I don't know why but it gives me an odd sense of satisfaction.

I do not feel tired – but a sense of serenity falls over me. If anything, I feel rejuvenated. Like I could sit here for eternity.

It is with an element of chagrin that I feel her stirring in my arms as she awakens to the morning sun.

Chapter 18

Vessa

"The morning sun looks stunning on you, love," he croons. The first words I hear as I wake up on the cliffside.

So, it hadn't been a dream.

For the briefest of moments, I linger in the blissfulness of his arms before reality catches up to me. I startle, breaking away from his embrace as I regain my bearings. My shirt is half torn, hanging loosely at my elbows, the bare skin of my chest exposed to the elements. My gills on full display.

I pull the fabric over my shoulders, rebuttoning what remains functional of my shirt. I drape my hair over my shoulders as well for good measure, though I know there is no possibility that he has not noticed them.

"No need to be shy, lass," he smirks. "Nothing I haven't seen before. Well, almost nothing."

I avert my eyes. My mind flounders, trying to craft some kind of lie that can get me out of this situation. But no possible explanation comes.

"Anything you want to tell me, love?" he asks, tilting his head in inquisition.

What bothers me the most is how much I actually *do* want to tell him the truth. How safe I feel in his company right now and how his presence last night was the only thing that has ever worked to drown out the calling voices of the ocean. It unnerves me just how much I wanted him in that moment because of it.

"Would you believe me if I said *it's nothing*," I ask.

"I would accept it as your answer if that is all you wish me to know," his reply is level headed. Utterly void of humor. "But I was under the impression I had earned a bit more of your trust than that."

I hate how calm he is. Seemingly unphased by the anomalies branded along my neck. Hate how they *responded* to him last night as he kissed and touched them. How *I* responded to him.

But there is a call of its own in his calmness. In the softness of his eyes as he looks into mine. A lulling sense of security that compels me to speak.

"I wasn't always like this," I start, my eyes drifting to a patch of tall grass beside me. "Months ago, seven or eight, I met a woman in a tavern. We started talking. Drinking. Wasting the night away. I had no idea who she was, *what* she was, or I'd have never spoken so openly with her. I should have known there was something off about her."

I absentmindedly rip a long reed from the ground and begin breaking it apart, tossing the severed bits aside.

"I made... a *wish*, I guess? I don't remember verbatim what I said. I know it wasn't for this." I spread one of my hands in full, displaying the webbing between each digit. "She took whatever words I uttered that night and twisted them, making me into this... *thing*."

I pause, but he does not speak. He is nodding slowly as he stares at my hands, which now feel as though they have been stripped of their skin and are being dissected one sinuous strand at a time. Eventually, his eyes lift to my neck though he cannot see the concealed gills.

"And what exactly are you?"

"I don't know, exactly," I admit. "*One of her creations.* That's what she called me." I shake my head. "I think I am still human, in every way that counts. But these," I toss my hair away from my shoulder and pull the fabric enough to reveal some of my gills. "These are quite functional. And these," I pull the stocking from my left foot and bare the full webbing between my toes. "I can swim as fast as any of the beasts of the ocean. Breathe at any depth without need for the air above. I'm," my voice catches. "I'm a monster, I think."

I chance an upward glance at him and regret it instantly. His eyes are fixed on me and I cannot read the expression. I'm trapped in his sharp gaze, unable to break from it.

"Who is *she*?" he asks. His tone darkens.

"I think you know who."

"*Who is she?*" he repeats, slower and more punctuated.

I swallow nervously. "Delesseria."

His jaw tics, a manic half-smile creeping up at the corner of his lips. "Is that why your precious Gareth was so interested in finding her?"

My heart hurts at the mention of his name in this new reality where I spent the night in his murderer's arms.

"Yes," I state. Not a lie.

An unnamed emotion slithers in the depths of his eyes. His jaw clenches and his eyes drop from mine, sliding slowly down my seated form before returning to hold my gaze. He releases a long exhale, forcing his darkness back down to the depths of his soul.

"Explain what happened last night," he growls the loaded question.

"The little *gift* she gave me was not without a price."

His eyes pierce into mine and I want to look away, but I won't give him the satisfaction of knowing he is unsettling me.

"Every night of the full moon, something calls me to the ocean. Voices. Her voice, but there are many. All at once, affecting me like a trance, compelling me to dive into the water. If I do, she can take control of me. Possess me."

"And you know this how?"

"I know because it happened once before. Before I knew the cost of her spell." The urge to look away from him is too strong and my eyes fall to my hands. "I lost time. There are bits and pieces of memories, flashes really, but not enough to remember the details of what happened during that time. The compulsion broke at the new moon, when her power is cut off and begins anew. I haven't been back in the water during a full moon since. Hence the..." I nod toward the ropes and chains still strewn at the base of the nearby tree.

"And this?" He draws a line with his fingers back and forth between us. I can feel his eyes burning against my cheek.

"You cut me loose," my voice gets quieter. "I told you not to, but you did. And then you..." I close my eyes, shaking my head. "And for some reason, the voices stopped. The compulsion stopped and my body was mine again to control." I look off over the cliff, finding it far easier to speak to the distant waves than to him directly. "When we stopped, they came back, so I... so we..."

"Did Gareth also subdue the voices with his *affections*?" His voice is low, simmering.

"I never thought to try," I answer without thinking, an undertone of humor saturating my voice. I hope that it goes unnoticed, but Calder latches onto it. His eyes narrow in contemplation.

"Who *are you*, Duvessa?"

"What do you mean?" My heart skips a beat at the finality of his line of questioning. At the inability to step back from it.

"No common strumpet can wield a blade in battle the way you did." His tone is snide. Inquisitive. "Who are you to Gareth? To Vayne?"

I consider my answer carefully, my mind pulsating, trying to latch onto a cohesive thought. To decide what to reveal and what might condemn me. I must take too long because he slams his fist into the dirt beside him in frustration.

"Damn it, Vessa. Who the fuck are you. And don't lie to me."

"I am the captain of the *Ocean's Shadow*."

I regret the words the moment they leave my lips. This was not the time. Not the place. I am alone with Calder in the jungle. Over an hour's walk back to the village. *Unarmed.* Divulging my identity to him was not a wise move.

Yet, it feels oddly *liberating* to admit who I am. For him to truly see me for the first time. In a way, he now knows me better than anyone. Living or dead.

With all of my past lovers, it always felt so empty. Mechanical. Last night, for the first time in my life I felt true desire. Not a mere basal urge but true, all-consuming desire. Felt the need for more in every sense of the word. For some reason he stopped me from taking what I wanted and that only made the craving stronger. Made me ravenous with unquenchable need. Even now as I watch him absorb the knowledge that I am the enemy he was meant to kill, I want him.

"Are you now?" That unidentifiable darkness returns to his eyes.

"Yes," I affirm, spine straightening.

"So, Gareth was..."

"My greatest friend."

Calder sneers, a judgmental laugh cutting me like a blade. "And you let him die for you?"

"I had no choice! You left me no choice," I repeat the platitudes that I have used to subdue my guilt.

"There is always a choice. Stop lying to yourself, *Captain* Duvessa," the honorific burns like acid. Standing, he strides away from me. He stops several paces off, turning to face me. "Was anything you told me the truth? Was any of *this* real?" He aggressively clutches at his heart, rabid with rage.

"You have to recognize that you left me no choice," I level my composure, speaking gently and with reason. "If you had known I was the captain you'd have killed me on the spot. It was your own assumption that made you think Gareth was the captain and not me. I just... didn't correct you."

Calder paces back and forth as I speak.

"Yes, I lied to you by letting you believe your assumptions. And I'd do it again in the name of self-preservation." I hate that he is making me feel genuine guilt. That I feel the absolute need for forgiveness even though I stand by my choices. "But much of what I told you was actually true."

He stalls his pacing to glimpse at me before diving back into the repetitive motion.

"Everything I told you about my family was true," I sound meek as I admit this fact. Even now, I still don't know why I opened up to him about the subject. "When I was fifteen, I stole the money given to my father by the man he arranged for me to marry. I ran off and Vayne found me and I joined his crew. He wasn't perfect, but he was good to me and saved me from a life I didn't want. Gareth was... he was the only friend I had ever known.

He was the family I always wanted. Him and Vayne. When Vayne was lost, I took his place with Gareth at my side. He was loyal to me until," my throat tightens. "Until the day he died." I choke out the words.

Calder is standing deadly still, his eyes cast down at the grass near his feet. I continue to kneel, facing his statuesque form. I feel cold. Completely exposed for all of my truths and all of my faults.

"Are you going to kill me now?" I ask. I don't know why, but I feel like I wouldn't stop him if he tried.

"I don't know." His voice is gruff. Quiet.

He stands there, staring away from me for seconds that drag on into infinity. Running his finger through his hair, he turns his head to face me, peering at me coldly through his thick lashes. His entire body emanates wrath and malice.

Jaw clenching, his eyes drop to my mouth.

Striking like a cobra, he eats the space between us until he is standing in front of me, lifting me by the neck until I am on my feet in front of him. His fingers tense around my throat and I am convinced he is going to strangle me to death here and now. Still, no sense of self-preservation compels me to do anything about it.

I hold his unyielding gaze.

After several seconds, he lets out a heavy breath, his fingers loosening their grip and I take in a gasping breath.

"Damn you," he curses before pulling my face to his in a rabid kiss.

There is no time to catch my breath and no mercy in his kiss. No forgiveness. It is angry. Punishing.

And I don't seem to mind. His lips, his tongue wipe away the pent-up anxieties from the conversation, leaving a sense of euphoria in its absence. I wrap my arms around his neck and pull him closer.

His lips drop to my neck, peppering it with desperate kisses. He bites harshly at the scaley skin of my gills, slowly licking over the abused flesh before repeating the act. The sensation causes my core to burn with fire. He lifts his head slightly, hovering over my neck. I can feel the caress of his lips and the breath of his words when he speaks.

"What do you want from me, *Captain Duvessa?*"

He bites my neck abruptly, then presses a kiss into the stinging mark.

"You," I moan. An admission. A wish.

I feel a shift in him as he holds me tighter, kissing more passionately against my neck. He brings his mouth to my ear and whispers. "And how badly do you want me?" He takes the lobe of my ear in his mouth and I hate that it elicits a groan.

"I *need* you, Calder," I admit and I've never meant words so much in my entire life.

"No, you don't."

As suddenly as it began, he pulls away, walking off toward the trail.

Chapter 19

It took everything in me to break apart from her. To keep from escalating the moment until there was nothing left in that jungle but she and I and the bare truth that she craves me more than anything in her whole damned life.

But I did. And for that, I deserve all the treasure in the world.

I have never wanted anything the way I want Vessa. She with no surname. She who renounced the scum of her lineage and started anew when the world did nothing but fail her. She who beat the odds of fate and circumstance and rebuilt the world into one completely at her mercy. Hers to own. Hers to control.

How I want to live in that world.

I should want her dead. *My rival.* The protégé of my greatest nemesis.

The one who lied to me for a month. The one who shared in my life for weeks. She who dined with me. Who warmed my bed and brightened the room with her glowing amber rage. She who mesmerized me in the simplest of moments, feeding my infatuation.

I should hate her. But... I don't.

All I feel is ever burgeoning want.

I make my way back to the trail and start walking in the direction of the village. I don't realize how fast I am moving, propelled onward by my agitation until I am already at the forest edge and making my way into the village. I see the woman from the night before, the one who told me where to find Duvessa. She gives me an inquisitive look and I nod at her in affirmation as I pass. I am in no mood for conversation, so I allow the gesture to act as the only verification that Vessa is alright.

I continue on to my ship.

Fritz tries to hand me something as I pass. *Food? Beverage?* I do not know, as I ignore him entirely and make my way to the dock.

But it isn't the deck of the *Queen Marie* I find myself standing upon. It's *her* ship. The *Ocean's Shadow.* I see her in a new light as I walk the length of the ship, replaying the events of that night with the lens of my newfound clarity.

A wave of emotion swirls through me, wrapping tighter and tighter around my throat, pulling me down in a whirlpool of my darkened mind. *Anger. Betrayal. Pain.* All these things I should feel for her she should feel for me as well.

Yet.

She kissed me. Wanted me. She knew from the very beginning who I am. What I've done. And still, even after everything, for some inconceivable reason, she told me that she *wants* me. *Needs* me.

Or maybe that is a lie as well.

All this time I thought I was her savior. Now I know I was the villain in her story. The man who stole her life's work. The man who killed her friend. Who trapped her in a lie and forced her to feign compliance.

For what?

I'm standing by the helm, staring at the plank. This is where I stood when she watched him fall to his death. That pathetic nobody who died for her in a way that only the truest of loves could do. I hate him all the more for it.

The scene replays in my mind when I hear her footsteps approaching.

"Calder?"

"What do you want?" I do not turn to look at her.

"I," she starts. She has stopped walking and stands at a cautious distance to my side. "I just want to know what to expect. Moving forward."

It sounds like she is going to keep talking, but I have no interest in her questions.

"What were you going to do?" I cut her off. "*Kill me? Take back your ship?*"

"Do you want the honest answer?" she asks.

"Honesty is always preferred, though you seem inept at the practice," I snip.

"Yes," she steps into view but retains her distance. "That was the plan. But..."

"What changed?" I demand, still not looking at her.

"I don't know," she shrugs.

"Try harder," I growl.

She is silent for a moment. "I don't know what changed, Calder." My muscles tense at the sound of my name on her tongue. "I should hate you but..."

I laugh abruptly, the sound cutting her off with a flinch.

"*But you don't?*" I turn my blazing gaze on her. "And you expect me to believe that?"

"Believe what you will. But it's the truth," she dismisses my goading.

"Because you have such an affinity for truth," I sneer.

"For fuck's sake, Calder!" she bursts, no longer leveling her emotion. No longer holding back. "You're a godsdamned pirate! Lying is the least of the offenses that go with the territory."

"One does not have to disavow all virtue to take up this trade."

"If you're looking for someone virtuous, go find a damn cathedral!" She throws her hands in the air, exasperated. "You'll find no virtue here. And certainly not within yourself."

Her eyes drift to the plank and I know she is thinking about him. *I hate the ghost of him in her mind.*

"I wasn't looking for anything," I say.

"Yet here we are," she replies. Her eyes narrow into an accusatory glare. Mine shoot back at hers and we stand in silence for a beat, trapped in a stalemate.

Her gaze is hard. Unyielding. A rock that won't be broken. I find her so compelling that I break against her instead.

"I'll return your ship to your charge," I offer as the only solace I can. The slightest flash in her eyes signals that I have surprised her.

"What's the catch," her voice sharpens.

"No catch, love." I savor the way she reacts to the endearment. Yet, I proceed with my contention. "Though I would not be surprised if your crew is less than willing to part ways with their new captain."

"Come again?" she inquires, knitting her brows together.

"You'd be surprised at how effective a little *ethical treatment* of your crew can be in assuaging resentment," I shrug. "I dare say they are downright loyal to me at this juncture."

"I wouldn't be too sure of that," she scoffs. "After all, they..."

"Led me here?" I finish for her. "Yes, well. While they had initially steered me on the reverse course, they ultimately chose to come clean about their previous deceptions. At that point, we had made so much progress in our journey, I opted to simply proceed and recheck the region to be certain."

Her eyes grow distant as she ponders their betrayal. I almost feel guilty at having told her.

"Sorry to be the one to break it to you, lass," I offer, with no measurable amount of regret. "For what it's worth, not a one of your men gave you up as their captain."

I step down from the helm and circle her as I speak. When I pass behind her, I lean closer to dramatize my whispering in her ear.

"But then again, not a single one of them inquired as to your wellbeing." I tsk and shake my head in mock sympathy. "In fact, I overheard many of them expressly stating how glad they were to be rid of their previous captain. Of course, I assumed they were speaking of Gareth. It makes far more sense why they were so emphatic about the various, shall I say, *grizzly fates* they hoped befell you after your transfer to the *Queen Marie*." I chortle. "I dare say, if I hadn't come along there is a very real chance that you'd have had a mutiny on your hands, lass."

Her hands are balled into fists at her sides. She clenches them so tightly that they shake against the strain. I push aside the whispers of remorse fluttering through my mind. *All I said was true.* Better she hears it from me now than get hurt trying to return to her previous station. The look of devastation on her face rattles me, forcing me to fight even harder not to feel guilt for putting it there.

"Be that as it may," her teeth clench as she speaks. "The *Ocean's Shadow* is mine. I will be taking her back."

"Of course, love," I smile, though the malice still simmers in the background. "Consider it done. Though I doubt you will get all too far without the assist of a full crew."

"I'll manage," she growls.

"Where will you go anyhow?" My voice softens a twinge.

"What does it matter to you?" she scoffs. "From the sound of it, I'll probably end up in Davy Jones' Locker before too long." She sighs. "Or worse. Back under Delesseria's control."

"That's worse to you?"

"I'd sooner die than let another person control me. Not again."

She walks to the edge of the ship and leans over the rail. For a brief moment, I think she is going to jump in. Out of instinct, I go to her side to stop her if she tries, though logically I know she'd be more than capable if she did.

"So, that's your plan then? Track down Delesseria and, what? *Bargain with her? Kill her?*" I lean into the rail, craning my neck to face her.

"Something like that." She stares out across the sea.

"You know, lass," I shift, inching a little closer, craving proximity in spite of the coldness between us. "I happen to be in search of Delesseria myself. In light of your... *circumstances*, you might consider joining forces with me in this endeavor."

She huffs her distaste.

"I am the one with the respect and authority over not *one* but *two* crews, lass. Given the gravity of your situation, I'd say it might be in your best interest to first sort out your little *puppet-of-a-sea-witch* problem before you rip apart your enterprise trying to regain its control." I lean further over the rail and grin. "There's strength in numbers and in that, you are sorely lacking right now. Fortunately for you, I'm of a benevolent mindset when it comes to you, love."

I brush my hand against hers but she pulls it away. I chuckle at her irritation. At the fact that she knows this is her best option and how much it pains her to accept it.

"Alright," she relents, teeth gritting. "But the *Ocean's Shadow* is mine. Even if my crew refuse to answer to me."

"Anything you say, love," I smirk. "I'll order them to abide by your orders, but if any of them give you grief, you just let me know and I'll take care of it for you." I prod at the open wound of her vulnerability.

"I'll manage," she snarls.

"Of that I have no doubt."

"I'll return to my quarters. You and I will regroup and we'll set sail together once we chart our new course." Her words ooze with assertiveness. I smile at how she is trying so desperately to reestablish authority when she so clearly has none to spare.

"Of course," I smile, stifling a laugh.

"I need to know," she pivots to face me. "I need to know that I can trust you with what you learned about me. What happened last night – my crew is not *aware* of what happens to me when the moon is at its peak. What Delesseria can do to me. They know *what* I am, but I have kept the particular details of it to myself. Only Gareth knew."

"Mum's the word." I try to hide my growing smile at the realization that I am the only living soul who knows this secret of hers. But I fail to keep the grin contained.

She nods, accepting the promise for what it is.

"Don't you want to thank me, love?" I playfully twist at her discomfort.

"Don't push me," she rolls her eyes.

"Why not? It's come to be one of my favorite pastimes."

Her eyes dart up to the sky behind me. She startles, ducking down as she abruptly takes a step back, raising her arms overhead. It is a quick, involuntary action. One that I do little to react to other than to laugh at the overreaction. I saw him coming earlier on in the conversation. Even if I hadn't, I've grown so attuned to him that I can always tell when he approaches.

I extend my right arm out to the side, letting Aero perch atop my forearm. His talons dig into the leather of my jacket as he lets out a single screech. Over the past several weeks, each of my messenger hawks have found their way back to my ship. All except my beloved Aero. One by one, each message brought me nothing but disappointment. No news of Delesseria's location.

Vessa straightens, eyeing Aero like he will swallow her whole at any moment. I laugh at her overt weariness.

"Come now, Vessa. You aren't afraid of a common hawk now, are you?"

As if on cue Aero screeches once more, causing Vessa to flinch. My ensuing guttural laugh is unpreventable.

"Shh, Aero," I reprimand the raptor. "Be nice to our friend."

Aero seems to eye Vessa just as warily and I cannot help but find the entire dynamic comical.

"Care to give him a little pet?" I extend my arm slightly in Vessa's direction. She instinctively steps back to counter the advance.

"I think it might bite my hand off."

"He might," I joke, but she seems to take it as gospel. "But only if I tell him to."

That would be a trick.

Aero has always been a free spirit. I raised him since he was a fledgling. In that, I find we have a far more special bond. All of my messenger hawks have been purchased, already trained in their craft. Aero was a surprise bonus when one of the female hawks laid eggs soon after I acquired her. She hatched and reared him until one day she went off and never returned.

None of the other raptors stepped in to care for the young scrap of a thing, so I ended up caring for him until he was old enough to stand on his own two feet and learned to soar. He learned how to be a bird from the others of the brood, but I fear too much of myself imprinted on the poor creature because he never could quite be contained. Though he was born and bred in captivity, he has the wildest spirit I have ever known. It is rare that he comes to the coop with the other hawks, though he has free reign to do so at will. While he is not a conventionally trained messenger bird, I trust him more than anything.

I lift my hand and he extends one of his legs to expose the attached scroll. I undo the leather binding and slip the parchment from its pouch. After redoing the buckle, he lowers his leg back down to my arm.

"Thank you, my friend," I nod at him and lift my arm. "Now off with you. Go rest."

He screeches and flaps his mighty wings, lifting from my arm and flying off toward the jungle of the island.

"Petulant bastard," I mumble as I watch him disappear into the trees.

I unravel the scroll, eyes quickly scanning the scribbles of ink that one of my inland connections considers handwriting. I read and reread the text.

"Well, love," I say, rolling up the parchment and slipping it into my jacket pocket. "It looks like we have some good news and bad news."

"What?" she asks.

"The good news is we no longer need to figure out Delesseria's location. I know exactly where we can find her."

Her face lights up with excitement.

"And the bad news?" she raises a brow.

"It looks like you're in for a bit of a family reunion."

Chapter 20

The prospect of returning to Lythren sets my stomach on edge. I have not been back since the day I ran away and have had no contact with any of my blood relatives in equally as long. I am not even completely sure that my father is still alive. But evil doesn't die so easily. And with the way my luck has been going lately, he is probably alive and well. Probably thriving in whatever life he's built for himself after I ran away. He always did have a knack for scamming his way through life. Surviving like the termite he is.

The news of my crew's betrayal stung less than I would have imagined. To some degree, I am not surprised that they would choose Calder over me. Not that I plan to take the defeat quietly. As much as I hate to admit it, Calder makes a fair point. Better to regain my freedom from Delesseria before inciting further dissonance within my crew. Better to use Calder as a resource then pick up the pieces of my shattered life when all is said and done.

Upon receiving the news of Delesseria's location, Calder ordered that the crew prepare to embark at dawn of the coming day. We will spend one more night docked at Torrence. The Torrencians were eager to offer help in stocking certain jungle fare to bolster our rations. Refusing to hide myself away in the shame of my crew's hatred, I chose to assist in this effort.

I am hiking through the jungle, collecting small game from snares the Torrencians set prior to the attack on their village. Having not been checked in days, there are ample catches to retrieve, though some have been snatched by advantageous carnivora. Insects buzz around the carcass of a rabbit that hangs by one foot from a length of rope. I hold my breath as I cut it down and toss it in the cloth bag slung across my shoulder, praying that by the time Fritz has worked his magic, it will be unidentifiable on my plate. I walk to the next snare and do the same with another regional quadruped, the species of which I am unfamiliar.

Around me in the surrounding forest, several men are doing the same with traps of various kinds. Harker is among them. I have not gotten the chance to speak with him since he lied to Calder about why he was so versed in Torrencian culture. Further, I haven't gotten the chance to speak with him since Calder stole my ship. Remembering our brief, silent exchange from earlier, I cling to a shred of hope that maybe he is still loyal to me. I wait for a moment when we are out of earshot of the others before I make my way to him.

"I hear the men are in no rush to reclaim my ship." I approach from behind, but he does not react to my sudden proximity. Nor does he turn to look at me when he responds.

"It seems you're in no rush either." He slices his knife through a length of rope.

"Don't think I do not note that absence of *captain* from your reply."

"Is that what you are? *Our captain?*" His words are even and dry. "Seems to me that ship has sailed."

"I've been a good captain to you all for years," I work to keep my own tone level, not wanting an ounce of emotion to leak out and tarnish my reputation. "I can't say I understand the animosity."

Harker's laugh sounds half-hearted. Tired. Almost unvoiced in its apathy.

"You gave us a few good years. I'll give you that." He tosses a carcass in his bag before heading to the next trap. "But you haven't been a captain to us for some time now."

"So, it is true then?" I follow after him, enraged that he had the audacity to walk away from me. That I had to follow in order for him to hear my words. "You all choose that scoundrel over me? Over Vayne's legacy?"

"I prefer to think of it as we choose ourselves over neglect. Captain Calder may be a polished prat compared to our former captains, but he treats us with respect and has looked out for us more in the short time we've been in his employ than you or Vayne ever did." Harker stops in his tracks and turns to face me for the first time. "We chose you as our captain. Back when you deserved the position. But you haven't chosen us a day since. We're sick and tired of being nothing but disposable lackeys to you. Sick of your damned secrecy and sick of being ordered on senseless quests that result in zero pay and never receiving an explanation as to what the hell we are even trying to accomplish."

"Cry me a river," I laugh in his face. "You're a pirate Harker. You live to serve your captain."

"Exactly, Duvessa." The disrespect of his using my name makes my fists clench. "We are pirates. But we don't live to serve our captain. We live to serve whatever means get us to our desired gains. *You don't pay us?* Great. Then we don't serve you. We didn't get into this line to cater to the whims of some flighty bitch." He stalls at his own insult, which would have previously resulted in a lashing for the insubordination. But now, all the power I have is to issue an indignant glare. "We all came to this life to get out from under the thumbs of regulation. The way things have been, we'd just as well return to those meaningless lives we all hated so much before."

"If you were all so unhappy, why not do something about it?"

He grimaces at me. "You really can't figure that one out for yourself?" He shakes his head in annoyance. "Fucking Gareth would have had our heads if any one of us laid a hand on you. You don't think we'd have loved to slit your damn throat and replace you. Guess who would have taken your fucking place. Gareth. But he wouldn't hear of it. Said we had to obey your fucking orders or else we'd pay the price. Kept telling us to hold on just a little while longer until he could fix things. Cagey as his answer was, we listened."

My face heats, jaw clenching so tight that I think my molars will crack. "You're lying."

"Think what you want," he shrugs. "Gareth was the only reason you are still alive. I'd watch your back if I were you. Now that you've been stripped of the formality of your title, I don't see much need to kill you. But I can't speak for everyone on the crew. I know at least some of the men have a much stronger proclivity to hold grudges than I."

"I will not be intimidated away from what is mine," I growl. "You ungrateful..."

"Suit yourself," he cuts me off. "Don't say I didn't warn you."

"Why?" I solicit.

"Why what?"

"Why did you even bother lying to Calder about our course?"

"Oh, that? At the start, we planned to take back our ship from the bastard for what he did to Gareth. For all our lost men. Figured you were already dead, and if you weren't – well, with Gareth gone, there'd be nothing standing between our blades and your throat." He speaks casually as if he weren't admitting conspired mutiny. "But the man grew on us. Ended up deciding to let bygones be bygones. Less additional bloodshed this way anyhow. Besides, the way we figure, the lives lost at Calder's order were taken in the line of politics. All the crewmembers we lost because of *your* flighty moods, I'd say those are just as much a marker of Gareth's ineffective leadership as it is yours. Calder is driven by reason, you by your own insecurity. And Gareth? Well, he was driven by something far more primal. I'll take reason any day."

My cheeks burn at the judgment. I want to argue, to tell him all the ways he is wrong. But in light of everything I've learned, and looking back at the recent past, I realize that the real reason for my hatred of his words is that they are absolute truth. Still, my anger keeps me from letting that realization fully settle within me.

"Why'd you lie to him about having lived on this island?" I deflect, trying to pry more truth from his lips, needing to understand every crevice of the crack that's breaking into my world.

"That was no lie," his voice softens, growing distant. "This place was once my home."

I try to give a shit about that, but the rage that whistles inside my head prevents me from such empathy. I should probably care that he likely knew some of the people who were killed in the slaughter. Possibly some were family. I should probably say something to emulate compassion to make him an ally for when I ultimately take back control of my ship. Something kind like Calder said to him the other day in the village. Instead, I find myself saying, "I hope you rot in hell," and storming off toward the village.

I do not stop until I am in my quarters aboard the *Ocean's Shadow*. A man is standing beside the bed, his back turned to me as I skulk in the doorway.

"Can I help you?" I bark.

"I should hope so since you're the reason I'm having to pack all of this up." The man beckons me to come closer.

As I step to the side, I see that it is Doryn, Calder's healer. Laying on top of the bed are dozens of glass vials and a leather case. He systematically takes each vial, carefully placing them in pocketed sections that line the inside of the case.

"There," he latches the buckles, lifting the case and setting it on the floor. "You can take that over to the *Queen Marie* for me. Put it in the captain's cabin for the time being. I can relocate it to my room from there."

"What is all this stuff?" I eye the various jars and vials that also line the top of my desk.

"Ointments. Salves. Elixirs." He doesn't look away from his busied hands. "The usual things you'd expect a healer to have in ample supply. Fortunately for you all, Azure does not scrimp on the essentials."

"You call him Azure," I note.

"Indeed," he swirls a vial of liquid, squinting his eyes as he examines it. "I've known Azure since... well, before he was born. Hell, I was the one who delivered him."

"You worked for his parents then?"

"That I did," he sets the vial aside and picks up another, repeating the action. "Azure... such an absurd name. But Marie refused to listen to reason and pick a more befitting name for a noble son. Then again, if they saw him now..." He shakes his head and tsks. "Said she could think of no name more befitting for the poor lad. Born on a cloudless day at sea, where the ocean met the sky in an orb of blue as far as the eye could see in all directions. Too poetic, if you ask me. Distasteful."

"Why are you telling me all this?" I quirk a brow, bewildered by the sociable banter.

"Boredom?" He shrugs. "Happenstance? You could be a literal statue and I'd still tell you the first hundred tales of Shahrazad. You just happen to be a human person in my vicinity and I am in a talking mood."

"You're a tad abrasive for a healer," I observe.

"And you're a bit judgmental for someone as despised as you."

"*Excuse me?*"

"I am a well-educated man, miss," Doryn looks up from his vials to glance at me. "Not just in medicine but in all scholarly pursuits. Don't sell me as short as these muscle-headed brutes. Of course I figured out you were the captain of this ship."

I stare at him in disbelief. "How long have you known?"

"Weeks." He returns his attention to his vials, having seemingly grown disinterested in the topic of conversation.

"Why didn't you say anything?" I ask, dumbfounded.

"Didn't see a reason to," he offers. "Unlike my cohorts, I am no pirate, miss. By trade, I aim to help people, not end their existence. I don't exactly revel in condemning someone to death. If Azure wants to play pirate, that's his prerogative. I'm just along for the ride."

"I... um," I stutter. "Thank you."

"Don't mention it," he smiles. "Besides, it seems like the kid figured it out. Odd that it went this way. Makes me glad I didn't tell the lad, otherwise I'd have had to leave this lovely cabin sooner."

"Why did you take up in this ship?" I step closer to one of the leather cases, absentmindedly running my fingers along its weathered handle.

"I've been tending to your crew. You left them in pretty rough shape, miss." His tone is level but it lands like a scolding.

"I," my eyes fall to my fidgeting hands, "wasn't aware of that."

"I can see that," he eyes me. "I hear a lot in my line of work, but I see even more. Usually, things nobody wants you to see."

"Oh," I say to break the awkwardness of the silence that follows.

"No matter," he deflects. "You best be starting on those cases, miss. If you want me cleared out of here by supper."

I walk to the largest of the cases. It is too heavy to lift with one hand, so I drag it towards the door and hoist it onto my shoulder once I'm in the hall.

"Oh, and miss," he calls over his shoulder. "I'd lock the door tonight if I were you," he warns. "I'm not sure I want to find out just how disgruntled your crew truly are with you."

Chapter 21

We are back at sea and nothing feels any better. I had hoped that once we were moving, once stagnation no longer forced me to linger in the present, I would be able to push her from my constant thoughts. *Out of sight. Out of mind.*

But even having her on an entirely different vessel has done little to purge me of the memory of how she felt against me. Beside me. Beneath me. Her bewitching taste is all I want in my mouth and no amount of whiskey can burn the essence of her that lingers on my tongue.

I find myself sleeping on my chair at night, staring at the absence of her. The bed does not feel inherently mine and, though we never shared it for a single night, it feels disquieting to be in it alone. The sheets strangle at my neck, the mattress pulling me down like quicksand.

I've only seen her once in the three days since we've set sail. Not that she is privy to this. It was by pure happenstance that my telescope glanced across the deck of the *Ocean's Shadow* as she came to stand staring out across the water. I watched her for a while before Corkin interrupted me with some minor inquiry. By the time my gaze returned to the vessel, she was gone.

I am now aboard a smaller, manually oared sub-vessel headed towards the *Ocean's Shadow*. I accompany Doryn, who insists he must check in on a few members of the crew who are still receiving his medical care. Though the effort is far from necessary, I tag along for the day under the pretense that I have business aboard the ship. Still, I cannot help if she is on my mind as I climb aboard the deck.

"'Ello cap'ain," several members of the crew chime. It is almost heartbreaking just how cheerful they sound, knowing damn well that the flip side to their approval of me is their hatred for Duvessa.

"Afternoon, chaps," I nod in greeting.

"Ah, doc," another member of the crew approaches. "Glad tuh see yah here." He clasps his hand on Doryn's shoulder, leaning in as he speaks to create the illusion of privacy, though his gruff voice takes little precaution to speak softer. "So, that little... *thing* you said weren't normal. Well, it uh... it turned this sort o' *purple* color and then it..."

"Whoa there," Doryn abruptly cuts him off with a chummy pat on the back. "Let's hold off on any of that until I get situated below deck. Don't want anyone losing their lunch over those details, mate."

Doryn's attempts to use seafaring terms always sound comical to me. So inherently out of place when said by such an educated man of aristocracy. Though he is much older than me, I find it reminiscent of a child playing make-believe that he is a *pirate doctor* off on grand adventures. It brings a smile to my face every time.

The man nods, looking completely vexed as he follows after Doryn. I make a mental note to never inquire as to the particulars of the man's condition.

I make my way through the crew, exchanging pleasantries and inquiring as to their well-being. I issue orders here and there for minor tasks to be undertaken for the day. Primarily, my goal is to foster a positive connection with each member of the crew, then establish authority by reminding them who holds the power. A delicate give and take. A manipulation of sorts. Especially since, in reality, I couldn't care less about any of the men I find myself conversing with.

Not at present.

My eyes impulsively flicker around the ship, despite my conscious efforts not to, scanning for her. I just want to see firsthand that she is alright. I ordered the crew of the *Ocean's Shadow* to treat her with respect and courtesy. There was much protest, but they ultimately agreed to play nice with their former captain, so long as they did not have to take any direct orders from her. While they swore that no harm would befall her, I am not in the habit of taking anyone at their word. Hence my presence here today.

I pass the afternoon communing with the crew. Some came forth with requests and questions they'd compiled for their captain over the past several days. I ended up putting in hours of work trying to address them all and by the time I'd finished, I found myself exhausted by people in general. Struggling to keep hold of my final nerve, not wanting to slip and undo my social efforts of the day, I excuse myself to go below deck.

I knock on her closed door, but there is no answer. I had not seen her come topside all day, so I assumed she was remaining in her quarters. I knock again and still there is no indication of her presence. I consider where else she might be, and my heart stalls briefly as I contemplate the possibility that something nefarious occurred.

My hand reaches for the door handle, finding that it is already unlocked. I creak the door open and enter the room.

"A lack of reply is not an invitation to enter." She sits atop her chest, gazing out the small window. She does not look at me when she speaks.

"I'll keep that in mind for the future," I reply, stepping further into the room and closing the door behind me.

"Come to gloat?"

"*Gloat?*" I raise a brow. "Whatever for?"

"You were right," her gaze remains fixed out the window. "They hate me."

"Ah," I smirk, sitting at the edge of the bed. "I hadn't realized that was still an uncertainty."

"It was a lie," she continues. "They never thought of me as their captain. They only listened to me because Gareth made them." She sighs. I've never heard her sound so defeated. So devoid of that fire that makes her so addictive. "Everything I thought I'd accomplished. Everything I thought was mine. I only had it because some *man* decided to give it to me."

I nod my head, digesting her words.

"What does that matter?" I ask.

"It matters."

"Does it?" I lean against the wall, crossing my feet at the ankles as I fold my arms over my chest. "It seems to me the only thing that really changes in your story is quantity."

She turns to glare at me, an element of confusion added to her animosity. "*And that means?*"

"You say that the only reason you had what you did was because one man gave you his support. That's not so different from what you thought to be true. How every captain gains control. Only now instead of a group of men who *comprise* the majority, you were backed by a single man who *controlled* that majority."

She stares at me, unblinking for a moment. "Is that supposed to make me feel better?"

"I thought it might, yes."

Her slow blink screams her continued discontent.

"I had no control over my own crew. Gareth did."

"And you controlled him. Sounds like a highly effective chain of command, if you ask me." I shrug. "You only had to control one person instead of dozens. Tell me where I can sign up for that brand of authority and I'd gladly make the switch."

"That's not the issue and you know it," she shifts her gaze back out the window.

"If that's how you choose to see it, that's your prerogative," I push myself to stand. "Take solace in that interpretation or not, it makes no difference to me."

She huffs, irritation bleeding through her breath like smoke from a dragon.

"Here," I step toward her, tone transitioning to a new subject. "You left this behind."

I reach into my pocket, producing the small leather-bound journal I'd given her weeks prior.

Her eyes narrow on the item, glazing over as her cheeks redden with fluster. "Did you..."

"Look inside?" I cut her off, with a smirk. I let her marinate in that possibility for a moment before answering. "No, love. I did not steal a glance into your private thoughts. Tempting as it was."

Tentatively, she takes the journal in her hands, setting it on her lap. She settles back against the wall and stares out the window in silence.

"You're welcome," I mutter under my breath.

Her silence persists as she continues to ignore me.

"So," I take a few steps back until I am sitting on the edge of the bed, facing her. Leaning forward, forearms pressing into the tops of my knees, I tilt my head in a theatrical indication that I am trying to get her attention. "How've you been getting on?"

"Leave me," she tersely barks.

"Come now, Vessa," I sing. "All I want is to ensure that nobody is giving you issue. Then I promise, I'll leave you in... well, if you call this *peace*."

"Your crew is abiding by their captain's orders." Her teeth grind as she speaks. "Not one of them will so much as speak to me."

"Not a direct reflection of my orders," I clarify. "And you are still content to remain on this ship?" I try and fail to sound uninterested in the question.

"Why?" she scoffs. "You expect I'd want to go back with you?"

"Why not?" I grin. "I think you'd find the time would pass far more pleasantly if you did."

My attempt at levity is unsuccessful as her shoulders slump forward. A twinge of some foreign feeling zaps in my heart. I do not enjoy seeing her this way.

"At the very least, there's ample supply of that whiskey you covet so dearly," I raise my brow, tilting my head as I try to force her to meet my imploring eyes.

She remains silent for a beat, but the urge to argue with me wins out. "I much prefer rum."

"Well, we are all allowed to be wrong from time to time," I smirk.

My heart flutters briefly as I note a faint smile on her face, but her eyes remain shrouded with gloom. Her continued refusal to accept my benevolence is starting to grate my thinly wearing mood.

"I answered your question, Calder. Now leave."

I stare at her for a heartbeat, calculating what words could be spoken that might transport us back to that night on the cliff. "*As you wish,*" I relent and make my way out of the room.

Chapter 22

Vessa

I am trapped. Only now it is by circumstance rather than by force. There are no choices to be made. No places I can go. My only move is to stay the course and ride the coattails of Calder. To *behave.* For the time being.

I try to focus on the task at hand. *Killing Delesseria.* But I cannot prevent my mind from wandering to everything that might come after. Calder gave me his word that the *Ocean's Shadow* is mine for the taking, though it seems I would be abandoned by my crew when the time comes to part. The knowledge that the ship was never really mine makes it even harder to swallow the fact that the only reason I am back aboard her now is that another man decided to allow me the privilege.

Has anything in my life not been decided by a man?

Every element of my life was controlled by my father in my early life. Up until I ran away. *My choice.* It was Vayne who let me join the crew. Vayne who decided my fate thereafter. Gareth who decided I was nothing more than a child to placate, letting me think I was in control when in actuality he held all the power.

But they chose me, at first. Hadn't they? In the beginning, I was their captain. Truth and reality blur in my mind as convolution reshapes the narrative. *Did they ever really choose me?*

My mind has been plagued with these thoughts for days now. At first, I tried to speak to the crew. Tried to force them to tell me every agonizing truth they'd been hiding from me. But they treated me like I never existed. None spoke to me. None looked at me. I was a ghost that haunted my own ship. Eventually, I relegated myself to my quarters where I could, at the very least, sequester myself from the chill of their apathy.

Here I have been ruminating ever since.

When Calder leaves me alone once more, I sit for the remainder of the evening. I watch the light fade into nothing. Ignore the person who brings a tray of food into the room, setting it atop my desk. I don't reply when he retrieves the tray from breakfast, the food cold and untouched, and threatens that if I do not eat by morning this will be the last tray brought to me. I do not so much as look at him when he snarls at me, "Fine, fucking starve."

The room is dark by the time I move, no lanterns having been lit. I don't bother to light any as I slip off of the chest and into my bed.

I do not bother to lock the door. I haven't since my return.

My mind races as I lay in bed. I find that I am talking to myself in my head, to the gods. Begging. Bartering. Trying to understand what I did in a past life for this to have been my existence. I must have fallen asleep as I did because I find myself somewhere else entirely.

I'm fifteen. Back in Lythren. My father's friend, Mr. Tenebrys, is sitting in a chair beside my father in the parlor of our house. Father made me polish the room until it almost looked as though we were not living in poverty. Mr. Tenebrys is the richest man in Lythren and Father always has me put in the effort to make the house seem respectable when he visits. He has come to visit many times, for the past several years.

I first saw him when I was thirteen and Father sent me into town for some flour and gin. Tenebrys appeared behind me as I brought the items to the clerk. He hovered over my shoulder and offered to pay. I let him. Father always took money from others whenever he could, so it felt like the right thing to do. I thought it would make Father happy to have the money returned to him and just maybe that would mean he would be in a good mood for the rest of the day. I didn't realize it was more than the flour and gin that this stranger sought to purchase that day.

Tenebrys followed me out of the store and asked me who I was. I told him I was **Corbin Foley's daughter. It didn't dawn on me to lie. He took the items from my arms and told me that someone as beautiful as me should not be made to work so hard – that I should be taken care of instead. I tried to take them back, insisting that Father** *had given me the chore and that I should really be the one to do it. But Mr.* Tenebrys was so much older, so much stronger than I that he easily brushed me aside and insisted I let him walk me home. I remained quiet the rest of the walk, feeling his watching eyes as he fell into step behind me. I remained quiet until we arrived at my house and he handed me the flour and gin, stepping closer to me as he did. He looked down at me, brushing a strand of my hair behind my ear, and said "Aren't you going to thank me, my pretty little thing?" I thanked him as I started to silently cry. He brushed the tears from existence, dissolving the evidence of my fears. He said he would see me again, before walking away, leaving me with a pit in my stomach that I could not name but knew I had to bury deep inside.

Tenebrys sought me out every time I went to the town thereafter. His wealth bought the eyes and ears of the town and any time I so much as stepped foot outside my father's house he knew. He always knew. Then one day he was in my home, having drinks with my father, who had me constantly refill their glasses of gin throughout the night. He became a frequent visitor of my father's home and a constant shadow over my life.

I am standing in front of them and Father is telling me that I am going to marry Mr. Tenebrys. Tells me that Tenebrys has admired me for quite some time and has waited for me to become of marrying age to ask for my hand. Father tells me it will happen in a month, the preparations having already been made for a ceremony with all the extravagance desired by someone of Tenebrys' station. Tenebrys' eyes dissect me from across the room and my skin is crawling off my flesh. I do not understand.

I am falling down a dark hole.

Falling...

Falling...

I am sitting on a ship, hidden from sight as I clutch the money I stole from my father's safe. A pair of boots appear before me. When I meet his eyes, I am no longer fifteen. I am an adult. I am me. And it is not Vayne, but him.

Calder.

Calder extends his hand to me and I take it, him pulling me up from where I am hiding.

"Come out of the shadows, love. You'll wither into nothing if you keep hiding from your past." He smiles.

"I'm not hiding from anything."

"Just because you hide it in the darkness, where not even you can find it, doesn't mean it isn't there."

"There is nothing there."

"Look," he takes my chin in his hand and turns me to face beyond him.

My vision is taken by total darkness. I see nothing at all. Hear nothing. My only anchor is the feel of him as he steps closer and pulls me against his chest. My heartbeat quickens as the darkness somehow grows even darker.

Deeper. Thicker.

"Don't you see it?" He whispers in my ear.

"I don't see anything."

"Liar," he purrs, gently stroking my hair.

"I don't..."

"Liar." He presses a kiss against my cheek and I start to cry. I press myself deeper into his embrace and let the feeling comfort me. I cry harder than I ever have before and I let him kiss the waterfall of tears as they pour. He does not wipe them away as something to be hidden but absorbs them as his own as something to be shared. Seen. Witnessed.

My heart feels hollow, like it is falling down a dark hole too and there is no bottom to break its descent.

"Wake up..." his voice is gentle. Beckoning.

But then it is no longer him.

"Wake up," another voice demands.

Fingers wrap around my throat and I am gasping for breath. I try to bring my hand to my neck, to fight to free myself from his grasp, but my arms are unable to move. All I can do is choke and count the tears as they slide down my cheeks in rapid succession.

"Wake up, you fucking bitch. I want to watch the life drain from your eyes."

I am awake now, lying in my bed. My eyes take a moment to adjust to the faint light of the lantern set on my desk and the lack of oxygen flowing to my brain. A man is kneeling over me, pressing my arms down at my sides with his shins. His hands are wrapped around my neck, squeezing so tight I think my spine might snap.

"That's a good girl," he loosens his grip on my neck just enough for me to inhale a shallow breath before he is strangling me once again. "That's right. Fight for your life, like you didn't fight for Gareth's. Like you didn't fight for any of us." Again, he briefly loosens his hold.

"You know what happens to a person when they sink to the bottom of the ocean?"

I try to buck him off of me, but the weight of him is too much and his position over me debilitating. I recognize the face. Bill. A member of the crew. His expression is deadly calm. His eyes, determined.

"Eventually your body just sort of... pops," his eyes flare. "If you don't drown first, all that pressure just pushes," he squeezes tighter around my neck. "And pushes." *Squeeze.* "And *pushes*," he squeezes so hard his hands shake. "Until finally," he traces a finger along my temple. "All those little veins just implode."

He releases my neck, though one of his hands continues to hover above. I struggle to breathe and I wonder if he crushed my trachea. I try to make a sound, to scream out, but his hands are clenching again before I can.

"Now, you'd have to make it pretty damn far down for that to happen. But our Gareth, he could hold his breath better than anyone. *Couldn't he?* Anyone *human,* that is."

I feel the vein in my forehead pulsating from the pressure.

"It's a real toss-up what got him first. The drowning or the popping." He presses my neck deeper into the mattress. "Now, I can't drown you, *you fucking freak*, but I sure a shit can take away your air. Let's see what gets you first, little fish. That or the pop of your neck."

I notice now that my gills are flailing as I am being strangled, my body trying everything to stay alive. Bill alternates between strangling me and split-second reprieves where I try to inhale as much oxygen as I can before he continues with full force. I can feel the pressure building in my head and hear the thunder of my racing heartbeat fighting to push blood past the obtrusion of his hands.

My eyes flood with involuntary tears and he must see the pleading in my eyes because he says, "You deserve to die for what you did to us. You don't deserve our ship or our loyalty. So long as you're alive, we can never be free of you *and* keep our home. They all think that just because you're a woman you should be treated differently. Gareth. Calder. They can't see past their own throbbing cocks when it comes to you. Any other captain behaves like you, they'd have been gutted and replaced long ago. You want to be treated the same as any other man? Well, it's your lucky fucking day, princess. I'm happy to oblige."

The details of the room are growing dimmer, narrower as my brain is increasingly starved for oxygen. The pounding in my ears increases until I can hear nothing else but my own blood panicking inside of me. There are no thoughts in my mind now, only pressure until...

Blood falls down on me like a rainstorm. The release of pressure in my head roars like thunder.

My senses come back to me in sequence. First, I feel the sticky warmth of blood go cold as it drenches into my clothes and the bed beneath me. I smell the liquid metal coating my skin, taste it dripping into my mouth as I gasp for air. I hear something hit the floor to my right, falling heavy with a sickening thud. I feel the dead weight collapse on top of me. Feel it dragged off of me as my arms come free from beneath its weight.

Lastly, I see –

Him.

Calder tosses the body to the floor, glaring down at it as he seethes with rage. He is covered in red and I realize through the shock that I too am drenched with blood. I start to sit up, coughing from the pain in my throat and gagging from the gore that saturates me. Only once I move, as if pulled from a trance, does Calder look at me, lividness still swirling in his eyes like blood diffusing through water. He rushes to my side, putting his hand behind my back as he helps me sit forward.

"Are you alright?" he asks, his voice simmering with a low growl.

I nod, unable to speak. But my breaths are starting to become less shallow and breath by breath I regain some semblance of composure. He pats between my shoulder blades as I cough up mouthfuls of blood, vomiting twice as I wretch. I notice once I stop that my body is shaking. Violently.

He is rubbing gentle circles across my back, reassuringly and soothingly. "Are you sure you're alright?"

"I'll be fine," I rasp.

My verbal confirmation is all he needs before he jumps from the bed, entirely possessed by his fury, in continuation of his rampage. He kicks the body as he crosses the room to retrieve Bill's severed head. Grabbing it by the length of its hair, Calder dangles the decapitated skull so that it faces him at just below eye level.

"Fucking bastard," Calder snarls before spitting on the horrendous face, forever frozen in murderous sadism.

He steps slowly toward the door, picking up his bloodied sword from where it leans against the bed.

"Follow," he orders me. He is out the door and starting down the hall before his words even register.

"Show a leg! All hands, on deck," he bellows, loud enough to wake the dead. "All hands. Now!"

I scramble off the bed and reach the door just as he starts ascending the steps to the deck. The head is swinging loosely at his side. On shaky legs, I follow.

Grumbles can be heard from the crew as they come alive in the bunks, filtering up onto the deck with varying complaints at having been awoken in the dead of night. The sky is overcast, but the moon slips in and out of view through breaks in the clouds.

Calder stands on the platform by the helm, facing away from where the rest of the crew are congregating. I can tell by the way he is standing that every muscle in his body is tensed. Standing awkwardly off to the side of the ship, my body and mind have still not realigned with the actual passing of time. As eyes fall on Calder, voices go silent until all that remains is the sound of the waves.

A repulsive sound echoes through the silence as Calder lifts the head high and brings it down into one of the wooden spokes of the helm. His arms drop to his sides, the head impaled and facing out toward the crowd of stunned men. A cloud shifts and the moon lights up the ship as Calder turns to face the crew.

For a time, he stares out at the crew in silence, though the devilishly manic look on his face speaks louder than anything he could possibly say. With a sharp slice, his eyes fall on me.

"Come here," he instructs, nodding his head to the space beside him. My feet obey the directive and I make my way to his side. I have barely reached the spot when Calder's head snaps to the side, fixing on two members of the crew.

"You," he nods to them both. "Your faces. You are surprised to see her?"

"No, Captain. Just..." one of them tries to explain, his tone sounding forcibly sincere.

"Quiet," Calder shouts. "Your words mean nothing when your faces are as readable as a book."

"We did nothing wrong, Captain. We would never..." the other one speaks.

"Oh, but you did," Calder cuts him off. "I don't give a damn what role you played in this attempt on Captain Duvessa's life. The mere fact that you knew about it and did not come to me immediately. Did not try to stop it. That is all I need to know."

"I'm sorry, Captain," the second man says, eyes dropping to the floor in an attempted sign of respect, or maybe pure fear.

"Apologies mean nothing to me. What matters is obedience. I *give* an order. You *follow* an order. Savvy?"

"Yes, Captain. It won't happen again," both men ramble.

"No. It certainly will not," Calder snarls. "Seize them."

Four members of the crew come forward and restrain the two men. I can't tell if any of them were once a part of my crew, their faces too obscured by the darkness both within and surrounding them. They drag the men toward us and Calder steps down from the platform, unsheathing his still bloodied sword.

There is begging, pleading from the two men as they are forcibly lowered to their knees. Not a single person says or does anything to stop the scene as it unfolds. Hands push each man by the back until they are bowed forward, held in place by heavy boots along their spines – necks vulnerably exposed.

He is speaking to the entire crew now.

"You mistook my kindness for weakness."

He brings his sword down on the first man's neck, severing it from his body. The second man starts to fight even harder against the hands holding him in submission, wailing for mercy.

"I assumed you all knew that I am not an enemy you want to make. *That?* ... That is on me. I will take the responsibility for your lack of understanding." He points his sword to the head spiked on the helm. "*That* is what happens to anyone who defies me."

His eyes fall on me and for a split second his face softens, before he turns back to the crowd, reinvigorated in his thirst for punishment.

"I *told you* all not to harm her. Not to *let* harm befall her. *Told you* what would happen if any of you tried."

He raises his sword overhead.

"Here is a reminder to obey that command."

He brings the sword swiftly down. The ship grows silent in the absence of the second man's screams, his head rolling forward to Calder's feet.

Calder uses his boot to turn the cranium until its dead eyes are staring, unseeingly up at the stars. He skewers it through one of the sockets with his sword, bringing it up to examine at eye level. There is a look of pure derangement in his eyes. Slowly, he turns his gaze onto the stunned crew.

"Any questions?" he taunts with a maniacal grin.

Eyes avert as heads shake in answer. Some dare to mutter simple responses. Calder slides the skull from his sword and lets it drop to the deck floor. Wiping the blood from his blade against his pants, he sheaths it.

"Hang their heads from the bowsprit," he orders. "Let them serve as a reminder to you all until they decay and fall into the ocean."

All move out of Calder's path as he walks straight through the crowd. My feet follow after him.

Calder stands beside a wooden raft, the one he and Doryn used to travel between the ships. He lights a lantern, places it in the boat then extends his hand to me. I stare at him, unmoving.

"Come along, Duvessa," he gesticulates his hand in a coaxing manner. "I have no intention of staying here a moment longer. If I do, I can't say with certainty that more blood won't be shed."

"No," I take a small step backwards. "I'm staying here."

"Vessa," he chortles lightheartedly as if he did not just decapitate three men in the span of a few minutes. "Your room is drenched in blood. As are you in case you didn't notice. Unless you want to bask in the juices of that noxious prat, I suggest you come along with me to somewhere a little more hospitable to you at the moment."

He extends his hand further to me, nodding to it invitingly with his eyes. I stare at his hand for a beat. Then at his manic eyes.

I have no doubts that even if I were to protest, even if I indeed did want to stay, it would not dissuade him from forcing me onto the raft and taking me, kicking and screaming, back to the *Queen Marie.*

But looking into his flaring eyes, I want nothing more than for them to burn me.

I take his hand and let him help me into the boat.

Chapter 23

It kills me just how stunning she looks with the moon reflecting off of her blood-coated skin. As she sits unmoving, stoically staring across the dark water, she looks like a statue embodying how I feel on the inside.

Broken and utterly confused.

Something snapped inside of me when I saw him trying to strangle her. All I saw was red and all I could do was paint the world that very color. Stain it in blood. I don't know why I completely lost control in that moment. Yes, I care for Vessa, and acting to save her was well within my right and well within reason. But why couldn't I stop there? Why did I kill the other two as well? Yes, I said the reason was to establish authority over my newly acquired crewmembers. Yet, deep inside, I know that this was not the primary motivation.

I wanted them to know that she is mine. That I would eliminate anyone for even the slightest transgression against her. I wanted the world to know that I would choose her over everything else.

And I didn't even realize that until now.

It was by fortune that I had seen the man headed toward her quarters. Having opted in the last minute to remain aboard the *Ocean's Shadow* for the night, rather than return to my ship as planned, I ended up in the crow's nest. A place I love to spend nights when sleep evades me, as it often does. I saw him head toward the steps and rationalized that he was headed to one of the storage rooms that are also down that hall. When he did not return in a timely manner, I went to check on her. *Just in case.*

It's amazing how powerful intuition can be.

We haven't spoken a word since the boat was lowered to the water and I started to row us toward the *Queen Marie.* My mouth twitches with the urge to say something. Anything that might break the fog of tension keeping us trapped in this limbo between moments. Manning the oars myself, with no aid from Vessa, the journey between ships is slow going.

We reach the ship just as the threat of the rising sun buzzes on the horizon. I tie the dinghy to the edge of the ship and prompt Vessa to start climbing the rope ladder up and onto the deck. I follow close behind, feeling the urge to stay close in case she slips.

Her every move is foreign, like a puppet going through the motions without concept of its actions. Weak is not the word to describe the utter void of her in each movement, but I can tell that there is a lag between her perception and her action. She clambers over the side of the ship and disappears onto the deck. Once I too find myself aboard the ship, I see that she has already situated herself atop a barrel and is gazing out across the horizon. Keeping her in sight, I make my way across the ship to speak with one of my crew, requesting a bath to be drawn in my cabin and for food to be brought from the galley. After receiving confirmation that each need would be tended to promptly, I saunter to Vessa's side.

I place my hand on her shoulder, but she does not react to me. Frozen in thought. I slump to the floor, pressing my back against the barrel as I sit at her feet, staring out across the ocean as well. We sit in silence and watch the sun start to rise.

We must look horrendous, both coated in red that has long since dried on our skin and clothing. The blood cracks and flakes as I flex my hands, examining them in the burgeoning sunlight. I find myself wondering if she holds any fear for these hands that kill so willingly. For I who feel utter detachment from the lives I so recently ended. She must know now that there is nothing on this earth that could make me harm her. She must know now that these hands are hers to control. *All she needs to do is ask.*

I hear a forced cough to my left.

"Yes?" I ask without removing my eyes from my upturned palms.

"Your room is ready, captain."

"Thank you," I reply, dropping my hands. "That will be all."

"Aye," the voice confirms before I hear footsteps walking away.

I muster the energy to move, forcing myself to my feet, though I'd be quite content to remain here for eternity. Turning, I face Vessa and take her hand in mine. Her eyes drop to our joined hands. She says nothing as I lead her toward my cabin.

I open the door and she steps inside without prompting. I too step inside and close the door behind me. The curtains are drawn shut, a platter of food set on the table along with several large candles that work to light the room in tandem with the lantern on my desk. A large wooden tub sits in the middle of the room. Steam radiates from the heated water inside, calling to my aching bones. The room is filled with a floral fragrance, courtesy of whatever oils and soaps were put in the drawn bath. I step toward my desk, slipping free from my jacket and feeling instantly lightened from the burden of its weight. I drape it across the back of my chair before reaching for the decanter and pouring myself a hefty slosh of whiskey.

When I turn around, she is standing in front of the bath. Facing away from me, she stares down into the water. Her feet are already bare, her shoes and stockings set neatly by the door. I try to think of something to say to break the silence that has been building between us for hours. But nothing comes to mind. Instead, I lean into my desk and watch her as I sip the amber liquid in my glass.

One by one, she undoes the buttons of her blouse. I can tell by the subtle shifts in her arms as she works her way down the shirt before slipping the loose garment past her bare shoulders and letting it fall to the floor. Her dark locks, starched with dried blood, hang long against her tawny back. Her hands slip down to the buckle of her belt as she unclasps the leather strap, then undoes the buttons of her pants, allowing the remainder of her clothes to slide down her form and gather at her ankles. She lifts one foot, then the other, up and over the side of the tub until she is lowering herself into the sumptuous bath.

Gently, she tilts her head back, until the nape of her neck is resting against the edge of the tub and she slips deeper beneath the steaming surface of the water. I watch her for a moment as I polish off my glass, setting it aside when I am finished. I unlace my boots, kicking each off to the side, tossing my stockings promptly after them. I release a heavy breath I didn't realize I'd been holding as I approach the bath. Rolling my sleeve past my elbows, I come to kneel beside her.

Her eyes are closed, but I can tell she registers my presence when she flinches ever so slightly as I reach across to grab the cloth that is draped over the opposite edge of the tub. Once I do, I dip the cloth in the water, beneath the thick layer of soapy bubbles, saturating it before withdrawing the sopping fabric. I wring the cloth slightly before bringing it to her face, wiping away the caked blood from her cheek. Her eyes remain closed as her face nestles against the cloth. When it is well coated in red, I rinse it in the bath before continuing to wash her face of the visual reminder of the event.

I find the entirety of her face beneath the layer of blood that painted it before starting on her neck. Once that is clean as well, her gills begin to rise and fall in unspoken appreciation as water trickles down her neck from the moistened cloth. A strand of her hair slips into her face, leaving a streak of water colored red on her cheek. I tuck the strand behind her ear before brushing away the red rivulet from her cheek with my thumb. Her eyes find mine the moment they open.

A mix of emotions swim beneath their surface. *Sadness. Anger. Gratitude.* A plethora of others I cannot name but cannot tear my eyes from.

One of her hands emerges from beneath the bubbles, taking mine in hers, drawing it from her cheek to her lips. She drags her pursed lips across the tops of my knuckles, pressing gentle kisses against them as she does. Sitting forward, she shifts until she is kneeling right in front of me, her breasts bobbing at the surface of the bathwater, like sumptuous apples ripe for the taking. But my eyes are too transfixed with her gaze to appreciate them as thoroughly as they deserve.

She takes the cloth from my hand and drapes it over the edge of the tub beside us. I hear trickles of water as they drip onto the floor. The mess does not register as she reaches up and unbuttons my shirt.

She slides the fabric over my shoulders, agonizingly slow. I make quick work of pulling my arms free of the garment, tossing it aside. Hooking two fingers beneath the buckle of my belt, she pulls coaxingly upward as she rises further from the water until she is on her knees and I am standing before her. My pulse quickens as I grow agonizingly harder for her, the confines of my pants becoming increasingly unacceptable.

She is excruciatingly slow to liberate me from my trousers, but the stifled gasp that slips past her lips when she does makes it well worth the wait. I cannot help the roguish grin that transforms my face into that of the devil himself. I have to fight the urge but manage to keep myself from making any quips that might sully the potency of this moment.

I kick my pants to the side and join her in the water, which has now gone tepid. Not unwelcome to my sweltering temperature as I burn increasingly wild. As I step into the tub, she shifts back to accommodate the space my size demands. I detest the way the water further conceals her form as its level rises when I seat myself in front of her.

But I am nothing if not a good sport.

What I cannot see I can settle for feeling. I cup my hand behind her neck, pulling her forward until she is flush against my nakedness, her legs wrapping around me as she sits on my lap.

She reaches for the cloth and begins wiping the blood from my face and neck as gently as I did hers. The water runs red as the blood washes from my body, mixing with that which has already been cleansed from hers. Only her hair remains slick with remnants of blood. Once she has finished, I take the rag from her and toss it aside. I kiss her neck and slowly lower her backward until her hair is fully submerged in the water. Elegantly, she draws her head side to side, sending the length of her dark tresses floating like seaweed dancing in the tides.

She sits up as I reach for the bar of soap on the table. I usher her to turn around and she does without protest. I wet the bar of soap and work it into a lather in her hair, massaging her scalp as I scrub the caked blood from her locks. As I do, she lays her head back against my chest, which makes the task all the more arduous, but I don't complain.

The view is far too titillating for such criticism.

When I finish, I slide her forward, lowering her back until her hair is submerged and her head floats above my lap. As she lavishes in the water, I work the bar into a lather in my own hair. After a time, she sits up, creating just enough space for me to lay back and rinse the suds away. I submerge my head fully beneath the water and scrub at my eyes, running my fingers through my hair as I reemerge.

She has pivoted to face me, sitting cross-legged at the other end of the bath. I lay my neck against the edge of the tub, draping my arms over the sides as our eyes lock. She lets out a shuddered breath, almost imperceptibly quiet, but I have been conditioned to notice even the smallest details of her existence.

Slowly, she starts to stand. Water falls from her like a statue of an alabaster goddess being raised from the depths of the ocean. Bare and purely flawless in her every feature. Even the scars that decorate her naked form seem like they were always destined to be there. Like medals of honor from every hardship she has survived, they tell stories of her bravery and resilience. Of tribulations and victories. Stories I'd very much like to hear again and again until I can recite them like my favorite poems.

I reach for her but she shakes her head, instead stepping out of the bath and reaching for one of the folded towels set beside the tub. Slowly, methodically... *tantalizingly*, she dries herself from head to toe,

273

scrunching her hair dry as thoroughly as she can before draping herself across the foot end of my bed. With the curl of a finger, she beckons me to follow.

"Vessa," I almost choke as I exhale, hating myself for the irritating chivalry I'm about to force past my lips. "Are you certain?"

She shifts forward, slightly, narrowing her eyes. "Aren't you?"

A soft growl rumbles in my throat before I stand. Her ravenous eyes drop to my hardened length and I know that, if nothing else, there is a burning desire between us. *But I want more.*

I step out of the tub, water pooling at my feet, not bothering to reach for the second towel.

"If we do this," I run my fingers through my sopping hair. "There will be no denying it any longer." I take a step forward and her breath catches. "No pretending that this *thing* between us is only physical. There is more to this and you know it." I continue walking towards her as I speak, the cool drops of water all but evaporating as they slide against my heated flesh. "If we do this, you can't pretend that my affections are something I'm forcing on you. That you aren't as drawn to me, as I am to you. The magnetic north that's dragged our wretched souls together since the moment we met."

I reach the edge of the bed. She has pushed herself onto her hands and is sitting, legs still sprawled to the side, looking up at me as I tower over her.

"I won't," she almost whispers.

I reach out and cup the nape of her neck with my hand, adjusting her head closer to me, angled more sharply up to meet my gaze.

"Say it," I order.

"What?" her eyes narrow in confusion.

"I want to hear you say it," my hand tightens, slightly, her neck feeling nothing shy of dainty. Fragile.

"I won't pretend that..." she starts.

"No," I cut her off, using the hooked knuckle of my free hand to tilt her chin further. She releases a sharp exhale at the forcefulness, but does not pull away. "I want to hear you say what it is you want."

"I want you, Calder." She involuntarily gulps after the admission, biting her bottom lip from the anxiety of her vulnerability.

I laugh.

"Well, if that's all you want," I release her chin with a flick. Her eyes flare with longing at the sudden absence of my rough touch. With excruciating tenderness, I brush a strand of hair from her face. "Mission accomplished. I'm already yours."

She quirks her jaw up, angling it just as I'd held it with my hand, her physicality trying to trick her into remaining in the previous moment that she so desperately longs to return. The thick vein that underlines my cock throbs at the anticipation of doing just that.

"What do you expect me to say?" she shakes her head.

"I want you to tell me what you want from me... *explicitly*," I smirk.

275

I see the understanding seep into her eyes, her cheeks blushing my new favorite shade of red.

"Verbal contracts and whatnot," I press with a grin.

"I... I think you know what I want," she inches closer to me, but I counter the advance with a step back, leaving her cold and wanting. I raise my brow and nod, baiting her to continue.

"Fine. I..." she lags, scathing with embarrassment.

"I'm waiting," I antagonistically sing.

"I... I'm no good at talking like this," she confesses.

"If you can't say it, how can you expect me to know what you want from me?" I am getting a rise out of pushing her in such a way. Flustering her.

"I..." she starts again, her eyes averting to her hands.

"Ah, ah," I reprimand. "Eyes up here, love."

Without moving the angle of her head, her eyes dart to mine. Her unique brand of fiery anger that seems to ignite against me burns in her eyes. I step closer to her, pulling her up against my chest as I tilt her head back once again.

"Come now, love. We haven't got all day." I press a kiss against her neck, biting playfully into the tender flesh.

"Please," she purrs into my ear, making me groan against her silken skin.

With one fell swoop, I push her back until she is lying flat on the bed. Clawing my way across the mattress, I don't stop my advance until I am hovering above her.

"Not good at following directives, are we Duvessa," I tsk, brushing the backs of my fingers across her clavicle, watching as her skin pebbles beneath my touch. "And after seeing just how personally I take such disobedience."

I nip the soft flesh of her earlobe.

"No matter," I whisper, lowering myself until our bodies are pressed together. "I much prefer you exactly as you are." I drag my cock along the wetness of her folds, growling at the ecstasy of the sensation. "Though I must confess, it riles me to no end when you beg for me," I rasp in her ear before biting it once again.

She lifts her hips as much as she can against the weight of me on top of her, trying to deepen the friction of our contact.

"*Please*," she says again, as if on cue.

I smirk at the overt manipulation of her pleading, but it proves effective in controlling me nonetheless. With the next jerk of my hips, I slide myself inside of her. Slowly and with great control, I inch my way deeper until there is no room left inside. Even then I continue to press, trying to fill parts of her that no man could ever access. Once I'm certain I have reached her very depths, I pull myself out to the hilt before thrusting back in as far and hard as I can.

Her back arches, a treble groan slipping from her lips. *And I am unleashed.*

277

Her hands dive into my obsidian hair, brushing it away from my face as her fingers snake their way to the back of my skull. Twisting and pulling, she forces my face down to hers and she commences nipping and sucking at my bottom lip. Her face is lost as she moves to the side of my neck, assaulting it with deep, lustful kisses, feeling as though she were trying to devour me whole. My pace quickens as she takes my earlobe between her teeth.

I shift my hips slightly to the right and on my next thrust, her body loses cognizant stewardship of her actions. Her head falls back onto the mattress, hands stretching overhead as her chest irrhythmically contorts from her building pleasure.

"*Yes,*" she moans, the words an involuntary admission. A truth pulled from a place that even she may not have known existed.

I smirk as I gaze down at her, watching as I unravel her from the inside out. "Like that?" I say rather than ask, punctuating the words with a mighty thrust.

"*Yes,*" she repeats with a wanton groan that could bring many a grown man to his knees.

"Yeah?" I playfully antagonize, memorizing the very spot that seems to ignite her ruination. "You like that?"

I pick up my pace once again until I am almost certain we will break the bed, the *entire ship* in two. If she doesn't scream from the ecstasy, I think I just might.

"*Yes!*" Her back arches as she shatters around me. "*Azure,*" she nearly cries my name.

As she does, I come undone. Hearing my name on her sensual tongue, I spill into her with a rush. A prolonged growl echoes from deep within me as I fight back a fully unhinged squall. *The release is absolute rhapsody.*

Her body stills beneath me. I lower myself to gently lay atop her, using my arms to keep my full weight from crushing her entirely. We breathe together in silence, unable to muster the drive to pull myself from the comfort of her warmth just yet. I press my forehead against hers and smile at the closeness I feel with this absolute vixen. Rocking my head gently, I brush my nose against hers, eliciting the softest of giggles from her velveteen lips. It sounds so foreign in her voice, but nonetheless welcome to my ears.

"Well, that was..." I start.

"Shh," she cuts me off. "Don't ruin it."

"Well, you have ruined me entirely. It only seems a fair exchange," I chuckle, but relent to oblige the request by pressing an insistent kiss to her lips, which she matches with soft fervor.

It is with great effort that I find the will to peel myself from the moment, rolling to lay beside her on the bed. She counters the retreat by draping an arm and a leg over me from the side, nestling her cheek into my left pectoral as she cuddles against me. I wrap my arm around her back, pulling her closer.

"That was..." she starts.

"Ah," I tsk, my words ringing with jesting mockery. "*Don't ruin it.*"

"You're incorrigible," she taunts.

"Not at all, love. You wanted to prolong the sanctity of the moment by maintaining silence. I'm just holding you to the same standard."

"A futile endeavor," she laughs. "You can't go five minutes without needing to hear the sound of your own voice."

"On the contrary. I find that you render me speechless quite effectively." I brush my nose against the top of her head, inhaling deeply the scent of her hair. She nuzzles against my chest briefly before pivoting herself to hover above me, gazing down into my eyes with a wry smile.

"Is that so?" she teases, lowering her face to gently nibble my ear before whispering into it. "Perhaps I could... continue to render you speechless."

"Look who's incorrigible now," I chortle, raising my hands to her hips, pulling her flush against my body. She huffs a laugh at the playful act, but rather than escalate the intimacy, she nuzzles her face into the side of my neck. Her body goes soft in my arms, her muscles slackening as though she released a heavy sigh.

"Calder?" her voice sounds velvet soft.

"You're locked into *Azure* now, love."

She's quiet for a moment, weighing the impact of the informality. "Azure," she sighs and falls silent once more.

"Yes, lass?" I press.

"I," she starts but hesitates before shaking her head and starting again. "It's difficult for me. To say it. Especially with a..." she trails off. "But gratitude where gratitude is due."

"You don't have to say anything. I did it as much for my own selfish need to keep you alive as I did for your benefit."

"Regardless," she says. I can feel her brows knitting together against the side of my neck. "Thank you for saving me. If you hadn't shown up when you did, I'd..." her voice grows quiet. "Well, *thank you.*"

"Anytime, lass," I tilt my head to rest against the top of hers. "I'd bring the world to its knees for you."

She laughs. "The whole world, huh?"

"Well," I smile wryly, drawing slow circles along her bare back. "If you'd prefer something more personal, I can think of other things that could be brought to their knees."

Her laugh becomes a gasp when in one quick motion I have flipped us over until she is flat on her back and I am hovering above. She smiles up at me, our eyes locking in silent desire. I crawl my way off the bed, pulling her by the ankles until her legs hang over the side and I am standing between them.

Squeezing the tops of her cream-white thighs, I drop to my knees.

Chapter 24

Vessa

I should be ashamed of how many hours passed as we lost ourselves in our intertwining flesh. Ashamed at how many knocks sounded on the door from various hands looking to speak with their captain, only leaving when the sounds from within the room left no doubt in their minds as to what was transpiring behind closed doors or what Calder would do to anyone who'd dare intrude. I should be thoroughly and utterly ashamed. But that would require an element of regret that I cannot seem to muster for the whole, toe-curling escapade.

I found it oddly liberating. Knowing just how little the members of each crew think of me. That even when I clutched to the reins of control and dignity, they looked at me with judgment and malice. Sleeping with Calder could not make them think any less of me than they already do. Why spend so much time trying to prove to them that I am no whore, no object of lust when that is all these men will ever see me as. Why not appease my own satisfactions when no amount of chastity could ever alter their imposed narrative? Nothing I could ever say, nothing I could ever do would mean a thing in the court of public opinion. All I can do is make it worse. Why not have fun while burning down everything I've worked so hard to build?

It is well past afternoon when I emerge from the bed. To my benefit, several articles of my clothing had remained in Calder's cabin when I'd moved back onto my ship. I dress in slacks and a tunic before pouring myself a mug of cold coffee. Having been sitting on the table with the untouched food that had been brought along with the bath, it has grown so strong that it is almost unpalatable. I grimace at the bold flavor but force the gulp down before retrieving the decanter of whiskey from the desk. I add a splash to the mug.

"That won't make it any better. But it will surely make it more fun to drink," Calder snickers. He is sprawled out in the center of the bed, still naked, though a blanket is lazily draped across his more illustrious parts.

"A connoisseur of fine sludge?" I ask, lifting the mug in a ridiculing toast.

"A connoisseur of fine ways to let whiskey improve the mundanity of life," he smirks.

"I see," I nod, taking a sip.

He sits forward slightly, patting the empty space beside him on the bed. I approach but sit at the edge. He takes the mug from my hands and downs a mouthful before handing it back. I continue to drink as he sits up, scooting close behind me. Brushing aside a strand of my hair, he gently kisses my neck.

"I don't know why you insisted on getting dressed," he coos in my ear. "I can think of a thousand ways to pass the time between now and our arrival in Lythren and none of them require clothing of any attire."

The mention of the place is enough to make me uneasy. Suddenly, his touch is less welcome. Too reminiscent of the ghosts from my past. I take another drink and allow the feeling to subside with the astringent burn of the alcohol.

"If I didn't get out of that bed, I think we both would have rotten away," I state, dryly.

"There are worse demises," he runs a hand down my arm, causing me to stand and walk across the room to the table. I top off my mug with more coffee, then go to the desk for another tot of whiskey. I lean against the desk and continue to drink.

"Is everything alright, Vessa?" Calder's brow is raised as he sits forward. I can feel his eyes trying to read my expression, but all they can do is stumble over the foreign text he fails to decipher.

"I'm fine."

"What's wrong?" He presses, ignoring the deflection. "Not having regrets, I hope."

"No," I reply too eagerly. "It just... It has nothing to do with you."

"Then you should have little trouble confiding it in me." His tone is level, but prodding. Not a request, but an expectation.

But this is my secret. One I buried deep within me long ago. From time to time, it tries to claw its way to the surface, but I've kept it interred by adding fresh layers of filth, weighing it further down in my soul.

"I said it's nothing, Azure," I snip. "Leave it at that."

"Aye," he tilts his head, lifting his hands in theatric defeat. "Whatever you say."

He shifts forward until his legs hang over the foot edge of the bed. His enormous feet, like the sturdy roots of a tree, meet the floor as he comes to stand. The blanket drops to the floor as he steps toward the table, fully nude. I cannot help but fixate in admiration at the mighty trunks of his strong, muscled legs as he gallivants across the room.

"Well," he says, picking a grape from the tray of cold food. "If I can't interest you in coming back to bed, I'll have Fritz whip us up something fresh to dine on before returning to the labors of regular life."

He procures a clean pair of pants from his wardrobe and slips them on, sauntering towards the door as he works the buttons shut.

"No shirt?" I ask as he reaches the door.

"I know, *truly scandalous*," he mocks. "Nothing they haven't seen before, lass. I assure you."

Laughing, he goes to pull the door open, but a tremendous thump from below sends a shudder throughout the ship. Calder falls backward from the force. Dropping the mug, my hands brace myself against the desk, keeping me stationed in relative place.

"What was that?" I ask, rhetorically.

There are yelled commands from on the deck as the crew jumps to various tasks in steading the ship.

"Starboard!" someone yells.

"By the gods, it's huge!" bellows another.

"We're all doomed!"

"Monster!"

Calder clambers to his feet, retreating deeper into the room, grabbing his sword before making his way back toward the exit.

"Stay here," he orders.

"Not going to happen, Calder," I spit. I walk across the room in search of a weapon for my own to use.

There is no time for him to argue with me to relent to his protective demand as we are hit with another monstrous blow. He steps out onto the deck, pulling his sword from its sheath.

"Fine," he nods toward a chest. "More weapons are in there, love. Help yourself." He disappears across the sea of scurrying men.

I scuttle over to the chest, falling to my knees as the ship begins to intensely rock against the building, chaotic waves. I undo the latch and lift the lid, exposing dozens of swords, knives, and firearms. I procure a humble sword with no ornamentation of the hilt, unlike the rest in the collection. Standing, I pull it from its sheath, dropping the leather covering to the floor. I step toward the door, but my eyes fall back on the chest. On a whim, I procure a pistol and tuck it into my belt before stepping onto the deck.

THE OCEAN'S SHADOW

Mayhem. That is the state of the ship and crew. It takes a beat to gather my bearings, the shrill cries of the men resonant with sense, dulling fear. The air rings with chaos.

The world expands around me and I can see beyond the ship itself.

Monster seems too childish a word. As though what it is describing is something that could be rationalized when, in truth, our human brains can barely conceive of the sheer horror of this creature, too large to be seen in a single instance as one visualized entity. This abomination of the abyss could only be that of the greatest depths of the ocean, the only place dark and wide enough to have given rise to such colossal a demon.

Thick, sinuous tentacles branch from the hefty body like bushes of tree trunks bound together in a mighty arm. Each lined with meaty suctioning disks so wide that any single one could fully encompass a grown man with ease. The tentacles wrap and whirl around the ship with such irregularity that it's difficult to tell if the creature has any intention other than destruction.

One tentacle wraps around the man to my right. He screams as it constricts around his chest. Squeezing tight, it cuts him off mid-cry as it snaps his spine. The body is tossed to the side like rubbish.

It isn't killing for food.

I don't have time to process the thought when another tentacle swooshes from my periphery, latching onto another member of the crew. Instinct compels me and my sword cuts deep into the beast's flesh. My sword but a toothpick compared to the size of the creature, I manage to catch it by surprise in my assault and it releases the man. He falls to the deck unharmed.

"Thank you," he cries.

"Look out!" I scream for him to duck, but it is too late. The man is pulled into one of the creature's suctioning disks, its pliant folds wrapping around him, prehensile, moving with such precision and intention that it seemed to have cognition all its own. The man has no further chance to cry out as the rubbery flesh suctions around his mouth. His eyes go wide with fear. I think they will pop from his skull when his gaze darts behind me with fatal intensity.

I hear the roar of the whipping tentacle and duck in the nick of time. Rolling into the direction of the offending appendage, I regain my footing, still crouched down closely to the deck. After a hastened scan in all directions, I rise, lifting my sword high overhead and slicing it downward. Once was all it took for me to partially amputate the disk. The beast rears its injured tentacle, dropping the man once more from its useless, dangling flesh. As soon as he hits the wood of the deck, I am rushing to save another person from a similar fate. If he tries to thank me again, I do not hear.

Time moves oddly when you are fighting an unwinnable battle. This... thing. It will win. If it wants to. All we can do is give it hell until it ultimately pulls us to our deaths. Picks us off one by one.

But why?

Why is it attacking if it isn't hunting? Why without provocation? Surely a creature such as this is not capable of pure malice. Of calculated wrath and destruction. Could it be one of Delesseria's creations, under her control? But why now? If she had the power to control such a monumental creature, why is she only now issuing this attack? It makes no sense.

"Vessa!" Calder appears at my side, sword raised overhead as he fights off another tentacle that swats at me from behind.

"It's useless," I yell over the sounds of the frantic clash. "We are barely hurting this thing with swords. We get one good slice in and all it does is pull back and regroup. We can't fight it off like this."

Kaboom.

"My thoughts exactly," Calder replies.

A guttural screech echoes as the creature shifts back, displacing a powerful wave of water. The ship turns erratically as water churns around it in the absence of the goliath sea monster.

"Cannons!" he shouts to me. "Its body was covering every cannon on the port side of the ship. It will take a moment to reload. Pray the blasts were enough to fend it off for a time."

"I don't think we're so lucky," I stumble back as I point at the sight. The creature jerks forward, hitting the side of the ship once more, sending all aboard her stumbling to the other end.

For the first time since the attack began, I think of my ship. "What about the *Ocean's Shadow*?" I say, clasping Azure's shoulder.

"I haven't seen it," he replies. "Then again, I can't see much of anything past this fucking goliath."

"What if the creature got to her first?" My emotions don't have time to catch up to that prospect as the slur of tentacles once again enwrap the ship.

"We can worry about that if and when we survive this." Calder springs into action, slicing the beast in any and all places accessible to him. "On men! Kill the beast! Send this feral swine to its watery grave!"

The battle renews with increased vigor. Swords slice. Pistols fire. But nothing proves effective to do more than temporarily cease the assault.

Then it takes him.

"Azure!" I scream, but it already is wrapped around him, his arms pinned down at his sides. It starts to lift him high above the ship.

It is without thought of anything but him that I jump onto the grimy tentacle. Palming the hilt of the sword, I struggle to climb its length toward Azure. While the bottom side of the creature's tentacles, lined with suctioning disks, is slimy and slick, the top is caked with grit and barnacles, which I use as handholds in my ascent. My presence on its appendage goes unnoticed by the creature as I cling and claw until finally, I am just below his dangling feet. He spots me.

"Vessa!" he calls. "Don't! Get down! You'll put yourself at risk!"

"You should have thought about that before getting yourself into this mess," I smirk, climbing higher. Once I am positioned beside him, I raise my sword overhead.

"Vessa!" Azure warns, but it is too late.

The tip of a tentacle slashes, sending my sword plummeting to the ground and me close behind. I manage to grab hold of Azure's leg, preventing me from falling the rest of the way to the deck. From this height, lifted just above the crow's nest, I fear such a fall might just kill me. *I had not thought this rescue through.*

"You alright?" he calls to me from above, his foot flexing as he tries to give me an easier handhold.

"I'm alright," I confirm.

"Ok," I can hear the panic in his voice. Hear him thinking. "There has to be a way to get you down safely. If I swing you over to the side, do you think you can grab hold and climb back down the way you came?"

"I'm not leaving you like this," I reply.

"Vessa," he almost pleads. "We don't have time for this. Just..."

"Wait," I cut him off. "I can..." I start, but there is no time to finish my thought.

"*Vessa...*" Calder draws out my name in anxiety as the creature's body shifts closer to us. A brown leathery patch of skin, as large as the *Queen Marie's* headsail, begins to writhe. Cracking and flaking, the lid is lifted until an ominous eye glares back at us.

The eye is level with my face and I swear it is seeing the very depths of my blackened soul. It thinks that I am small. Insignificant. That I can be easily broken. But what it does not know will be its demise.

I wrap my right hand in a death grip around Calder's ankle, digging my nails for added security in my free hang. The other drops to the gun in my belt. I cock the pistol at my side, not wanting to risk the possibility that it, or whatever might be controlling it, will notice the weapon before I take my shot.

Raising the pistol, I fire a single bullet through its eye.

The screech is deafening at this proximity, the impairment heightened by the rush of adrenaline that comes with our ensuing freefall after it releases its hold on Azure. So loud is its cry that I cannot even hear my own screams, though I feel them scraping my throat like shards of broken glass. Even as we fall, I cling to Azure's leg, yearning for some proximity to him in the final seconds of our lives.

And then the rope goes taut. And we are no longer falling.

"Grab the rope, Vessa," Calder prompts. "At your side."

I see the rope and grab it before my brain has finished processing. Azure lowers himself beside me on a separate line.

"How did you," I start.

I look to my left as we swing and see that we are halfway down the mainmast, clinging to free-swinging ropes that had come undone in the skirmish. The sheer distance we had fallen...

"Rope burn is a small price to pay for our lives," Azure brandishes one of his palms, revealing his torn, bloodied skin. "Shall we?" He nods and begins climbing down the rope. I take his lead and do the same.

He reaches the deck before me, an impressive feat considering the state of his hands. I reach the literal end of my rope, my feet meeting the open air beneath me.

"The line's been cut," Azure calls up to me. "Grab the... *Vessa, jump!*"

The beast has collected itself from the gunshot and is barreling at full speed back to the ship. Tentacles flail in an expression of rage. My hands barely release the rope by the time one of the appendages whips the line above me, sending it lashing so hard against the mast I'm certain I'd have cracked my skull.

I fall, longer than I expect, before strong arms are wrapped around me. He assesses me with his eyes, cradling me for a moment before setting me on my feet and asking, "Are you hurt?"

I feel a twinge as the soles of my feet make contact with the deck. Lifting my right foot, I note a smudge of blood staining the wood. I must have cut it on one of the barnacles.

"I'm fine," I say. "Where's my sword?" My eyes dart across the deck in search of the weapon I'd dropped, but it is nowhere to be found.

"Take mine," Azure forces the hilt of his sword against my chest. He leaves me no time to argue before he runs off to continue fighting.

His is a slightly heavier sword than I am used to, but I manage to wield it successfully. Our efforts do little more than buy us time, which we immediately spend trying to defend the ship. I see the toll the battle is taking on the crew before it even registers in my own body. We are growing weary. Losing strength. I know in my bones that we won't be able to keep this up much longer. And once we break, we will lose everything. Including our lives.

A tentacle sweeps at my feet. My knees buckle from the assault and I fall forward onto my face. It takes every ounce of willpower to push myself up onto my hands. To find the will to keep fighting.

A nagging voice in the back of my head tells me to stop. To let it all go. It would be so much easier to let it all go. All my plans, all my troubles, they seem so small, so insignificant in this moment. If I let myself go, it would all be over. I heave a sigh at the thought of letting it end here. I hate how much comfort that prospect gives me in this instance. Hate how much I want it.

But there is more than me at stake. If I cease fighting, then all these people will die. Everything Azure has worked for will be lost. *He* will be lost. And I just can't let that happen.

I force myself onto my knees, reclaiming my sword from the floor beside me. I lift my gaze in the direction of the creature's massive body. Only then do I see it. Like a beacon in the darkest night the outline of an unknown ship coming straight for us.

I don't have time to ask. I don't have time to tell anyone about the ship, to see if they see it too. All I know is I cannot let the creature notice it before it has a chance to strike. To save us all.

I push myself onto my feet, a wrath filled cry emanating from deep within me. I find my legs leading me closer to the beast until I am standing beneath its uninjured eye, the one that still can see.

"Hey, you oversized cephalopod!" I stall, flailing my arms in the air as I try to attract its sole attention. "Recognize me? The one who stole that eye of yours." I take several steps backward, its eye tracking the movement. When it narrows in recognition, I know I have it lured. "Come and get me! An eye for an eye."

With that, I sprint toward the center of the deck. The moment I reach the mainmast, I start climbing the rope ladder up. Tentacles lash and bat at me. Swinging Azure's sword, I fend them off enough to make my slow ascent. Having witnessed my baiting display, Azure works to fight the creature from below, protecting me to the best of his ability.

"Come and get me you one-eyed bastard," I taunt.

I nearly reach the crow's nest when my plan starts to fail. One moment I am reaching for the rope above, the next I am being enwrapped by a slimy tentacle. The way it glides over my skin, slipping and sucking, is the most unsettling, the most violating sensation.

It pins me to the mast, wrapping around the wood and my flesh, squeezing my spine roughly against the grain. I grimace from the pain, sneering at the restriction. As it tightens its hold, I am transported back to last night. To the hands wrapped around my neck that pressed and squeezed until my skull threatened to pop. Rage fills me and I try to roar my hatred. But there is not enough space in my chest to do more than growl. My vision grows darker and I think I will lose consciousness, until...

Its grip around me loosens, just enough that my lungs are able to breathe more deeply. It does not let me go but it is no longer crushing me.

Why?

Why has it not killed me when every other of its victims were crushed almost instantly?

"What are you?" I almost whisper. The way its eye narrows at the question, I think it heard me. "What controls you?"

Its eye softens and for the first time, I see the creature as more than a monster. It becomes something more than myth and fear. It becomes something born. Something mortal. Something that exists beyond this instance of destruction, in the quiet in between.

I think for a moment that it sees me too. But I do not get the chance to know. A deafening scream echoes so loud in my face that my hair blows back from the sound. Its grip starts to loosen even more until I am able to free my hands and grab hold of the rope once more. Its tentacle unravels from around the mast, retreating back from the ship. Only once that barricade to my vision is gone do I see the wooden skewer sticking out from the body of the creature.

That phantom ship had made its way to us. Had skewered the beast with its bowsprit. A clean shot through.

The creature falls backward, each of its tentacles retreating from the *Queen Marie*. A thunderous cracking of wood echoes in the air as the phantom ship cracks in two under the weight of the dying creature. Sailors jump from the broken vessel trying to swim against the rush of water pulling them down with the sinking ship. As the beast slips beneath the surface, its appendages flail, batting at the remainder of the wreck, dragging it along in death.

I hasten my way back down the mast, tracking the carnage as I do. Once I reach the deck, I find Azure at the edge of the ship barking orders.

"Drop the rafts! Hurry!" he bellows. "No man left behind!"

He spots me approaching, stripping my tunic from my body until I am in nothing but my trousers and undershirt. He has no time to question my motives as I run for the edge of the ship and dive into the water below.

One by one, I drag each man up to the surface, leaving them there to be picked up by the crew before diving back down for another. I do not waste precious time conversing with them as I fight to keep each man from drowning.

In the distance below, I spot what remains of the ship. Diving deeper, I reach the halved vessel and start to swim my way through the chambers in search of any remaining sailors. My gills lift and lower as they filter in a steady supply of oxygen, keeping my heartbeat even as I work my way from the severed center of the ship. No sailors are found.

The heap had turned on end, with the captain's cabin, which had been at the back tip of the ship, now being the closest thing to the surface. I again find myself outside the ship, floating beside what was once the deck.

I swim to the window of the cabin and peer into the room.

The cabin has not yet fully flooded, with a pocket of air remaining as water continues to seep in through the cracks in the door. I almost miss the pair of legs that remain practically motionless where they float at the surface. They lightly flutter, slowly but methodically, appearing calm when any ordinary person should be panicking.

I do not dare open the door, lest the remainder of the space flood instantaneously. Instead, I knock lightly on the window, trying to gain the person's attention. When they do not move, I try a series of irregular knocks, fearing that a rhythmic knocking pattern might be mistaken as something emanating from the ship itself.

The legs stall for a moment. My heart skips a beat as I consider that this person may just have passed into the great beyond. My worries are put to rest when, in the next instant, a face slips beneath the surface and meets my gaze.

Doryn.

My mind is too focused on the task at hand to question what he is doing aboard this unfamiliar ship. Instead, I raise and lower my hands, signaling him to breathe, then enacting a retained breath before pointing up to the surface. He nods his head and I pray he understands my meaning. If he doesn't take a hefty breath, he might not make it all the way back to the surface.

And even if he does...

His face disappears in the pocket of air. A few moments pass before one of his hands falls to his side and signals the okay.

With that, I push in the door and swim to him as fast as I can. Grabbing him by the ankles, I pull him down to the entrance, slipping us both out to the open water. His eyes narrow in on my neck and he nods, seemingly in understanding as to how I am able to come to his rescue.

And taking it quite nicely if I might add.

As he kicks toward the surface, I know he will run out of oxygen long before he makes it to safety. I position myself behind him, hooking my arms beneath his before letting my back fins kick with every shred of power they have, and beseeching some they don't. Doryn's arms cross gently across his chest, legs extended long beneath him. Once he does, we progress even faster toward the surface. I feel his heartbeat pounding against my chest as he forces himself not to take an involuntary breath, his lungs desperate for air.

All I can do is kick, and kick, and...

Gasp.

As precious air fills his lungs, manic laughter forces its way from Doryn's lips. As such, he is in a loop of gasping for air only to lose it all in a fit of laughter.

"Aye," I wave a hand above the water, beckoning to the nearest life raft. "Over here!"

The men aboard row in our direction. I only release my grip on Doryn once a set of hands reach for him and start to hoist him aboard. One of the men extends a hand to me, and I stretch my arm to take it.

Before our hands touch, I feel a hand briefly wrap around my ankle, before it slips away. I snap my head down just in time to see the face of a man, hands stretched overhead, reaching for the surface as he is being pulled down.

I scan the immediate area.

No one is left in the water but me. I had not seen another person at the surface when I emerged with Doryn. Nor had I seen anyone else underwater.

Wherever he came from, he is still very much alive.

And I can keep him that way.

Diving again, I spot the man just out of sight below, slipping deeper into the depths.

I follow.

I don't know what has a hold of the man. I can only assume the colossal beast somehow managed to grab hold of him in one final strike of cruelty. Or perhaps some other creature of the deep stumbled upon the shipwreck and took advantage of the free meal, picking off the unsuspecting sailor as he waited for rescue.

I pass the remnants of the ship, which now rest on a shelf at the ocean floor. Craning my head, I search for any sign of the man, but see nothing around but open water. Bubbles rush up at me from below and I catch a glimpse of the man before he disappears in another swirl of blinding bubbles. I swim down, further still, and find a foreboding emptiness. A pit of darkness that somehow stretches past what I thought to be the very bottom of the ocean.

THE OCEAN'S SHADOW

With but a moment's hesitation, I follow. The blackness swallows me whole, the light disappearing behind until the only reason I know I'm still moving is the gentle pull of the current that builds stronger with each passing moment. I try to reroute, to turn back and return to the surface. But the strength of the current becomes so strong that no amount of thrashing proves effective in preventing my descent.

The musk of the water grows sulfurous in my gills. These waters feel ancient in their aura, sending a chill down my spine that isn't entirely credited to the decreasing temperature. One moment, there is utter darkness. The absence of sight entirely. The next, a blinding light engulfs me. It shoots through me until there is no up, nor down. No direction. I feel as though I do not exist in time or in space.

Then...

"Hello, Duvessa."

Chapter 25

Vessa

I am sitting in a parlor. The walls, the ceiling, the floor are all carved and polished rock. A cavern I can only assume is at the very bottom of the ocean. I am no longer submerged in water, though off to the side of the room I see a pool that dips down into an underwater hallway of sorts. I imagine that must be where I came from since there are no other exits from the room that I can see.

Had I lost consciousness?

The cavern is adorned with all the fineries of a palace. Gold plated sconces adhere to the walls, candles lighting the room in a radiant glow of warmth and invitation. I sit atop a red velvet chair, outlined with intricate gold that matches the sconces and various other chairs and couches that complete the extravagant set. A quick scan of the room and I can tell that any single item here could set a person up for a life of lavish luxury, with excess wealth that could last to support one's children's children without so much as pinching a single penny.

"It is not every day I welcome a soldier of my daughter into my home." His voice is gruff and booming. Yet, an aftertaste of something almost grandfatherly lingers beneath his words. He sits across the room on a similar, but more ornate, throne-like version of my own chair. Beside him, an amber fire burns in a magnificent hearth, adorned with regal carvings of majestic sea creatures. His chair is turned to partially face the fire, while still being able to address me with little perceived effort.

"*A...*" I start to reiterate, but my words fail to form.

"I know of your dealings with my Del," he explains, resting his chin on his balled fist, donning a bored expression.

"Your... *Del*. Delesseria?" I discern. "That makes you... Triton, Lord of the Seas." My mind races with trepidation.

"*God*, actually. If you want to be technical," he scoffs.

I awkwardly shuffle to my feet and half curtsey, an action I've never done in my entire life. If the act itself doesn't *feel* wrong, I'd wager it certainly *looks* it in my sopping wet gentleman's clothing, hands floating oddly out at my sides with no skirts to occupy them.

"Your majesty," I say, nodding my head out of ceremony.

I knew it was foolish even as I said it. I'd never met a king, much less a god in my entire life. Not knowingly, anyhow. And from my position, which I wager is indeed the very bottom of the ocean, if not the center of the earth itself, I recognize that I am in no position to upset this... deity.

Triton laughs heartily, brushing the air in dismissal. "None of that, child. You'd be surprised at how quickly one tires of such formalities after centuries of groveling and doting acolytes."

I shuffle back to my seat, crossing my arms as I lean forward against my knees.

"Your majesty?" I start.

"Triton, my dear. Just Triton."

"*Triton*," I restart, feeling like a child that just called their parent by their first name. "Why am I here?"

"You know," he smiles. "This isn't our first meeting, actually. I've known you for some time, Duvessa." Something familiar glints in his eyes, but it disappears as he continues. "I doubt you remember your little, shall we say, triste with Del all those months ago."

"Can't say that I do." My jaw tightens at the mention of those lost weeks. "If I... *did* anything during that time that..."

"Bygones, my dear," he shakes his head, reassuringly. "If I blamed every pawn Del sacrificed in her little games, I'd have to slaughter half the population. Human and aquatic species alike."

"You haven't answered my question, Triton."

His demeanor shifts. Hardens. I can tell, while he claims to prefer informality, that desire is superficial at best. A disguise.

"Indeed, child," he forces a grin, that does not quite reach his eyes. "I've brought you here out of courtesy. To appeal to you as a father."

I huff. *If only he knew how misplaced that approach is with me.*

"I consider myself a tolerant man, Duvessa," he rises from his throne and steps toward me. "If not, I'd have done away with pirates like you long ago. Loyal to none but yourselves."

The closer he gets, the heavier the air in the room becomes.

"There was a time," he sighs, "how long ago it seems – when the likes of you would honor the reigning god of the seas. You'd brand the slaughters enacted for your own gains as offerings. Homage paid in blood and death."

Storm clouds shroud his eyes and somehow darken the room as well.

"Now, the most I get are the infrequent, whispered prayers spoken in last resort. But even those are woven between others voiced to false idols and lesser gods. The disrespect is enough to warrant a purging or a plague."

Triton towers over me, even if I weren't still seated. Dressed in seemingly human garb, I note the gills that run the length of his neck, so similar to my own. He crosses his arm over his chest, allowing me a view of his heavily webbed fingers. If not for his leather boots obscuring my view, I'd wager his feet mirror my own as well. Besides these abnormalities, his form is not unlike any other man, though the imposing nature of his size and musculature is enough to strike any mortal as preternaturally endowed. His greying hair falls loosely against his shoulders, the corresponding well-groomed beard clinging more predominantly to the remnants of dark strands that must have been lost to the ages.

"But I've resolved to, how should I put it, *take a step back* for the time being. Let humanity run its course by its own volition. Stand at the helm, as it were."

"How benevolent of you," I mutter.

"Indeed," he casually leans against the arm of his throne. "Indeed."

"What does this all have to do with me?" I press.

"She made you in the image of me, you know. The image of her true self, before I cast her out. She too once bore the markings of a sea god," he traces the back of his fingers along the side of his neck. "Stood on two legs more powerful than any creature. Had abilities the likes of which the world had never seen. But," his throat catches and I glimpse the twinkle of a tear in the corner of his eye. "But her demeanor was not fit for such strength. When she killed her mother... when she cast that spell and her magic augmented into something that even I could not vanquish. Well. All I could do was bind her magic. Limit it as best I could. When I disavowed her, she became the sea witch she so desperately wanted to be. With one terrible decision, I lost my only daughter and the woman who gave her to me."

His eyes fall to the floor and he goes silent for a spell, lost in thought.

"That's a lot to lose," I acknowledge.

"Loss is something you are acquainted with as well, I believe."

I nod.

"Perhaps then it is through loss that I hope to appeal to you," his eyes lift and meet mine across the room. "Do not kill my daughter. I have lost too much already."

I consider my words before I speak.

"Everyone is someone's child, Triton. You can't ask me not to seek revenge for what she's done to me."

"I am asking you to spare her."

"And what can you give me in return?" I have to work to keep my tone from heating with anger.

"My undying gratitude," he says with sickly sincerity.

I consciously struggle to keep from rolling my eyes. Can he really be so far removed from humanity that he thinks his approval holds any bearing in our mortal lives? That his mere gratitude could buy him a life?

"Can you break the curse she cast on me? Can you keep her from being able to control me?" There is a flicker of hopefulness in my inquiry.

"No," he replies plainly. I wait for him to elaborate but he stares at me as though this is all the answer I should warrant.

"Then what is it you propose I do?" I shake my head in exasperation.

"Go far from the ocean. Live the rest of your days landlocked, far from Delesseria's reach. You can live a bright, long life that way," his eyes fill with ethereal knowing. "If you go up against her, you may not live long enough to enjoy your freedom."

"Fear tactics don't work on me," I snort. "I'd rather die for my freedom than live with the knowledge that I was too much of a coward to fight for it."

"Duvessa, I ask that you see reason." He rubs his temple in irritation, as though my inability to yield to him is causing his distress. I can't help the way the act makes me feel as insignificant as a bug in juxtaposition to him.

"Why haven't you just killed me? You're a god. I'm sure it is in your disposition." I stand and start to pace the room. "Instead, you brought me here. And that monster? Was that..."

"Not mine," he cuts in. "One of Delesseria's no doubt. The carnage brought upon those ships was a stroke of misfortune for you all, but I had nothing to do with it."

I stand at the edge of the pool, peering down into its reflection. My mind returns to the face in the water for the first time since arriving in this room. I can't seem to recall his features, though they were nothing shy of vivid at the time. "And the man I followed down here?"

"An illusion, my dear. One I *will* take credit for." I jump slightly as Triton appears by my side, having not heard him move. "And as for killing you. It may be in my *disposition*, but it is not in my best interest."

"What do you mean by that?" I ask. My eyes narrow, head tilting to glance in his direction. I catch a brief glimpse of his gaze trailing my neck. When he registers that I've noticed, his eyes meet mine, brows raising.

"It means it's your lucky day, my dear."

I cross my arms as I turn to face him head-on.

"Your daughter ruined my life. And I don't even know why."

"Never mind why," Triton smiles down at me, speaking as though he is placating a child. *"A bit of advice?* Do as I ask. Find a quiet little town somewhere. Settle down. Enjoy what little time you mortals have in your lifespan."

"There is no..." I begin to protest, but he cuts me off again. My face heats at how little weight my words seem to have on him. How callously he brushes them aside, *unheard.*

"Think again." A darkness riles beneath his eyes. Something ancient and cruel that bubbles to the surface. "When a god gives you advice, *pet*, you take it." He articulates the derogatory term, a denotation of just how lowly he thinks of me and my kind.

He takes a step closer until he is practically standing on top of me. It is an effort not to step back in retreat, instead holding my ground against the intimidation tactic. I need to crane my head to continue holding his glare.

"Muse on that before you risk that pretty little life of yours."

He snaps his fingers and the world goes black.

Chapter 26

Panic doesn't begin to describe it. That feeling you have when someone you love disappears and there is nothing you can do about it. All you can do is feel useless as you wonder if they'll ever return and mentally berate yourself for all the ways you could have prevented it.

I know she is alright. She *has* to be alright. I remind myself of her unique condition. Remind myself that she is not bound to the same restrictions as the rest of us. Still, my mind races with every possibility of misadventure. Every detail of her condition I still don't understand in full.

I'd gone into the water. Helped pull the survivors to the lifeboats and back to the *Queen Marie*. I'd seen her emerge with Doryn. Seen the men on that boat pulling him aboard and seen her dive back down.

I haven't seen her since.

A sense of calm has yet to return to the crew, the lingering buzz of prolonged fear still coursing through their blood and through the air. Around me, people lounge in varying states of waterlogged disarray. Some are tending to the wounded. Others attempting to establish order after the battle, securing rogue items and taking stock of the dead.

I stay glued to the rail, overlooking the water until...

"Uh, Captain?" a tentative voice sounds behind me.

"Can't you see I'm occupied?" I say without removing my eyes from the sea.

"I think you're gonna want to see this."

I sigh in irritation. "Whatever it is..."

"It's *her*, Captain," he cuts in.

His dramatized vagueness is doing nothing to soothe my agitation, so I direct my pent-up aggression at him. I turn on my heels and approach him. Grabbing the collar of his shirt, I pull him close to my sneering face, a rabid dog itching to strike with barred teeth.

"Show me."

He lifts a shaky hand and points to the opposite side of the ship. "Over there, sir."

The moment I am provided direction, I release him, striding across the deck. He follows close behind.

"She appeared out of nowhere. One minute she isn't there. I turn around and the next she's just... lying there."

When my eyes find her, she is propped up against a pile of loose rope, cracking her neck as she snakes her spine into realignment.

She sees me coming and flashes a smile as I drop to my knees beside her. Urgently wrapping my arms around her, I pull her tight against my chest.

"Are you alright?" I press elated, relieved kisses against the top of her head. I cannot stop their dire successions, feeling as though if I stopped, I would never get the chance to kiss her again.

"Fine." Her arms can't wrap around me fast enough. "You?"

"I've been worse," I dismiss, far more interested in her wellbeing.

It scares me realizing just how much of me is bound to her. How much of me would have been lost if something happened to her. We haven't had the chance to talk about it. The meaning of last night's dalliance. I know what it meant for me. *But her?* I want to pry open her mind and siphon that information from her. I want to know, but not to ask. Asking seems to cheapen it somehow. Diminish it.

She pulls away from me and my skin misses her proximity. Looking around the ship she asks, "Who are these people?"

"The ship that came to our aid," I answer. "It was one of mine. The *Victor's Trove*. She and the *Cannon's Wrath* returned to our party a few days ago. The *Victor's Trove* just happened to be the nearest when we were attacked."

She nods as I speak, absorbing the information. Her eyes fill with worry and her eyes dart around the perimeter of the ship. "Wait. What about *my* ship? Is she..." She pushes herself to stand as she scans the surrounding water for the *Ocean's Shadow*. She takes several shaky steps toward the rail, but her legs give out beneath her on the fourth.

"Whoa!" I catch her before she manages to hit the deck, tucking my shoulder beneath her arm and holding her close to my side. "Your ship is fine. Look."

I help her to the starboard rail and point to where the *Ocean's Shadow* sails parallel to us off in the distance. "I'd imagine the crew were not too motivated to come to either of our aide after last night."

I know it is not for the lives of her crew that she sighs with relief upon seeing her ship safely gliding across the water. She smiles faintly as she watches the ship, my heart warming at the simple expression of happiness as it lights up her face. But like all joy, it fades into neutrality and we are left with the reality of all that must be done moving forward.

"I should help with the crew," I say. "Maybe you should rest while we..."

"No," she shakes her head. "I can help with..."

Her hand raises to her temple as she sways, the foundation of her legs once again failing her. This time, I scoop her into my arms and carry her back to my cabin.

"I'm sorry," she says, her eyes closed as she continues to slowly shake her head.

"Why are you sorry?" I ask.

"I don't know. It's just. I'm sorry." She sinks deeper into my arms. She must well and truly be drained if she isn't bothering to protest my carrying her.

"Sorry that you helped keep my ship from being destroyed by that sea creature? Or sorry that you personally saved my life and those of the men that almost drowned?" I chortle.

"I don't know why I am so lightheaded. I should be able to help." Her words are quiet. Simple. They should mean nothing. But her tone breathes death into her soul. A black smoke of self-deprecation.

"It's ok to not feel well. You're allowed to be human." As if undergoing some identity crisis, her gills flutter in rebuttal to the identification. I step into the cabin, shutting the door behind us with my foot.

"No. I'm fine." The forced cheer in her voice scratches at my ears, the stark juxtaposition of two extremes. "I just need some water and I can help."

"The crew will manage." I step over to the bed and set her down at the edge. My eyes narrow as they examine her face. "Why is it so hard for you to admit when you need rest?"

"I don't need anything," she scoffs. Her brows scrunch at the perceived insult.

"Yes, you do."

"No, I..."

" *Vessa,*" I place my index finger against her lips in a silencing gesture. Her cheeks redden as her eyes pierce with irritation. "I don't know what happened to you in your life exactly to make you feel this way, but your strength is not measured by your weakest moments. Everything needs balance. And that includes your energy and well-being."

As I spoke, her face hardened into statuesque indifference. An expression that now stares back at me through hallow eyes. She does not move. She does not breathe. The only sign that she is more than a block of molded clay is the pulsating vein in her temple as she clenches her jaw. I brush my thumb against her cheek, and then...

Like a dam breaking, I see the crumbling infrastructure before the water falls. The muscles in her face release their survivalist hold on control. The tears flow silently, as she turns her head away from me. Tipping her chin back toward me, I smile down at her, taking in the briny rivulets as they actively stream across her face.

"It's ok," I tell her.

A whimpered squeak escapes from where it's been clenched in her throat. She cries harder.

I sit beside her on the bed, wrapping an arm around her shoulder and squeezing gently. Some things are meant to be experienced rather than discussed. Whatever thoughts or memories have brought her to this release, they feel too intimate for my inquiry. Even if words would alleviate my own discomfort in the immediate.

I sit with her in silence for a time, her crying tapering out as the moments pass. Eventually, she grows quiet as she lays her head against my shoulder, her stillness only interrupted by the occasional hiccup brought on by the enormity of her purge. She reaches across my lap, taking my hand in hers. When she does, she flips it over on her lap, tilting her head to examine it.

"Your hand," she exclaims, fussing over the bloodied skin. "I forgot about your rope burns."

"It's fine." I try to take her hand again, but she continues to examine the wound.

"Do you have any bandages?" she asks, already standing. Though she still appears fatigued, she is steadier on her feet. "Or I can get Doryn. *Doryn!* Is he okay? Did he make it back alright?"

"He's fine," I lay back onto the bed, propping myself up with my forearms, smirking at the way Vessa has gone from openly weeping to fussing over mine and Doryn's wellbeing in the course of a few seconds. I find the uncharacteristic compassion to be a charming look on her. "No need to bother him, though. He is rather occupied at the moment."

"Alright. Then *I'll* tend to those wounds for you," she starts heading toward the door. "I'll just ask him for some..."

"Top drawer on the left," I cut her off, anticipating what she was about to say. "My desk. There are a few items in there you can use."

She locates a roll of linen and a clean cloth from the desk drawer, procuring a bottle of whiskey as well before nestling back on the bed beside me.

"An exquisite call," I smile, taking the bottle and drinking.

"To clean the wound," she scolds, grabbing the bottle back with exaggerated forcefulness.

She places one of my hands palm up on her lap. Saturating the cloth in whiskey, she begins to dab at the tattered flesh. I wince at the biting sting of the astringent liquid.

"Your lightheadedness seems to be waning," I note, trying to distract myself from the burn as she cleans the wounds.

"Uh-huh," she affirms, not looking up from my hands. "I still feel... *lethargic*, I guess. But I'm no longer dizzy." She sets the cloth aside and lifts my hand up toward her face. "Hold it there," she directs and begins to wrap it in linen. "It must have been the depth. Being so far below then all of a sudden being back on the ship. It doesn't usually bother me. Not since, well. You know." She gestures to her gills. "But I've never been... I think I was... *teleported?* Or something."

"Excuse me?" My brows are likely in my hairline based on how taken aback I am by her claim.

"When I went back down that last time. I saw something. A man. But it wasn't a man. It was a trick to lure me to Triton's lair." Her tone is casual. Matter of fact. As though what she is saying is not indicative of insanity. She ties off the end of the bandage and taps my forearm to signal she is done with it.

"Maybe you aren't as well as I thought," I place the back of my unbandaged hand against her forehead to check for fever.

"No," she pushes my hand away. "Listen. Triton used magic to lure me to him. I blacked out and when I regained consciousness, I was in this throne room, somewhere beyond the ocean floor. Triton, he wanted to talk to me. Asked me to spare Delesseria. Told me to flee to dry lands and just *live out my days* avoiding the water. The next thing I knew I was back on this ship and the world was spinning."

"Are you going to?" I ask, deciding to take her claims at face value.

"Going to what?"

"Listen to him."

Her eyes lose focus as she ponders her thoughts before replying, "No."

"No?"

"No," she repeats with more assuredness.

"Vessa," I place my bandaged hand on her knee, wincing at the slight sting of the pressure. "Maybe that would be the better option. If you go up against Delesseria and lose..."

"Azure," her voice softens as she holds my gaze. "I have spent the majority of my life being told what I could and couldn't do. Having other people control the outcome of my life. Even when I thought it was me holding the reins." Her hands fidget on her lap, eyes dipping to feign interest in the motion. "I can't live the rest of my life like that. I have to fight for what I want."

"I understand that," I tip her chin up to look at me. "Let's say you succeed. You defeat Delesseria and everything goes back to normal. You will still have Triton to contend with. Do you think he will allow you to live freely? Every ocean in all the realms. It's all his domain. Do you really think he would think twice about killing you?"

"I... don't think he will."

"Why?"

"He could have killed me now. Could kill me at any time. But he hasn't. For some reason, he hasn't."

She seems to ponder her statements as philosophical riddles.

"That doesn't mean he won't seek retaliation if you don't do what he asks," I release her chin, shaking my head in exasperation. "Everyone knows the lore about the wrath of the old gods. Just because he's passive now doesn't mean he can't revert and regress on a dime to a more oppressive version of himself."

"I'll cross that bridge if and when I get to it."

"These are immortal beings we're dealing with," I say. Vessa takes my other hand and begins to clean it as well. "Maybe this isn't a fight we can win."

"Even so," she reaches for the gauze and begins to wrap my second hand. "It's a fight I am going to face."

"It's suicide." My words are half whispered. An accusation. A realization.

And her silence confirms it.

Before I can speak, the door to the cabin opens.

"Don't mind me, kids," Doryn enters the room toting a leather satchel. "Just coming to see if either of you need tending to." His eyes fall to my now bandaged hands. "Looks like I am a bit late to the game in here."

"Good as new," I smile at Vessa, raising my hands to brandish her handiwork. "But she might benefit from a once over."

"I'm fine," Vessa dismisses, but Doryn is already setting his bag on the table and pulling a chair out for her to sit. His years at sea have done a number on his bedside manner. Namely, he doesn't take no for an answer when he is used to a troupe of rugged rapscallions all trying to prove how tough they are by denying their need for medical attention. Doryn has worn them down, but they too have worn away at his previously unwavering patience.

"You bandage two hands and you think you're an expert," he mutters, his curmudgeonliness laced with a twinge of repartee. "Come now. Sit." He pats his hand on the back of the chair. "I'll be the judge of that."

Begrudgingly, Vessa rises from the bed, makes her way to the chair, and sits in silent discomfort. She has barely stilled before Doryn begins his assessment. He takes great care not to touch her gills, though I note how his eyes linger on them with a gleam of interest. After an initial scan revealed that she has no superficial wounds, he began testing her range of motion. Lifting and lowering her arms and legs in various directions. Having her eyes track the movement of his index finger. Listening to her lungs and heartbeat through his odd little contraption.

I try not to smile at the clear discomfort she is displaying through her body language and how ineffectively she is trying to hide it. When she can take no more of the awkwardness she breaks the silence. "Glad to see you aren't worse for wear."

"Ah. What's a little drowning," he continues to work as he speaks. "How many fingers do you see?"

"Is that really necessary?" she objects.

"Just trying to see if there is anything wrong in there," he taps his finger against her temple. "Unless of course, you can't count on a good day."

I am taken aback by how goadingly he jokes with her and wait for the blowback. He is always quite informal, teetering on careless with his speech, a trait I presume would not bode well with Vessa's temper and generally stern demeanor. It surprises me when all she does is crinkle her face into a scowl and say, "Three."

"There," he smirks. "Was that so hard?"

"Excruciating," she mockingly smiles, tilting her head to the side.

"Alright," he steps aside and returns to his bag. "I'm done with you. You next, kid," he calls to me.

"I'm fine Doryn, really," I find myself hypocritically denying his request.

"Don't make me ask twice, lad."

No one talks to me the way Doryn does. I wouldn't allow anyone but him to do so, and only because he and I both know it is in good humor. And he would never do so in front of the crew.

There is mutual respect between us. He knew my parents before I was even born and they considered him to be a good friend until the day they died. Besides Braun, he is the only link I have left to them. He is the one constant presence I have to remind me of the fragility of life and humble me as the child I once was. Be that good or bad, it's nice to feel that connection from time to time.

I huff, but make my way to sit, as requested.

"You kids and your brooding dismissal. I swear, I am at more of a risk of dying from the sheer stress of dealing with you than I am of actually drowning."

Doryn makes quick work of his assessment of me, finding nothing wrong beyond the burns on my hands, which he unwraps to further examine. After adding a layer of some kind of ointment, he rebandages each, wrapping them more loosely than Vessa had done. When he finishes, he repacks his satchel, tossing it over his shoulder before stepping for the door. His hand wraps around the handle, but he hesitates, lingering in place.

"Thank you," he says, without turning away from the door. "For pulling me from the ship. I don't know how you knew I'd gone to the *Victor's Trove* this morning. Or maybe it was pure, dumb luck you found me."

"Of course," Vessa nods.

The silence that follows is potent, but brief. The weight of it lingers even after the next words are uttered.

"Why didn't you jump ship with everyone else?" The tone of Vessa's question is gentler than I thought her capable. "You weren't exactly trapped in that room."

"I," Doryn's hand drops to his side in a fist, his nails digging into the flesh of his palm. The only overt sign that emotion swims beneath his calm surface. His voice is collected – an unbreakable stone. "I went back for a picture of my family. The only one I have."

"Did you manage to get it?" I ask, knowing the importance of the emblem to him.

"A little worse for wear, but it should dry alright."

"And that was worth the risk?" Vessa asks in earnest. There is a childlike purity in the question. "You almost died."

"Without question," Doryn glances over his shoulder at Vessa, examining her expression inquisitively. He seems to find his answer in the emptiness of her face. "I'd rather die than forget their faces. Without that, I have nothing left."

Doryn sighs, opening the door and stepping back out onto the deck.

Chapter 27

I hate my traitorous heart as it beats in anxious thrums in my throat. I've only ever seen the shoreline from this perspective one time in my life. And that was when I was fleeing. Now, watching the blurred horizon take shape as we approach, I detest each unchanged element I recognize from my childhood.

In the days that passed since the attack on the ship and the attempt on my life, I have remained aboard the *Queen Marie.* The dynamic between Azure and myself has been tentative, to say the least. And I know that is my own doing.

The silence between us makes me uncomfortable now. After everything that happened, everything that was said and everything that was not, it feels like he has a piece of me that I didn't realize I was giving him. And I don't know what he will do with it. He could crush it. Break it. Toss it into the ocean and never think twice about it. He knows an intimate part of me, and not because we've entwined our bodies in carnal lust. No. In fact, that has continued to occur with great frequency. Partly from desire and partly as a diversion from any further inquiry into my mental or emotional state.

He saw me cry. I never let anyone see me cry. And certainly not like that. I hardly said anything, but when he looked into my eyes it felt like he was seeing my thoughts dancing like ghosts in my mind. It felt like he understood, on some level. But I refuse to let either of us make it real by discussing it with words.

I know that there is a very real possibility that I will die going up against Delesseria. And I know that it is irrational, but I would rather die than simply bow my head and yield to yet another man's orders. Even if that man is a literal god. I hate how petulant that makes me seem, but it is the last shred of control I have over my life.

It might even be simpler that way. If death took me. One final show of strength, then I never have to be strong again. I can just be... whatever it is that comes next. *That's the stone of truth that Azure took from me.*

I can feel him watching me. Thinking. I can feel when he is rearing up to reopen the subject, to try and prompt me to tell him about my thoughts and feelings. And every time he does, I stop him. With my lips. My tongue. My body.

And every time, it works.

By not talking to him, by not opening up in this way, I feel him growing distant, uncertain as to how to handle me. I think he thinks I'm fragile. And maybe I am. Maybe I am on the brink of shattering. But I have been dancing on the edge of that brink my entire life and

I have held myself together thus far, kept myself in one piece. *Maybe I only need to do so a little while longer.*

For now, he is my reward for a life of holding everything together. I am letting myself enjoy him for however long it lasts. However long I have.

Despite the moments of awkwardness between us, the sex is earth-shattering. When the details of my darkness are pushed from my mind and it is just us, riding each moment for all that it's worth, I almost feel at peace. Liberated in some ways. Trapped in others. But that is when the details start to creep back into view. In these days, I've tried so hard to fight off the details and enjoy these beautiful moments of life and lust.

The prospect of seeing my father does something to me. I find the sensation too repulsive to put into words, not wanting to linger on the emotion or explore it enough to clearly define it as one thing or the other. I don't even know if he is still alive. After all these years, *I hope he is dead.*

To the starboard side of the *Queen Marie* sails the *Ocean's Shadow*. Port side, the *Cannon's Wrath*, completing his fleet. I can tell that the loss of the *Victor's Trove* was felt deeply by Azure. Fortunately, the loss of lives was minimal after the attack and the shipwreck. The bodies of those that were found had been ceremoniously buried at sea. A fine celebration of the lives lost. In Calder's usual fashion, he spoke charismatically and compassionately about his fallen crew and threw a jolly celebration of music, food, libations, and dancing. I learned that several members of his crew are proficient fiddlers, all of which played rousing shanties throughout that night. Once more of the whiskey flowed and inhibitions wavered, another crewmember joined in on the spoons, playing irrhythmically against the kept time of the more skilled musicians while others clapped and hollered in merriment.

For the most part, I tried to keep to myself, leaving the men to their festivities. Gazing out across the night sky by the stern I could see the lights of the other two ships and hear similar sounds of celebratory hijinks. I assumed it would be Calder who tried to drag me into the heart of the affair. And when I felt an urgent tapping on my shoulder, I assumed it to be him.

"I don't want to dance, Azure," I said without turning from the twinkling lights.

"Ah, come now miss," an unfamiliar voice blared.

I turned to see the vaguely familiar face of a man who was swaying so dramatically as he attempted to stand, I knew it had more to do with the quantity of liquor he had consumed and less with the gentle swaying of the ocean.

"I just," his speech briefly ceased as he half hiccupped, half burped in my face. "On behalf of the crew, I just wanted to," he swayed so much that I reached a hand to steady him. "Thank you for pulling us all from the water. If you hadn't, well, I don't think as many of us would be standing here on this *beautiful night.*"

On his final words, his attention drew up to the night sky, mesmerized, as if he had never seen the sky before. He stared in awe at the stars as though his thoughts of gratitude had been but a fleeting moment that he no longer recalled. As suddenly as he lost his attention, he returned it to me.

"Come, dance with us! This would be a much more somber occasion had you not been here to help today."

He lifted the bottle of amber liquid to his lips, dribbling a fair amount down the sides of his face as he attempted to take a drink. With his free hand, he reached for me, taking my wrist and jerking me forward to follow as he started back towards what the masses deemed the dance floor for the evening.

"Woah!" I registered Calder's voice before I saw him, emerging from the shadows. An impressive feat on such a starry night.

He placed a hand on the man's shoulder, towering above as he peered down at him with darkened eyes. Though the inebriated crew member was slow to process the development, upon registering Calder's presence, he released his hold on my wrist, jovially grinning at his captain, presumably misreading Calder's domineering intent.

"Ah, Captain," he raised his bottle. "I am trying to convince the lovely lady to join us all in the festivities."

"Hmm," Calder growled. Only then did the man take a step back with unease, averting his eyes.

"Maybe you'll have more luck, captain," the man said, already heading back to the rest of the crew. He dared one final glance at me. "Truly, though. Thank you." He half nodded, half bowed before turning entirely and stumbling away. I doubted he would remember the conversation the next day.

Calder took a step closer to me, softening his gaze as he looked down at me through heavy lashes. "I can attest, it is a far more somber occasion without you."

"I am not much for rowdy celebrations," I confessed.

"Come," he took my hand in his, weaving his fingers between mine and urging me to follow. "If not for your own enjoyment, or to appease this sudden urge I have to force you to have a good time and spin you around until you fall *joyously* into my arms, then perhaps you can find it in yourself to do it for your rank."

"My rank?"

"Did it ever occur to you that in order to have people follow you and want you as a leader, just maybe you need them to like you? Play the game. Schmooze. Who knows, you might find yourself begrudgingly having a good time." He had the nerve to wink at me before pulling me after him towards the dance floor.

"You're drunk, Calder." I tried to pull away, to retreat back into the shadows, but he did not relent.

"I thank the lucky stars for that," he cheered, grabbing an open bottle from someone else's hands and taking a sloppy swig. As he gulped the bottle down, the rest of the crew hailed their merriment.

I hate that I had a delightful evening. Drinking. Dancing. Singing. Not just with Calder. In their drunken stupors, the crew welcomed me with open arms and open bottles. And I dare say a part of me opened up to the experience.

The juxtaposition of then and now is stark and painful.

Calder tried to broach the topic of my family once again this morning, which I *artfully* evaded in a manner that occupied the entirety of the day thus far. It was only moments ago that I left him in a state of undress on the bed, hair tousled and half asleep. Redressing, I slipped out onto the deck to be alone with my thoughts.

As gratifying as the throes of passion were, breaking down our barriers and ravaging each other to the core, I need a moment to collect myself. I need my walls secured around me to face whatever treads the shores of **Lythren**.

The closer we get, the calmer the waters seem to become – like a snake stilling before it strikes. A sense of doomed foreboding shrouds me in its weight. He only emerges from the cabin as we approach the dock, exchanging words with the crew that do not register with me as I continue to stare ahead.

As the crew secures the lines, I note how little the docks have changed. For a brief moment, I close my eyes, wanting a reprieve from the deplorable sight. Taking in a shallow breath, the smell itself transports me to a past that my physical self is struggling to reconcile with the present. I open my eyes and unlike my nightmares, the village is still here. *I am still here.*

I make my way off the ship and almost float toward the steps that lead up to the main road. The pebbles beneath my feet seem to remember me. Remember the last time I stepped across them. They seem to ask me where I'm going. Seem to stall my forward motion, pulling me back toward the ship. But I quell their protests with each strike of my heels.

"Vessa?" Calder grabs my hand as I reach the steps. I turn to face him, pulling my hand away for the sole reason of not wanting to be touched. By the look on his face, I can tell that he had been talking to me, though neither his words nor his presence registered with me until he grabbed my hand.

"What?" I narrow my eyes.

"Where are you headed?"

I tilt my head in confusion. "Into town."

"The ship had barely stalled before your feet hit the ground running," he motions back toward the boat. "Give me one moment to speak with the dock foreman and I will join you. Remember, I have business with Delesseria as well."

I nod my confirmation, stepping down from the stairs and sitting on a bolder several paces to the side. I watch as he makes his way back across the rocky beach toward the moderate hustle of the dock. Whether I actually intended to wait for him or if I knew I would leave the moment his attention was fully away from me, I cannot say. But I find myself standing, walking up the steps, and stepping onto the main road before I consciously realize I am doing any of it.

Seeing the town center from this vantage, I cannot help but notice just how much has changed. As I walk deeper into town, I wonder if it has changed enough that I might even be able to tolerate being here. Wonder if I might not be as broken by this place as I thought.

That all changes when I see the store.

It looks as though it was placed in a time capsule. Untouched since the day I stepped inside a child and came out with the attention of a predator. A part of me feels like I too must have been placed in that capsule all this time, that I am still that young girl, but far from untouched.

I stand, unmoving, staring at the haunting fixture for what seems like my entire childhood, but is likely no more than a few minutes. A horse-drawn cart passes in front of me, breaking me free of the trance that held me captive. I shake my head as I regain my hold on the present. When my vantage clears, I take one final glance at the storefront.

Only...

I catch a glimpse of something seemingly mundane. A head of wild locks falls in tangled waves down the back of a small girl. Her hair is pulled half up from the back with a yellow bow that frays and fringes along its edges. The chocolate brown glows golden as the sun illuminates her like a beacon of purity in this otherwise dank town. Though she faces away from me, walking with a large bag in hand in the opposite direction, I can't seem to shake the sense of familiarity that obligates me to follow.

My feet take me down an all too familiar path that feels like a nightmare. Yet, I cannot bring myself to stop my shadowing of the girl. Her dress too is familiar. It looks just like one from my youth. While the dingy grey fabric denotes a level of impoverishment that few else experienced in this town, it is the various patches that verify it.

The girl is wearing one of my childhood dresses.

I pray that she will stop walking with every house we pass. That she will turn and enter one of these simple homes where no monsters lay in wait. But with every one she walks on by with heavier steps than any child should endure. I see the growing apprehension, the way her feet grow leaden the closer she gets to the place where all my nightmares began.

She turns and approaches my childhood home.

She stalls momentarily on the porch, sighing before her hand reaches for the doorknob.

"Hey, kid," I call to her from the walkway, unable to stop myself or consider the possible repercussions of my intervention.

She turns abruptly and drops the bag. She gasps, both at the sudden awareness of a total stranger and at the bottles that fall to her feet. One of the bottles shatters entirely, emitting the astringent smell of gin into the open air. Another bottle of the same vice rolls down the steps and stops at my feet.

Silent tears burn in her eyes. The girl cannot be more than ten, though the sad expression that seems a permanent fixture on her face makes her appear older than she is. In another way, it makes her seem so much younger in my eyes.

"It's alright," I tell her, bending to pick up the bottle. "This one is unscathed."

I extend the bottle by the neck for her to take as I step closer to the porch. She shakes her head so slightly it almost doesn't register. I can see the muscles in her neck tensing as her silent tears refuse to fall. When she does not reach for the bottle, I set it on the step near her feet.

"No," she says. Not to me but to the placating sentiment. She glues her eyes shut, as though trying to shut out the world. "He'll be mad."

"Who?" I ask, already knowing the answer.

"My father," her soft voice whispers.

She presses her eyes closer together. I want to tell her that it never works. That she can close her eyes to the problem but that won't make it go away. Won't keep her safe.

The muscles in my neck contract as I swallow.

"Who is your father?" I ask, though I already know the answer.

"Corbin Foley."

The world closes in around me as I blankly stare at the child, who slowly opens her eyes. Something in my expression must scare the girl because she takes a step back and presses herself against the frame of the door. I force my expression to soften, lifting my hands to the girl to signal that I mean her no harm.

"It's alright," I lie with every ounce of compassion I can feign. "Everything is alright."

"Not for you it isn't," the demon from my dreams laughs behind me.

Then everything goes black.

Chapter 28

Vessa

I wake in the place that transcends time. The place I go on many a night when sleep is more of a torment than a solace. And just like in those horrid dreams, he is sitting in the chair across from me.

"Father," I growl, the word leaving a bitter taste in my mouth.

It takes a moment for my senses to catch up with my mind. I start to lift my hands, wanting nothing more than to wrap them around his neck and shake the abhorrent smirk from his face, but the ropes cut against my wrists where they are bound behind my back.

"Father?" he mocks. "After what you did, you lost the privilege of my being your father."

"The only privilege you could ever offer is my watching the life drain from your eyes." My voice sounds deep. Feral. I almost don't recognize it as my own.

"Oh, she has venom now? And here I thought she only had claws."

"You'd be amazed at just how many weapons a victim has in their arsenal. So much time wasted thinking I was helpless," I snarl.

"Victim?" His tone almost sounds genuine. "You really think after what you did you can call yourself a victim?"

"Some wrongs are justifiable to make things right."

"Spoken like a true criminal," he laughs.

"Takes one to know one." My eyes pierce him with unconditional hate.

"On the contrary, Duvessa. Between the two of us, I am the only one who has never committed an actual crime."

I huff.

"All I ever did was try to give you the best life I could." His tone is nothing short of poisonous. He doesn't even bother to try masking it in feigned sincerity. "Perhaps I did fail you by not breaking you of the evil that fills you instead of a soul." He shakes his head, tsking at me with condescension. "A mistake I vowed not to repeat."

His eyes fall on the girl as she steps into the room. Maybe she has been here the entire time. He lifts his glass which is so permanent an extension of himself that I didn't even realize he was holding it. She refills it with the gin bottle she carries in her hands. As she does, her baggy sleeve slips down to her elbow, revealing bruises of various colors all across her forearm. A hatred I didn't think could grow any larger boils within me.

"How old are you?" I ask the child.

"Eleven," she replies in a meek voice.

"Don't talk to her, Malle," our father dictates. I note her subtle flinch at his sharp tone and hate how much it took for me to keep from doing the same.

"Malle," I repeat, testing the way it sounds and hating the way it burns my ears. When I continue speaking, it is to him. "Waited a whole four years before replacing your milch cow. I'm surprised it took you so long. What, couldn't find a woman desperate enough to fall for your tricks?"

"Never stopped me before." His sneer is nothing short of evil. "How do you think you got here?"

An involuntary roar bursts from my chest, from the inferno of my rage. The sound is guttural. Visceral. It contains so much power that when the door swings open, I think it is from the sheer will of my voice.

But the nightmare only worsens.

"Don't mean to barge in, Corbin, but I heard a very concerning scream. Thought it best I let myself in given the circumstances."

The stocky man steps into my line of vision, unhurried by his lacking perception of urgency. That or his portly frame only permits him to move so fast. Regardless, the gun in his hand that is fixed on me becomes my primary focus.

"Sheriff," my father smiles as he remains seated. "Impeccable timing."

I do not recognize this lawman. Likely a new resident since I last stepped foot in Lythren. It wouldn't matter if he did know me personally. Even if this man knew the nuances of my childhood, like the rest of the town, it would not make a difference.

"Would have come sooner, Corbin. But the lad you sent to fetch me when you spotted her in town took a bit of a detour trying to find me." The sheriff comes to stand beside my father, gun still raised on me. "This must be her then?"

"Indeed, sheriff." Evil flares in his eyes and I wonder how it can be that I'm the only one who sees it.

"*Ungrateful little...*" The sheriff's insults fade into oblivion as he shakes his head in judgment. He tilts his head, examining me more closely, in a way that makes me want to cut his eyes from his skull. "Pretty little thing, isn't she? Pity such beauty has to go to waste."

"Hmm," Father nods.

When I think I cannot withstand the burn of their stares a moment longer, both men dart their eyes to the door behind me. The sheriff lifts his gun as Father shuffles to his feet with a startle.

"Sorry to intrude on this sentimental reunion," his boots sound with easy steps as he enters the parlor. "*Daddy dearest*, I presume?"

Calder comes into view in my periphery, sword lifted as he makes his way toward me.

"Stop right there," the sheriff orders, cocking his gun. Calder ceases his approach, looking at the sheriff through the sides of his eyes with a purely wicked grin. "State your business."

"Me?" Calder turns, speaking with a sickly-sweet mock innocence. "Oh, I'm just here to retrieve my *friend*. We have business to attend to in this," he pans his gaze around the room, "*charming* little town of yours."

Father snickers, seeming to relax, though Calder has yet to lower his weapon. "Thought you were too good for everything, yet you still found your place beneath a man. Only place for a girl like you, Vessy."

The sheer speed at which Calder swoops his sword to point it at my father's throat could claim the head of a dragon.

"Don't you *dare* talk to her like that," he snarls.

"Drop your weapon, son," the sheriff steps closer to Calder nodding to his handgun as his final reminder. When he does not comply, he redirects the gun to point at me once again. "Or maybe this is more of a motivation to you. Drop the weapon or I will shoot her and then you."

I see the muscles in his back almost shake against the tension of his rage. He lowers the sword to his side, lifting his other hand in signaled defeat.

"Good," the sheriff keeps his gun on me. "Now drop it and kick it off to the side."

Calder stalls for a moment, but begrudgingly obeys.

"Now son," the sheriff asks, "are you going to behave?"

"That all depends officer."

"Sheriff," he corrects.

"*Sheriff*," Calder derides, turning enough to the side that I can see his face once again. "Tell me, what is going on here exactly?"

"Son," the sheriff's tone almost sounds comforting as he speaks. "Your girl here is a wanted criminal in these parts."

"That I know," Calder chortles, changing his tone as he changes his tactic. "I am well aware of her, shall we say, past indiscretions."

"Then you know I have to take her in to stand trial."

"Surely an arrangement can be made, sheriff?" Calder's voice becomes melodious in his feigned comradery. "Whatever amount she stole from this man here, I am sure I can repay with interest."

"I'm afraid no interest can be repaid on murder."

Calder's head cranes toward me, a bewildered expression on his face. Hot tears start to run down my cheek as he learns the truths of my past. It's not his sudden knowledge of the murder that brings me shame. It's everything that lies beneath that truth.

"Duvessa Foley, you are under arrest for the robbery of Corbin Foley and the murder of Cyril Tenebrys."

Calder does nothing as the sheriff lowers his gun, stepping forward as he drags me from the chair. He does nothing as he cuts the rope that binds my wrists and clasps iron shackles around them in their place. He does nothing as my father takes a step toward him and places a hand on his shoulder.

"I'm sorry you had to find out this way, lad." My father examines the side of Calder's face while he continues to stare at me with an unreadable expression. "You seem like a good man," my father continues. "But she is not worth your time or your pity. She's replaceable. Trust me, you will move on from this and find some other woman. Someone more agreeable. This," he points at me.

340

"This one's defective. Broken in ways no one can fix. Better to let this one go and start again."

Calder's jaw feathers as I am pulled from the room. I fight against the rough hands of the sheriff as he pulls me by the arm. I kick and fight in silence, choking down all the sounds that build inside as burning tears streak my face, knowing damn well that if I release a single cry, I will unleash a hurricane of tears, and screams, and wails that not even I would be able to distinguish from rage or fear. Being here, being trapped, being at the mercy of others, unable to control my fate. It brings me back to *then*. It strips me of my power. It makes me vulnerable in a way I haven't been since that night.

I am not safe. Every particle of my being knows it. And knows that there is nothing I can do but be dragged along by the will of another.

The world whirls. The hands that are on me are not the sheriff's. They are his. They are leaving their mark on me the way they did that night.

They burn me.

They own me.

And I need it all to stop.

I feel the eyes of the townspeople as I am dragged toward the jail. I cannot help but acknowledge that this is the most I've ever been noticed in this town. I lived here for the first fifteen years of my life. Grew here. Suffered here. I walked these very streets covered only by rags and bruises and all they ever did was turn their heads from me. Only now, when there is no risk of fault to their consciences, do they feast their eyes on me. Only now, when I am just a spectacle, a cautionary tale instead of a walking cry for help.

A criminal instead of a victim.

The musty smell of the jail permeates my nostrils before it registers that I am now inside. A rat runs past my feet as an officer fumbles with the keys and the sheriff shoves me inside. My hands are still bound beneath my back, so I am unable to break my fall as I faceplant into the rocky floor. My knees become wet as moisture absorbs into the fabric of my pants. The entire cell is damp and I don't think knowing why would set me at ease.

Gruff hands grab me by the arms and pull me back to my feet.

There is nothing in the cell. Not a cot. Not a chair. The only thing besides the stone and bars is an iron ring that hangs from the back wall. The officer unclasps one of my cuffs, looping the chain through the ring of iron before reclasping it on my wrist overhead. The ring is just high enough that I'm standing on my toes to keep the cuffs from cutting into my wrists.

The bars slam shut, and I am left alone.

Chapter 29

Azure

The hand on my shoulder radiates cold indifference. Every word from his mouth, every feigned emotion is nothing more than a replication. A carefully observed and practiced behavior used solely for manipulation.

Duvessa's father is worse than I imagined. At the very least, I thought that his cruelty stemmed from anger. Hatred for the world, for his circumstances. A need for *more* that blinded him to the suffering he inflicted. I thought maybe the pain he caused stemmed from a pain he felt inside. That I could at least comprehend.

But the man that stands before me is filled with nothing at all.

The sheriff left with Vessa. My feet started to follow, but Corbin's icy hand stalled me. And his cruel, rejecting words for his daughter planted them firmly in place. I will be able to find her at the jail quite easily. Better I do not follow right away. There is nothing I can do in the light of day. Better to play the part of the now dismissive suitor than to storm in and set them all on guard for an attempt to liberate her. *Which of course I will do the moment I get the opportunity.*

As he speaks, it becomes more challenging to fight the urge to slaughter him where he stands. But that is not my craving to satisfy. No one but Duvessa deserves that luxury.

Corbin squeezes my shoulder once before dropping his hand, which I've been fighting the urge to sever from his arm. I step across the room to retrieve my sword, sheathing it as I turn to face the door. The loathsome crocodile is eyeing my adornments – my gold rings and tailored clothing that screams refinement. My propensity to remain well-groomed certainly helps to disguise my profession and leaves me more than presentable as a man of my fortunate lineage. *Corbin is enamored by it.*

"You know," he starts, forcing his eyes to meet mine. "I myself found it *earth-shattering* to lose my Vessy all those years ago. You must think I'm heartless seeing me so numb to it all now."

"I did note a certain... *coldness*," I work to keep my tone level.

"Hmm," he nods. "A mask I must wear. Painful as it may be sometimes. But alas, I must."

"Is that so." The hair at the back of my neck raises at how well this vacant shell of a man can emulate emotion.

"You know why?" he asks. "Why I do it? Why I was able to move on with my life? To," he pauses to simulate emotional distress. "To *heal* from everything that Vessy put me through?"

When I don't take his bait he continues, unprompted.

"*My youngest daughter.* My dear, sweet Malle." He raises his arm and points to the shadows of an open doorframe, leading deeper into the house. "Come here, darling."

I had not noticed the girl in my haste. Maybe she hadn't been there when I entered. The kid is just that. Gods know how old. Probably still plays with dolls and dreams of a life filled with happiness instead of apathy.

Her features are so reminiscent of Duvessa, those green eyes near clones in their darkness. Upon initial glance, the largest denotation of their difference is the color of their skin. While Duvessa is as pale as the summer moon, Malle is a radiant umber – her skin a shade darker than the golden brown of her hair. The way she stands so brokenly still, she almost looks as though she were molded of earthen clay. A shattered fragment of a work of art.

But it is the resemblance that strikes me most. And I find the resemblance to instill in me an instant desire to protect her.

"I don't want to say that she *replaced* Vessy. But," he wraps his arms around her docile frame once she stands by his side. "It has been so healing for me to see pieces of Vessy in Malle throughout the years." He plants a kiss on the top of her head. The girl, Malle, remains vacant in her expression, though she does not pull away. A compliant doll in his arms. "Sometimes it's almost like she's still with me."

"I can see the resemblance," I note.

My skin crawls at the opposition between the girl and her father. His vacancy lies within, but hers is skin deep. He *projects* false character. *Hers is buried alive.*

"You know," he releases the girl, who instantly retreats until her back is pressed into the corner of the room, arms wrapping around her middle as she stares at her feet. "I am a humble man with very little to offer. As a father, all I have ever wanted is a better life for my children. That is all I ever tried to give Vessy, and that is all I want for Malle."

He steps toward a small table beside a chair and retrieves a glass of clear liquid. He swirls it twice before taking a sip.

"It seems that *timing* is something I have never quite gotten right. Sometimes I wonder if Vessy had experienced some semblance of luxury, the kind of security that can only be bought with coin, just maybe she wouldn't have become... *what she became.*"

I cross my hands behind my back, hiding the unpreventable clenching of my fists at his manipulating perspective.

"Perhaps, if I had found her someone wealthy. Someone like *you,* for instance." He feigns levity at the implication of my wealth. "Maybe she could have been saved."

"The way I hear it, she was fifteen when you tried to do just that."

"Cyril. Yes. Unfortunately for Mr. Tenebrys, the effects of our life of poverty had already taken its toll on my poor Vessy." He dramatically sighs. "Each day, I fear the same might befall my Malle. Women are so *susceptible*, don't you think?"

He is not asking my opinion. He is looking for endorsement of what he assumes to be a perceived fundamental.

My jaw tics – the only indication of my disgust.

"Be frank, Mr. Foley. I have no temperament for games."

"A man of business. I can respect that," he smiles as he leans against the wall beside Malle. "I feel it would be in my Malle's best interest if I could *secure* her a suitable life. A future where I know she will be well cared for." He strokes the side of her cheek with his thumb. "Of course, it would be only reasonable to arrange some kind of monetary exchange to compensate for the *insurmountable* pain I would suffer in losing my only remaining daughter."

Bile rises in my throat. The look on Malle's face is unchanged, nor has she moved. I pray to the gods that she is too young to understand the implications of her father's words. But knowing the demons that still haunt Vessa, I fear those prayers are far too late.

"A tempting offer," I vomit the lie. The words feel grotesque on my tongue, but I want this man to feel a false sense of security with me. "Perhaps we can reach some kind of arrangement."

The cat-like yellow that speckles his eyes gleams at the prospect of fortune, as if mother nature herself knew that nothing would hold value in the eyes of this man but gold.

I want to wipe all expression from his face and see him for what he is. I want to watch as Vessa runs a sword through his heart and destroys him the way he destroyed her. I want to get this child free from him and find a way to bring life back to her broken soul.

All in due time.

I feel my control slipping. I need to get away from this cretin before I wring the life from him.

"As I said before," I start toward the front door. "I have business to tend to here. Once I have settled that, I'll return to discuss said arrangements with you, Mr. Foley."

I make my way to the door, feeling his presence following behind me. Once I have stepped onto the porch, I turn to face him.

"Until tomorrow?" I force a smile.

"I will be eagerly awaiting you, *Mr....?*"

"Carmichael," I say, claiming Braun's name in case my reputation precedes me.

"Until then, Mr. Carmichael."

The door shuts behind me, but I am already making my way down the steps and onto the footpath back to town. As I walk, I envision all the ways I could torture and kill him, each one progressively more brutal and deranged. I start to question my sanity at just how unhinged my mind becomes when Duvessa is at stake.

Eventually, my mind settles back on the charges against Duvessa.

She killed that man, the one she was supposed to marry. I wonder why she hadn't told me. After all, taking lives is not exactly taboo in our world. Hell, the first time we met, I murdered her friend in cold blood as she watched, and somehow still, we are... *whatever we are to each other.* Why would she not tell me about this specific instance?

Perhaps it simply meant so little to her that it didn't dawn on her to mention it.

But that reaction. The way she wouldn't look at me when they read the charges. The look of *shame* that seemed so foreign on her face.

No. There is more to the story. Whatever piece I am missing, whatever part has been intentionally withheld from my knowledge, it is of no consequence to me. I am unconditionally on her side. No matter how right and no matter how wrong, hers is the side for which I fight.

Once I reach the edge of town it is all too easy to catch her scent. Not so hushed whispers are exchanged between the townspeople of the procession they had just witnessed.

I overhear two women standing at a streetcorner and chatting, casually stating the Foley name.

"A thousand pardons, dear ladies," I politely bow, brandishing my most charismatic smile. "I just arrived in your lovely town – a brief stop on my travels across the realm. Permit my inquiry. What was all that commotion? Nothing too serious, I hope?"

Both women's faces briefly go blank when I start speaking. Their eyes rove over me, and – as is custom with most women where I am concerned – bright smiles and warm eyes light up their faces as they shamelessly flirt with their body language. Half the time, I'm not even certain they realize they're doing so.

"Nothing that isn't under control, sir," says one.

"Just old news finally coming to a close," says the other.

"How do you mean?" I press, taking a measured step closer. I almost lose composure at just how drastically such a small action affects them. My effect on women is an invaluable asset. One that I do not take for granted.

"Well, you see. Mr. Foley. He is from an old family that's been in this town since, well, since it became a town. Well, he had a daughter. Crazy little thing. Lost her mind and killed an esteemed member of our community. She fled town and was gone for *years*. Apparently, she came back, and well... now they're finally going to be able to have her stand trial." The first woman, a rotund blonde of maybe forty, leans toward me as she speaks, as if her words are a secret. Though she is far from whispering.

"Just what this town needs," says the second woman, a rail-thin redhead with infinite freckles. "It'll be good to see some justice. I think closure is just about the best thing we could hope for now."

"I see," I nod, matching their gossipy energy. "Is the town *safe?*" I lean in as if I don't want anyone to overhear my inquiry, knowing very well how they will react to my encroaching proximity. "I mean, two lovely ladies such as yourselves unattended as you are out here in the open. What if she were to escape?" I cross one arm in front of me, bringing the knuckle of my other hand to my mouth as if overtaken with concern.

Both women practically swoon.

"Your concern is too kind," the redhead says as she bats her lashes so swiftly that I fear she might take flight. "Lythren has a very sturdy jail and immensely resolute guards."

I note the direction in which she nods when speaking of the jail.

"That is a great comfort to hear." I lower my hand to my heart and bow slightly. "Thank you for your candor, ladies. Good day to you."

I leave them to their gossip and try not to think about how old they must have been when Vessa was being abused. How many times they turned a blind eye to her suffering. If I allowed myself, I'd burn the whole town to the ground and shoot anyone who tried to escape the flames of damnation.

No time to spiral.

I continue down the road, overhearing more conversations about Duvessa. I hear whispers of desired sentencings, none of which paint the people of Lythren as anything close to merciful. It doesn't feel real until I turn a corner and see the gallows, a noose being raised like a sail.

Fuck.

"Excuse me," I approach the man erecting the noose. "Is there going to be an execution?"

"A visitor, huh?" The man ties off the rope and hops down to be at eye level with me. "Sorry you have to see the town like this, my good man."

"When?" I ask, too emphatically.

He raises a brow at my concern.

"I just mean," I lick my lips and avert my eyes in fake shame. "I am not good with death. Never could stomach it. If there is to be a hanging, I'd rather not the ladies see how squeamish I can be. Not good for the image you see." I smile meekly at him.

He coughs out a hearty laugh and pats me roughly on the back.

"You pretty boys and your *dispositions*." He continues to chuckle. "Tomorrow at dawn, steer clear of the area. I'd clear out of the whole town if I were you. The townsfolk, they get pretty worked up over these things. They can get darn rowdy if they have a mind to. And I have a feeling they just might be getting pretty worked up over this one."

"How do you mean?"

"Oh, you know. The guy that was killed, when he died, his money and assets went into a trust. Became untouchable until 100 years after his death, since he had no heirs to speak of. The guy was a bit of a nut that way. But I guess when you're that rich, you can do whatever the fuck you want. Without his money, the town fell on hard times. Took a long while for people to get back on their feet."

"Seems like they've managed," I eye the surrounding buildings, noting those that appear fairly new and well-tended.

"We've done alright," the man nods.

"Tomorrow at dawn," I repeat his earlier words as I take my first steps to leave. "I appreciate the warning. I'll make certain to avoid this place like the plague."

Dawn.

That doesn't leave much time. But I wasn't planning on letting her spend the night locked away from me anyhow.

The jail is easy enough to locate. After all, it is the only building with bars in the windows. The dark stone building looks as old as the town itself. Like it has been a fixture of the community, bestowing judgment and invoking punishment since the very beginning.

I play the lost tourist of the town to perfection. Few people look twice at me beyond to smile and exchange polite pleasantries. I make it a point not to let the sheriff or any officers see me to avoid raising suspicion. I circle the perimeter of the jail from a distance, occasionally stopping to feign fixation on adjacent buildings or to ask irrelevant questions of passersby about local cuisine and accommodations.

It troubles me how normal the citizens are who are so willing to watch the death of a woman they wronged in childhood by letting her suffer for years. I don't care what hardships they faced themselves. Someone at some time could have helped her. There were choices to make, and they made them to her detriment. *Every time.*

When I am certain that I understand the jail's layout, I return to the ships, not wanting to further press my luck or risk arousing suspicion. I take inventory of the crew's efforts to replenish supplies and instruct them to be back aboard the ships, ready to sail well before sunset. I take Corkin aside, instructing him to lead a small handful of men in asking around about Delesseria. Though she is the reason we came to this place, I've decided that I cannot risk inquiring about her myself – not now that my face needs to remain in the shadows and unremembered. At least until nightfall. It may even work to my benefit if a few of my men draw attention to themselves by making a stir about the sea witch. It just might take away any unknown interest in my presence near the jail today.

As the rest of the day passes, I pace around my ship waiting for the cover of nightfall. I cannot bring myself to rest, though I know expending my energy so uselessly accomplishes nothing productive. Still, the pacing continues.

Gradually, the crew filters back to the ships until everyone is aboard and ready to set sail at my command. There is some grumbling from certain members of the crew who wanted to spend more time at port, as was my original intent. But plans change when an unscheduled hanging gets in the way.

Corkin and his cohorts are the last to return.

"Captain," he nods me over to the relative privacy of a quiet corner of the ship.

"Aye, what did you find?" I ask in a hushed tone.

"We couldn't find her, per se," he shrugs. "But we found – oh, fucking gods, I don't even want to say."

"Spit it out, man," I growl my impatience.

"We found an *oracle*," he almost chokes on the word with how clunky it sounds in his voice. Immediately after he says it, he gets embarrassed, cheeks reddening.

"I'm not saying I buy into all that. They're all charlatans if you ask me," he babbles.

"I didn't ask you, Corkin," I fix him with a pinning stare, my voice an unnerving calm.

"Aye, captain," he lowers his head in respect before continuing. "This one, I didn't even go to her. She found me. Walking down an alley to get to another pub. And she stopped me. Pinned me against the alley wall.

Me." He gestures to his stocky frame. "And she was nothing more than a whisp of a thing. Didn't even touch me. It was like... *magic.* Witchery of some kind."

"What did she want, Corkin?" I press. "What did she say?"

"Some fruity rhyme type thing. She said, and I quote: *I know the one you're meant to follow is looking for the master. If there is any hope to find her, retreat and do it faster.*"

I stare at him, expecting more. "Is that it?"

Corkin blushes, "Not exactly."

"What then?" I shake his shoulders in exasperation.

"She, uh. Well, she kind of... kissed me."

I cannot help whatever look possesses my face. Some cross between confusion and disgust.

"Why?" I find myself asking.

"Believe it or not boss, women have been known to find me attractive from time to time," he snorts. "But uh," he rubs the back of his neck with his hand. "It was strange. When she spoke in that eerie verse, it was like she was some kind of puppet. Not a real person, like she was physically there but there was no one at the helm, if you know what I mean. Then all of a sudden, her eyes, they animated. She looked like a real person that was seeing me for the first time in that exchange. And when she did, she reached for me and kissed me. She seemed scared. Like she was trying to get a hold on me to keep herself from disappearing back to wherever she was when her eyes were nothing but white."

Corkin looks at his feet for a moment, haunted by the memory of her eyes.

"When it stopped, she whispered something in my ear. Not in that strange ethereal voice from before, but what I think was her *real* voice. She said, and again I quote: *The sea witch is waiting for them at an island off-shore. Mortals can only find it if she allows them entry. Don't let them go. There is no escaping her. All they can do is run. No deal is worth this, it's too late for...*"

Again, I stare at Corkin, waiting for the end of the sentence. "Too late for what?"

"I don't know. Her eyes went white and she walked off all possessed like. I tried to get her to snap out of it. Get her to talk, but she almost floated away like she was sleepwalking or something."

"Did you follow her?"

"I tried. I followed her out the alley and down the street. She crossed the road, and I was cut off by a wagon. She got ahead of me. I don't understand how. She was moving so slow. Before I could catch up, she turned a corner, and when I followed, all that was there was a dead end. There was nowhere she could have gone."

"Hmm," I nod slowly, mulling over the information as it settles in my mind. "Good work, Corkin."

"Thank you, Captain." He straightens his posture. "Anything else I can do for you, sir?"

"Aye, alert the crews of the *Ocean's Shadow* and the *Cannon's Wrath*. Have them set sail the moment night falls. I want them on their way to open waters before I retrieve Duvessa. No sense in using three ships to flee with an escaped convict. They can wait for us to catch up once they reach a safe distance. Be prepared to take out any pursuing vessels that may be in our wake."

"Yes, sir," Corkin nods. "And what of the oracle's words?"

"We'll reconvene on that matter after we get everyone out of this hellhole." I glare at the townscape.

"Aye," he replies, setting off to complete his task.

"If all goes to plan, we might all just get out of this alive," I say, more to myself than the already retreating Corkin.

Night falls, but the town is far from quiet. I force myself to wait even longer on the ship until the last of the dockworkers have cleared out for the night. When I leave the ship and make my way to the steps, the bustle of the streets has finally died, leaving the town to look like nothing but a hollow carcass.

Just like her father.

One man. One town. One and the same in the eyes of the woman I'd do anything to protect. I set off under the cover of shadow in the direction of the jail, smiling in anticipation of watching her destroy her demons.

Chapter 30

Blood drips down my arms so far that I feel it on my shoulders. I can't tell if the numbness in my fingers is from blood loss or from my hands having been chained overhead for so many hours. I stopped trying to move my hands a long time ago. All it did was make the cuffs cut harder and the blood drip faster. The numbness is painful, but far more tolerable than it was before.

My feet no longer support me from below. Part of the reason for the aforementioned numbness. The arches of my feet and my legs started cramping so severely that I had no conscious choice when they gave out beneath me, letting my full weight pull down against the cuffs. I have been alternating between standing on my toes for a time whenever I've recovered enough strength to do so, but these are short and equally painful reprieves.

I haven't moved from this cell since they tossed me inside and strung me up like an insect on the wall. They didn't take me to my hearing. I doubt they even bothered to have one at all. Part of me thinks they did, just to continue the spectacle of my punishment. Part of me thinks they wouldn't have wasted their time on the likes of me. They never had before. *Why start now?*

I've been left alone all these hours. That has gotten into my head more than I care to admit. I don't know what is worse, *feeling* alone or truly *being* alone when you're in this kind of broken state. I've experienced both and honestly cannot say which I would prefer over the other if I had to choose.

The only time my solitude was broken was when my father came into view and told me I was to be executed at dawn. It felt fitting it was he who told me. He was drunk, as is his usual state.

The smile on his face didn't surprise me. He always smiled when he was hurting me and didn't feel like pretending that it didn't bring him joy. But it was his eyes that bothered me most.

His eyes were as empty as the distance I so desperately pursued in my years at sea. *I wonder if there is something in that.*

He told me all the horrible things he used to tell me about myself. One last time, for the sake of sentimentality, I guess. I was grateful, in a way, for the bars that kept me locked inside. They also kept him out. As he polished off his bottle of gin, he told me all the things he used to do to me, as though I needed the reminder. The same things he threatened to do to me now if only he had the key. The more he spat his venom, the more I pictured the face of that little girl. My sister, I guess, by definition. *Malle.*

I didn't mean to do it. Didn't intend to think of her. I guess it's just easier to care about the fate of someone else than it is to care about yourself. Or maybe that's just me. Maybe part of me knows I'm not worth saving. But part of me knows that little girl is. And, be it a twisted sense of self or be it true, there is a small part of me that, in a way, is still the same as her. And *that* little girl is worth saving too.

He left when he finished the bottle. Unsurprisingly, he could not depart without leaving a physical scar to accompany the emotional. Though truth be told there is nothing left that he could say that could hurt me now. It's all repetition of words already spoken. Words already committed to memory.

He threw the bottle across the cell from between the bars. It shattered against my left leg, a shard of glass cutting into the front of my thigh. I bite back my cry at the pain, not wanting to allow him the satisfaction of seeing or hearing my weakness. At this, he tsked and said *disappointing to the very end, aren't you Vessy?*

I waited to make sure he was gone before I let myself cry out loud.

The tears ran dry by the time darkness fell. Dehydrated and exhausted, the only thing that fills me now is hatred. An absolute drug for the damned.

They say that in your final moments your life flashes before your eyes. I wonder what I will see come dawn when all I see now are visions of all the ways I want to punish the people who have wronged me. Watch the town burn to the ground. And one of the faces in the crowd I see as I watch them burning in my mind...

Calder.

I don't know why it bothers me so, him letting them take me. Arrest me. Condemn me. It's not as though I am anything to him. It's not as though he owes me anything.

In a way, his dismissal of me hurt more than everything else that happened today. Because the only thing I feel about him now is sadness. And that, to me, is far less palatable than hate.

If I die tomorrow, as fate seems to have decided, I've made peace with dying with hate in my heart. *But this?* I cannot die with such weakness in my heart for a man. I try to push it from my mind, to fixate on the hate for my father. For the town. For the pain in my leg and the numbness in my hands. Try to make it spread to my heart and feel nothing. I try to forget about Calder entirely in these final hours of my life.

But his face keeps materializing in my mind.

"You do look stunning all tied up, love."

Great. Now my ears have conjured his haughty fucking voice.

I groan at the irritation, rocking my head lightly from side to side, trying to shake the sound from my consciousness.

"But I'd much prefer we reconvene back on my ship, lass." A rattling clangs above my head and my eyes dart open. "This place is vile. Even for a slumming scoundrel like you."

I crane my head to look up the length of the wall, meeting his all too corporeal eyes. His hands are wrapped around two of the bars of the window above, face pressed between them as he looks down at me.

"Calder!" I exclaim with multifaceted relief.

"Why, were you expecting someone else?" his roguish grin makes my stomach flutter. "I hate to be the one to break it to you, but the people in this town? Hate you. If you can bear it, you may have to settle for my rescue," he jests.

The corners of my lips twitch upward. "I'll find a way to live with it."

"I'm counting on it, love. And for quite some time."

I try to wet my mouth with saliva that I can't quite summon. "Any idea how to get me out of here? I don't know where the keys are being kept."

"No need for keys, Vess. I brought something a little more versatile."

From his finger, he removes one of his gold rings. It is fairly large, adorned with an ornate squid crest. When I'd seen it before, I had thought it to be a cumbersome adornment. A family heirloom, I assumed. I hadn't bothered to ask about it, not wanting to stroke his ego at my noticing his garish treasure. Now, as he fiddles with it in the light of the moon, he unscrews the coin-sized crest from the top, revealing a stash of white powder.

He pinches the powder between his fingers, sprinkling it along the windowsill, putting extra where the bars meet the stone.

"What are you doing?" I ask as he dusts off his hands, wrapping them midshaft around two of the bars.

"Close your eyes and tuck your chin," he instructs.

I do as he says without hesitation. I hear him mutter something under his breath just before I feel cold pebbles crumble down my neck. The sudden sensation startles me, but I keep my eyes shut and head tilted down.

He grunts in strain as something squeaks above. Then more stone crumbles onto me.

"You can open your eyes now, love."

I peek warily through my lashes before opening my eyes entirely. Calder lowers himself in through the window to my right. When his feet meet the cell floor, he dusts his hands on his sleeves before settling in front of me, eyes assessing my various wounds. Darkness curls beneath his eyes.

"I will kill them all," he vows. Not a statement, but a warning.

Before I can reply, he presses his forehead against mine, pinning my head against the wall. He does not kiss me, but his nose brushes against mine in something far more intimate as his brows pinch together.

"Hold still, love," he whispers, so close that I breathe his words into my mouth. One hand wraps around my waist, pulling me flush against his chest. The other raises above me as he tinkers with my shackles.

"*Kuvantchee*," he mutters, the same word from before, and when he does, I feel my arms go slack. They fall like dead weight to the sides, catching on his shoulders as my elbows bend around his neck. The shackles clatter to the floor. Most of the blood on my arms has dried, but my wrists are still slick around their wounds. Blood is getting in his hair, but he doesn't seem to mind, and I don't seem to have the will to move from this position just yet.

When I stare into his cerulean blue eyes, I wonder how I could have doubted he would come. I want to cry at just how much he sees me. Just how much *of me* he sees. Even the parts I thought had died a long time ago. He sees me in a world where no one ever cared enough to try. Beyond that, he did not run from what he saw. Was not repulsed by the broken, mangled parts of me that have brought me nothing but shame.

I feel a sudden release, like a long-held breath, and I am flooded with a thousand emotions. I cannot tell if the overall sensation is good or bad. Something bubbles in my chest, like words that want to be spoken. But I can't seem to figure out what they are. Instead, I wrap my arms behind his neck, pressing my lips against him. *His lips. His cheek. His neck.*

He ceases my manic pecking by pressing one long kiss against my lips, briefly biting my bottom lip between his teeth before pulling away.

"As much as I'd love to stay here and revel in this *precarious position*," he smirks. "We've no time for that now. You, my dear, have a date with revenge."

Clear, concise words return to my brain and I remember that we are not yet safe.

"What was that stuff?" I ask, pointing to the window.

"Ground pixie dust. Hexed by... well, let's call her an alchemist."

I raise my brow.

"It's a long story for another time," he nods toward the window. "For now, I suggest we leave these quaint accommodations behind and get a move on."

Calder boosts me to the window, and we climb into the alleyway. When we turn the corner into the square, my feet stall when my eyes fall on the gallows, the rope noose swinging in the mighty wind. My hate and rage are reinvigorated, seeing the tangible evidence of my intended fate. Of how the town intended to break me one final time.

Calder watches as I transform into a thing of nightmares. The transformation is internal. It is silent. It is subtle. But Calder sees it. Witnesses it in all its broken glory.

And he smiles.

"Do you have a plan?" he asks.

"I've been planning this my whole life." My vision blinds to my periphery as I set off down the road.

I always hated how secluded my childhood home was from the rest of the town. It meant that no one would ever hear my cries or come running in aid at my screams. It wasn't until I got older that I learned it wouldn't have mattered if anyone did hear them. The result was always going to be the same.

Tonight, I am thankful for that seclusion.

I kick in the front door, beaming as the wood splinters beneath my boot. Calder falls into place behind me as I lead the way to my father's room. I kick in that door as well, and somehow it feels even more satisfying than the first.

He startles awake and I can't help but laugh at the terror in his eyes when he sees the dark shadows skulking toward him. Perhaps a better version of myself might be worried by how much I am enjoying this role reversal. But that version of myself is not here. *Only me.*

Calder stops at the side of the bed, stripping the blankets that father clutches like a child afraid of the monsters beneath their bed. Those monsters were once my only friends.

"Wh-Who's there?" his voice shivers.

Calder seizes my father's arms, ripping him up and onto his feet. "Oh, you know. Just a couple of *defective, broken, replaceable* souls." Calder recounts my father's previous words with vitriol.

"Mr. Carmichael?... I don't..."

"Quiet, you slimy bastard." Calder pulls him close to his face, sneering down at him with mere inches between them as he lifts him by the collar of his shirt. "I wouldn't concern yourself with who *I* am when your reckoning is in this very room."

Father's head strains to turn toward me, still dangled above the floor by Calder. "Vessy?"

"Don't call me that," I seethe. The nickname had always struck a chord. Like the full extent of my name, passed down to me by my mother, wasn't worth the effort it took to say it. Every time he called me that throughout my life, it was like he was underhandedly stripping me of my final connection to her.

"But, Vessy, you don't understand I..."

Calder violently shakes him by the collar, effectively silencing him.

"I don't think you heard her, mate," he snarls through gritted teeth. "Call her that one more time. I honestly dare you. Give me an excuse to cut her name into your flesh so you always remember."

"Listen," Father lifts his hands in defeat. "I don't know what she told you but..."

"Don't talk to me," Calder spits. "This is between you and the lady over there. If you know what's good for you, I recommend you shut up and behave."

With that, Calder shoves him so hard that father crumples to the floor in a heap. Pushing himself onto his hands, he looks me dead in the eye. No ounce of remorse to be seen. No fear.

He smiles.

"So, what is it you want, girl?" Calder kicks him in the side, but it doesn't seem to faze him. "You got this poor lad wrapped around your little finger. Got him to *rescue the damsel in distress* or whatever you think you are in all of this. Why bother coming here?"

"What happened to my mother?" my voice comes out cold as stone.

"Your *mother?*" he snickers. "What does that have to do with anything?"

"What happened to my mother?" I staccato my words with impatience.

"She ran off with..."

"Don't lie to me!" I yell, taking a step toward him. He doesn't bother to flinch.

"She sprouted wings and flew away to a magical..."

I raise my hand and strike him across the face with the back of my hand as hard as I can. His hand goes to his jaw as he massages around the blotch of red that now mars his cheek. He clicks his jaw, cutting his eyes to me like daggers. Smiling, he spits a mouthful of blood on the floor beside my feet.

"You know what happened to your mother," he sneers.

I swallow, the grief carving my throat like a razor. "Why?"

"She got to be a problem. One that wasn't worth solving," he shrugs in apathy – as if his words are nothing but logical.

"She was going to take me away from here," I say. Part question, part statement.

"The rat was pocketing my money. And planning to steal you away from me."

"You had your little schemes. The cons you'd run to keep your pockets full. Why not just let her go? Why not do anything else? You didn't have to kill her. She – "

"She learned too much of what I planned to do. *That damn Tenebrys.* All I had to do was get you to give him a child. An inheritor. Then I'd have killed *him, you,* that damn *baby* if I had to... anyone that stood between me and that fortune. Your mother? She was just the first thing to get in my way. I wasn't about to let her take my greatest asset from me. Couldn't risk her going to the sheriff."

My throat constricts so hard I think my neck might snap in two. I almost wish it – to keep from feeling the anguish.

"You sick fuck," Calder seethes, face contorting in disgust. "Your own flesh and blood? Is that what Malle is to you? A second take on pure treachery?"

"Why Mr. Carmichael," Father feigns astonishment. "I thought I wasn't supposed to talk to you when my... *reckoning* is in our presence." He laughs.

Calder clenches his fists, rearing up to land a kick, but I raise my hand. He stalls his assault, turning on his heels, unable to look at the pile of filth at his feet. He runs his fingers through his hair in exasperation, muttering hateful words under his breath.

"Where is she?" I demand.

My father turns his head to face me again. "The kid?"

"My mother."

The word hurts more than I can stand.

His eyes drop to a spot on the floor. "She always liked to be outside," his tone shifts to something softer than I've ever heard him speak. The change is so dramatic, so unsettling, it sets me askew and I feel out of place in my skin. "I don't know if you remember that. In the beginning, she used to say *we don't have much but nature has everything.* Stupid little thing, she was. Used to sit in the back of the property, beneath the old ash tree for hours and just stare out at the landscape. Watching whatever critters passed on by. So content in that simplicity."

He smiles softly to himself. For a moment he almost seems sentimental. But then the smile morphs into something cruel and wicked.

"She always did love that ash tree," he sneers.

Repulsion lances through my bones. I had always known, at least on some level, that he had killed her.

Hearing it voiced aloud, that did not wound me the way I thought it would. But this. *This skewers me.*

All this time.

All this time and she was so close. She was buried beneath the tree where I, like her, would sit in the sun and wriggle my toes in the grass. Where I would stare at the sky and dream of a day when I might leave this place, the way I was supposed to with her.

The times I'd cursed her, thinking she had left me when her bones were crumbling to dust beneath me.

I step back until my back is pressing against the wall beside the doorframe, hand raising to press against my temples, trying to keep my mind from spiraling. Trying to push back all the thoughts and memories of all the times I stood above her, not knowing that just beneath me she was rotting in the earth.

I see the worms crawling through her decaying flesh.

I sink to the floor and shake my head. Tears burn in the back of my eyes, but they refuse to fall.

In the recesses of my mind, I hear a faint voice. My voice. Telling me to push it down. Not to let myself be vulnerable around him. Not to let my weakness show. But that voice is drowned by the rush of the empty. I see nothing but blurs of red and hear nothing but the thump of blood pulsing through my body. I think I may pass out entirely when...

I am pulled to my feet by my hair. Before I can react, I am spun around, a revolver pressed to my temple as my father steps backward into the doorframe. I thrash against the binding hold that pins me against his chest, but the barrel pressing deeper into my skin forces me to still.

"Ah, ah," Father derides as Calder raises his gun. "I'd lower that weapon if I were you, boy."

Calder hesitates, lips curling as his jaw all but quakes from the tension of his gritted teeth.

I hear the click beside my head as the gun is cocked.

Calder cocks his in an echoing response.

I feel my father's arm tensing around me where it crosses over my chest, his fingers digging into my shoulder. "If you think I'm bluffing, just remember the gallows they have waiting in town. I have no qualms about being the one who gets to end her."

Calder's eyes cloud with reluctance, lip twitching as he tries to master his initial instinct to pull the trigger. Slowly, he lowers the gun to the floor, eyes catching mine in a piercing stare.

"Now, son. I see this going one of a few ways. On the one hand. I could kill her here and now. Maybe you'll get to your gun first and shoot me dead. Maybe I'll drop you before you manage to do that. But you see, I don't like the odds of that. Too much *risk* for my blood."

My eyes narrow as Calder continues to glare at me. I try to find meaning in his eyes but fall short of deciphering any message he might be trying to convey. Perhaps he too is panicking at the prospect that I've fucked this up irrevocably.

"On the other hand, I could just wait out the rest of the night with you at gunpoint. When they find that Vessy here isn't in her cell come morning. Well, this will probably be the first place they go. But that seems time consuming if you ask me. And while I have the upper hand right now, a lot can change in a short amount of time. Which leaves me with a third option."

Calder blinks for what seems like the first time in ages. When his eyes reopen, he addresses my father. "And what is that?"

"You simply walk away," he coos. "Leave this place and let justice run its course. Don't let yourself become collateral damage in all this."

Disgust crinkles between his brows. "I won't leave without her."

"She's not worth the dirt beneath your boots, kid. Don't throw your life away for some animate piece of trash." My stomach curls as he hooks the barrel of the gun beneath my chin, using it to tilt my head to the side so he can look me in the eye. "The only reason I didn't hunt her down and kill her myself was that she wasn't worth the time or energy. She's a murderous whore and by sunrise, she'll have paid for her sins, one way or another."

Knuckles crack as Calder balls his fists. "Over my dead body."

"Suit yourself." The pressure releases from my chin as the gun is pointed in Calder's direction.

I need no time to think as muscle memory from years of combat training kicks into action. Whatever self-deprecating divide I have between mind and body when it comes to my own well-being disintegrates now that the threat is directed at Calder. I slip the hold my father has on me as his attention is divided between myself and his target, forcing his arm to the side a millisecond before the gun fires. The bullet grazes past Calder's head as he ducks to the side. Snaking my arms around my father's, I pivot to face him, sliding my arm down the length of his as I force the pistol from his grasp. Puffing my chest, I raise the gun to his forehead.

He lifts his hands, an empty expression settling into his features. No fear. No anger. No concern. Just pure, consuming emptiness.

"I won't bother to ask you to admit to all the things you've done. You don't deserve to assuage your guilt with repentance." I cock the gun slowly. The only reaction he gives is a weighted blink from the sound.

"Who said anything about repentance?" he scoffs.

"No one yet. But don't worry, you'll be made to atone for your sins once I send you to the hell you tried so hard to emulate on earth."

I do not offer him the opportunity for last words. I do not prompt any further questions or seek anything resembling closure for myself.

Here I stand. The product of a lost childhood, facing the shadow of my demons point-blank.

I absorb the emptiness of the face staring back at me. And I pull the trigger.

The bullet blows clean through his skull and with its power and proximity, his death is likely immediate. But sometimes, even after death, the body refuses to believe its mortality and it moves out of sheer will to keep fighting beyond the point of defeat.

A smile flickers on his zombie lips, cruel even in death. His hands cradle the flesh of his abdomen, holding in them something glinting with silver and red.

But the image shifts and he is not holding anything at all.

As the body succumbs to inevitable release, he falls to the floor. Eternally still.

Blood pools from his skull.

And from his abdomen.

And the little girl stands in the doorway, hand still extended from when she plunged a knife through her father's back.

Chapter 31

Malle's eyes are distant as she stares down at the body on the floor. I'd be remiss to say that the strike she inflicted on her father occurred posthumously, his hands having clutched the wound, his eyes seeming to have registered the infliction a split second before the bullet shattered his skull. I'm unsure if I would rather that she attained her vengeance or for her young conscience to be assuaged from the finality of having taken a life.

Regardless, the look in Malle's eyes tells me the only thing that matters. She *believes* that she has taken a life.

It's rather poetic if you ask me. Two daughters killing their abuser simultaneously. Neither one knowing the other, other than through their mirrored fates.

Looking at Malle, I feel as though I am seeing Vessa as a child, though consciously I know that they are strangers to each other.

Vessa is calmer, more collected than I have ever seen her. After staring blankly at the corpse for a few moments, she saunters to the door, stepping over his outstretched leg. She brushes the stoically stagnant Malle out of the way, neither acknowledging the other, as she proceeds into the parlor.

"Let's move," she calls to me without looking back.

I pick up my pistol from the floor, securing it in my holster as I too step toward the door. But unlike Vessa, I stop when I reach the child.

"Malle?" I kneel beside the girl, softening my eyes as best I can. When she doesn't acknowledge me, I speak again.

"Malle, darling," I place a tentative hand on her shoulder, hoping the act will pull her out of her distracted state. It works too well as she gasps and startles backward, darting her eyes at me. I pull my hand back instantaneously, trying to instill a sense of safety between us. "My name is Azure. I am here to help you."

"You're the man from before?" she asks.

"Apologies for the deception," I nod in affirmation. "I am a friend of your sister's." I gesture over to Vessa, who is standing by the front door pretending not to overhear our conversation.

"I don't have a sister," she squints in confusion.

"It turns out you do, lass," my face contorts in an uncomfortable smile. "Regardless, you can't stay here, kid. I know you're probably confused and scared, and you don't know us but..."

"Can I come with you?" she asks over my shoulder, directing the question at Vessa.

"Of course you can," I answer for her. But Malle keeps staring at Vessa, waiting for a reply.

"Vessa," I prompt, shooting her a glare.

Begrudgingly, Vessa turns her head in our direction but does not make eye contact with either Malle or myself. "She can come."

I internally roll my eyes at Vessa's belligerence toward this child but try to cut her some slack, given the circumstances.

I stand and walk toward the front door, placing a comforting hand on Vessa's shoulder. She hardens beneath my touch, so I step past her into the night. I lean back in through the open door to address the child.

"Pack what you can carry. Only what you need. We will wait for you outside. Hurry, though. We need to set sail before sunrise."

Vessa follows me out the door, stepping down from the porch and onto the grass. She continues walking until she rounds the side of the house, making her way to the expanse of land behind what had been the home of her formative years. I follow only so long as it takes me to realize where she is going. When she stops beneath a lone ash tree, I return to the front porch, where I sit in wait.

This is not a time for my intrusion.

It is a matter of minutes before the child emerges carrying a small cloth bag.

"That's it?" I quirk a brow.

"Don't have much," she shrugs, her cavalier nature so reminiscent of her sister.

Vessa reemerges from the side of the house.

"Everything alright, love?"

"Just had to say goodbye," Vessa stares ahead as she replies, continuing past us and starting down the road toward the town. I nod for Malle to follow. She keeps pace with me as we walk side by side.

The sky softens into a navy-blue hue by the time we reach the docks and board the ship. We are barely past the breakwater when the first glint of sun kisses the horizon.

Vessa took no time before barricading herself in the cabin, leaving me to contend with the accommodations for the child. I brought her to a private room just below deck. It's small but clean. And she can lock the door from the inside so she can feel safe in this new and strange place. I gave her the key and told her to consider it hers to do with as she likes. Told her that she alone decides who can or cannot enter her quarters. I didn't bother explaining to her that I have the master key for everything aboard the ship. That truth isn't important when I'm trying to instill a sense of safety and control for her.

I leave her to rest, smiling as I hear the door lock behind me. I don't go far, stopping at the adjacent door and knocking. Doryn was less than pleased to be woken up so early in the morning. Despite the many years he's spent at sea, he has yet to become the type to rise with the sun.

I step inside, smiling at his irritated yawning. I explain to him the situation. The barebones details of what transpired and who the young girl is inhabiting the room beside him. I instruct him to keep an eye on her. I trust my crew implicitly, but I trust Doryn with more than my life. I trust him to make sure she is taken care of. Despite everything, he was once a father. And a damn good one from what I remember. He had his children young. They died when they were not much older than Malle. Had they not passed, he would likely be a grandfather by now. I know that weighs on his mind whenever things grow silent.

I take this sentimentality into account when appointing Doryn as her caretaker. After affirming my plans to return in a few hours to bring the girl food and make their introduction, I leave Doryn to return to his slumber.

By the time I enter my cabin, Vessa is sitting on the edge of the bed, wearing one of my button shirts that hangs long against her thighs. Her hair is down, falling over her shoulders as her elbows press into her knees, face cupped between her hands. She doesn't stir when she hears me, knowing the footsteps to be mine.

"I want to ask if you're alright, but it seems too loaded a question given the circumstances," I half joke, coming to sit beside her.

"I'm fine," she voices, face still buried in her hands.

"It's alright if you are not fine," I put a hand on her knee.

She drags a long breath in through her nose, exhaling as she straightens her spine. "That's just it," she looks straight ahead. "I am honestly fine."

"You are?" I challenge.

"Really," she turns to face me. "I feel... relief." She smiles. "Like this *tether* I've had that kept at least a part of me trapped in the past is just *gone*."

I examine her features and find nothing but sincerity.

Her eyes harden, gaze falling to the floor in front of her. "I want to tell you something. Just once. And then I never want to talk about it again."

"I'm listening," my brow quirks.

"I don't want you to say anything. I don't want to discuss it. And more than anything, I don't want your pity."

"You have my word," I assure.

She swallows the energy of the room, my fingers tingling with the desire to comfort her beneath my touch. But I fight the urge, trying to be the set of ears she needs me to be.

"I was young. *Really young* when I first met Cyril Tenebrys. He was a," she seems to search for a word. "*Much* older man. Older than my father, I think." She sighs. "But the point is, I was young. And he liked young. And my father? Well, *he liked money.* He never had it and he was always after it. But of course, he refused to work for it. Felt he was entitled to it. So, when Tenebrys expressed his interest in me, they struck up an arrangement. A *monetary* arrangement. He was *rich.* Not just in comparison to everyone else, but *filthy* rich. And the amount he was willing to part with so he could *have me* was absolutely shameless."

She goes silent for a few moments and I think she may have changed her mind about telling me her tale. Just as I'm about to speak, she continues.

"The worst thing about it was I actually thought it would be better that way. Tenebrys repulsed me. But he was gentle. Nothing about him seemed cruel. And all I knew at that point had been cruelty. Where my father left bruises, he left compliments. Though honestly, those left bruises in the pit of my stomach that took far longer to heal than tangible abrasions."

I grind my teeth, running my palm against the tops of my legs and digging the nails into the flesh above my kneecaps. I tether my urge to react. To start seething and hurling cursory words at all who hurt her. Start threatening the gods themselves for letting harm befall my Duvessa before I even knew she was mine to protect. But I temper myself, knowing damn well that my reactivity is not what she needs.

I continue to listen.

"I was going to go along with it. Parts of me believed what my father conditioned me to think. Other parts rebelled. But *those* parts, the ones that felt worthless. They kept me trapped."

"What did..." I unthinkingly start to ask, but she raises a hand. I silence myself in honor of our agreement.

"The night before the wedding, Tenebrys climbed in through my bedroom window. He'd been out. Drinking." She stares at a point on the floor, eyes hardened, lips pursed in tension. "Said he wouldn't wait another night – that he had to have what was his. Bought and paid for." Her throat tries to swallow the confession, hating that it is out in the ether. But the deed is irreversible.

"I tried to fight him. But I was small. And I didn't know how. I was so terrified I couldn't even bring myself to scream for help. But it wouldn't have made a difference anyhow. The only person that could have heard me wouldn't have done a thing. And it was nothing that wouldn't have happened the following night, regardless.

"He passed out on the bed beside me. I can't even put words to the change that happened inside me. Can't name the thing that broke in me. I don't remember if I even knew what I was doing when I went into the kitchen and got that knife. But I do remember – there was a moment when I was standing over him, beside my bed, when I thought about the consequences. And then I slit his throat. He didn't even wake up.

"That bothered me. His final memories were..." she shudders. My eyes watch as goosebumps flush across her skin. "And he never even knew that I found my strength."

She sits up straighter, eyes narrowing in revelation. "It may be sick and twisted. But," she presses her eyes together, wrinkles forming at the corners. "If that never happened - didn't play out the way that it had, I may have never gotten away."

Her eyes relax but remain shut as she lets out a nervous laugh.

"So, yeah. That's what I wanted to say. I've never told anyone about that," her voice falls soft and gentle, like a twilight snow. "Vayne knew, I think. Maybe not the details, but he understood what was broken in me. He may not have been the warmest of father figures, but his distance and his structure were all I think I could have tolerated from men at that point in my life."

A fog of silence embeds itself in my lungs as I contemplate her words.

"Anyway," she rises to her feet, letting out a dramatized sigh. She turns to me and shines a smile so false I want to bite her lip to prove it isn't real. "I am going to sleep. When I wake, can you have a bath..."

She continues talking, moving on so effortlessly from the darkness she just spewed. My brain does not process her words as she climbs into the bed, pulling the blankets up to her chest and laying on her side. She goes quiet. Her wrists cross on the mattress beside her face and she stares at the cuts and bruises left by the handcuffs. Neutrality takes hold of her expression once more.

"Duvessa," I say, still sitting at the edge of the bed.

She reads my dark and heavy tone for what it is and understands that I have not dropped the subject. "Azure, you promised."

Ignoring her, I continue. "I don't pity you," I say.

"What?" she sounds surprised.

"I don't pity you, Duvessa," I avow. "I *revere* you."

She does not speak but releases a breath. Her hands fidget with the tops of the sheets for a moment before she turns and faces away from me. I watch her for a while. She doesn't seem to move or make so much as a sound, but I know she is still awake. After watching her for a while, I kick off my boots, toss my jacket on the floor, and curl up beside her under the sheets.

I place a hand on her hip. When she does not flinch away, I wrap my arm around her and pull her closer to me. Burying my face in the nape of her neck I lay there, simply holding her as she falls asleep.

I am too wired to do anything but lay quietly and consider everything she just told me.

Only me.

I feel a selfish sense of fulfillment that I am the sole person she has opened up to about her past. Not Vayne. Not Gareth. *Me.*

I'm not sure that I deserve every depth and intricacy of this magnificent creature. Understanding her as I do now, I cannot help but bask in admiration at just how far she has come – how much she has accomplished in the wake of so much suffering. She crawled from her prison, bloodied and bruised, and kept on fighting until she got what she had always been denied. *Power.*

Strength is something she always had – even if she didn't always know how to wield it. But *power.* That is something that only exists between two people. It can either be taken or given. When you have it, it's yours. And when you don't, only the strong can fight to make it theirs.

Power was always hers to take.

Hours pass with her in my arms. I devour her scent with every breath, feeling her chest rise and fall against me as she sleeps. When I finally muster the will to untangle myself from her and rise from the bed, I can still feel her breathing against my chest like phantom waves, lulling like a siren's call that beckons my return to her side.

Exiting the room, my eyes linger on her briefly before shutting the door behind me.

Corkin's words from the previous day replay in my mind.

Provided Corkin carried out the orders I gave in secret at the time of our boarding the ship, we should be arriving soon.

Chapter 32

I wake to an empty bed. For the briefest of moments, my panic rises as I recall the events of the previous night. Not for any reason that one might think. But because of a split second of fear that I have never before experienced.

No, I remind myself. I moved the gun before he could harm Azure.

In that split second, when the gun was turned on him, I realized something I hadn't been able to admit.

I couldn't bear to lose Azure. I don't think I could survive it. I am not ready to name this feeling I feel for him – this thing that radiates between us in potent fumes. But I know in my core that if I ever lose it, it will destroy me.

I feel nothing over the death of my father. Nothing proximal to a negative emotion, that is. And though I feel sadness for the absence of my mother, it is a vacancy I have long since learned to live with. Now that the initial shock has worn off, I realize that what I feel now is closure.

But *that* tiny moment, one so small it could have been missed in the blink of an eye when I saw the barrel pointed at Azure, and everything seemed to click into place - *that* tore through me like lighting.

My body aches for the warmth and comfort of the hard plains of his body. I want to fall back asleep only to wake again, properly this time, with his arms still wrapped around me and his breath stroking my neck.

I sit up from the bed, feeling a lightness in my chest.

I didn't have to tell him.

He had no inherent right to know my secrets. He was owed no explanation. But I have no regret for sharing it with him.

The weight that is now absent from my heart, I realize now, is from finally voicing it all. The things that happened. The thoughts that have kept me prisoner in my own mind. In my own body. The dark fog feels thinner now that it is spread between us, no longer contained to my lungs alone. Now it is out there in the open swirling around us like ethereal bonds that can now be carried off by the wind.

Perhaps it is more than lightness. I feel *cleaner.* More whole.

Maybe that is why I can't bring myself to acknowledge her.

A sadness settles into my heart with greater ease now that there is more room inside.

I find it too hard to look at her. Woven into her features, I see parts of him. The same parts I've always seen in the mirror. The parts of me I despise the most.

Acknowledging her makes it real. Her existence. Our separate but all too shared trauma. And I don't want it to be real. Not now that I have finally purged myself of all the darkness.

She is a stranger, and I don't have the strength to even *want* to know her. Her darkness mirrors my own, and I have barely found my bearings in mine as it is. Why should I be responsible for putting her back together?

If she is anything like me, we would only ruin each other anyhow. Better not to hurt her more by being not enough.

As I slide the covers to the side and clamber to the edge of the bed, my wrists scream in protest. Scabs wrap my wrists like briar vines, shaded with hues of purples and reds. Even motionless, the bruises pulse down to the bone.

I see that Calder had a bath prepared and a meal set on the table. I couldn't have been sleeping long, the lightest billow of steam still radiating from the tub. My cheeks heat at the idea that someone besides Calder was in this room while I slept, unaware of their presence – though I doubt Calder would have permitted such an intrusion without his being here as well.

My lips play a game of tug-of-war as my mind flutters between feeling comfort in Calder's protectiveness over me and my core drive to reject such reliance on a man. I bite into an apple, an all-consuming smile winning out as I make the conscious decision to let myself be unapologetically happy.

I push a chair to the edge of the bath, placing the tray of food on the surface of the seat. I pour a mug of still hot coffee and place that beside the tray as well. I undo the top button of Calder's tunic, which I used as a nightshirt while I slept. My wrists burn from the subtle contractions of my wrist muscles, so instead I slip the entire thing over my head and toss it on the floor.

Careful not to put pressure on my wrists, I lower myself into the tub. The cut on my leg isn't as deep as I had initially thought. I almost forgot about it entirely until the brief but zapping sting as it is submerged in the hot bath. The pain subsides before I even settle at the bottom.

The displacement of the water sends wafts of jasmine and sandalwood whirling into my nostrils. The sigh that escapes in my exhale is involuntary, but I embrace it as I shut my eyes and sink deeper beneath the surface. I sit in peace for a few breaths before the desire for coffee wins out and I reach for the mug. As the water warms me from the outside, the coffee bleeds life into my veins. I palm two links of sausage from my plate and devour them with great relish.

I remain in the bath, downing the contents of my mug and polishing the plate clean. The skin of my hands and feet have pruned by the time I pull myself from the tub. Drying myself with the provided towel, I find myself turning my hands beneath my scrutiny, admiring the simulated aging from the wrinkled skin. I wonder if this is how they will look when I am truly old and weathered by time, instead of just bathwater.

I dress in slacks and a tunic of my own, brushing through my wet locks and twisting the length of hair into a rope braid that falls heavy between my shoulder blades. I notice it more now that the intrinsic weight is lessened.

Sitting on the foot edge of the bed, I lace my boots. Not yet wanting to relinquish my quiet afternoon, I lay back on the mattress. Staring up at the ceiling, I indulge myself by thinking of absolutely nothing. Just feeling comfort and calm.

Only when the calming nothing turns to churning thoughts do I sit back up and head for the door.

I do not have to look far to find him. Calder sits atop a barrel, back turned to me. He is speaking grandiosely to whichever people are standing in front of him, their forms and faces obscured to me from my vantage. As I approach, I cannot quite make out the words being exchanged, but I can tell from his tone that the conversation is light and friendly. His casual posture makes him seem as though he were any other man, speaking to a group of friends. Not a supposedly ruthless captain ordering his crew.

Once I take up the space to his side, I see why he is being so amiable.

The girl is standing in front of Calder, facing a crowd of smiling faces. Members of the crew have gathered around, some coming and going as they say hello in passing. The pleasant looks on their faces seem genuine, though part of me wonders if the kid might be off-put by the apparent effort they are taking to exchange pleasantries with her. I know I certainly find it somewhat unnerving. In the back of my untrusting mind, I search each set of eyes for malintent, but all I see is genuine kindness. Admittedly, the time I have spent with Calder's crew has warmed me to these men. While I wouldn't say I trust any of them implicitly, I have more faith in them than I do my own crew at present. Or what used to be my crew.

"Ah, Duvessa," Calder smolders when he sees me, taking my hand and guiding me a step further into the mix of people. "How kind of you to join us. Doryn and I are just introducing our new friend here to the rest of the crew."

Calder places a reassuring hand on Malle's shoulder, shaking her gently in comradery. I grimace at the action, knowing how I would have reacted if a stranger had done that to me in my youth. But contrary to my anticipation, the girl does not pull away. Instead, she steps closer to his side, glancing at him and *smiling*. She looks almost *content*. Her eyes meet mine for a split second before she returns her attention to the people in front of her. From her new position, I can examine her face as she answers frivolous questions asked of her, such as what her favorite color is and if she has ever gone fishing.

Doryn materializes at my side, leaning in to speak quietly in my ear.

"I thought it would make the transition less terrifying for her if she could put names to the faces of everyone on the ship. Turns out the kid is fairly adaptable. Doesn't seem to have a modicum of apprehension about her circumstances."

Doryn sounds perplexed, honing his attention on the girl's mannerisms.

"I guess she is just less fragile than I was," I try not to sneer, but my words sound more bitter than I intend.

"Possible," Doryn nods, his mind seeming far off. With a tilt of his head and a quick glance at me, he backtracks. "Not that I think *fragile* is the appropriate word."

"I take it Calder told you about what happened?" I avert my eyes to the floor beside my boots.

"He filled me in on a bit of it. Not much in the way of details, pertaining to your past." I feel his eyes releasing the side of my face. "Nothing I hadn't already figured out myself."

I peer at him, brows furling.

"I see more than most, remember?" His smile thaws my discomfort.

"You know," he knocks his arm against my shoulder. "If you find you need a sympathetic ear to talk to, I'm a fairly adept listener." His smile twists into something lighter, more playful.

"I'll keep that in mind," I smile back, warmth spreading through my heart. The offer feels like more than an obligatory reply. It feels genuine and welcoming.

"Thank you," I add beneath my breath.

Doryn nods with a quick grin before stepping forward. "Come, child. Let's get you more to eat. I'll show you to the galley." When the girl's eyes pinch in confusion, Doryn leans down until he is at eye level with her.

"That's the kitchen," he whispers with a wink. "You're welcome to fetch your own grub from there whenever you feel peckish. Just make sure to check with old Fritz before you take anything."

Doryn ushers the girl from Calder's side, guiding her across the deck to the steps leading below. Once she makes her leave, the remaining crew disperses and returns to their various tasks, leaving me and Calder in relative solitude.

"You're looking well rested, love," Calder stands and presses my shoulders between his hands, his eyes flickering with amusement as he stares down at me.

"I'm feeling much better. Thank you. For the food and the bath." I run my hands along the sides of his forearms, letting them rest in the creases of his elbows.

My mind fixates on how well-adjusted the girl was. Not even just compared to how I acted at her age. She, overall, seemed as normal as anyone else. Is it possible that she was not subjected to the same tribulations as I had been? Maybe all the hate and mistreatment had been saved just for me. Maybe her life with him hadn't been as terrible.

But she ran a knife clear through him. Children who feel safe and loved don't do that sort of thing.

Unless of course the same cruelty that animated my father had been passed down to her.

Had it not been passed down to me? After all, did I not kill a man and then immediately integrate myself into a life that not only accepts blood and violence but requires it?

Maybe the violence courses through our blood.

But how could she appear so comfortable and collected? After a life of abuse? After killing her own father?

Maybe she isn't as broken as I was. Maybe she hadn't suffered as much or as long as I had. *Or maybe she is just stronger than me.*

"What's the matter?" Calder's brow quirks as he leans his face closer to mine. "Where did you just go?"

"Nowhere," I seal my lie with a smile. "Just feeling a bit lagged still after yesterday. My body needs a moment to catch up with the rest of me, I guess."

"Hmm," he doesn't drop my gaze. Calder doesn't seem to quite believe me, but he doesn't press any further. "Doryn prepared an ointment for your wrists. Here." He pulls a small vial from his pocket and hands it to me. "He said it should help with pain and prevent infection."

I open my mouth to speak, but he presses a finger to my lip before I can utter a word.

"And before you reject the help and claim that the pain doesn't bother you, don't waste your breath. You will be using it until you've healed, even if I have to hold you down and apply it myself." He brushes his thumb against my lip, brandishing a devilish grin. "And trust I wouldn't mind the task."

My throat bobs as I swallow the implication.

"I don't know," a husky rattle settles into the playful tenor of my voice. "I'm not sure that I need it. I have a fairly high threshold for pain."

Both arms wrapping around my waist, Calder pushes past the remaining space between us, pressing into me in a way that is nowhere near appropriate in such a public space. He twirls a finger in the loose hanging hair at the end of my braid, tugging the strands ever so slightly.

"Oh, I have a passing familiarity with that information," his grin widens. "But I'm always happy to explore the boundaries of just how much you're able to withstand."

I love the way my heart tumbles from my chest and burns deeply in my core.

No other person could drag me from the mental whirlpool that pulls me under and somehow flush every particle of my being with impassioned lust. No one else could make the dark thoughts seem as though they'd never existed at all.

I tilt my head up, pressing my lips into his, savoring the taste of his lip as I take it between my teeth. The skin of his lip slides against my teeth as it stretches into a haughty grin. He runs his jaw across my cheek, the black stubble rough and the line so sharp it could cut me open and bleed me dry.

My heart stutters, loudly pounding against my chest, the beat of his reverberating through my bones.

"Land ho!" a voice bellows above us.

Azure pulls back at the remark, looking off into the distance behind me.

"Land?" I contest. "But there are no lands so close to Lythren."

"Are you so sure of that, love?" Calder jerks his head in indication.

I jaunt to the bow, gazing out at the mass of green that speckles the horizon of blue.

"What in the realms...?" I stutter in fascination.

"I suppose now might be an opportune moment to fill you in on what we learned in Lythren," Calder settles beside me.

"Perhaps I can shed some light on that," an unfamiliar voice echoes behind us.

THE OCEAN'S SHADOW

In synchrony, Calder and I whirl around to face the most stunningly beautiful woman I have ever seen.

Her silver eyes grow heavy when she meets my baffled gaze.

"Welcome to Neverland."

Chapter 33

Corkin did not do her justice in his description.

A sheen of silver saturates her ethereal form. Her hair falls like liquid silver down her shoulders, skin so white it looks as though she were carved from stone. Her eyes too are silver, with a sparkle that rivals any diamond I have ever before seen. But that sparkle is only a visual simulation, no joy seeming to lighten her heavy aura.

"Who are you?" Vessa's voice is laced with confusion. "How did you get on this ship? Are you a stowaway?"

A shallow smile plays at the corners of the woman's lips, but it recedes like a broken wave.

"My name is Yara. And I assure you I am no stowaway."

The woman steps towards us - no, *floats* - with all the elegance and hesitation of an entranced specter.

"Who I am is of little importance." She comes to inhabit the space beside Vessa. I try to downplay the way I wrap my hand around Vessa's arm and lightly pull her a step closer to me. "*What* I am, however, is the gatekeeper to Neverland."

"How did you..."

"The moment you reached the boundary I was able to materialize aboard your ship and guide you safely across," Yara answers Vessa's previous question. "Had I not, you would have sailed straight on into the open waters of the material realms, like all other ships that are not welcome. As the other ships in your fleet have done."

Darting my glance across the horizon, I realize that the *Queen Marie* is alone on the open water. The other ships are nowhere to be seen,

"The materials realms?" I query.

"What we call the human realms," she offers. "Neverland exists outside of time and space. It is everywhere and it is nowhere. Few ever set eyes on its shores, much less set foot there. The souls that do are usually lost and only find it when it's their last remaining hope." She flutters her glance between Vessa and myself. "Others are simply in the wrong place at the wrong time."

Vessa's eyes narrow. "What does that mean exactly?"

Yara's eyes dart to the open water, her shoulders tensing up to her ears. "I shouldn't speak so openly. There are ears across the ocean and all report back to her."

"Delesseria?" Anticipation saturates Vessa's voice.

"Yes. She instructed that I bring you to her. She felt it was time you reconnect."

Vessa twists out of my hold stepping closer to the woman as she leans deeper into the rail. "Why are you working for the sea witch? What exactly are you?"

"Those stories. Those details. That's what makes me who I am. And as I've said, that is of little importance now." Her eyes pool with liquid silver before she slams her lids shut. "Delesseria will explain everything to you once you arrive at her castle on the island."

"She's here? In Neverland?" I press.

"Of course," the woman furrows her silver brows. "This has been her home ever since she *became* the sea witch. It exists just outside of Triton's reach."

"Does that mean that..."

"Save your questions for Delesseria. I will not answer any more." Yara raises her hand to silence Vessa's attempt to continue speaking.

"Sail straight on toward the island. I will meet you there as soon as you arrive."

Before she even finishes speaking, her aura begins to shimmer. Within seconds, she fades into nothing, and we are left alone.

"Neverland," Vessa mutters to herself. "I've never heard of such a place. And I have never seen it mentioned in any of the texts written about Delesseria."

"Nor have I," I offer. "As the silver woman said, it exists out of time and space. Maybe that somehow has kept it secret from the *material* world."

"Perhaps," Vessa nods, though her eyes are oceans away. "*Neverland.* Such an odd name."

In the minutes that follow, we do as the silver woman, Yara, instructed. In an amount of time that seems uncharacteristically short, we arrive at what may have once been a quaint dock. Now, it is overgrown with mosses and vines to the point where I question the soundness of the wooden structure beneath, but as Vessa and I make our way onto the dock and down the boardwalk to the sandy beach, I tentatively come to trust the foundation.

"You have arrived." Yara materializes several yards ahead of us. I think I see her shoulders flinch briefly as we step down into the sand from the boardwalk, but I push that detail from my mind. "Delesseria instructed that only the two of you are invited to proceed beyond this point. The rest of your crew will need to remain aboard your ship."

"She expects us to walk into the witch's den without enforcements?" Vessa sneers. "What? So that she can strike us dead and swallow our ship and crew with one rogue wave?"

"No harm will befall you while you are on Neverland. Unless provoked. The same courtesy is extended to the members of your crew."

I steal a glance back toward my ship, kicking myself for not strategizing with Corkin before disembarking.

"If you agree to those terms, you may follow me now." Without waiting for our reply, Yara turns and starts float-walking across the beach toward the distant tree line.

I flash Vessa an apprehensive glance before we both start after her. The sand is deep and soft, making our effort to cross far more time-consuming than for our ethereal guide, who waits patiently beside a tree for us to catch up. We have barely transitioned into the grassland terrain when she disappears into the forest.

The forests of Neverland are not too dissimilar from those of Torrence, with one main difference. The humidity is almost nonexistent here, the gentle heat being countered by a near-perpetual cool breeze. As such, the bugs that usually swarm and bite in places such as these are nonexistent, though other less affronting insects creep and crawl at a respectable distance. We hear in the jungle depths hoots and hollers of various primates and the clucks and calls of infinite avians. The foliage is so dense that we are not able to see any of the individuals from which these sounds originate, though the occasional rustling of branches and bushes tells us they are not far.

Another unique feature of Neverland is the deep red coloration of the soil. The dirt that now cakes the soles of my boots makes it look as though I have been traipsing through puddles of blood, thick and coagulated. Whatever minerals comprise this earth pump buzzing life into the surrounding flora, which emanates energy just as potent as any breathing creature I have ever encountered. Just walking in these forests revives in me a sensation of youthful exuberance I thought to be long since lost to me in my adulthood. I find myself examining Vessa, searching for a similar reaction to the energy of the forest. But she appears to be unaffected.

In what I am coming to accept as the usual fashion of Neverland, the trek through the jungle is both shorter and longer than it seems before the forest breaks, leaving us standing at the precipices of the castle.

A grassy meadow dotted with purple wildflowers spans the distance between the tree line and the rocky castle walls. Cobblestone walkways line a path that takes us straight to the towering fortress, others diverting into circling paths around the castle and throughout the garden meadow. The heavy wooden door, old as time itself, creaks open without provocation as we approach. An inexplicable sense of welcoming encompasses me, pulling me forward and through the threshold.

From the outside, the size of the castle rivals that of any mortal royals. The inside does not disappoint.

Two sets of wrapped staircases roll up from either side of the grand entry. The floors are paved in pearls. Every scrap of metal is gilded pure gold, every jewel authentic and undoubtedly costly. And I know my treasure.

Intricate sconces that are somehow lit by perpetual flames are carefully crafted to resemble voluptuous mermaids, tails frozen in powerful strokes and hands forever bearing the torches they raise like the Promethean emblems they are. A heavy jeweled chandelier hangs from the ceiling in the center of the room, so far from the floor that I have to squint to make out the craftsmanship of the metalwork. Labyrinthine carvings tell unspoken stories in the scenes that unfold across the golden limbs of the light fixture. I could spend years deciphering the subtle details of each individual and their place in the greater design.

"Azure." Her voice breaks me from my gold-induced trance.

Vessa waves a beckoning hand from where she stands across the room, in the vast space between the two staircases. Her voice echoes in the ambient silence, the second and third rings so complete that it sounds as though she's calling me over and over again. When she sees that she's gotten my attention, she turns and follows Yara through another set of grand wooden doors.

Despite my anticipation of another room so close to the entry, these doors open into a vast courtyard. The cylindrical stone walls that form the space are so wide I can almost not distinguish their curves as they wrap around the expanse. More cobblestone pathways lead around the perimeter, another trudging straight ahead. Vessa has disappeared into the lush vines and shoulder-high grasses when I follow.

The courtyard becomes a small lagoon. At the center, a narrow waterfall flows against all logic, forming a throne out of the rushing waters. Despite its liquid foundation, the throne is itself solid. Regal in its improbability.

Rivaling the regality of the throne is the woman sitting atop it. The sea witch herself.

Delesseria.

Red hair falls like flames that lick against her skin in turbulent curls. The contrast of the immaculate white of her flowing dress brings out the subtle hues of molten red in her otherwise pale complexion. Embers buried just below the surface. The thin straps of the dress leave her arms and shoulders exposed, the silk fabric pleated like shells across her breasts and plunging at the center of her chest. The rest of the fabric falls long across her slender form, not unlike a silken waterfall that emanates from the seam fitted around her waist.

Despite the rush of water that comprises her throne, she is bone dry, untouched by the spraying water misting around her.

Her eyes are the color of whiskey, just as enticing and just as debilitating. I feel myself stalling beneath the thickness of that amber gaze. I fear that if I don't move, even a little, I may be frozen entirely.

"You," Duvessa's voice pulls me from my trancelike state. I hear the sound of sliding metal as she unsheathes her sword. I turn my head just in time to see the sea witch effortlessly lift her hand, looking almost bored as the sword goes flying out of Vessa's hand and clatters onto the stones behind her.

"I will pretend that didn't happen. But consider that your one and only lenience."

The lilt of her voice sounds older than she physically appears. While I recognize that she is an immortal being, and the rules of age likely hold different consequences for her, she looks to be no older than I. But her voice rumbles with the intrinsic knowledge of time itself in a way that shakes my bones and rattles my bravery. Yet, her tone holds the slightest twinge of youthfulness that makes her voice seem more befitting of her appearance. But it isn't *quite* youthfulness. It is *hope*. Somehow, that is more disquieting than anything else.

"Now," Delesseria divides her attention between Vessa and myself. "If we are quite done with theatrics, let's get down to brass tacks. Shall we?"

Vessa's entire body is a clenched fist. Though disarmed, she does not appear so easily dissuaded from attacking the sea witch. She takes but a single step forward when Delesseria fixes her with a glower, effectively stalling her in her tracks.

"Remember the terms of your invitation into my home, deary. If you try anything, there is an entire ship filled with your people waiting for me to pick off one by one." The intensity of her tone sends a chill down my spine. She shakes as though trying to rid her body of raindrops, and when she stops, her face is locked in a mask of pleasantry. "I do hate being forced to play the villain like this, but you have to understand, you'll leave me no other choice if you try and attack me in my own home."

"I would say you've done more than play the villain," Vessa spits.

"What on earth gave you that impression?" Delesseria's spine lengthens as she presses further into her throne, a gesture of contentment in the power differential between us.

"Oh, I don't know. Perhaps the spell you cast on me."

"Spell? My dear sweet child, you asked for this. Wished for it. You vilify me for giving you exactly what you wanted?" She quirks a brow in genuine confusion.

"I never asked for *this*!" Vessa pulls at the neck of her shirt, exposing her swirling gills.

"Can you honestly say that the gifts I gave you have not proven useful to you? Saved you? Let you play the hero for others? Are you truly that ungrateful?" Her fingers curl into the arm of her throne, causing water to spurt forward as it rushes past.

"Am I supposed to be grateful that you can control me at will?" Vessa's hands clench, her forearms quaking as she tries to temper her rage.

"I don't want to control you," Delesseria's voice goes calm as a stilling sea. "I want you to choose me."

"Choose you?!" Vessa dry heaves the words. "Choose you for what? You have given me no choices in any of this. You tricked me, controlled me like the wicked, heartless viper you are."

Delesseria sits forward on her throne so swiftly that I flinch, but she does not rise. Vessa holds her ground, unaffected by the suddenness of the gesture. She is a vision of strength as she stands in the face of a wrathful goddess.

"I may be wicked in the eyes of some. And I may even be a viper, if that's the form they want me to take. But I am *anything* but heartless." The temperature seems to drop with the pointedness of her words. She exhales a slow breath of frost, muscles slowly untensing as she forces herself to relax. "I give people what they want most in this world. Is it so wrong that I ask for something in return? That *is* how the human realms work, after all."

"What do you know of the human realms?" I ask, the first time I find words to voice in her presence. I regret speaking when her eyes return to me. Her look of disgust shoots through me like a bolt of lightning.

"I know more than you," she scoffs. "You are nothing more than a fetus in the grand scale of time."

Turning her attention back to Vessa, she softens.

"Believe it or not, I used to adore humans." Her eyes glow as memories replay in her distant gaze. "Centuries ago, before everything happened. It seems like more of a dream now, before I ever stepped foot in the material realms. The humans, they worshiped me. I was a goddess, after all, and that is what humans did. That was the natural order of things. The humans worshiped and groveled. And the gods, well, they drank it down like ambrosia. Others were content to revel in their adoration, their fear. But me? I was fascinated by them. All I wanted was to understand them. I watched. And I listened. And I learned as much as I could about them from the safety of my father's kingdom.

"Eventually, it wasn't enough. I had to experience it firsthand. I wanted to taste the air they breathed. Feel the sand beneath my feet. I wanted to *be* them, so I could *understand* them. So, I crossed the threshold. I would steal away any chance I could to the material realms. I learned their customs. Lived among them."

Her eyes turn to stone, her tone growing cold.

"And I learned just how cruel they could be. Even in that I was fascinated. I couldn't understand how they could be so malicious, so evil at times when they had so much at their disposal. And then I realized, they weren't at fault for their cruelty. We were. The gods had forgotten them long ago. Stopped hearing their prayers and pleas. All they did was take. Take their love and adoration with greed and gluttony. These humans turned cruel because of the cruelty of their circumstances, forced upon them by the apathy of the Divine. And that cruelty became an evolutionary trait that spread through humanity like a plague. The crueler they could be, the easier it became for them to survive."

"So, you spent some time with humans. You think that gives you the right to control them?" Vessa spits back at Delesseria as though fear and consequence hold no structure in her soul. My heart races at her boldness and stills as my concern for her well-being clenches around the overworked muscle. "The gods may be apathetic, but at least they haven't tampered with free will."

"I haven't..." Delesseria pinches her brow between her fingers, slightly shaking her head. "Why do you keep accusing me of such things?"

"Well, excuse me for taxing your delicate system, my lordship," Vessa taunts with mock courtesy. "But I think my weeks of lost time have entitled me to some criticisms."

The sea witch stalls the rubbing of her brow, hand lowering as she stares at Vessa. I fear she may well smite her where she stands and mentally prepare to throw myself between them if it comes to that.

"Your memories of the events are false. I have no control of how your mind chooses to process reality." Delesseria sighs. "But... since you've come back of your own volition, I can return to you the broken pieces I took. Maybe then you will see me in a more truthful light."

The sea witch procures a copper clamshell from her pocket. Extending her hand, it opens on its own, a pearl of bright light floating out from it and drifting toward Vessa so quickly that she has no time to react before it hits her. When it does, Vessa's entire body goes ridged, back arching as her head flies back.

"Vessa," I yell, running to her side and taking her shoulders between my hands. "What have you done to her?" My previous trepidation of the sea witch disappears entirely at the assault.

"Just restoring her memories, dear boy," she waves a dismissing hand. "She is not in pain, only traipsing within the boundaries of her own mind."

"Duvessa!" I shake her, trying to pull her from her trance. "Vessa, come back to me!"

I feel her body go slack in my arms, her eyes livening back to the present.

"Are you alright?" I pull her close to my chest, hugging tightly as her feet regain purchase beneath her.

"I. Remember. Now." Her voice breathily whispers in my ear.

"What do you remember?" I pull back to look her in the eye, hands still clenching her shoulders, afraid that if I let her go, she will be taken from me again.

Vessa steps out of my grasp as she walks past me, stopping a few paces closer to Delesseria than she was before.

"You," she stares up at the sea witch, eyes watering. "You were right."

"I told you I would never lie to you." Delesseria's voice turns warm, almost maternal.

"What do you mean?" I step toward Vessa, trying to catch her eyes, but they do not leave Delesseria. When it is clear she will not answer, I turn to the sea witch. "What is she talking about?"

"Do you want to tell him, or shall I?" She smiles warmly at Vessa, who remains silent as her eyes fall distant, almost meekly upon the lagoon.

"Tell me what?"

"She never forced me. I know that now," Vessa starts. "I was there voluntarily. She was teaching me. *Training* me. And when I wanted to leave, she let me."

"I had to take those memories, Duvessa," Delesseria's voice is laden with apology. "I could not risk your sharing what you learned with the wrong people." She leans forward imploringly. "I always intended to restore your memories when you returned to me."

"Training you for what?" I tilt my head, trying again to ensnare Vessa's eyes.

"When I discovered the origins of the cruelty in man, I found the most remarkable group of humans," the fire in Delesseria's eyes reignites. "True revolutionaries of their times. They have existed in various forms over the ages and across the realms. Given various names and held various titles. I, however, have always been partial to the one your realm uses to brand them."

"Witches," Vessa says beneath her breath.

"Indeed," Delesseria smiles wide, again entranced with her reminiscence. "I took up with a group of mortal witches. A coven of wise and aspirational women who were trying to fight back against the Divine powers that kept humans compliant and trapped. I took up with their cause and when my father found out about it, he threatened to kill my mother."

"Legends say you were the one to kill your mother," I state dryly.

"Do you believe everything you read? Who do you think wielded the quills that committed the tales to history? Of course, the truth got lost in the translations of man," Delesseria sneers at me.

"Triton tells the same tale," Vessa lifts her eyes to Delesseria, averting from the lagoon, questioning, accusing. "According to him, you killed her for the spell that transformed you."

"It wasn't like that," Delesseria's throat catches. "He threatened to kill her if I didn't stop my efforts with the coven. If I didn't come back and follow his every rule. I came there... *to rescue her? To call his bluff?* I was just so angry. And I tried to free her from him, but he," a sob dies in her heart, her voice growing silent while she forces down a stuttered breath. "He used her as a shield from my magic. She died instantly."

"If what you say is true, how did you transform into the sea witch?" I inquire.

"The rage of true grief is a powerful thing, child," she looks at me for the first time without malice, but with... *longing.* "To not know its bitter taste is to be truly blessed." A faint smile haunts her face. "Intent does not negate outcome. The truth of the matter is that my magic *is* what killed her. At that moment, when I realized the irrevocability of my actions, all the anger and sadness of the cosmos collected inside of me. Like the eye of a hurricane, my world blew apart around me, and everything within compressed and twisted until I just *transformed.*"

A nervous laugh slips past her lips.

"It was magic indeed, but none conjured by choice. It was inflicted. It was inevitable. And in that same moment, the moment when I transitioned, Triton disowned me. How truly fated it was that those two instances overlapped, for if they had not, if I hadn't become the original sea witch in that precise moment, his disownment would have stripped me of my powers entirely instead of merely binding them to the moon."

Delesseria's eyes snap to mine, her fingers snapping in the same instant, and I am jerked upward. Invisible hands wrap around my throat, feet dangling above the ground as I kick and claw to free myself, to no avail.

"Let him go!" I can hear the threat in Vessa's voice, but Delesseria pays her no mind.

"I can feel the judgment coursing through your veins, boy," an insincere smile brushing across her face like an impressionistic painting. "I *am* vicious. And I *am* abrasive." She spits the words pulled from my mind like a venomous threat. "But this is the shape I've taken from years of adaptation. Triton disowned me. Humans came to fear and despise me. And those that still came knocking on my door, well, all they wanted was to use me. So, in a way, I started using them back. Making deals. Making it so that if ever I did decide to share my power with someone, I would always get something in return."

The invisible hands tighten around my neck.

"*You* spend eons having everyone and everything *take, take, take* from you." Her eyes compress like coal, filling them with a sparkle of madness. "Feel yourself wearing so thin you think you might snap. Then tell me you don't understand my perspective. Existence is a quid pro quo endeavor. Even the air you breathe is taken from the trees. The foods you eat from the earth. Lives for lives. Survival for dismay. The sooner you realize that, the easier your lives become."

As quickly as it started, she drops me to the ground. I break the fall with my hands, coughing as I remain crouched in the dirt. Vessa rushes to my side, rubbing her hand gently between my shoulders as I struggle to catch my breath.

"Do *not* hurt him," Vessa growls.

"How strange it is to see you so taken with this man," Delesseria all but sings. "He is truly a surprise. Especially after all I told you would come to pass."

Vessa's eyes dim with sadness. "He has nothing to do with any of that."

"Doesn't he?" the sea witch chortles.

"Yes," Vessa stands. "You were right. I returned to my ship only to lose everything. *Yes*, it turned out that all the power I thought I had was a lie. And maybe you are right. Maybe there is some cosmic lesson to be found in that. That *none of us* have any power. That all of it is a lie we tell ourselves to trick us into thinking our lives hold meaning. But," Vessa's hand brushes against my cheek. I look up to see her staring down at me. "But there is more meaning to be found in life than power. There are other things to live for. Other ways of living."

Delesseria starts to slowly clap her hands in condescension. "Bravo, my dear. You found *love*. How truly quaint of you." Her clapping stops and she sits forward on her throne. "But are you truly content with just that? Given everything you know. Everything I taught you. Can you really walk away from me and all I fight for, for *this*?"

Delesseria points at me, a look of disgust and judgment saturating her face.

"Why does it have to be a choice?" Vessa asks in earnest. "Why can't I have both?"

"What I am trying to do is start a revolution. To create and train a coven all my own. One that draws its powers from the waters rather than just the lands and can conquer both. Witches of land and sea that can help me fight to reclaim the realms from the neglect of the Divine. Soldiers I can mold into warriors to bring about my rule. I am the *only one*, that in all of this, still answers wishing prayers. At the end of the day, *I care*. I can fix all of this. I just need your help to get there."

"What makes you think he can't help?"

"I assume that *because I know* won't be a good enough answer to you?" she huffs. "How about the mere fact that he reacted as he did to the effects of Neverland? When average people step foot on Neverland, they revert to feeling the energy of their youth. Many revert so completely that they find their answers in the simplicity of forests and never make their way to me to cast their wishes at my feet. Half the time, they forget what they even wanted before."

"What happens to them?" I ask through gritted teeth, wondering why we encountered no other people on our journey to the castle.

"They spend their lives in the forests. And since Neverland exists out of time and space, their lives are...

413

long. If they do no harm, I let them stay and live whatever quiet, simple existence they'd like, without interference. They live in a way they no longer can in the material world." She eyes me with scrutinizing judgment. "If it weren't for your company Duvessa, I think this ape may well have never made it out of the jungle, much less into my castle."

I snarl as I clench my jaw, trying to bite my tongue. This only makes her antagonistically laugh.

"Why was I not affected like that?" Vessa barks.

Delesseria sighs. "Broken people cannot be fixed. Not even the magic of Neverland can fix the truly broken."

Vessa's face conceals how deeply these words affect her. She swallows her pride and asks, "How do the broken heal?"

"My darling child, if I knew the answer to that question, I doubt any of us would be standing here today."

Vessa shakes her head, trying to gain purchase on a deviated subject. "So, he isn't broken like us. Does that make him useless to you? You won't even give him a chance?"

"You should know by now that what I want are allies. I want my coven to choose me. I want them to understand me. To know me. I will not force loyalty. And I will not risk halfhearted kinsmen whose allegiances aren't fully devoted to me." She sighs. "Do you know how I found you, Duvessa?"

Vessa's answering stare of defiance is her only reply.

"The death of my mother and the role I played in it were the greatest losses of my entire existence. In one I lost a life. In the other, I lost parts of myself that I have never gotten back. *Loss* was how I found you, Duvessa. I could hear your heart calling out to mine, singing the same song of sorrow I learned in my past.

"I only hear that song from those who have experienced the kind of broken heart that comes with their *greatest* loss, the kind that leaves you forever changed. Very few people experience their greatest possible loss in life, and fewer still consciously realize it when it happens. The heart does not die but shatters into a million pieces. Feeling too much. Sometimes, too little. *Intensified.* Somehow *wrong.*"

The look on Vessa's face says it all. She is all too familiar with what Delesseria is describing.

"And I can only make witches from those who have blood on their hands," The sea witch continues. "Taken by choice. The blood on my hands that turned me belonged to my mother. I chose to strike against my father, and that resulted in her bloodshed. I don't have to tell you whose blood made it possible for your transition."

Bile rises in my throat at the memory of what Vessa told me of the man she killed years ago.

"Before that blood was shed, you were but a whisper echoing across the oceans in all directions. But when you took his life, I could hear you clearly. Sense you across the realms."

"If you could sense me, why did you wait so long to find me?" Vessa sounds almost aggrieved by the lost time.

415

"By the time I found you, you were tightly wrapped beneath your Captain Vayne's wing." Delesseria's eyes soften, again exuding something maternal. "How young you were. Just a child. The choice you made to join him was barely a choice at all. And when you did, you clung to him like the father you'd always wanted. You taught yourself to feel safe, and you credited him for that comfort. You would not have chosen me if I had approached you then. And as I said, I have no interest in forcing your compliance."

Vessa's hands clench into fists at the mention of her mentor.

"So, I waited for you to grow into the astounding woman that you've become. I waited until your song was all but blaring in my ears, and I could no longer ignore its call." She smirks. "You say you never wished for this, but you did from the very depths of your soul, with every fiber of your existence. And deep down, you know this to be true."

"You claim that you have no control over me. That you have no interest in forcing my hand," Vessa presses. "Then why is it I hear you - *feel* you calling to me every full moon? If you think hypnotizing me with your magic and compelling me to do things isn't manipulation..."

"Duvessa," Delesseria cuts her off with a laugh. "That has nothing to do with me. You feel the call of the water on the full moon? Feel the need to jump and swim and find me? That isn't my control wavering, it's yours. That is *you* fighting your own instinct and desire to join me. You feel my call just as much as I feel yours."

"That doesn't..." she starts to argue.

"You know that it's true, child," Delesseria scolds. "No point in denying it further. Not now that you have your memories."

Vessa stares blankly ahead. After a long silence, she sighs. "So, what now?"

"Now?" Delesseria smiles. "You rest. I had rooms prepared for you and your guest in the west wing. Stay the night. Processes what we have discussed. Take the night, the week, as much time as you'd like. And when you've reached your decision, I'll be waiting."

Chapter 34

The ghostly woman leads us to our rooms. I pay little attention to our trajectory through the castle. I remember perfectly well how to navigate the palace from my previous stay on the island. Besides, I have a feeling that Delesseria will find me when she senses I am ready.

But already I know what my answer is.

I will stay.

The moment those memories came flooding back to me, she was no longer my enemy. She was my ally.

My savior.

My deity.

She was the thing that was missing in me all my life. The promise of something better. Fulfillment incarnate. She was that unnamed feeling I would get whenever a person would tear me down, knowing I would rise above them from the ashes of their disrespect.

I don't quite know how to express this to Azure, his pestering questions having not relented since we left the courtyard. In deferment of my answers, I take to questioning Yara.

"How did you come to know Delesseria?" The question gives me a sense of déjà vu, the image of her face itching at the back of my mind as I wonder if there are other pieces of my memories still missing from my recollection.

The look of disappointment on her face does little to subdue my paranoia.

"Like I told you before..."

"Yes, I know. *It doesn't matter who you are.*" I mimic her self-deprecating tone from before, something about the exchange feeling all too familiar. "I'm just curious."

"You warned us away from this place," Azure chimes in. "I find myself equally curious as to *why* if the sea witch is as *well-intentioned* as she claims to be."

"One person's good intentions are another's nightmare," Yara does not stall as she continues to float in front of us.

"How ominous," he scoffs.

"Let's just say that I made a deal with Delesseria once," she speaks plainly but with palpable reminiscence. "At the time, I thought it was the right thing to do. Now? I would do anything to return home."

"Where is home?" I ask.

"You two do ask a great deal of questions."

"If you are trying to warn us of something, you are doing a horrid job of it," Azure exclaims. "It seems the sea witch has made a compelling argument for Vessa to stay. If there is one to be made for her to leave, I dare say you should speak plainly before it's too late."

I try to ignore the notes of urgency he fails to hide from his tone. But, for reasons I cannot begin to explain, I find myself latching onto the conflict.

"Too late?" I cut. "I take it you would not *approve* of my choosing to stay then?"

"I didn't mean that," he exasperates.

"Because last I checked, *Calder*, I do not require your approval."

"I just meant..."

"Tell me," I turn my attention back to Yara. "*Is* there a reason I shouldn't stay?"

Though she is floating, Yara still manages to shift on her feet under the discomfort of my outburst.

"Everyone's path is their own. I cannot say what is the right choice for you." She stops walking and I have to catch myself before falling into her. She turns to face us, eyes searching to see if we are alone. When she detects no one, she relaxes.

"You may have noticed my comparatively unique features." When we nod, she continues. "I am what you might call a moon sprite. My people - they say we were created out of moonbeams, more of an illusion than a tangible form, though we can become more corporeal at will. As you have witnessed." In exemplification, she fades and rematerializes before our eyes.

"What we do - the reason we exist - is to bring the light of the moon to the realms. Each night, we dance across the sky, breaking through the barriers between realms and finding a way to deliver the light wherever it needs to go."

Her eyes twinkle with memory before darkening.

"I always had a fascination with the water – how the moonlight would reflect against it. How dark and mysterious it seemed to me, as someone who only knew light. And that was how I met him. Agwe. Prince of the waves. Not a god, mind you, but an ethereal entity like myself. I fell for his darkness, and he fell for my light.

"Ours was a *tumultuous* love. Only able to be together in the night and only ever from a distance as I was bound to the moon itself – it coursing through my very existence and tethering me to its pull. He professed his love for me every night across the broken waves. Spoke sonnets of how he yearned for us to one day unite. By design, we were cosmically fated to be apart but yearned to be together against the odds."

Her shoulders slump as her eyes drop to the floor.

"But when I made my deal with Delesseria, when I broke my bonds with the moon and found my way to him in the tangible realms, he turned me away. Pretended like everything we'd shared, everything he promised had never happened. And when I refused to accept his dismissal, he disappeared entirely." Yara sighs. "Turns out he did not love me at all. All he loved was the idea of someone wanting him but never being able to have him. He loved being someone's unattainable passion. He loved the pain in my eyes that showed brighter than the moonlight I delivered each night."

The story, her words, they ring as faint as a bell in my mind. *Had I heard this story before? Some legend as old as time itself?*

"Is that how Delesseria controls you? The price of your deal?" Azure asks. I fight the urge to scoff at him for being so blunt and not so much as acknowledging her pain. Truthfully, I wouldn't begin to know how to do that either without it sounding forced.

"No. When I made my deal with Delesseria, it was long before she became the sea witch. Before she started demanding remittance. When Agwe turned me away, I couldn't return home. I had rejected the moonlight, and in return, it rejected me. It was still a part of me, as I am comprised of it. But the pathway home was closed off to my return.

"So, instead, I wandered across all the material realms, able to slip between them. I found myself walking across the water in constant search of a love who didn't want to be found. Eventually, I lost the will to continue."

Yara looks at me with a mixture of sadness and hope, searching for something in me I don't seem to have.

"Delesseria found me sometime after her transition. She has been able to control me ever since. I say it is because she's now bound to the moon, but part of me thinks it is because I lost myself somewhere out there across the waters. And I don't care enough to get it back."

I stare at her, my brain unable to think of a single word to reply. So much information has been shared with me today. All of a highly emotional nature. I hate how drained I feel beneath the weight of other people's burdens when all I want to do is say something, *anything* to alleviate it.

Yara doesn't seem insulted by the silence that follows. In fact, she seems oddly comforted by the absence of words. I know from my own experiences that false sentiments are nothing but salt in already unbearable wounds. Sometimes, silence is better.

"It's been quite some time since I've spoken of all this," she sniffles. Only now do I realize that she had started to silently cry. "Thank you."

"Of course," Azure tries to place a reassuring hand on her shoulder, but it goes straight through her fading form, which had started to ebb and flow in its tangibility during her emotional state. I stifle laughter at how awkwardly his hand retreats as though something gooey is dripping from his skin.

"That is all to say - I regret my choices. Some things are better left as they were always meant to be. What Delesseria is doing, I don't know if it is *right* to try and alter the cosmic design. Sometimes, that only makes things worse. I would do anything for the sadness I knew when I felt trapped by the moon, for the sadness I feel now is far more painful." She smiles faintly. "Take whatever morals you can from that."

Yara leads us the rest of the way to the west wing, instructing us which rooms to take when we arrive before fading away and leaving us alone in the hall. Calder and I are given separate rooms across from one another. I open the door to the room that is mine when I feel Calder stepping behind me.

"Your room is over there, Calder," I pull from his embrace, stepping into my room.

"Yes, but yours seems so much more hospitable than mine," he leans into the doorframe, a wry smile lighting up his face.

"I really want to be alone right now," I explain. "There's a lot to think about and I need space to do it."

"You aren't upset with me, are you?" His grin drops.

"No," I shake my head. "I just. Now that I remember, I need some space to consider everything that's happened. To see if it changes anything."

"Changes anything between us?" Azure's jaw tics as he tries to conceal his anger at the possibility.

"I don't know, Azure," I confess. "I just. Need space to think. The memories are back, but jumbled. I need to sort through it all."

He only moves from the doorframe when I start to push it shut. I hear him kick the door once before footsteps teeter off into silence, leaving me alone with my thoughts.

Chapter 35

That wasn't how I wanted my final moments with Duvessa to go. I wanted to go with her into her room in the castle. I wanted to make love to her and tell her just how deeply she has rooted herself in my soul. I wanted to tell her that if she wanted to leave, all she would have to do is say the word and I'd carry her to the ship, if that was what she wanted, abandoning all else as we set off into the horizon and never look back.

That I would forget my quest to save Braun if it meant I wouldn't lose her.

I was not prepared for the possibility that she may decide to stay. I was not prepared for how starkly she seemed to change after having her memories restored.

I was not prepared for how she slammed the door in my face. How she ripped the rug from beneath me, leaving me to question everything I thought was shared between us.

I stormed across the hall to the room that I was given. Its luxury was not lost on me, but I found myself unable to enjoy any of the provided amenities. Instead, I passed an hour pacing the room and drinking the last of the whiskey from my flask – my mind spiraling at the prospect of Duvessa deciding that whatever happened in her missing weeks somehow negated everything that has happened since.

When the whiskey is gone, I find an unopened bottle on the liquor cart beside the bookshelf and drink straight from the source.

Another hour passes and I am writhing with irritation. I consider storming across the hall, busting down her door, and reminding her just how much I've come to mean to her. I am halfway out the door when I decide that is a horrible idea and return to my pacing.

From the window, I can see that darkness has fallen. Yet, I do not feel the slightest bit tired. Maybe that is accredited to my fucked-up sleep pattern from leading a practically nocturnal life the past few days. Or maybe it is due to the oddity of time on this godsforsaken island.

The longer I am in Neverland the more I come to despise it. More than anything, I detest the hold it seemed to have over me when we traipsed through its jungles. Perhaps I should be grateful that I am not one of the irrevocably broken few who cannot be fixed. Perhaps that is a compliment in itself. But I cannot help but feel slighted that my pain was deemed *not enough* by some entity that has no clue what I have endured in my life nor what I feel inside. Then again, are they not omnipotent, one way or another?

And was I not relatively fine after the deaths of my parents?

What was it that she said?

I only hear that song from those who have experienced the kind of broken heart that comes with their greatest loss.

Even in this angered state, I recognize that the loss of my parents was never going to be my greatest loss.

Maybe it won't even be losing Braun. Maybe the greatest loss that looms ahead of me is losing Vessa now that I have found her.

As I pace the floor, anger flowing, emotions whirling, I cannot say which might strike the mortal blow on my heart. Braun or Vessa.

But only one of these outcomes is within my power to control.

I take one more swig of whiskey before slipping out the door and down the hallway. I retrace the path that Yara took on our jaunt to the west wing. The halls are filled with shadows and chills, but I maneuver the castle with relative ease. Only briefly do I hesitate at the heavy wooden doors before swinging them open and stepping into the courtyard.

The moon shines high on the lagoon as I approach. I find myself wondering if Yara sits out here on quiet nights and stares up at her lost home, praying for its forgiveness.

The throne is empty. I thought it might be. But still, I hoped she would be here waiting. When she looked into my eyes, I knew she already understood how I ended up in Neverland.

"I thought you might have changed your mind. Found something else to live for."

The voice behind me is gentler than before, at least compared to how she'd spoken to me. I feel her aura gust around me, but before I even start to turn, she materializes on her throne. She is even more devastating in the moonlight, both her beauty and her intimidation. I stiffen my spine, swallowing the desire to back away from my intentions.

"I heard your whispered prayers across the waters," she tilts her head like a predator sizing up its prey. "Your friend. Braun. You came looking for me a desperate man about to lose the last remaining thing he truly loved. But then you found something else to love. Didn't you? *Someone.*"

She scoffs as her eyes scan me head to toe.

"And you know from experience that the heart heals so long as there is love lingering inside. You thought Braun's death would break you. That losing him would be the final straw to send you over the edge. But you found *her.* You fell in *love.* And you know down to your core that with *her* at your side you could survive another loss."

I open my mouth to speak, but she raises her hand, and I no longer have the liberty.

"Don't bother trying to deny it. I know more of your truths than even you care to admit." She releases her hand, and my mouth is mine again.

"So, tell me, *Azure Calder.* Why are you here?"

"I'm here to make a deal," I assert, my liquid courage giving me a sharper, more assured edge.

"Yes, that much is evident."

"Braun's life. What will that cost."

428

"Ah, ah," she tsks. "That's not how this works."

"Then enlighten me as to the process," I sneer.

"First, I need to decide if you have anything to offer me."

"What is it that..." I start, but she cuts me off again with her invisible hand. Anger heats my face at the absence of respect in how she interacts with me. I am nothing more than an insect to her. Her eyes burn beneath my skin as she assesses me.

"Hmm," she hums. "Alright." She releases my mouth again, my hand rubbing along my jawline from how tightly she held it this time. "I can work with you." She nods. "Tell me then, why risk throwing it all away with your dear Duvessa? Does this Braun really mean so much to you? Or is it that Duvessa means so little?"

"Don't presume to understand what either means to me," I snarl, trying to contain my reactions. "You may be able to see inside my mind, but you're too broken to comprehend the depths of emotions we mortals possess."

"Hmmm," she chortles. "I enjoy just how slow you are to learn your place."

She smooths the silk of her dress across her lap, taking great care to subdue her snide smile and restore stoicism to her expression.

"But you haven't answered my question. *Why?*" She asks with genuine interest.

"You say that I could survive losing Braun," I shrug. "And you are right. I could survive it. But I couldn't live with myself for not saving him when it's in my power to stop his death."

"It's not within *your* power, boy. It is my power you covet. And if there is any hope that I'll show mercy to you I suggest you bow before it."

My muscles tense as I glare at Delesseria, a broad smile pulling her face. My stomach riles as I realize she means this literally.

I bow before no kings – no masters and no gods.

But she will not grant me my bargain if I do not comply with her demands.

I do not break with her eyes as I force myself to lower to my knees, jaw feathering from my clenching teeth. When I stop there, she nods in indication – a command for more. Flames of humiliation whipping at my face, I lower my chest prostrate to the ground. Only then am I forced to break eye contact.

"Better." I can hear the pleasure in her voice. "I will cure your Braun of his illness, and he will live a long and healthy life. No trickery in my wording. No catch."

"What is it that you want in return?" I ask, pushing against my hands as I start to rise. But something hits me hard in the center of my back, forcing me back down.

"Why darling, it's already begun."

Snap!

She is the first thought in my head when I regain consciousness. Not the first thing I *think* of, for the thought of her is always there it seems.

The stone surrounding me sweats moisture, leaving the air musty and the cuffs of my pants sopping wet. As far as prisons go, this one is not the worst I've ever seen.

There are no windows, only three stone walls, and a fourth constructed entirely of bars. Pushed against the back wall is an unmade cot with rolls of blankets stacked atop the center of the thin mattress. I am surprised to see not a latrine but a functioning toilet in the back corner of the cell, though I am less than delighted by its lack of privacy. I silently praise the running water of the sink that somehow manages to be the exact temperature I desire upon turning the faucet. The simple luxuries of a magical island, I presume.

Cupping the tepid water in my hands, I clean my face of the dirt and grime that marks the memory of my groveling before her.

This is it then.

I awoke in this place with the understanding of the price I will pay for Braun – as though my sentence were branded into my bones. I will live the rest of my days as Delesseria's indentured servant.

I will never leave the island again.

Neverland. How aptly named. A conscious choice.

I see that now.

For we *average* people, those that the sea witch feels no kinship with, the moment we step foot on these shores, whether we make it to the castle or get lost along the way, our fates have been sealed. We will never leave this land again.

A drip of cool sweat sends goosebumps shooting down my spine at the realization.

I swallow the burgeoning doubt that rises from the pit of my stomach. What's done is done. My choice is made.

I wanted this.

I do not regret trading my life for his. Trading my freedom for him to have the chance to live out the rest of his days the way that he deserves. He gave up so much for me, it was all I could do to return the favor after all these years of letting him down.

What I do regret is how it happened. I should never have gone there in that state. Inebriated, and angry, and feeling vulnerable. Right about now, Vessa is likely waking up. Knocking on my door to tell me what she decided in the night. Whether she chooses me or I lose her for good.

But that choice is no longer viable. Whatever she ultimately decides, I am no longer hers to have. I took that choice from her. And that I do regret.

I wonder if she will find me. If she chooses to leave, would she think I abandoned her? Will the sea witch tell her of our deal? Hold my captivity over her in hopes that it will make her stay? Selfishly, I hope she does, if for no other reason then I might see her again.

Or maybe she decided that there was nothing between us at all. Maybe she will learn of my bargain - my eternal fate - and will set off aboard my ship, taking all that is mine with her. If anyone is to have what's mine, I want it to be her.

Maybe that would be the best possible outcome. What kind of man would I be to want her to stay when we can never be together entirely? When we can no longer have a life.

What I want...

No. It is not a matter of what I want. What I *need* is for her to forget me. I need her to go, and live, and have all the things she wants out of her life. I need for her to not be anchored down by the decision I have made.

I try to snuff out the escalating remorse before it consumes me.

I love her.

And I need to let her go.

That is the best thing for her now.

I use the provided blankets to fashion the cot into something resembling comfort. When I sit on its edge, a metal spring digs up into my thigh. Leaning forward, I bury my face in my hands and sigh.

Whatever life awaits me, there was no other outcome. Even if I hadn't made my bargain, the island would have never let me leave. I made it here to the castle with my consciousness intact because Vessa had been at my side.

My anchor.

Even if she had chosen to leave with me, I doubt that Delesseria would have allowed me to go. I tell myself that this is so.

From somewhere down the dark stone hall, a single cough echoes.

I lift my head at the sudden break of silence and listen for further sounds that do not come.

"Hello?" I call out into the silence.
But there is no reply.

Chapter 36

The night passes slowly, and I am anything but rested when I climb from the bed.

I have no concept of time here, but when I first arrived in the room, I noted a table full of decadent foods and bottles full with my favorite libations. For hours I picked and nibbled at the various plates and sipped conservative glasses of rum. All the while wading through my newly regained memories.

Everything that I remembered from that time, what I *thought* I remembered, was nothing more than a shadow of a dream. Fragments of a mind that had been wiped clean - but a heart that remembered something life-altering had happened in the interim.

The moon had called to me, and that first and only time, I answered. It was not the pull of a chain but the calling of one heart to another that every piece of me begged to answer. When I slipped beneath the surface, the call became so much clearer. Suddenly, I knew down to the last coordinate which path I was meant to take - which direction would lead me to her.

There was no fear when I swam. Away. Down. So inconceivably deep until I found my way past the barrier between my world and Neverland. A green light shone bright when I crossed the threshold, and when I ascended, I was in the lagoon before her, staring up at her magnificent form.

How easily she entranced me with her words and with her cause. I'd never cared much for the world, so how could I not want to watch it burn? Bring justice to those like me who the Divine had failed to protect. How could I not bow and fight to restructure the hierarchy of the cosmos, to place her atop the throne to rule them all?

She taught me how to fight. Taught me what I'd become. She taught me to draw magic from the elements and from within. Taught me what it means to be part of something bigger than myself. What it means to be a coven.

At the time, it was only us. Neverland, our playground. When I asked about the others, no answers were ever offered.

I chose to leave, I did. And I don't remember why. Like a pebble missing from a rocky shore, the absence of the memory almost goes unnoticed among the piles of other thoughts and feelings from that time.

But I did. I told her I wanted to return to my ship. That I did not want to continue with her. As I consider it now, I can't imagine why.

She allowed me to leave. Taking these memories from me to preserve her secret. I agreed to the terms and awoke on my ship none the wiser of my time in Neverland.

But before she did, she told me what would happen. She told me that if I were to return to my mortal life, I'd learn how little power I truly held. That I would no longer be able to live with the emptiness I'd come to accept. Told me that I would be betrayed by my crew and lose everything I thought I knew.

And she was right.

She told me I'd return to her once I learned how little can change without a full revolution. She foretold that I would realize how badly I need her, as she needs me. And somehow, even without my memories, I found my way to her.

But what does this mean in the now?

I know in my mind that I want to stand beside her. Fight for her rule. The power I feel in my indignation is enough to wage wars and win battles.

My mind is set.

But my heart refuses to fall in line.

Despite everything, I care for Calder in a way I never thought I could for another. When I am with him, I almost forget all the reasons I have to hate and to destroy. I can almost live entirely in the moment and forget everything life and humanity has done to me.

For that, I can almost walk away from this.

My sleep is restless, and I spend the entire night tossing and turning and dreaming of a million different scenarios of what the future might hold. When I finally rise in what I think to be the morning, my heart and mind have fallen in unison.

I slip from the silken sheets, still dressed in the matching silk sleeping trousers and tunic the room provided. The table has been magically reset, the dirtied plates cleared from the night before, and a new platter of sausage and eggs set in its place. I know it to have been magic from my previous stay in the castle. Enchanted as it is. Even if I hadn't, I'd kept the door firmly locked throughout the night so no one could have gained entry to tend to the room manually. I take the plate, pour myself a mug of hot coffee, and sit cross-legged on the brown fur rug in front of the lit fireplace. Despite the eternal summer of Neverland, the air inside the castle has a soothing chill, and the fire wraps around me in a warm embrace.

I take my time enjoying the luxuries of my room. I forgot how much I missed it in my time away. During the weeks I'd spent here, which amounted to over a year in the island's time, I came to love this room more than anything. The enchanted castle transformed it upon my initial entry into the exact vision I'd had as a child for what a home should look and feel like. The walls and floors are rich cherry oak, the hearth a stunning fixture of large earthen stones.

My bedframe is crafted from thick twigs and branches that stretch toward the ceiling at the four corner posts. A sheer veil of gold fabric hangs loosely from the canopy, resembling something I'd always imagined a woodland fairy might sleep in – if I'd believed such things existed as a child. The various tables are works of art, hand-crafted wood carvings that swirl and bend in elegance. The muted gold silk of the bedsheets matches the upholstery of the dining chairs and the various sofas and sitting apparatuses that encircle the fireplace.

In spite of the vast luxury of the room, I prefer sitting on the fur rug, having always wished for one as a child.

When I've finished eating and have drunk my fill of coffee, I step into the large bathroom, not bothering to shut the door behind me. I drop my pajamas to the floor, stepping into the tub that magically prepared itself for me. The rich oils smell of roses and waterlilies, with petals from each floating delicately on the surface. I sigh into my relaxing muscles and slip beneath the surface, fully saturating my hair. Lathering my strands with the thick soap, I wonder how I could have ever left this place.

Once finished with my bath, I wrap myself in a towel, approaching the mirror hanging above the sink. I reach for a second towel to dry my hair, but it has already dried into flawless curls, the likes of which it never could look without the aid of such magic that flows through the castle halls. I smile, looking into my own eyes, not hating what I see staring back for the first time in ages.

Everything feels easier here. Not perfect. But easier.

When I return to the bedroom, I find my clothes are nowhere to be seen. Instead, a long black dress is laid atop my freshly made bed.

I slip it on, letting the loose silk fabric fall across my form. It is the mirror image of Delesseria's – only mine is pure black. I relish the feel of the fabric against my skin, remembering how much I came to love the power and freedom I felt while wearing this dress. It was all I wore the last time I was here. Unless, of course, our training took more of a combat form. Then it was my usual attire, which I assume is now cleaned and hanging in my closet.

But this? This is the uniform of our coven.

I opt for bare feet, knowing now that the stones and brambles of the earth will soften beneath my soles and yearning to feel connected to its energy with every passing step.

Unlocking the door, I step into the hall.

I knock for several minutes, but Azure does not answer his door. If he is inside, he is either still asleep or is actively ignoring me. I don't blame him if it's the latter. He was so angry with me after last night. Perhaps I should care more than I do, but I can't seem to feel regret for taking the time I needed to sort through my thoughts alone. And I'm certain that he'll have come to understand by now.

I knock one final time, calling his name through the door, but when I am again met with silence, I decide to press on.

I don't need him for this anyway.

I make my way back to the main entry, not needing to pay attention to where I am going as muscle memory guides me back to the courtyard. Entering it now, it feels a bit like coming home.

"Do I take it by your attire that you have made your decision?" Delesseria sounds nothing short of thrilled.

I bow my head the slightest bit in reverence.

"Sister," I move to the very edge of the lagoon looking up to where she sits on the throne. "You were right. Everything you said was true. I never should have left. But," I shake my head. "But I think I had to."

"That's all very well, my dear, but that doesn't answer my question." I can tell she is trying not to get impatient.

"My time with you, it changed me," I continue, tentative in my approach. "I hadn't even realized how much until I'd gone off, and come back, and all my memories came flooding back and I got to see firsthand just how starkly altered I am between then and before."

"But?" she presses.

"But I have changed since leaving here, too," I admit, shuddering from the anxiety of my vulnerability. "My entire life, I've felt like I've been at a distance. Growing up, I was kept at a distance. And when I wasn't? Well, I learned pretty quickly that distance was safety. Distance was survival. And when I got out, that conditioned drive to be distant – it never went away. I never let anyone get too close to me, and the few who did, I kept them distant too."

A tear burns the corner of my eye as the confession tears my heart, leaving nothing but sadness for the child I was and the person I never got to be.

"In these past few months, I learned all the things you told me I would. I lost my hold on control and realized I never had it to begin with. And maybe you are right. Maybe that is because, at its core, humanity is built on pillars of cruelty and greed. Maybe the darkest parts of people are the things that make the biggest impacts on the world."

My voice shakes as I struggle to keep from going on a pessimistic tangent.

"But also, in these months," a glimmer of hope warms my tone, "the distance I used to keep myself safe – it was shattered. For good or bad, that distance was closed and I was made to see a few hard truths in a new light. Face demons I tried so hard to forget. And you know what? I learned that beneath all the bad, there are other things too. Small things that make them deserving. Make *us* deserving. I can't abide by any amount of human life being lost as collateral damage."

"You still feel kinship for them?" Delesseria narrows her discerning gaze, looking hurt by my proclamation.

"I still feel *something* for them. No matter what I've become, I was once human. Still am in every way that counts. I know you feel the same way about yourself. Why else would you have modeled me after the markings of the oceanic gods." I feel the storm brewing in her fury, but I cannot help but provoke her further. "You chose to hide those parts of you, but I know they're still there. Skin deep. But I can see them. I can see you."

Delesseria sits forward, a slight transition so abrupt one might have missed it if the entire energy of the room had not become turbulent. For a split second, I can see the writhing of her gills, pinned down beneath the glamor of her choice to be something less than what she was born to be. But they fade, leaving her skin unmarred by her inner self.

"You don't know a thing," she spits.

"Don't forget that what I've regained is far more nuanced than the superficial memories you've returned to me," my voice is meant to comfort, but it seems to dig beneath her skin. "You know me, but I know you too, Delesseria. Don't discredit that."

Her preternatural stillness is that which only one in total mastery of the elements can attain. It chills me to the bone.

"What we are is more than anything either of us ever came from," she finally breaks her silent stare. "What we are is the better way."

"I don't know if that's true," I avert my eyes, almost ashamed at the admission.

"If your only qualm is the loss of human life, I can," she swallows the quiver of need that builds in her throat. "I can *try harder* to prevent it."

I startle slightly, this being the first time I have ever known Delesseria to even attempt to compromise. I cannot help the flutter of pride it gives me, her offering such a gesture of respect. I know she can sense the way it bolsters my spirits. I also know that she can sense that it isn't enough.

"The way things are, there is no justice to be found," she continues to argue, trying to further convince me. "The way things are, all there is for your precious humans is pain and emptiness. Don't you want to be the *more* they so desperately need?"

"I do," I shake my head. "I did."

"Well, which is it? *Do* or *did?*" she snaps. "Are you going to return to me, to everything we were working towards, or are you going to again run from your destiny?"

"I want to," I confess, searching for the right words and the courage to say them.

I clench my fists, the weeds at my feet growing and wrapping in protective vines around me as though they could somehow keep my vulnerable heart safe.

"*But?*" she prompts, her eyes flooding with glee at the vision of my powers coming out to play.

"But," I brace myself against the prospect of being denied my truly deal breaking request. "I want Calder to remain with me."

I feel exposed with the words dangling between us.

"He can be of use to your cause," I add for good measure, trying to appeal to her need for control.

"Oh, darling," she smiles. "Didn't you know?"

"Know what?" My heart goes hollow at the uncertainty.

"Last night, he came to see me - to make a *deal.* His life for that of his dying friend," her forced sympathy is sickly sweet. I see it for the manipulation it is. We may be allies, sisters in power, but I remember all the flaws she tries so hard to conceal and deny.

"His..." my heart starts to race.

"He is still very much alive," she clarifies. "But the cost of his wish is that for the rest of his days, he will serve in the castle."

I stare in shock for a beat. *His dying friend.*
"Who?"

"Turns out you don't know your Captain as well as you thought." Delesseria shrugs. "If you want to know more about it, ask him. I care not about the man he chose to sell his life for. But, if I were you, I would focus on the most important lesson in his choice."

"And what is that?" I scoff.

"He chose this friend over being with you. He didn't care about the cost of his wish, only that he could save his friend. Rather telling that *you* were not the thing he'd throw everything away for. Turns out you were just one of the things he was willing to part with."

No.

My heart sinks to the depths of my soul. He would not have chosen this. He'd have never sacrificed us for anything else. He would never have chosen to leave me.

"Per your request," Delesseria continues. "If you choose to return to our work, you may see him whenever you please. Provided it doesn't interfere with my uses for him."

My stomach rolls.

"Where are you keeping him?" I force my voice to remain composed.

"Does this mean you'll return to me?"

"*Where is he?*" I practically growl.

"An answer for an answer, darling," she purrs.

My heart beats uncomfortably in my chest when I answer. "Yes."

"How grand," she claps her hands in fervorous delight. "I *have* missed you, Duvessa."

I wait for a beat, regaining control of my composure before asking again, knowing damn well that she does not respond to the clashing of others against her authority.

"Where is he?"

"The dungeons," she scrapes a speck of dirt from beneath her nail. "But they are only accessible by magic. And since yours is only partially formed, only I can bring anyone in or out."

"I want to see him," I guise the demand as a request.

"That can be arranged," her face remains neutral. "But I need your word that you will not interfere with his end of the bargain. He made his choice, darling. Now he must pay the price."

"I promise." I don't bother to fake a smile.

With the snap of her fingers, I am transported. My sight is taken, but I feel the sensation of slipping between the warding of the dungeon, like being pushed through miles of thick molasses in a matter of seconds. I cannot breathe, neither from my lungs nor through my gills, and my head spins with every passing second. I am on the brink of the unconscious when I hit the stone floor in a crumpled heap.

"Duvessa?" His voice is laced with shock and concern.

I cough on my first few breaths of air, and he is at my side in an instant.

"What are you doing here?" He lifts me onto his lap, hugging me close as he rubs gentle circles across my back. "I thought I'd never see you again." He peppers my face, the top of my head, with urgent kisses.

"How could you, Azure?" I push away from his embrace, too furious with him to allow either of us the comfort of each other's arms. "Why did you do this to yourself?"

"Don't be mad, my dear sweet Vessa," he presses my face between his palms as his eyes examine my face. In spite of my anger, all he does is smile at me with a longing gaze. "I hoped that after all this time, you might have found a way to forgive me."

"All this time?" I quirk my brow as I force myself to my feet. "Azure, it has only been a few hours."

"Hours?" Azure sighs, bringing himself to stand as well. "Is that all? Time really does move strangely here," his voice is lethargic, broken. He steps closer to me, taking my shoulders in his hands and drinking me in again with starving eyes. "For me, it has been months since the last time I laid eyes on you, love."

"Months?" my eyes widen. "You've been trapped in here for months?"

"Not exclusively," he tilts his face down, pressing his forehead into mine and rocking it side to side, arms locking behind the small of my back. His touch is so gentle, it almost feels unreal. "Sometimes I am here. Sometimes I am with her. Sometimes, I don't know where I have been or what I have been doing."

He breathes in deeply through his nose, taking in my scent as though it were the last bit of oxygen on earth. "I've missed you with every particle of my existence."

He feels so weak. So thoroughly broken down. As he embraces me, I feel like I am holding a husk of his former self. An empty shell that's been worn against by the changing tides and unable to keep itself from sinking deeper at her command.

Seeing him like this, feeling him, it unhinges me.

"Azure," I shake him by the shoulders, trying to rouse something in him besides resignation. "We have to get you out of here. I can't leave you like this."

"No, Vessa," he dismisses. "I need to stay. I had to. You don't understand. I had to. For Braun. I had a chance to save him, so I took it. I took it, and I can't allow myself to regret it. If I regret it, what kind of man does that make me?"

A single tear falls down his cheek and splashes against my bare shoulder. He runs his hand along my neck. Across my shoulder. Down my arm. I lean into the touch, though I try with every bit of strength to keep from being sucked into the trap of his comfort.

"I don't know who this Braun is, but..."

"He raised me. After my parents died. He raised me and I left him alone to die, having never given him anything in return. All I did was take. And leave. *Take* and *leave*. And now he's dying." Azure's speech grows fast and erratic. "But now he's *not* dying. *I* am dying. Slowly and in my soul. But he is *living* and that is all that matters."

"Azure, listen to me," I snake my face beneath his, forcing him to meet my stare. "This *Braun*. He wouldn't want you to do this. He wouldn't want you to throw your life away like this. *We will find another way.*"

"There *is* no other way," he shakes his head with eyes pinched shut. "And what is done is done."

"I refuse to believe that," I shake my head, frantic for a solution.

"You have to, my love," he pushes me away, turning his back to me. "You have to let me go."

My eyes burst into a storm of burning tears that sear my cheeks as they fall.

"Azure," I clench my jaw, trying to keep the pathetic begging twinge from my tone. "Do you love me?"

He stands motionless, a powerful energy rippling through his statuesque form. He does not speak, but I can tell I've broken through to him.

"Do you love me?" I repeat in sharp staccato.

Like a predator striking, he turns in one swift motion, eating the space between us before he is on me. Pulling me flush against his body and crashing his lips against mine. His soul is lost in my mouth and mine in his, each warring to be the first to claim the other.

"I never knew the meaning of love until I met you. Until I lost you these past few months," he professes before diving back in for an even deeper kiss. "My love for you is stronger than my desire to live and breathe."

This time, I am the one to devour *his* mouth, pressing into him so hard that he falters a step, and his back presses into the stone wall behind him. I thread my finger through his obsidian hair and pull his face so close to mine I cannot tell where I end and he begins.

When I think I just might drown, I force his skull back by the hair until our faces part.

"Then come with me. Don't make me live a life without you," I cannot mask the vulnerability in my voice.

"That's beyond my control now, Duvessa," he sobs. "Now matter how much I may want to."

"There has to be something..."

"How are you here?" his eyes narrow in interrogation. "There are no doors to this place. No keys to the locks."

"Delesseria sent me through."

"She let you come to me?" he nods in somber understanding. "Does that mean you chose her after all?"

"I... You don't understand. What she is doing is..."

"If you plan to follow her, why bother trying to break my deal?" He shakes his head in frustration. "What do you expect will happen?"

"I can reason with her. I can have it both."

"You can't have it both," Azure steps away from me. "You know she won't let you."

"I don't know that at all," I argue.

"Well, I do, love," he brushes his hand against my cheek. "For you, it may have been hours. For me, these past few months, I have come to know precisely what Delesseria thinks of me. *I am your weakness.* Just as you are mine. Even if not for my deal, she'd have sent me away. She doesn't want to share you."

I step closer to him, letting his arms swallow me whole as I lay my head against his chest.

"Whatever time I have left, it's borrowed. And eventually, she will come to collect." Gently, he strokes my hair. "Do what you must. And in whatever time you have, come to me. I'll be waiting for you always."

"It won't be enough," I cry, my tears soaking into his shirt.

"It will have to be." He tilts my chin, pressing a kiss against my lips.

"Vessa?" He pries his lips from mine, leaving them cold and longing. My eyes remain closed as he brings his lips to brush against my ear, whispering. "Do you love me?"

There isn't a molecule of doubt in my entire being when I reply.

"I love you, Azure."

Chapter 37

As suddenly as I was sent to the dungeons, I was ripped away from his arms.

I choke just as much from the deprivation of air during the transportation as I do from the whirl of emotions that overpower me after giving voice to the feeling I refused to acknowledge fully.

I love him.

It's more than lust. It's more than comfort. If I taught him the meaning of love, then he is the word itself. If his love for me is stronger than his need to live and breathe, then I'll gladly give him my very soul and the last remaining breath in my body.

I love him and...

"How touching."

I am once again standing in front of the lagoon, Delesseria propped on her watery throne.

"A little too melodramatic for my tastes, but I guess your mortal loves don't feel as redundant to you as they seem from my perspective."

"Bring me back to him," I urge. "Please."

"Time and time again you humans meet your *one true love*, as you like to call them. You fall madly in love and think that for whatever reason yours is the love of centuries – that yours is the tale of the ages. But every time, it is the same exact story. Nothing new. Nothing special. *You love. You lose. You die.*"

"Please," I repeat in desperation. "Let me see him again, I wasn't finished."

"You will see him presently. I promise."

"What do you want from me, Delesseria," I take a step back. "I already told you I would stay. Why toy with me like this?"

"I'm not toying with you, child," she sings. "I am training you."

"Training me?" My hands thrash in frustration. "How is this training me? If you want to train then fine, teach me what it is you want me to learn. But do not manipulate me. Be straight with your intentions, or I won't be so receptive to your lessons."

"I think my point is rather straightforward, deary," Delesseria sneers. "The problem is you refuse to accept this final tenet. *This.* This final step in your transition. This is where I lost you last time."

"I don't know what you mean," I jeer.

"Love is not eternal," she stands at the base of her throne, the rushing water parting around her feet. "As much as they like to think that it is, love is as mortal as the flesh you wear." Slow, methodical steps bring her to stand in front of me. "*You love. You lose. You die.* The only certainties of life. There is no love without loss. It is an inevitability."

She cups my chin in her dainty hand, lifting it to forcibly hold my stare.

"The greatest liberation you can find is losing that love that holds you back, binds you from taking your true form." She releases my chin and smiles, her eyes exuding genuine warmth and compassion. "*You love. You lose. You die,*" she sighs. "Darling, don't let this hold you captive. Take control of your destiny. Become the everything you were always meant to be. Don't make the same mistake again."

With that, she reaches out and taps a finger against my skull. My final missing memory comes surging back to me.

"Gareth," I whisper. "You wanted me to kill Gareth."

She nods.

"You brought him here. My ship. You taught me that spell, the one that killed your mother."

Delesseria hisses at the mention of her mother.

"And I..."

"Refused," she finished my sentence. "You griped and argued and sobbed. Said you couldn't bring yourself to do it. Though both of us know you have the capacity to kill, you just wouldn't. Even when I warned you of his impending death should you return to your mortal world."

"But the spell..." I shake my head, trying to unwarp the memory as it replays in my mind.

"The spell only works if you kill the thing you love most," she laughs. "At the time, all you had was Gareth. And you did love him - in whatever way you could. I didn't know for sure that what you felt for him would be enough to transition you fully, but based on how strong his love was for you, I was willing to go on a little faith."

"Love?" my arms wrap around my waist, trying to hold myself together, all the guilt and sadness threatening to explode from the pit of my stomach.

"I had my suspicions when you brought him here. Your Captain Calder," she almost chuckles in her contentedness. "But now, after your little display in the dungeons, there is no room for doubt."

The courtyard echoes like thunder as Delesseria snaps her fingers. A wooden structure materializes behind her, two beams forming an X on top of the small platform. Bound by wrists and ankles at all four points is Azure, who pulls against the restraints. When he sees me, he tries to call out, but with another snap of her fingers, he is gagged and rendered unable to do more than mumble muffled grunts through the thick fabric.

"There. That's much better." She smiles giddily. "Now we girls can continue our little chat."

"Azure!" I explode, trying to push past Delesseria to get to him. With the raising of her arm, an invisible force glues me in place.

"Look at you, darling. You're a mess. Unthinking. Uncalculating. Just blindly trudging forward, and all because of the weakness you have for this *thing*." She half turns over her shoulder to spit the insult at Azure, whose growling protests barely make it through his gag.

"Beastly little mongrel, isn't he?" she chortles. "At least that Gareth was easier to put in his place."

I twist and pull against the force that holds me hostage where I stand, unable to gain the slightest bit of mobility.

"It fascinates me that you came to love the one who sent your Gareth to his death. How you can love them both." She walks toward Azure as she speaks, fisting his hair at the top of his head and pressing it back against the wooden beam. "You know, centuries ago, during my travels in the human lands, I encountered many cultures. Some of which believed that they took on the energies of the things they killed." She tilts Azure's head to one side, examining the musculature of his neck as he seethes. "Perhaps that is how you can still love him after everything he's done?"

I give up trying to fight for liberation from my invisible bonds. The moment I do their hold lessens, though not entirely letting me go.

"He's weakness, Duvessa," Delesseria releases Azure, turning once more to face me, standing off to his side. "You didn't have the strength to follow through last time. To shed yourself of your last remaining weakness. And all you did was find yourself another one."

I am trapped in Azure's gaze, his eyes screaming words I cannot decipher.

"So, what will it be?" the sea witch tilts her head.

My heart pounds so loudly that I struggle to keep from retreating into the comfort of its rhythmic tune. I want to hide from it all - to keep myself from having to make this choice. A choice that, no matter what, will mean I have to lose.

"There is no other way?" I break my eyes from Azure, sending them to the ground in contemplation.

"This is the only way." Her words are etched in stone.

I force my eyes shut, listening to the sound of my breath as I feel the blood pulsing through me.

"Alright," I lament, lifting my head and looking her in the eye. "I'll do it."

I watch the grin grow on her face like mold. See the sharpness of her eyes slicing through the final barrier that has kept us apart.

"Do you remember the spell?" she asks.

I nod, feeling its memory twitch at my fingers like a regret waiting to happen.

Stepping forward, I feel the full release of my invisible bonds. There can be no interference for this spell to work properly. She has to stay at the sidelines.

I am resolute in my decision as my eyes fall on Azure.

"I'm sorry," is all I manage to say before raising my arms and casting the spell.

Chapter 38

The blast of light is all I see before my eyes pinch shut out of reflex.

I'd often wondered what my last thoughts might be before I meet my maker. Wondered what memories would resurface. What state of being, what emotion would be my last. Fear? Anger? Maybe even resignation.

But all I feel is *pride.*

Whatever turbulent emotions had been warring for dominance within me, the moment I saw her step forward, seeing the look of total sovereignty glowing in her eyes and radiation through her aura, I couldn't help but marvel at the woman she's become. The woman she had always been, but who I'd never had the pleasure of meeting. Even if I had to die for her to rise above.

How glad I am to have met her in my final moments.

The light collected around her, channeling down her arms, through her hands, until it shot forth in my direction. Even with eyes locked shut, I can see its burning glare draw closer in a flash.

And then...

"Azure!"

Soft hands stroke the sides of my face and I know I am in heaven. I open my mouth to speak, but all I do is taste the bite of dry linen in my mouth.

"Azure!"

My eyes shoot open.

By the grace of the gods, I am standing on the platform, still bound on Delesseria's executioner's block.

I am not dead, and this is far from heaven.

I am...

Covered in something red. Blood-red pieces of torn algae shards fall like snow around me. *Delesseria is nowhere in sight.*

Vessa slips the gag from my mouth before seizing my lips with hers.

She chose me?

She chose me.

My mouth tries to devour her like a starving man on the brink of death. Pressing, reaching, desperate to gain proximity to her that the laws of matter themselves could not permit. *But laws have never held much sway with me.*

She pulls away and again I am starved, needing the taste of her lips in my mouth. But they do not return.

"I don't know how much time we have," she maunders as she works to undo my bindings. "I don't know the permanence of that spell for someone as powerful as the sea witch, but I doubt she would have trusted me with one that could cause her an ultimate death."

"I thought you decided to align with her cause?" I use my newly liberated hand to untie the other, while Vessa starts unbinding my feet.

"I did," she states. "But not at the cost of losing you. Change is needed in the realms. And maybe Delesseria *is* the answer. But I will find another. *We* will find another."

My second foot released, I step forward, ripping the linen gag from my neck and tossing it onto the pile of algae that I assume was formerly Delesseria.

"Aye, love," I smile. "In the meantime, I suggest we make haste to the ship and get the hell out of this place."

Together we run across the courtyard, slamming through the doors and rushing out of the castle. By the time we reach the open meadow that circles the tended property, the sky is blood red. Neither day nor night, the island rages around us in a time that does not exist. Tempestuous clouds threaten and stalk as we run, hand in hand toward the jungle.

As we scuttle through the thick foliage, the wind whistles through the treetops above like a siren blaring an ominous warning. From all around me, I hear voices. Some in languages I do not speak but find no difficulty understanding.

Come, they call to me.

The sounds of comrades never met but that I've somehow known all my life plead and beckon me to join them in their eternal Eden. They offer nothing more than the promise of pure and unending bliss. And all I want is to oblige them.

But the hand in mine grounds me. Roots me to the memory of why I carry on. Why I endure all of the darkness and all of the mundanity of our flawed realm. The reason I'd been looking for in wealth and prosperity, but only ever found in her.

Love.

Who we are, what we feel, all of it is flawed. We are broken disappointments of our own potential. But we are the carved creations of free will – fixtures of crumbling art.

We are hideous and we are blemished. Flawed and faulty.

But we are an unaltered truth. The reality of the dream.

And I will choose this broken life with her over any promised fantasy, in this and every lifetime.

I breathe a sigh of relief when the ship comes into view. Part of me had expected her to be gone by the time we returned to shore. Her sails are raised, prepared to embark and I wonder how much time has passed for those aboard. For me, it has been ages since I last set eyes on the *Queen Marie* and the homesickness that I felt for her eases from my heart with every approaching step. And when I set foot on her deck, I truly feel like I've come home.

"Captain," Doryn smiles. "Back so soon?"

"Aye," I flounder past him, trying to get the attention of Corkin and the rest of the crew.

"Avast! Unfurl that sail!" I command to those who had just now started to roll the mainmast sail. "Quickly, now. Weigh anchor! Haul wind! We have no time to waste, lads."

"What's wrong, Captain?" Corkin asks, approaching me with great haste.

I explain the gist of the situation, expressing the need for a quick escape. Corkin sets off to bark further orders throughout the ship. I then turn back to Doryn as I recall our adolescent guest.

"Is the child safe?"

"Of course, son," he quirks his brow. "Or at least I assume as much. You've barely been gone an hour. I haven't had the chance to check since we docked."

I nod in understanding, grateful that such limited time has passed for the crew. Less opportunity for folly in our absence.

"Good," I reply. "Leave her be. No point causing her concern if we manage to leave this place unscathed."

The wind takes the sails and we are on our way, nautical knots incrementally increasing as we glide between the waves.

"Captain," Corkin returns to my side. "How do you expect that we will be able to leave this place?"

The barrier.

"Is there any chance the magic you learned is enough to have us cross out of Neverland?" I address Duvessa.

She shakes her head. "Last time I was here, I was guided in and out by another creature. They were made of magic, so they could cross at will. All I can do is harness it from the elements. And as far as I know, that isn't enough to cross between realms."

462

"Then we sail as far as we can. Go wherever we can. Even if that keeps us within the parameters of Neverland." I proclaim.

"We could be trapped here for eons," Vessa contends.

"Then we will spend every moment searching for a way out of this place."

"You may not have to search so hard, Captain." Corkin points behind me.

"Yara!" Vessa exclaims.

"Duvessa," she smiles for the first time with sincerity. "It's nice to see that *all* of your memories have been restored."

"It's nice to remember," Vessa's eyes light up as she stares at the moon sprite.

"I've come to help you across," Yara states. "You managed to erode her physical form, but she is rematerializing even as we speak. So long as she is not fully regenerated, I can maintain enough control to bring you safely across the threshold."

"Come with us," Vessa reaches out and takes her hand. "You used to roam freely. You can do so again."

"I couldn't," Yara's aura dims.

"Yes, you could," Vessa prompts. "You've grown so much since the first time we met. Changed for the better. If there is even a chance that you can start again, you have to take the risk. *Please.* At least try."

"If I try and fail, it will only get worse for me here," a silver tear traces Yara's cheek. "The only reason I have so much freedom now is because I don't try to fight her. She knows she has no risk of losing me."

"All the more reason to leave now," Vessa brushes Yara's tear with her thumb. "Don't wait for things to get worse before you make them better."

A disembodied cackle echoes across the ship.

Delesseria?

"How?" Yara pulls back from Vessa, eyes darting around in fear. "She couldn't have regenerated so quickly. It's not possible."

A small figure steps into view from the shadows, armed with an insidious grin.

Malle is dressed in a sky-blue frock, hair braided down either shoulder, tied off at the ends with matching blue ribbons. In her hands she cups a pale pink conch, the horn of the shell opening up toward us.

"Malle?" Azure exclaims in bewilderment.

"Did you think I couldn't sense her?" Delesseria's voice emanates from the shell. "Did you think I couldn't hear her song belting out to me the moment she crossed into Neverland? That sweet, twisted, eerie melody. So different from any other I've heard. So dissonant. So enthralling."

Malle's face beams at the sentiments.

"Malle," Azure steps toward her. "You're being manipulated. You don't have to..."

"Manipulated?" Malle laughs. "What I am is *special.* Powerful. And Del promised to teach me."

"There are other ways to be powerful," Vessa speaks to Malle for the first time.

"All you are is weak," Malle snarls at Vessa.

"What she is, my dear, is unprepared," Delesseria chimes, like a mother smoothing over a petty rift between her children. "Very few are born ready to make their own fate, like you, my dear sweet Malle."

A crack of thunder roars across the ocean.

"Lucky for you, Duvessa, we are fated to be together. You, me, and Malle."

Gusts of wind whip against the side of the ship, causing it to sway violently to one side. Vessa stumbles backward into my arms and we both slide clear across the deck until my back slams against the mast.

"And I am nothing but patient."

A gust comes from the other direction and we fall forward onto hands and knees.

"You will come around, my dear. And when you do, I'll be waiting with your precious Azure."

Vessa pushes herself upright, shuffling back until she is blocking me from the edge of the ship with her entire body.

"In the meantime, enjoy watching every member of his crew perish. I know I will."

With a girlish wave, Malle disappears where she stands, leaving nothing in her place. There is no time to respond as a giant sea monster emerges beside the ship.

"It's back!" the crew wail. "The beast!"

"I thought we killed the bastard!" Vessa cries beside me, rising to her feet.

"Looks like it didn't take!" I bellow back.

Corkin clambers from my quarters, stumbling with great difficulty toward me as the ship surges back and forth.

"Here, Captain!" He reaches out and hands me my already unsheathed sword. Pulling his own set of guns from their holsters, he sets off shooting at any part of the creature in range.

"Here," I toss Vessa a knife that I steal from another member of the crew.

"No," she throws it back. "I have something better in mind."

With that, she closes her eyes, raising her hands in front of her in a sluggish, methodical arc. The wood beneath my feet begins to vibrate, buzzing with whatever remaining energy she is drawing from its depths.

Her closed eyes wince as her hands begin to shake. My stomach drops at the worried expression on her face as the trembling works its way up her arms, and still, nothing happens.

Her hands clench harder. Her spine goes rigid. And as quickly as the doubts had come, all signs of worry recede – the slightest of smiles building on her face.

With the flick of her wrists, light shoots forward, harpooning the beast in its side.

The creature flails backward, displacing water in frothing rapids. The beast seems smaller now compared to the first time we faced it in battle. No bigger than the ship herself. Within its clutches, the beast wraps several of my men in its suckered limbs. It starts to descend into the depths when my eye catches one of its captives.

Doryn.

I swing my sword into the mast, severing a length of rope. Without much in the way of a plan, I hold it tight and run for the edge.

My feet embrace the open air beneath them, and for a moment, I fear that I will fall into the water. But then the line goes taut, and I am swinging in full force. My feet smack against its rubbery hide, my legs wrapping around its slimy tentacle. Sword in hand, I slice the beast just below where it holds Doryn. Its hold on him falters just enough that he is able to wriggle himself free, grabbing onto the rope that is still firmly clutched in my left hand. Together, we heave ourselves from the creature's limb mere seconds before it crashes beneath the water's surface. I climb the length of the rope back up to the deck, Doryn practically nipping at my heels as he follows suit.

I try not to think of the men I wasn't able to save.

By the time we crumple onto the deck, the creature has reemerged on the other side. Vessa is beaming it with her magic, again and again. I see the toll the effort is taking on her, but she continues her attack without hesitation. I slip off my jacket now weighted from the water it absorbed, regrip my sword, and rush to her side.

The moment I take position beside her, its attention fixes on me.

The beast's eyes almost narrow in recognition. Perhaps it recalls me from our previous dance. *Good.* If I can force its attention on me, maybe that will give Vessa a chance to regroup and regain her waning strength.

"Remember me?!" I taunt.

It tilts its head, seeming to recall my features. Its eyes narrow into something almost human. *Rage.*

It swings its appendages wildly, all seeming to focus on its targeted prey. I dive out of the way, rolling just in time to avoid being squashed beneath its battering limb. Another comes sweeping above me, and I stab my sword through it to the hilt. When it pulls back in pain, it rips the sword from my hand, still deeply impaled in its tentacle.

I scramble to my feet, shuffling back as I flounder, looking for another weapon. Anything I could use to fend off the onslaught of strikes.

"Captain," Doryn roars from off to my right.

I turn just in time to see him toss a sword in my direction. I reach up to catch it, but before it reaches me, the creature bats it out of the air, sending it careening to the side. It lands tip first in the shaft of the mizzenmast, wriggling side to side as it contends with its forced stagnation.

I run to retrieve it from its wooden prison, but the moment I take a step, I am encircled by a punishing grasp. The creature constricts its sinuous tentacle, yanking me off from the deck and into the air.

It toys with me for the next several minutes, whipping me under the water and holding me down until I am close to losing consciousness. Right before the blackness overtakes me, it pulls me out, allowing me to gasp for just enough air to keep me alive but also preserve the ardent burning in my lungs. It repeats this, again and again, until I almost wish for death - just to make my lungs stop burning through my flesh.

When I think that sweet release is just around the corner, it lifts me high in the air, pulling me close to its open eye.

My body shakes against my will. Not from terror but from the aftershocks of my torture.

As I glare into its deep brown eye, a somber sense of recognition settles. At first, I think it is the kind of recognition one has for the very thing that will end them. A resignation, of sorts, for an unavoidable fate as you stare it down the barrel and wait for it to pull the trigger.

But then it hits me...

"No!"

I hear Vessa's cries for the first time, though based on the rasp that cuts through the air, I think she has been screaming for a while now.

A blast of her light hits the creature, but it is unaffected by the assault. It squeezes tighter around my chest and I hear the popping of one of my ribs. I cringe at the echoing crack, the sound more daunting than the sensation.

"Please!" she shrieks, sending another blast of magic spearing toward it.

This time, the creature flinches slightly at the hit. Turning its head, it focuses on Duvessa.

"Please," she repeats. "Let him go."

The air goes still. All fighting stops. Duvessa does not break her binding stare with the creature.

I feel the moment it loses its aspiration to destroy, its hold on me loosening enough that I can take a full breath into my abused lungs. My head spins from the deprivation of air, the world whirling around me. I think I must be hallucinating as the creature starts to shrink.

Smaller.

And smaller.

Until...

We are standing on the deck. Vessa is mere inches from me. I want to ask her what is wrong, why her face is white as death. But the fist is clenched around my throat. The fist that was previously long, and slimy, and wrapped around my chest.

"How are you alive?" her eyes grow watery as mine start to blur.

"How are you with him?" a distinctly male voice spits through gritted teeth.

"Let go of him," Vessa hisses. The grasp on my neck does not relent. "Let him go, Gareth."

His arm shakes violently, but in a matter of seconds, I am stumbling backward, gulping in painful breaths that don't quite want to oblige.

"How are you...?" Vessa steps forward, taking Gareth's hand in hers and pressing it against her cheek as though trying to see if he is real. It isn't lost on me that it is the same hand that was clenched around my throat.

"The sea witch. She came to me in the water," he glowers at me with malice. "Right before I drowned. Offered me my life if I was willing to pay any price." He fixes Vessa with a painful stare. "Figured I had nothing left to lose. I've been trapped with her ever since."

"You've been here all this time?" she asks, a whirl of emotions catching in her throat.

"I have," he replies dryly. "Said she was keeping me here for some ritual."

Vessa's eyes flare with embarrassment. "I..."

"She explained it to me, Vessa," he cuts her off, and I want to cut off his hand for the disrespect. "I love you too."

Now I want to cut his throat.

Vessa bites her lip, brows knitting together in some unreadable emotion. "Gareth, I..."

"We're about to cross the boundary," Yara configures beside me. "Gareth!" she exclaims. "You... you fought her compulsion. How did you...?"

"I saw something worth fighting for," his eyes never leave Vessa's face. Her cheeks redden at his admission, eyes averted to the floor.

Yara's face overflows with worry. "But if we cross the threshold..."

But there is no time for her to finish voicing her concern.

The boat surges, causing everyone aboard to stumble. The sky is suddenly dark, no longer drenched in red, lit only by the light of the waxing moon and stars.

If there was any room for doubt whether we had crossed back into our realm, it is quickly washed away.

Gareth stutters back. Dropping Vessa's hands, he claws at the neck of his shirt, pulling it away from the tensing muscles of his neck. His face turns red, then purple, eyes bulging as he struggles to breathe. I try to subdue the budding smile that's threatening to brand me as a full-blown sociopath as I watch Gareth drown above water.

He drops to his knees, water spilling out from his mouth in reverse gulps, as if that would save him from the ocean of water pooling in his lungs.

"Gareth!" Vessa sobs. "What is happening to him?"

"It's his bargain," Yara explains. "Since he crossed over the boundary his deal was negated. He reverted back to the state he was in when he made the deal."

"He's drowning?" Vessa wails.

I don't know what compels me. It cannot stem from sanity. But the sound of Vessa's agony, the broken look that's frozen on her face, I know I cannot leave her to suffer this loss again.

I kneel beside Gareth, pushing him to lie supine on the floor. He fights me at first, but I am stronger and force him to comply. Hovering over him, I begin to perform compressions on his chest. When more of the water spills from his lungs, I pinch his nose shut and press my lips against his, puffing long exhales into his mouth. I repeat the abhorrent series until my arms and lungs burn from the effort.

Even as I fight to revive him, I hope that he dies.

When he sits forward, choking down air as the last bits of liquid spill from his mouth, there is only one word on my mind.

Fuck.

Chapter 39

He didn't have to save him.

What's worse? I had the ability to do it myself.

I watched as the water spit from his lungs, watched his eyes fill with the kind of fear that comes in those thin moments between life and death. I watched. And I waited. And I have to believe that I'd have done it. Stepped in and used my powers to pull the water from his lungs. Coax it out of him so that life-giving air could fill him once again.

But I didn't. Even as Calder worked to save him, I stood by and watched. Not frozen in fear, but indecision.

Part of me has to have wanted Gareth to live. After all, I mourned his passing when I'd thought he died. He was my friend and in my own way, I loved him. Even the Divine seems to have known I loved him. *Love him?*

Another part of me, the part I'm not sure I can admit to aloud, wished he would have stayed dead. His being back changes so much. But if I am being honest, that's not what bothers me most. Part of me wants to punish him for the control he held over me when I wasn't even aware he had it. That part of me feels violated in a way that doesn't seem logical but rips through me like shrapnel coursing through my veins, working its way to embed in my heart.

I had a choice to save him or let him die, and I didn't even make it. But in that, I guess I did indeed make my decision.

How befitting that Azure was the one to save him. Not just as the man I professed my love to not an hour ago, but as the man who sent him to his death in the first place.

The wrong that I grappled with as I slowly fell in love with Azure has been wiped clean from his conscience with the saving of a life. Nothing lost, but everything gained.

Azure looks equally as baffled by his noble actions, refusing to meet my eyes. He rises above Gareth, extending a hand down to him as he sits on the deck. Instead of taking the offer of truce, Gareth swipes Azure's legs from beneath him, causing him to fall backward. In an instant Gareth is on him, throwing punches at his face.

Calder lifts his arms to block the blows but does not return the offense. "I saved your life, mate," he sneers between blows.

"Yeah, but you were the one who tried to end it in the first place," Gareth lands another jab on Calder's chin.

Calder catches Gareth's wrists, shoving him away until he falls backward across the deck. Gareth is already coming back as Calder makes it to his feet.

They continue to spar, throwing hook after jab.

"Come now, lad, get it out of your system," Calder provokingly bates him.

"You fucking bastard," Gareth spits.

"Boys," Yara scolds with the kind of maternal voice that could only belong to a being as ancient as time. "Stop that."

They continue their fighting, romping their way closer to the edge of the ship. I tell them to stop, but my words fall on deaf ears, each man too swept up in the tension of their brawl. I fear that without intervention, their skirmish won't end until one of them is dead.

Clenching my hands, I summon the water below, making a forced wave crash over their heads, completely saturating them. Both men cease their fighting, freezing in place as they turn to look at me.

"Will you two quit it?" I snip. "Regardless of how we got here, Gareth, he did just save your life."

Gareth glares at me, lowering the hand that was raised mid-swinging at Calder's jaw. "He only did that to manipulate you."

"Oh, a mind reader now, are we?" Calder taunts, his forearm still wearily lifted to block the previously impending punch.

"Maybe you've forgotten, but time is of the essence here," Yara interjects. "Who knows how much time we have before Delesseria fully regenerates, and when she does, we need to be prepared. That place. The reason she calls it Neverland is that those who find their way there never leave that land again. Not unless she lets them. The fact that we now stand on a boat full of fugitives who all escaped against her wishes. We've upset the fragile balance of that realm. Who knows what repercussions might arise from that? If that is not enough of a concern, I doubt Delesseria will ignore the slight."

Azure and Gareth each take a step back but continue to monitor the other warily.

"What do we even do now?" I shake my head, completely exhausted.

"Now," Yara smiles faintly. "I suggest we rest. Regroup in the morning. Decide if what we want is to try and fight back or simply flee with our lives."

I lift my head to look at the moon, wondering how many nights have passed in Neverland. Considering what Delesseria told me and wondering, now that I have my memories, if I will be able to fight the ocean's call at the next full moon. Whether the call is indeed my own inner voice or if that was merely a lie, I will find out soon enough.

But that is still days away from what I can tell.

"It looks like you did it, Yara," I turn my attention to my friend, pushing my own worries briefly from my mind. "Look at you. Free of Neverland and free of her control."

"For now," Yara huffs. "Who knows what will happen when she returns to her full strength."

"I believe in you, Yara," I offer in earnest. Because I now remember that I really, truly do. With that final memory, a series of smaller moments that all connected to my decision to leave came flooding back, like a single fabric being rewoven into a tapestry. I remember our friendship. I remember everything. "Whatever comes, we will face it together."

She smiles, eyes twinkling in the moonlight that formed them. "And for now?" she smirks. "I am going to enjoy my first free night at sea in *far too long*."

With a radiant giggle, she fades into the night, leaving me alone with *them*.

After threatening to throw Gareth in the brig if he so much as thinks about stepping out of line, Azure instructs Corkin to bring Gareth below deck to the room he had given to Malle. I can see in his eyes just how bothered he is that the girl is back in Neverland. I can tell that he feels like he failed her.

As for me, I cannot say I feel much of anything at the loss. Her methods may be unorthodox, but what Delesseria has to offer, the vision she has for the world, even now I cannot say a part of me doesn't wish I could still stand by her side and fight the order of the universe. But she is unyielding in her need for control. Unwilling to allow any deviation from what she decides to be the way. Too willing to sacrifice the innocent.

Yet, if she hadn't insisted that I kill Azure, and Gareth before him, I think I might have overlooked it all. A dark part of me knows I would have.

But as I am, I am not enough. She tells me that my powers are but a fragment of what they could become if only I follow through with that final spell. And maybe it makes me selfish, but I am not willing to give up my small fragment of happiness when I have only now found it. Not even for the betterment of all the realms.

While Azure made arrangements for Gareth and instructed the crew to treat him as their own, with the caveat that all bets are off if he so much as lifts a finger against them, I excused myself to our quarters. I slip out of my black silk dress, hanging it immaculately in the wardrobe and redressing in my usual pants and tunic. By the time I reemerge, Azure is standing across the ship, looking out along the calm dark waters.

"Penny for your thoughts," I slide next to him against the rail. He lifts his arm, pulling me close against his side as we gaze out at the stars.

"I'm thinking about Braun," his voice is low, quiet.

"Your bargain," I gasp internally. In all the commotion, I hadn't even considered how crossing the threshold would impact Azure's friend.

"I made a choice," his arm tenses around me, holding me even tighter. "Once again, I chose myself over him. Chose my happiness at his expense."

"He wouldn't have wanted you to..."

"With all due respect, Duvessa, you've never met the man. You haven't the faintest notion what he would or wouldn't want." His eyes darken, rivaling the depths of the ocean below. "I'll hate myself for that later."

He shakes his head before turning to face me, wrapping his other arm around me as well as we stand beneath the stars.

"For now," his tone brightens, "it would almost be disrespectful not to enjoy the bounties of such a selfish choice." Azure brushes his lips against the tip of my nose. "I apologize for snapping at you. My grievance is not with you."

I make the conscious decision not to broach the topic of Gareth. I am not ready to discuss what happened, the fact that he is alive and that he claims to love me. I'm not ready to sort through my feelings about any of it. All I want is to live in the stolen moments that we will never get back. The moments right after Azure told me he loved me, and I returned the sentiment. But instead, we are here, pretending everything that happened between then and now is nothing more than a distant memory.

So, I tilt my chin and press a claiming kiss against his lips. And the kiss that is returned claims me in equal measure.

"We will find another way," I promise, pulling back from his lips.

"For what exactly?" His eyes smile softly, craning his neck as he playfully tries to reclaim my lips.

"For all of it. For Braun."

"Yeah?" he kisses along the side of my neck. "Like what?"

"Neverland," I suggest. "Neverland exists out of time and space."

Azure straightens at the thought. A knowing grin begins to rise on his face.

"We could defeat Delesseria. Take the island for ourselves," I continue.

"Bring Braun there where time won't progress his illness. He could keep living," he adds, chortling with merriment at the prospect of restored hope.

"The problem is," I admit. "I don't know how. My powers alone, as they are, they're not enough. Especially if she trains Malle."

"Hmmm," Calder quirks a brow.

"What?"

"If what you need is to magnify existing powers, I just might have an idea," he smiles wryly.

"Care to elaborate?" I coax.

"Do you remember the powder I used back in the jail? The words I used to break through the bars and locks?" As he speaks, his finger traces along the golden ring on his left knuckle.

"I remember," I nod, eyes narrowing. "Pixy dust ground into powder. You said it was *enchanted,* or something?"

"*Or something,* indeed," he affirms. A look of sheer delight enraptures Calder as he smiles down at me. "Well, love, I think it's time I introduce you to an old friend of mine."

Epilogue

There is something profoundly sad about staring into the eyes of someone you have known your entire life and realizing you don't know them anymore.

The person you are no longer sees the person they once were. Maybe you've changed. Grown. Maybe you have left them behind in your own journey of self-development and what you see is the same image, just through a different lens.

Or maybe it was you who was left behind. Maybe you are the one who never changed and the face staring back at you is just as dissociated from what *used to be* as you. Maybe the space between you is more than the inches that separate you, but is actually measured in years and experiences.

As I stare into the looking glass, one line resonates in my mind.

I don't know you anymore.